Esteban

&

Marialena

To Chris!
Happy reading!
♡♡

Eve Corso

eveCorso

Publisher's Note: This is a work of fiction. Names, characters, places, and incidents are a product of the author's imagination. Locales and public names are sometimes used for atmospheric purposes. Any resemblance to actual people, living or dead, or to businesses, companies, events, institutions, or locales is completely coincidental.

Esteban & Marialena

A contemporary romance –
the kind movies are made of.

EVE CORSO

For my mom.
I love you with all my heart.

Chapter One

As the hostess seated the two women, Roxanne whistled under her breath. The two girls knew how to draw attention. Both were curvy, though Marialena had more of a voluptuous body. The dress she had borrowed from Roxanne was just a little too tight up top and she couldn't stop tugging at it when she felt no one was looking. Roxanne, her cousin, had curly long hair and wore hers up, lest it get in the way. Both girls were of Mexican descent, though Marialena had features that made her look like she could be from anywhere, and people often assumed she was Middle Eastern or Indian. Marialena wore her wavy, thick brown hair down that night. She had voluminous hair, a look that men loved. Her hair, combined with her dark skin, thick eyebrows, full lips, and big almond-shaped eyes made men lust after her. But Marialena was over it. She wasn't the type who used her looks for attention. Her cousin Roxanne didn't share her views and was more of a troublemaker.

"Oh my god, this place is amazing. How have you not been here before?" Roxanne asked her cousin.

Marialena shook her head and shrugged. She looked around the darkly-lit restaurant and tried to breathe it all in. "I've driven by it a million times."

"You need to get out more," Roxanne said.

Marialena nodded. "I know, I know…" she trailed off.

"After I leave, you're going to have to promise me you will take yourself out every once in a while."

"You're right, I should. I will," Marialena said, reading the menu. "Except it's all so expensive," she added.

"Oh, it's not that bad for Beverly Hills. There are some places in Nashville that are more expensive than this. There's one restaurant that Brian and I went to for my birthday last year. The food was pretty good, but it was way more than this." She looked around again. "This place is nice, though. I like it."

Marialena smiled and looked down at her breasts to make sure they were still inside her very tight dress. She laughed to herself.

"I'm not sure which is better. That you're the only date I've had in months, or that you're the cutest date I've had in a year."

"I swear I am going to cancel your Netflix subscription when you're not looking."

Marialena opened her mouth in mock surprise. Roxanne nodded enthusiastically. "Oh, don't think I won't. Remember, we are family, not friends. I don't have to be nice to you."

Marialena stuck her tongue out at her cousin.

"Charming," said Roxanne, and went back to the menu.

"Ooh, the sandwiches actually look pretty good," Marialena said.

Roxanne put down her menu and lowered her voice. "You're going to order a sandwich? Look at all these amazing choices. Don't order a sandwich. You can make that at home."

"Not like this, I can't."

A waiter walked by and Roxanne sat up a little straighter.

"I forgot that every single waiter in L.A. is *hot*."

"That guy?"

"Yeah, you don't think so?"

"Yeah, I guess. He's not my type, though."

"No, I guess you're right. *Who is* your type? Let's have a look, shall we?" Roxanne rubbed her hands together and looked around the restaurant.

"Okay, what about that guy sitting in the corner?" Roxanne looked at him from behind her menu.

Marialena turned to look at him and shrugged. "Yeah, he's okay."

"*Okay?* That guy is *hot*. God, what's wrong with you?" Roxanne teased her cousin.

"I don't know. He just doesn't do it for me. Besides, it's all in the personality. I have to get to know them first."

"Maybe that's your problem." Roxanne thought for a bit. "You don't actually *meet* a whole lot of guys. We need to introduce you to someone. There's got to be someone here, though...someone you could be into." Roxanne looked around again. That's when Roxanne noticed someone sitting with a small group of people. She squinted her eyes and looked at him.

"Oh shit, Marialena. Don't look. The table to your left, I'm pretty sure you can see him from where you're sitting. Just past the plant. I think it's that director you like. What's his name?"

Marialena's heart started to beat faster. "Who?" Marialena liked a lot of directors.

8

"Your *favorite* one."

"Esteban Gutierrez?! No way! Wait, how do you know what he looks like? *I* don't even know what he looks like."

"Yes!!! It's him! Don't look yet, he might see you! Hold on for one second."

"It can't be him. Here?"

"Okay, you can look now. He's reading the menu. They must have just sat down."

Marialena sneaked a peek. "The guy in the suit sitting with four other people?"

Roxanne looked again. "Yes!"

"How do you know it's him?"

"You made me watch one of his movies. Brian was over that night and he wanted to watch the special features. That's totally him! How have you not Googled him yet?" Roxanne pulled out her phone. "How do you spell 'Gutierrez?'" she asked. "Nevermind, I'll just Google the movie." She typed in 'director Last November' on her phone and his face came up. She clicked on 'images' and showed Marialena, who examined the face. It was definitely him, here in this restaurant. Marialena was surprised, though. She didn't expect him to look the way he did. He was handsome. He had a long face, gray hair, and a great smile from what she could tell in the pictures, but Marialena always pictured someone more Hispanic looking.

"I guess that IS him. That's CRAZY. I love all of his movies. He's not like a big-time director or anything, so I never knew what he looked like. But I always pictured him, you know, less white."

9

Roxanne shook her head. "No, you can't tell based on names anymore."

Marialena stole another look and at that exact moment, he looked back at her and held her gaze for what seemed like an eternity. In reality, it was probably only a few seconds. She quickly averted her eyes, but when she looked back at him, he was still looking at her, and he smiled this time.

"Oh shit, he's flirting," Roxanne whispered, witnessing it all.

"No, he's probably just flattered." Just then the waiter came by and took their food order. When he left, Roxanne had forgotten about the waiter's good looks and jumped right into the situation at hand.

"What are we gonna do?" Roxanne asked excitedly.

"What do you mean? *We* aren't going to do *anything*!" Marialena said.

"We have to do something!"

"He's *with* people."

"So?"

"So, that's *rude*."

"Okay, wait. First things first. Do you think he's cute?"

"Let me see those pictures again."

"No, Marialena. He's right there. *Look at him.*"

Marialena stole a glance, and he caught her looking again. This time he chuckled to himself.

"Shit Rox, I can't look over there anymore," she said, turning red. She picked up her wine glass and took a big sip.

"Oh my god, calm down. What is wrong with you? You're just looking at each other. *Jesus.* How could you be so bad at this, when all this city does is look at one another from a distance?"

"Not everyone."

"Clearly."

"Look, he's Esteban Gutierrez. He's my favorite writer-director. And he's dining, *with people*. I'm not going to be that fan that interrupts him while he's having dinner."

"No, you're going to be the girl that bats her eyelashes at him, hoping he'll get the message. Then I will leave. But *you*, you will go the bar after dinner. You'll stay long enough for two drinks. If he doesn't come to your side by then, forget about it...but he just might."

"Two drinks?" Marialena cringed.

"One, if you can drink it very slowly."

Marialena thought about this.

"What if someone else comes to take the bait at the bar? My boobs *are* popping out, you know? Or what if he doesn't even see me at the bar?"

"First of all, if he likes you, he will see you. It's on the way out...and if someone else comes, shoot them down. You are here for one man and one man only. If he doesn't show up, fuck it. Call me and I'll come back."

"And where are you going to go?"

"There's a bar right across the street."

The food came and they marveled at the quality of what they ordered. Before she took a third bite, Marialena felt a hand on her shoulder, a man's voice in her ear.

"After dinner, meet me at the bar. Say in about an hour." She looked at him as he walked to the restroom,

11

but only caught his back. Her heart was pounding. She took a deep breath and looked blankly at Roxanne.

After a moment of silence (and after he was out of earshot), Marialena asked, "Oh my God. Did that really just happen?"

"Yeaaaah, he's definitely cute up close," Roxanne said. "I must admit, that was one of the sexiest things I have ever witnessed. *He is smooth*. He actually winked at me when he was whispering in your ear. He has this twinkle in his eye, like he knew that he was making you a little nervous." They both looked at him briefly as he walked away. He was tall and made quite the impression. He was the kind of man you definitely noticed in a room full of people.

"Oh my God."

"It's okay, relax. Just eat your sandwich and act normal. You can do this. Don't look at him when he walks back. Play it cool. Or no, try this. When he's close, give him a sly smile, nothing else. That will get his blood flowing."

"I can't pull that off."

"Okay ssshh sshhhh, don't think about it too much. Let's talk about something else." Roxanne thought of a distracting conversation. "Tomorrow, when we go to the beach, can we push it to around one? I might want to stay out late tonight."

Marialena nodded. "Yeah, we can have happy hour afterward. There's this Mexican place I love near the pier. Let's do it." They talked about beaches for a bit, comparing beach restaurants and beach shopping, when Roxanne noticed him walking out of the corner of her eye. She looked at Marialena, making sure she was playing it cool. As he walked toward the girls, Marialena gave him a very small smile. He winked back and she nodded. He smiled all the way back to his table.

"Oh. My. God." Marialena exhaled.

"Wow. You did it."

"I did something." Marialena stared at her sandwich. It looked appetizing, but now she was all nerves.

"I can't believe he beat us to our plan. Like, that doesn't even happen in the movies."

Marialena nodded. "What are we gonna talk about? Should I bring up his movies? Should I admit I know who he is?"

Roxanne made a face. "I don't know. You probably should, right? Maybe lay off any 'I'm your biggest fan' type shit."

"Well, I mean, I love his work. But hello, I'm not creepy about it. I didn't even know what he looked like."

"Yeah, but he won't know that."

"Okay, well, it'll come to me. Thinking about it now is making me way too nervous."

The waiter came by to ask if the ladies wanted to place another drink order.

"No, I'm good, thanks."

"No, thank you."

Marialena looked at her phone. There was still some time. She needed some more distractions.

"Hey, so what's up with you and Dave? Are you thinking about hooking up with him?" Marialena asked as she picked at her fries. Dave was an old friend of Roxanne's; he and Roxanne had hooked up a few times when Roxanne came back to visit.

13

Roxanne shook her head. "No, I don't think so. I mean, he's all right. He's too moody, though. Fucking musicians, why do I love them so much?"

Marialena shrugged. "Because you've always loved music."

"I need to find a DJ or something. Not the club kind. Like a radio station DJ. I've never dated one of those. Think about it. They know a lot about music and they have sexy voices. I mean, most of them do. I'd make him leave long, drawn-out voicemails..."

They moved on from music and men to what they'd do the rest of the week Roxanne was in town.

As the two girls finished up their meals, Marialena's heart started beating a little faster. The time was drawing near, and soon she'd be sitting right next to her favorite director—the man who captured love so perfectly in 'Paris in the Dark.' The man who won her heart in 'Alone, Together.' The man who made her laugh and cry in 'Dinner for One.' She had just recently watched his film, 'The Promises We Keep' a few months earlier, but her favorite was his last one, 'Paris in the Dark.'

Roxanne paid the bill and stood up. She leaned over to give Marialena a hug and a kiss. "Knock 'em dead. Call me if you need me. Don't come home if you like him, and if you do come home, don't wait up for me."

All Marialena could do was nod. She thought about what Roxanne said. *Don't come home if you like him.* She couldn't even imagine it. She and Esteban Gutierrez, she thought. It was weird, because she didn't know a single thing about him, and she cursed herself for not watching the special features on his films. She didn't even know his movies had any special features. Still she knew enough

14

to know that she loved the way he wrote. She thought he was brilliant.

As she approached the bar, she looked for the quietest corner. Thankfully, there was only one couple sitting at the bar.

She pulled out the chair and sat down. She checked her boobs again to make sure they were still inside of her dress. The bartender approached.

"Hey, what are you having tonight?" he asked.

Marialena took a deep breath. "Wine. Red. A Pinot, please," she said, forgetting to be specific.

"Coming right up." He came back with a glass half full. "Waiting for someone?"

Marialena looked up from her phone and smiled politely. "I am." She took a sip of the wine.

A few minutes later, she heard footsteps. She took a deep breath and closed her eyes for just a moment. She did not turn around. She did, however, feel a hand on her shoulder. That was her cue to invite him to sit down. She turned to face him and smiled. She wasn't sure if she should stand up or not. She looked into his bright blue eyes and found cheeriness. She immediately liked that about him.

"And who do I have the pleasure of skipping dessert for?" he asked.

"Hi. My name is Marialena." She stuck out her hand, and he looked down at it and smiled. He took her hand in his.

"Well, hello Marialena. Tell me, do you have a last name?"

Marialena smiled. "I do. It's Villanueva."

15

"Villanueva," he replied. "Marialena Villanueva…it has a certain ring to it. I like it."

"Thank you," Marialena said quietly in her glass.

The bartender asked him for his drink order. "I'll have one of what she's having, please."

While they waited for the drink, Marialena could feel Esteban looking at her. She took a sip of her wine and glanced at him. He was taking her in with an intensity she wasn't used to. Finally, he broke the silence.

"Marialena, I noticed you looking at me, and I couldn't resist the urge to find out who you were."

Marialena swallowed, averted her eyes, and looked around, searching for something to say to fill the silence. She had nothing, so she just came out and said it. "It's just that I recognized you." She swallowed. "My cousin recognized you, actually. I happen to really admire your work."

"Aha!" he said, a little too loudly. "So, you're a fan of the arts?"

"Well, sure. Isn't everyone? But your work is different. I think you're absolutely brilliant." Shit, she had said it. Strong choice of words that she couldn't take back.

The Bartender came back with the wine and caught her last words. She smiled nervously.

He scoffed under his breath and watched the bartender pour the wine. "Oh, I don't know about that. In fact, I don't want to prove you wrong, not so early into the night. So please, let's start with you. Tell me, Marialena, what brings you to this fine restaurant tonight?"

"Well, my cousin Roxanne is in town from Nashville, and we're just going down the list of places she wants to visit and restaurants where she wants to eat," she said, hating how basic it sounded.

He took a drink of his wine and let it sit on his tongue for a second. "Ooh, this is very good. You have a great nose for wine."

"It's a Pinot Noir," Marialena said, feeling like a child pretending to be a grown-up all of a sudden.

He nodded. "Very nice. Nashville is great. You ever been?" he asked.

"I have, yeah. I've gone to visit her. Great city. I still love Los Angeles, though. It has a little bit of everything. It's not just one thing, you know?"

"Oh, I don't know if Los Angeles has everything. New York is preferable, I think," he said matter-of-factly.

"You're here, aren't you?" she asked, flirting a little bit.

"My work brings me here," he said.

"Lucky for me," she replied, feeling the wine in her blood.

He laughed heartily. His laughter was big enough to fill the room. "Tell me, what else is on this list for you and your cousin?"

"Okay, so we only have one more restaurant to try out. The one at the Bonaventure. Have you been?"

"I have. It would be quite lovely right now. The glow of the city lights on your face would light you up in a way that you couldn't even imagine."

Well then, Marialena thought. *He's* definitely flirting. All she could do in return was hide her blushing cheeks in her glass of wine. She took the smallest sip.

17

"Maybe she and I should save that one for last, then," she said.

He smiled. "Maybe you should."

Marialena was suddenly very aware of how the alcohol was affecting her and flagged down the bartender. "Hey, may I also have a water please?"

"Of course," said the bartender.

"What do you do for a living, if I may ask?"

"I work for a temp agency. I interview and hire people with certain job skills and fit them to specific jobs. I've been there for six years and I guess I've gotten good at reading people and figuring out where they'll succeed."

"Oh, wow. So, I imagine you have to have a sense of what people's skills are?"

"Not skills so much. I mean, it comes into play for sure, but mostly I try to figure out what people are passionate about. I ask them the questions I'm supposed to ask, but I ask them a few extra. Try to figure out where they'll be happy. It's not something I can do all the time, but I try to when I can. But you know what? I can't sit here talking about myself when *you* are sitting right in front of me."

He laughed.

"Okay, sure. So, you know who I am. I'm honored. What do you want to know?"

Marialena blushed. "Let's start with something that won't give me away as a fan. What brought *you* to this restaurant tonight?"

"It was a business dinner with the money for my next project. And I'm really glad they picked this place. I didn't know they had a dessert option I really wanted to get my mouth on," he said hungrily.

She paused for a second when the bartender returned with a water. "Anything else?" the bartender asked.

"Maybe in a bit, thanks," he replied.

Marialena was embarrassed. Flattered and embarrassed. The bartender had overheard. When he left, she said, "Well, this dessert isn't quite on the menu." She said it with a smile to suggest that maybe she could get talked into it depending how the night went.

"Do you have a boyfriend?" he asked, not beating around the bush.

"No. I just don't normally do this kind of thing."

"Of course. My apologies. It was a silly thing to say. No, you're not on the menu. You're more like the exquisite gem someone finds once in a lifetime. You see it once in passing and spend the rest of your life looking for it, only never to find it ever again."

"That's very kind of you to say." Marialena smiled, shyly. "You have a way with words. It's no wonder you're my favorite director."

"Oh, so I'm your *favorite* director?" he laughed.

"Why is that so funny?"

"I doubt I'm anyone's favorite. My films are sad. Beautiful, sure, but they're sad." He searched the room. "My latest project will be different. But a girl like you shouldn't respond to the kind of sadness in my previous work."

"Well, you don't know anything about me. But I don't think they're sad. I mean, I can't be the only one who appreciates the way you captured new love and the

19

excitement and nervous energy the first time two mouths came together. That was amazing. And the way you captured Paris at night, in the dark? So beautiful. It's so tempting to film it in all its beauty and splendor, but you went another way. And the lovemaking scene? Wow. Just wow. Even I felt like I was invading their privacy. It was so dark you could only make out shadows and the candlelight. I loved the way you could hear the street performer playing the guitar just outside of their window. *You see beauty.*" She took a deep breath. She had gotten excited for a second.

He was silent, listening to her. He looked down into his glass and smiled. "I can see that *you* see beauty." He let that sink in for a moment. "But I don't think I can take credit for all that."

Marialena didn't respond right away. She racked her brain, trying to figure out what he meant. She looked at him for an explanation.

"I believe you are referring to 'Paris in the Dark.' Great film," he admitted. Marielana squinted her eyes at him, trying to figure out where he was going with this. "Esteban Guttierez," he said.

"Yes, I know," Marialena said, confused.

He laughed loudly and boastfully. "I can assure you I am not Esteban Guttierez."

Marialena panicked. She looked around, trying to figure it out.

"Oh, I know him. Sweet guy. Short, quiet, very kind. How in the world did you confuse me for him?" He was getting a kick out of this.

"What? Oh my god? You're joking!" Marialena felt herself getting red. She finished the last of her wine, then

20

switched to water and ordered a second round of both. She was going to need this. "Okay, so who are you then? God, I am so embarrassed."

"My name is Patrick Denny."

Marialena put her hands to her mouth. "Patrick Denny?"

He laughed.

"So, you have heard of me?"

"You did 'Last November.'"

"I did," he said, smiling.

Marialena laughed in spite of herself. She thought for a minute. What the hell was happening here? So this *wasn't* Esteban Guttierez...which was funny because he didn't look like an Esteban at all.

"When my cousin and I sat down, she immediately recognized you. She said you were my favorite director. And that's when I said 'Gutierrez?' and she said 'Yes.'" Marialena paused for a second, trying to figure out what happened. "I guess she knew what *you* looked like because I told her to watch 'Last November' and she watched the special features...but I never had. She must have confused you with Gutierrez, since I also made her watch 'Paris in the Dark' around the same time."

Patrick smiled the entire time she was telling the story. At least he was a good sport about it. "But she showed me your picture on Google." Marialena thought back to that moment. She suddenly remembered that Roxanne had asked her how to spell Gutierrez and then said she was just going to type in the movie. "Oh god, she must have typed in 'Last November.' Oh shit. I am so sorry about this. This is so embarrassing." She put her face in her hands.

21

The bartender finally came back with her wine and a separate glass of water for the both of them. It took a little longer since two more groups of people had come to the bar. She had to admit, this bartender had a knack for arriving during the strangest parts of a conversation. She peeked from behind her fingers, said "Thank you," and smiled as he set the water in front of them.

Patrick touched her arm gently and laughed. "Hey, don't worry. It's humbling actually. Thanks for keeping me grounded. All this 'you're my favorite director' stuff was getting to my head."

Marialena put her hands down and smiled at him. She could still feel the redness in her cheeks, but it was fading.

"Hey, I loved 'Last November!'" She racked her brain trying to come up with something genius about the film. She remembered trying to explain it to Roxy over the phone. *It was about an older woman in her 80's on her deathbed...and how one holiday, the daughter comes to visit. The mother is well enough to talk most of the time, and they talk about memories from that one specific fantastic holiday from years earlier. But the daughter's memories are from her childhood with her mom, while her mom's memories are different. She remembers an affair she had that year. It's just incredible and it's a good reminder that your parent is a person who isn't just a parent. They had this whole other life that didn't always revolve around you.* She remembered telling that much to Roxy. "Your film really made people think."

"Thank you," he said quietly.

"No, really. I'm not just saying that. I recommended it to my cousin, remember? And you won the Oscar for

22

that, didn't you? I didn't watch that year, but I remember being happy for you. That's incredible! I actually bought it the day it came out. I loved it so much in the theater. It was a movie that really, *really* made you think about your own memories and that of your parents'. And the performances...oh my God. I remember how I felt I was doing it all wrong. Life, you know? I wanted to look back on my life and remember the kind of things Gloria, your character, had remembered, even the kind of things her daughter remembered. With my luck, I am going to look back and it's going to be a series of swiping left. All these images of men I'll never know haunting my thoughts."

She glanced up at him and he had this very serious look on his face, the twinkle gone from his eyes.

"Swiping left? That's the dating app, right?"

"Yeah."

"You're not mentally swiping left right now, are you?"

Marialena shook her head. "No." She gave him a small smile.

"You need to delete that app from your phone as soon as you get home. You don't need that crap," he said matter-of-factly. "From what I can tell, you're better than that and you deserve so much more," he said, bluntly. Man, he was really smooth.

23

"You're probably right. I should." She took a deep breath. "Your film was very beautiful, though. And I love the way it was shot, the lighting, the dialogue. Gloria's memories, and just the concept overall. I remember I tried to explain it to Roxy and I couldn't do it justice. How you pitched it, I'll never know." She was rambling now and made a mental note to slow down.

"Thank you. Yeah, that one meant a lot to me. I'll tell you one thing, though. I've never wished I was Esteban Gutierrez. But tonight, I do." He smiled sadly. "It's good, though, it's good motivation." He laughed suddenly. "Just wait until I tell him this story."

Marialena put her hands to her mouth. "No, you wouldn't."

He smiled. "Oh, I'm going to."

Marialena cringed.

"You are right, though. *He is good*. He's like that in person, too. Very tuned to nature and personable. Very soft around the edges, lovable, and down to earth."

Marialena smiled at that thought. That seemed to better fit Esteban's films.

Patrick drank the last of his wine while Marialena watched him. He glanced at his watch.

24

"Marialena, how about we grab the check?" He put his hand on her knee, just underneath her skirt.

Marialena noticed how he had first checked the time, and she realized she had no idea how much time had passed. Out of curiosity, she went to her purse to check for her phone. She felt around for it but couldn't find it.

"Um, hold on. I think I've misplaced my phone."

Patrick flagged down the bartender, asked for the check, and also asked him if a cell phone had been turned in.

"No, sorry. Have you tried calling it yet?" he asked Patrick.

"Not yet," Marialena answered, searching her purse again.

Meanwhile, Marialena was very embarrassed. She had been nervous meeting him. Something like this was bound to happen.

Patrick asked Marialena for her phone number. He called it, and Marialena heard her phone ringing. It was faint, but it was definitely her phone. She walked toward the ringing phone, and bent down to find that it had fallen underneath the table she was at with her cousin, out of eyesight. Relieved, she picked it up. Thankfully, the table was empty of customers.

"Found it. Thanks for calling it," she said to Patrick.

At first, Patrick was nervous about his number showing up on her phone. But she didn't seem like the crazy type. She was a genuinely nice girl. He decided to go for it, and he bent down to whisper close to her ear.

"How about I get us a room at that hotel you mentioned?"

"What hotel?" she asked, looking into his eyes.

"The Westin Bonaventure," he replied, smiling coyly. "The night is young, so why not?"

Marialena took a deep breath. She searched the room briefly while she thought of an answer, but couldn't come up with anything.

"I just need to use the restroom. Give me about two seconds," she said.

Inside the restroom, she exited the stall and took a look at herself in the mirror. She searched for the answer in her reflection, staring into her own eyes.

When she came out, she squared her shoulders. She took Patrick by the arm in the parking lot, stopped, and looked at him. He leaned down and kissed her softly on the mouth, his hands on her waist.

26

After, Marialena looked away. "You know, I'd like to go with you, but I don't think it's a good idea."

Patrick Denny nodded. "I understand."

"You're great, though. I'm sure tomorrow morning I'll be kicking myself."

Patrick laughed. "Call me any time you find yourself regretting it." He hadn't let go of her yet.

She put a hand on his cheek and kissed the other side. "Thank you for this, for even thinking of me. You've been very kind."

"I have a feeling I'm going to be thinking about you for a long time."

Marialena smiled at him and turned to leave. She headed toward the bar where Roxanne said she'd be, and smiled to herself the entire way. He had been lovely, but no, she wouldn't go with him. It wouldn't have been right. Besides, how embarrassing was it that she had confused him with someone else? She knew Roxanne would get a good laugh out of it though.

Chapter Two

Marialena heard her phone ringing. She noticed that the caller was not in her contacts, but in her area code. She lowered the volume on the TV and answered.

"Hello?"

"Hi, Marialena?" asked a deep older male voice.

"Yes, this is Marialena," she answered, unsure of who she was speaking to.

"Hi, this is Patrick Denny."

PATRICK DENNY. *Oh shit*. Marialena looked for the remote and fumbled with the buttons, trying to turn it off.

"Sorry. Listen, I know it's been a few months and that we didn't necessarily get off on the right foot, but something about that night has stayed with me. I was wondering if I could have a few minutes of your time to propose something to you."

"Yeah, sure." She wondered what he was going to say next.

"I haven't caught you in bad time, have I?"

"No, no...not at all."

"Okay. I'll cut to the chase; I'm starting my next film soon, and I remembered what you said about being good at reading people, at seeing people. This film, it's a little on the unorthodox side, for me anyway. I'm going to have a small budget for this one. I have casting people I always use, but I was wondering, hoping really, if you would like to join the team."

Marialena was quiet. He couldn't be serious.

"It would just be for a week or two. I need someone to look at auditions. I would like your eye. Look, I know you have never done anything like this before, and if I disagree with you, then I disagree with you and I go with my gut. But I think I need someone slightly younger, someone like you, who might be able to see the things I may not see in today's youth. I want to get this one right. And seeing how the topic of this film is youth, well, I would like you to help me."

"You want me to help you cast?" Marialena's mind was racing. She was shocked he kept her number, and she couldn't believe he was asking for her help.

"I was hoping you would. We could work around your schedule. Or if you're able to, a week off of work would help. We'd pay you for your time, obviously. Two weeks would be better than one, but whatever you can do would be great."

"I would love to. What's the film?" She could take two weeks off easily. She never went anywhere, never took vacations. She went to Nashville once, two years ago. Since then, she'd only taken small fragments of time off to get errands done or to stay home. Staycations, Roxanne had called them.

"The idea came from my son. He lived with me years ago. He's older now, twenty-two actually. But when he was a teenager he stayed with me, and even under my roof there was so much I didn't see. He was a troubled individual then. I think a lot of teenagers go through this period of their lives where they feel unloved, unwanted. This film digs into that a little bit." He paused, allowing her to digest it all.

29

"I'm going to include a song that he wrote in the beginning of the film, or maybe the end. The film is about a boy, a teenager actually, who comes to Los Angeles to stay with his aunt. His own father needs to time to start his new family. My son is bisexual, and so the character is as well. It's an important topic and one that matters a great deal to me."

"Wow that sounds like a wonderful idea for a movie. So, the main character is based on your son?"

Patrick Denny sighed on the other end, thinking of how to answer. "In a way, he's the inspiration, but the character is a different person altogether. And that's where you come in. I want the character, Julian, to be...distraught. He's confused, conflicted, someone who is just trying to figure out the kind of person he wants himself to be."

"Like James Dean?"

"Well, yeah he comes to mind. It's interesting that you'd say that; he keeps coming up as an example."

"Any time anyone says distraught teen, I mean, that's what James Dean was all about..."

"Yes, but he wasn't a teenager. I'd like to go for someone younger if possible."

"Okay."

"Younger and maybe more innocent."

"What about sex appeal?"

Patrick Denny thought for a second. "No, that's not necessary either. I want the audience to be able to relate to him, but they don't have to be in love with him. He can be handsome, and that's a bonus for us, but not a priority."

"I know what you mean. So, when are the auditions?"

"Whenever you're available, the sooner the better. We have the green light on our end. Just say when."

"I'll need a script."

"Of course. I can have one overnighted to you. I would also like to get together for a lunch or a dinner, to hash out some more details, if you're okay with that."

Marialena's head was reeling. A Hollywood business meeting.

"Marialena, are you free for dinner this week?"

Marialena had to admit, she loved the way he asked. His voice was deep, older, and sophisticated. He spoke like a man, much different from all the guys she knew at this stage in her life.

Marialena paused for a second before answering. "Yes. Let me read over the script. I'll see what I can do about work, but I'm pretty sure I can take time off. I can meet you Thursday of this week."

"Thursday sounds perfect. Same place as last time?"

Marialena laughed. "I would love that."

"Okay...can you be there at seven? It may be a long dinner. We have a lot to go over. Plan on ordering dessert and a few drinks."

Marialena liked the idea of that. "Yes, seven is perfect. Thank you for thinking of me. I'm looking forward to it. I only hope that I won't let you down."

"Well, I seriously doubt you will. Thanks for doing this for me. I don't always ask for help, but I certainly know to ask when I really need it. This film is very dear to my heart, and you *feel* things. From the way you described your love for that *other* director—I'm still trying to forget that by the way—I can tell that you see things from the heart," he said.

"You're trying to forget that? I still want to crawl under a rock. But thank you, again."

He laughed loudly. "Don't worry about it. I'm only kidding. But yes, let me take down your address for the script and I will make sure my people get it over to you immediately."

She gave him her address, and they confirmed their dinner later that week. When she got off the phone, the TV show she was watching was far from her mind. She sat there, staring blankly for a few minutes. She couldn't believe this was actually happening to her.

***

When Marialena arrived home the next day after work, she saw a package at her front door. It had to be the script. She picked it up and went inside.

She threw the package on the table, went to the bedroom to change out her work clothes, made a sandwich, and poured herself a glass of wine.

She took the script out and saw that the first page was a poem.

Keeper

When you've lost your way
Say you'll find a way
Read between the lines

Of your broken mind

Smoke frames your face
Smiles fade away
As you contemplate
What led you here today?

Don't fall behind
Don't fade away
You'll find your way

Don't fall behind
Don't fade away
Stay here today
And you'll find a way

Marialena realized that those must be the lyrics Patrick's son wrote. She wondered what genre of music it would be. From what she could tell, the lyrics went with what she knew of the story so far. Marialena bit into her sandwich and turned the page.

After an hour of reading, she refilled her glass of wine and thought about the main character, Julian. She liked him. He was someone you wanted to protect and love, someone you wanted to stand by. Someone you'd feel proud to call your friend. Marialena was also curious about the girl in the story, Rosa. On paper, she was sweet and energetic, honest and real.

She went back to the script and read the rest. When she was done, she looked at her phone to check the time

33

and marveled at how quickly time flew. She stifled a yawn and stretched. When she slept that night, she dreamt of Julian. He looked just like James Dean, only with black hair. Marialena was playing the part of Rosa. In the dream, she had gone to his room and it was bare, except for a bed and drawers.

The next morning, she remembered the dream and her heart broke for Julian a little more. That gray room and its emptiness screamed out to her. "Love me," it said. It said the words that Julian couldn't, or didn't know, to say. She loved the way Julian looked in her dream. Messy dark hair, crazy beautiful smile, eyes you could fall into. Yes, she could see him clearly. Now all they had to do was *find him*. Later that day, when Marialena went to the supermarket, she caught herself searching for someone who could play Julian. She looked at every guy there, and wondered if that was why everyone in Los Angeles was looking at one another. Were they trying to cast one another in some project? She thanked her lucky stars she wasn't a professional casting agent. The hunt would eat her alive. Her dinner with Patrick was coming up the following night. She wasn't nervous. She was anxious to start and excited to see what faces came her way.

***

Marialena arrived at the restaurant a little early, despite a few mishaps. She had to stay at work longer than expected, a client kept her on the phone, traffic was worse than usual, she couldn't seem to find the right outfit, and she was now nervous and rushing. The more she rushed, the more mistakes she made. For instance, she tried hanging up a dress after she tried it on, and the hanger got caught on another hanger. When she tried to unhook them, she pulled a little too hard, hurt her elbow on the closet door, and twisted her ankle when she tripped over the shirt that had fallen on the floor. After that debacle, she rushed through her makeup. She had to take it all off and start again.

When she arrived, she gave Patrick Denny's name. He wasn't there yet. Marialena said she'd wait at the bar, and that's when she saw the same bartender from before. She smiled to herself, remembering how embarrassing that night was. Confusing Patrick for Esteban Gutierrez, losing her phone. But tonight was a fresh start. She took a deep breath, squared her shoulders, and walked toward the corner of the restaurant to the bar. She sat down and nervously tucked her hair behind her ear.

The bartender smiled at her, but she couldn't tell if it was his everyday 'How can I help you' smile or if it was a 'Hey, I remember you' smile.

"What can I get for you?" he asked warmly.

"A wine, red. Surprise me."

The bartender smiled. She had gotten better at this.

"Here on business?"

"Yes, I'm meeting someone, actually." Her phone buzzed. A text from Patrick.

"Sorry, running a few minutes behind. Traffic. Have a drink at the bar."

She smiled at the text. *Beat you to it*, she thought.

35

"Traffic out there is so bad tonight," she said to the bartender.

"I think they're closing down Hollywood Blvd for a concert tonight."

"Oh, who's playing?"

He shrugged. "Not sure, actually," he said, pouring her wine.

Marialena nodded, unsure of what to say next.

"So, this wine is actually my favorite. Try it and tell me what you think," the bartender added.

Marialena swirled the wine in her glass. She took a sip and closed her eyes. It was good. Not as good as the one she had before, but she definitely liked it. Smooth.

"It's really good," she said, looking him squarely in the eye. "But I have one here I like better. I had a Pinot Noir last time."

He laughed. "I remember. Just thought you'd like to switch it up."

Marialena smiled. "Well, this one is still very good."

"No problem. Let me know if you need anything else."

Marialena thanked him, and she took the script out of her bag to review it until Patrick got there.

"Hey, so I think your guy is here," the bartender said, nodding to Patrick checking in with the hostess.

Marialena turned around. "Yep, that's him. I should probably close out, but is it okay if I take this to the table with me?"

"Yeah, that's fine."

Marialena flagged down Patrick. He walked up to the bar and kissed her cheek. "Hey, thank you so much for meeting me. It turns out I wasn't as late as I thought

I'd be. And listen, I really am excited about this. Thank you for agreeing to do this, despite what happened last time. I hope you know that's not what I'm after. But I must say, you look wonderful tonight."

He looked at Marialena, who was more conservatively dressed in a pencil skirt that went past her knees and a red blouse. He was more casual than he had been before. He was wearing black jeans and a dark navy blue sweater which looked great with his sparkling blue eyes.

"Thanks. You do, too. I'm actually really glad you thought of me for the project. I finished the script. It's incredible. I loved it."

Patrick Denny was beaming. She could tell it was close to his heart.

"Let's get a table and order some dinner."

The bartender came back with the tab and Patrick took out his wallet to pay for Marialena.

"Oh no, I can get this," Marialena intervened.

"Nonsense. You're here doing me a favor. It's the least I could do."

Thank you," she said kindly.

"So, you said you finished the script?"

Marialena nodded. They were seated at a table. Marialena perused the menu, thinking about getting a salad.

"Tell me, what were you thinking for the main character?" he asked.

"Well, as I read it, I couldn't get James Dean out of my head. I had a dream about it, actually."

Marialena proceeded to tell him about her dream, the empty room, and the loneliness she felt for him.

"That's actually pretty great for the character. We need to write that in. A bedroom with no personality. It's perfect. He moved in not that long ago, but he feels no need to change anything or to add anything of his own, because he feels there isn't anything permanent. I love it. That really does add to the character development. When Rosa comes over, their friendship builds, and so does his confidence. He starts to come out a little more and with each step in the right direction, he adds something to the wall."

Marialena nodded, smiling. Her dream was going to be a scene in the movie! "So, I was thinking for the guy, he should look young, I agree. Doe-eyed, maybe. I want him to be the perfect balance between innocent and hardened. We have to make him approachable, but he's hurt, too."

"Doe-eyed? I like it. But we really just have to *see* him."

The waiter came by and they ordered.

"Have you cast Rosa yet?" she asked.

"Not yet." Patrick was hoping that she would be able to help with that too, but wanted to hold off on asking her until he saw how she worked with casting the part of Julian. "When are you free for the auditions?"

"How long does the process usually take?"

"It varies, depending on how picky we are and who we get. Our Julian could be the first guy to walk through the door. We need to pick a few anyway, for screen tests, once we find some Rosas."

"Okay. I could take some time off of work."

"It can also be scheduled for the weekends, if that's easier for you."

"You know, I actually have a ton of vacation hours. I never go anywhere."

"Marialena, that's a shame. Why haven't you gone anywhere?" he asked, allowing himself to take her beauty in. She looked absolutely stunning. It was like she didn't know her own beauty and he wanted to show her. But he knew he couldn't. He had reached out to her for business and didn't want to mix the two, at least not this time. He could tell she was more sensitive, and he liked that about her. Plus, he had a feeling she was perfect for what he needed. He didn't want her to become distracted and he didn't want to become distracted himself.

"That's the problem. I want to go everywhere," she answered. "But I don't want to go alone and I'm not big on traveling with a big group. I guess I just want that special someone to go with, and I've been single for a while."

"You should just *go*. I have this great place in New York. All you have to do is say the word and I could arrange for you to stay there." Patrick didn't know why he offered his place to Marialena. He barely knew her and he wasn't the type to invite strangers. But there was something trustworthy about her and he knew he didn't have anything to worry about.

"That's a sweet offer. New York? I think I might want to stick to my original plan. See, I've always wanted to go to Flagstaff."

"Flagstaff?" He laughed. "Why Flagstaff?"

Marialena shrugged. "I drove through it once and I fell in love with it. I've just always wanted to stay in Flagstaff and drive to the Grand Canyon. See the stars at night, that kind of thing. Of all the places I want to visit, that may be at the top of my list."

"You can see the stars from much closer places than the Grand Canyon."

Patrick didn't know Marialena very well, but he enjoyed her company. So far, there hadn't been a dull or awkward moment between them. He hadn't seen what she was capable of in a business capacity yet, but he was glad he hired her for this project.

"Sure, but I'd also like to see the Grand Canyon. And I will. But not before we cast this movie." She smiled and they moved back on topic. "Can you picture Julian's face?" Marialena asked.

"Not, yet. I just think of my son. You?"

"Yeah, actually. There are two versions of him in my head. The James Dean dream version, and the younger softer version. I'm a little worried that I am stuck on those two images."

Patrick shook his head. "If it's a good casting call, Julian will make himself known to you and it will erase those images from your head. When do you think you can start?"

"I can start on Monday, actually. Is that okay?"

"That's incredible. It was just what I was hoping for. Meet me one more time this weekend before Monday. I'd like to make this transition smooth for you." She wondered if he wanted something more, but it didn't seem like it. He appeared to be all business this time, which Marialena was grateful for. She couldn't picture herself with someone like Patrick Denny. It wasn't that he was older, but she couldn't put her finger on it, not yet.

40

"Thank you. I'd like that." They talked about the project for the rest of the dinner. She could tell Patrick was excited. It was a great screenplay with a great message. She couldn't wait to be a part of it. When Patrick finally convinced her to order dessert, he brought up Esteban Gutierrez.

"You know, I've been meaning to call him. I'd like him to come out when we start filming."

"Really?" Patrick noticed how Marialena's eyes lit up at the very mention of his name.

"You were right about him; I went back to watch his movies again after I met you. He's pretty great at capturing emotions."

Marialena smiled from ear-to-ear. "Yeah, he really is."

"Look at you, the way you light up. He's doing something right, if he can make you glow like that."

"Oh, it's nothing. I'm just a fan," she said, embarrassed.

"No, it's not nothing. It's exactly what I want for my film, a feeling that my audience can relate to the characters. He's managed to do it so well." Marialena smiled at him. He was right, Esteban Gutierrez had an eye for that kind of thing.

The rest of the night, they talked about Patrick's movie. It was still untitled, and they threw around names, but didn't settle on anything. When dinner was over, he stood up and shook her hand.

"Welcome aboard," he said. "I'm looking forward to seeing what you can bring to the table."

"Me, too."

When she walked to her car, she was ecstatic. She couldn't believe this was really happening to her, and on Monday. It was so soon. When she got home, she called Roxanne, who was back in Nashville, two hours later than Los Angeles.

"Don't screw it up, darling. This is a real opportunity. Once in a lifetime."

"I know, I know." Marialena took a deep breath.

"I have faith in you, though. I think you'll be great."

"Thanks, and thanks for you pushing me to get myself out there. I never would have met him if it weren't for you."

"Well, I sort of screwed it up though, didn't I?" Roxanne laughed, remembering how she had confused the two directors.

"It all worked out," Marialena said.

"All right, I have to go to bed. Listen, I love you and I am so happy for you."

"Thanks. Love you, too."

Chapter Three

Patrick Denny was in his office when his secretary announced a visitor. He finished up an email and stood up when Esteban Gutierrez was shown in. They shook hands and Patrick patted him on the arm. He was at least five inches taller and about five years older than Esteban.

"Hey, thanks for stopping by." Patrick sat back in his chair, inviting Esteban to do the same. Esteban looked at his surroundings as he sat down, his hazel eyes taking it all in.

"No problem. This is a nice little setup you have here," he said.

"What can I say? It's my home away from home. In fact, I may spend more time here than anywhere else," Patrick said, at ease.

Esteban nodded, knowing full well what Patrick meant. When working on a project, there was time for little else. Esteban missed those days. He hadn't written in over a year and wondered if he ever would again. He had gotten hit with writer's block and hadn't been able to get back to writing, no matter how hard he tried. Being here in this office with Patrick made him feel a little uneasy. He wasn't sure why he had been invited. He had only met Patrick once or twice and was surprised when he received the phone call. Patrick Denny hadn't said much on the phone. Still, he wasn't doing anything with his time, so why not take him up on his invitation?

"I like it," Esteban continued. "It's cozy, the lights aren't too bright. It has that vibe, you know? Good for writing. Nice artwork, an espresso machine in the corner for those late nights."

"And a much-needed corner set aside for some liquor. Can I get you something?"

Esteban eyed the liquor behind him. "No, I'm good. Thanks." He wasn't sure if Patrick was offering him coffee or alcohol.

"So, how's..." Patrick paused, struggling to recall a name, "...Laura, was it?"

"Oh yeah, Laura," Esteban said a little uncomfortably, shifting in his chair. He remembered that Patrick had met Laura at Sundance last year, or maybe it was the year before. "Laura and I are no longer together, actually."

"Oh, I'm sorry to hear that."

"It wasn't pretty, but it happens. What can you do?" he said, as Patrick watched him the way directors sometimes tend to do, looking for something they could use one day. Patrick liked the way Esteban's eyes spoke the truth. He wasn't trying to hide anything, didn't put up a wall. He was genuine, and you didn't find a whole lot of that here. It made him think of Marialena.

"There are plenty of fish in the sea," Patrick said hopefully.

"Yeah, sure," Esteban replied, trying to be agreeable. "I've heard that." He gave him a small smile.

Patrick nodded. "You know, I can think of one woman in particular who thinks you're the bee's knees." Patrick laughed to himself. "In fact, it's a funny story. When I met her, she thought *I was you*."

"How is that possible?" Esteban smiled despite himself. The two were nothing alike. Esteban was short, Patrick *tall*. Esteban was American of Spanish descent with olive skin, while Patrick was American of Irish descent. Patrick had gray hair, Esteban still had dark brown hair. He had a warm smile, while Patrick's was more mischievous.

"Well, I met her a few months ago. Someone had mistakenly told her that I was you or something to that effect. When we met, she went on and on about how much she loved my work and this and that, but she thought she was talking to you." Patrick laughed again. "I couldn't get her to sleep with me that night, but I might have if I let her go on believing I *was you*."

"This really happened?" Esteban asked. He didn't believe it.

"It really did." Patrick shook his head. "I was this close to claiming your work as my own," he said, holding up two fingers an inch apart.

"Well, at least someone wanted to. So, who's the woman?" he asked.

"Beautiful Hispanic girl. Sadly, she's not interested in me. But she has a good head on her shoulders and I actually hired her as a consultant for this project."

"No shit?"

"Yeah, I should introduce the two of you. In fact, she's here somewhere."

Esteban laughed. "That's one hell of a story. She actually thought you were me?"

"Oh, you should have heard her go on about you."

Patrick laughed and proceeded to tell him why he was invited. He described his film to Esteban who nodded and listened intently.

"Anyway, this woman I met sort of inspired me to reach out to you for your work. She's right about you, you know? She loves your work because you know how to capture people, young people. And I was wondering if there's anything you could tell from my description of this film to you. I'm wondering if you could pick up on anything that I might be missing. I don't want to take any chances or make a mistake on this one. It's too important to me."

"Aren't they all?" Esteban asked. He was curious and flattered that he was being asked for his advice.

Patrick shrugged, his voice deep and passionate. "I want this film to resonate with young people. You seem to have done that. There's a romance to what you've done. I seem to have become jaded, and I want to try to recapture the feeling of young innocence. Young love, young romance. How did you do it?"

Esteban shifted in his chair. "I don't know. I mean, I don't think I lost that sort of romantic innocence within myself."

"Is that so?" Patrick leaned back in his chair. "I remember what it felt like, but I feel like I'm grasping when I try to reach for it. It's not a hunger so much as a need to be loved, a desire to be loved."

"Well, if you understand that, then you've hit the nail right on the head. Your story sounds pretty good. Try to see it from their eyes, your characters' eyes. It will help when you cast the film, when you meet them, and when they start putting in their own emotions. It turns into this crazy mix of your feelings and theirs. That's when the creative energy starts to show itself, as I am sure you already know. I mean, hell man, you won the Oscar. You must have done something right."

Patrick nodded absentmindedly, lost in thought. After a few moments, he snapped back into reality…"Will you come to a few shoot days, take a look, tell me if I'm missing something?"

"Yeah, sure." Esteban nodded. "Whatever you need."

Patrick stood up. "Let's meet for lunch or dinner next week. We can talk more. I appreciate you taking time from your busy schedule to see me." They both stood and Patrick walked him out the door. He spotted Marialena sitting on a sofa in the corner with a cup of coffee in her hand, reviewing photographs. It was only her second day on the job. Patrick leaned into Esteban.

"There she is," he whispered, as if she were a doe he didn't want to disturb out in the wild. "Let me introduce you. I'm sure she could get some of your blood pumping."

"Her? What is she, like twenty-years old?" Esteban whispered.

"Oh, come on. I'm sure you've dated women in their twenties." Patrick led Esteban over to Marialena.

"Yeah sure, *when I was in my twenties,*" Esteban whispered back.

"Marialena, I'd like to introduce you to someone." Marialena took a large sip of her coffee and looked up. She recognized Esteban this time, having properly researched him after the whole fiasco of confusing him with Patrick Denny.

"Esteban Gutierrez, I'd like you to meet Marialena Villanueva. She's going to help me cast this picture." Her face felt flushed as he stuck out his hand to shake hers. His handshake was firm, his hand warm. She set her coffee down and straightened her skirt. She hadn't noticed this before, but he was quite handsome. His pictures didn't do him justice. And he looked much younger than his age, forty-nine, if Marialena recalled correctly. He was wearing an untucked white dress shirt, a light brown corduroy jacket, and dark jeans. Marialena was glad that she had gone shopping for new clothes. She felt confident in her white button-down shirt and black pencil skirt.

Esteban looked her right in the eyes. Marialena found his stare piercing, like he could see inside of her soul. She didn't know this before, but she could see that his eyes were sparkling hazel and she felt it difficult to turn away. She was suddenly very hot and didn't know what to say, where to start. To gush, or not to.

"Pleasure to meet you," he finally said. He leaned in. "I hear you're a fan." Patrick was right, Marialena was beautiful. Long brown wavy hair. The biggest brown eyes he had ever seen, with great lips.

"Yeah," she said, looking from Esteban, to Patrick, then to Esteban again. "I don't know where to start actually. I'm honored."

Patrick's cell phone rang and he excused himself to answer it. Marialena found herself alone with Esteban. She cleared her throat.

"What brings you to these parts?" Marialena asked, trying to be polite.

"Oh, it would seem that I have you to thank for that. How is it that you got one of the most talented directors of our time to come to *me* for advice?" Esteban asked with a raised eyebrow.

"Oh, I don't think I had anything to do with that." She kept her head down, staring at a young man's headshot. She couldn't bring herself to look at Esteban Gutierrez. It wasn't just that he was handsome, it was that he was a talented writer and director and his films really moved her, and here he was.

"I think you and I both know that you're wrong," Esteban said. She looked up and he winked at her. Marialena smiled back and tried to relax her shoulders.

"Who can blame him?" Marialena asked. "You're as gifted as any one of them," she said under her breath, feeling a little daring.

Esteban nodded. "Yeah, I think so and apparently so do you. But you know what? I don't think anyone else knows." Esteban laughed. "Thank you, though. It means a lot that someone out there gets it." Marialena nodded, smiled. She couldn't believe she was standing in Patrick Denny's studio and that she was talking to Esteban Gutierrez. He looked over at some of the headshots. She had two separate piles, the ones she liked and the ones she didn't.

"May I?" He reached over to pick up one of the piles, not wanting to leave right away. There was something he immediately liked about Marialena. He could tell that she was genuine and honest.

"Yes, of course." Marialena sat down next to him.

"Wow, you're going for the really young ones."

"Well, yeah, I want him to be a believable high school kid."

Esteban nodded. He saw one that he liked and pointed it out to Marialena. "Hey, this guy is great." He inched toward her and their knees touched, but Marialena didn't move away. She looked at the headshot, nodded, and smiled.

"Yeah, I am looking forward to seeing him in person."

"He has those eyes, you know?" Esteban said, turning to face Marialena. She felt something there, and within her stomach, too. This was definitely the man she had given over endless hours to, watching and dissecting his films. This was the man who made her feel like she wasn't alone in this world. Alone in her thoughts, hopes, and dreams. It was a different feeling from when she had met Patrick. He had a presence that spoke to her in a way she couldn't explain, a softness around the eyes. The mere idea of wanting to get lost in his eyes made her look away.

Patrick came back out of his office, but the two of them remained seated. "Marialena, I am so sorry but I have to cancel our dinner." He turned to Esteban. He wanted to give him some kind of signal that he wasn't chasing Marialena, not anymore. "We were going to go over some photos before the big day on Thursday. But Marialena, we'll reschedule tomorrow. Listen, I have to get going. Esteban, thanks so much for stopping by." Esteban stood and shook his hand.

Patrick started to walk away but then turned, remembering about Marialena's car. "Marialena, I was going to be your ride home tonight. I am so sorry. Will you be able to make it home?"

Marialena shook her head. "Oh yeah, I will be fine." Patrick nodded and was out of the office in a blink.

Esteban and Marialena both sat back down. "It's just frustrating knowing that half of these are going to be duds. I mean, a picture doesn't really capture a person's essence."

"Yeah, and there's always one that kind of surprises you."

Marialena nodded. She took out her phone and contemplated, then decided to ask Esteban.

"Uber or Lyft? I've never used either. Which one would you go with?"

"I have no idea," he replied. "I've never used either of them."

"Same. My car had a flat this morning, but I am so old-fashioned that I called a taxi and ended up being over an hour late."

"Where do you live?"

"Los Feliz."

"I'm not doing anything, let me take you back."

Marialena laughed. "No, no, no. Los Feliz is on the other side of town. There is no way I could let you do that. Plus, you're Esteban Gutierrez!"

This time Esteban laughed. "One of my favorite restaurants is over that way. Please, let me take you back. It will give me something to do."

Marialena looked at him long and hard, gauging whether or not he was joking, but he looked dead serious. "Well, I can probably take some of these home with me. Okay, sure. Why not?" Marialena gathered up her belongings. Esteban watched her, unable to get what Patrick said out of his head. She didn't seem too young after all, and it had been months since he was with anyone romantically. He was certainly pining for that physical touch, but Marialena was way out his league, not to mention age range. Still, he couldn't imagine *not* taking her home.

"Okay, I think I have everything."

"Here, let me help you with that." Esteban grabbed the files from her arm. When she stood next to him, she noticed that he was about an inch shorter than she was, which put him at 5'6".

"Thanks. So, where do you live?" she asked him.

"I have a place on this side of town, but I haven't been getting out much lately, so this will give me a nice excuse."

"There will probably be some traffic at this hour."

"Oh sure. That's okay, it will give us a chance to talk," he said as they got into the elevator.

"I can't believe this. Here I am, with my favorite director." Marialena stopped to look at him and felt her cheeks getting red. Esteban smiled back at her but didn't say anything. "I'm sorry. I needed to let that out," she admitted.

"It's okay, I get that all the time," he replied.

"Do you? Oh gosh, does it ever get old?"

Esteban laughed. "I was kidding." He was quiet for a second. "People do tell me that they're fans. But I don't really surround myself with it, so it's nice to hear every once in a while."

They got out of the elevator and Esteban led the way into the garage. He drove a gray Maserati. Esteban held the door open for her and she took her files back.

"Thanks so much for this."

"No problem," he said and closed the door.

Esteban sat down in the driver's seat. "Okay, so I have a question. What is it about my work that gives me favorite director status?" He held his parking ticket in his hand and handed it to the attendant as he drove out into the bright November sunlight.

"Oh gosh, where do I start?" she asked, smiling from ear-to-ear.

Esteban laughed. He could feel himself getting nervous as he waited for her to answer. "You know what? Forget I asked. We'll hold off on that for a while. Different question. Besides my films, which others do you like?"

Marialena took this time to watch him as he drove. He was dressed nicely, for someone claiming he had nothing to do. He looked very handsome, and she liked how he wore his hair. Short, almost boyish. He was going gray around the temples, but Marialena thought it looked sexy. She was attracted to her favorite director. She didn't see that coming.

"Hmmm, what other movies? Well, I am a big fan of 'The Graduate.' Oh, I also really like 'Rebel Without a Cause.'"

"Oh yeah, 'The Graduate' is a great choice. Actually, I might have to share that one with you. I love it. 'Rebel Without a Cause,' I don't know. That one doesn't do it for me, but it seems to work for a lot of people."

"You don't like 'Rebel Without a Cause?' What, were you never a teenager?" she asked, laughing.

"I did just say 'The Graduate,' remember?" They both laughed.

"Yeah, but you just stole that one from me," Marialena said, playfully.

"I didn't steal it. It's a favorite of mine, too. Honest. In fact, I just watched it last week. When was the last time you watched it?"

"Last year," Marialena admitted.

"Well, those are pretty solid choices. I'll give you that. A lot of people love 'Rebel Without a Cause;' I'm just not one of those people. It was shot well, but I don't know, the movie doesn't speak to me. Why do you like it?"

"Well, you have to admit, James Dean is hard to ignore. He steals every single scene and he's so fascinating. And for that time, to tackle what they tackled. I mean, wow."

"Sure. Maybe I need to give it a second chance," he said, trying to be amicable. Esteban fiddled around with his music. "What kind of music do you like?"

Marialena shrugged. "This is fine. Classic is always good." He had left the station on a Jimi Hendrix song.

"Classic it is."

"So, what's this restaurant you like?" she asked.

"It's a Mexican place. It's called Guapo's. Ever been?"

"No, but I know of it. It's actually walking distance from my place."

54

"Wait a minute, you've never been and it's in walking distance?" Esteban shook his head in disbelief. "Please tell me you just moved yesterday."

"I've been meaning to try it, really," she replied.

"You have got to go," he insisted.

"I will, I will," she said, smiling. Talking to Esteban Gutierrez was so easy, she almost forgot who he was.

"You know, people always say that, but I bet you won't go." Esteban looked at her from the corner of his eye. He was feeling playful and hadn't felt that way in a long time. A very long time.

"I will, in fact I'll go tonight. You've inspired me."

"Oh no, you can't go tonight," he said seriously.

"Why is that?"

"Well, I'm going tonight. Right after I drop you off. Why do you think I came out *all* this way?" he asked, teasing her.

"Because you're a nice guy," she said, teasing back. "I see how it is, though. I guess we'll both just have to go." Marialena's heart skipped a beat. Did she just invite herself out to dinner with him? Was she flirting with him? What if he didn't want her to go? She turned and looked out of the window, wanting to avoid looking at him for fear that she'd gone too far.

"Yeah, I guess we'll just have to go together then," he said without hesitation.

"I mean, is that okay? I could try it another time," she said quietly, daring herself to look at him.

"Don't be silly. I was going to extend the invitation to you anyway. Thanks for one-upping me."

"Good, because I'm starving." Marialena was a nervous wreck. She was going to have dinner with her favorite director. Already, he felt like an old friend. It didn't help that she was attracted to him. Could this really be happening? She stole a glance at him as he drove. He was squinting in the sun a little, so he flipped the visor down. His hair was dark brown and the only signs that showed his age were the graying at his temples and a few lines around his eyes. Otherwise, he looked pretty great and had a youthful face. He was probably one of those men who always looked young.

They both listened to the music and he looked around for his sunglasses.

"So, do you get mobbed when you go out? I mean, this restaurant for instance? Do people come up to you all the time?"

"You mean like fans?"

"Yeah."

Esteban chuckled. "No, not really."

Marialena shrugged. "I wasn't sure. I don't follow celebrities too much. I didn't know if people knew who you were."

"Gee, thanks."

"No, you know that's not what I meant. I just meant that..."

"It's okay. I know what you meant. I was kidding. A few people recognize me from time to time." Esteban laughed. "I have to admit, being confused for Patrick Denny is a first, though."

Marialena cringed. "He told you about that?"

"How do you not know what your favorite director looks like?" he asked, clearly teasing her. He suddenly remembered what Patrick had said about Marialena sleeping with him if he had continued to let her believe

56

he was really Esteban. Esteban suddenly wondered if he had those same chances. He stole a glance at her low-cut blouse and found himself wanting her. He longed to put his mouth on her young flesh, to inhale her kisses. She was beautiful, but more than that, she was genuinely kind and had this innocence and softness in her eyes that he adored. You didn't find women like that anymore, at least not in the circles he moved in.

"I just don't follow that whole Hollywood scene," Marialena said. "I mean, I love your films but it's not like I went online right after one of your movies to see what you looked like. That kind of thing just doesn't matter to me. I adored you for your work. That's what counts."

Esteban nodded. "Yeah, I agree. I live here in Los Angeles, but I'm not really the Hollywood type either." A Bob Dylan song came on and Esteban talked about his love for Dylan. He wanted to make a film with a Bob Dylan soundtrack, but he wasn't sure what the premise would be.

"It could take place at a smoky bar, circling the lives of wanderers who come in and out," she said, giving him an idea.

"That could be interesting," he said.

"Yeah, somewhere remote. A place where nothing much happens to the outside world, but when you look closely you see how rich the lives are...or something like that." Marialena realized how silly she sounded and apologized. "Sorry, someone must always try to pitch something to you."

"No, that was good actually. You just came up with that?"

Marialena shrugged.

"You could write it. Who knows, you could be the next big writer-director, and I would be out of a job," he said.

"Oh, no way," Marialena said, laughing.

"I don't think I'll actually make a Dylan-inspired picture. I am afraid that I'll get sick of him in the process, and I really don't want that happen."

"You might get sick of him for a while. But maybe when your film is done and you've given it some time to marinate, he might find his way back to you again."

Esteban looked at her. He was stuck at a light, and she looked thoughtful and hopeful. "Yeah, maybe...," he finally said.

The conversation drifted to music that inspired her, and he was surprised to hear some artists they shared in common. Maybe she really wasn't that young after all. A few minutes later, he got off the freeway and headed toward the restaurant.

"Is it okay if I leave these here?" she asked, referring to the files.

"Yeah, sure." He got out of the car and walked over to her side to get the door.

"Thank you," she said, unaccustomed to his charm.

They walked side by side to the restaurant. "You're going to love this place."

"It's so weird. I live like a block away. To think that I might have been in my apartment watching your movies while you were here, eating."

Esteban laughed. He leaned in to her, "I doubt you watch my movies as often as I come here."

"You'd be surprised."

Esteban took his sunglasses off and put them in the pocket of his blazer. "I'm flattered," he said. She held his penetrating gaze for a split second before looking away, tucking a loose strand of her hair behind her ear. When they got inside, they were seated right away. Esteban ordered a beer for the both of them.

"Is that okay?" he asked when the waiter left. "You could order whatever you want, but this kind of food demands a Mexican beer."

"Well, if it demands it then who am I to say no?" Esteban laughed. "No, a beer is fine. It's wonderful actually. Thank you." She opened up the menu. "Okay, so what's good here?"

Esteban didn't even have to look at the menu. "Everything. Everything is good here. Why do you think I've recommended this place to you?" He said it stone-faced, but Marialena could see the twinkle in his eye.

The waiter dropped off the beers and they each took a sip, holding each other's gaze. Marialena could feel something there between them. She remembered reading that he had a girlfriend on his Wikipedia page. And of course he did. He was successful and good-looking. Besides, what would he want to do with her? She was half his age. Marialena told herself she was being foolish and convinced herself she was misreading the signals.

"I have had everything here, actually. Twice. So, take that."

"All right, so I'll just have whatever you're having. I trust you."

"Uh-oh. The pressure is on. I like that."

"It shouldn't be hard, I mean...if everything is as good as you say it is."

"Yeah, but I want to wow you," Esteban said. He wanted to wow her in more ways than one, he thought to himself.

"You don't have to try that hard." Marialena said, testing the waters. She was surprised she had gone there, but the beer on an empty stomach was making her brave. Esteban was surprised, too. He looked at her with a raised eyebrow, but continued to speak in food euphemisms.

"I can think of a few options that will have you begging for more."

Marialena smiled at him, blushing.

The waiter came back and Esteban ordered for the both of them. He ordered two platters in perfect Spanish and Marialena felt herself falling for him. There was just something about him. She could tell that he wasn't putting on a show for her. He seemed relaxed in this environment. He told the waiter to hold the onions on his tacos de carne asada, and he looked over to Marialena who nodded and also said to hold the onions. She excused herself to use the restroom. She looked him up on her phone in the bathroom stall and saw that his Wikipedia page confirmed he had a girlfriend. Oh well. Maybe it was just harmless flirting. Marialena decided to ease back a little bit.

"So, tacos? I have to admit, tacos are my favorite," she said, returning from the restroom.

Esteban smiled. "They're mine, too. But sometimes the onions take away from the *carne*."

"Oh, I agree."

"You haven't had tacos like these, though. They're incredible. Perfect handmade tortillas, the meat is sublime, and the sauce they bring out is to die for."

Marialena nodded. "Hey, so I noticed your Spanish," she said, smiling. "Were you born here?" she asked, not quite sure.

"Yeah, I was born here, but my parents are from Spain. How about you?"

"I was born here too. About a stone's throw from Dodger Stadium. As you can see, I haven't gone very far," she said. "But my parents are both Mexican." She paused for a tortilla chip and dipped it in salsa. "My mom has Spanish roots, though. Her parents were Spanish and moved to Mexico."

Esteban nodded. "It's okay that you stayed near home. It's not a bad place to grow up. I grew up in New York, but I consider this my home now."

"Did you ever want to end up somewhere else?" she asked.

Esteban shook his head. "I haven't really thought about it. I like it here, but I'm not dying to spend the rest of my life in L.A. Who knows where I'll eventually end up?"

"I like that. The future is wide open for you."

Esteban didn't agree with her. "I don't know. It honestly feels like I'm fast-forwarding through my future. But it also feels like I'm on pause." He shook his head. It didn't make sense. He was slightly nervous. "I guess I'd like to feel settled eventually, to belong somewhere. I don't know. My career doesn't make things easy. It's not like a nine-to-five Monday through Friday thing. I go where my work is. When that's done, I just come back and wait for it to begin again. I have no idea how to turn that into some sense of belonging somewhere."

"I always thought that home was where your loved ones were," she admitted.

"Well, my brother is in Temecula. I don't know. Maybe I am settled and just didn't know it."

The food arrived and the conversation went from heavy to light again. They talked about how amazing everything was, and Esteban jokingly complained that she had more meat on her tacos than he did.

"Oh, come on," she said, playfully. "Do you want to trade?"

"No, it's okay. You get to be wowed this time, remember? If there is a next time, though, you better believe I'll expect a trade," he said.

Marialena moaned as she took a bite. He was right. It was amazing. "Wow. These tacos are divine. And the tortillas, oh my god."

"See, I told you," he said. He was thinking about making her moan like that again.

"You're so right. I'm glad we did this," she said. "I need to figure out how to keep from coming here every day."

Esteban looked at her, thinking. He took a sip of his beer and ordered another one for the both of them. "Hey, so I have this thing coming up. Next Friday actually. It's a fundraiser. You think you'd want to come with me?" he asked.

"Me?" Marialena downed her beer in anticipation of the next one.

"Yeah. I was planning on going alone, but I'll probably be bored out of my mind. Come with me, keep me company." It wasn't a question this time.

Marialena looked at him. She set down her fork. He looked back at her, held her gaze. God, she looked beautiful. He watched her take a deep breath. "You don't want to go with me. I'm just a regular person. That work I'm doing for Patrick? It's temporary. This is not my world. In fact, I don't even know why I'm there, or *here* to be honest. I'm not qualified in the slightest. I'm just an ordinary girl."

"We're all ordinary. Me? I'm as lost as everyone else. Besides, I'd like for you to come. I like your company."

Marialena resisted asking him about his girlfriend.

"Hey, listen," he said. "There is an obvious age difference between us. I mean, if that makes you uncomfortable, I totally understand. You could come as a friend. I don't have any expectations, so please don't worry about that."

"No, it's not that."

"So, then come."

"Okay, then. It's a date. Wait, is it a date?" Marialena asked, her stomach in knots.

Esteban waited for the waiter to drop off the new round of beers and as soon as he left, he said, "It could be a date if you wanted it to be. I could arrange that." He smiled.

Marialena blushed at her plate of food.

"I think it starts at eight. I could swing by your place at around seven-thirty?"

"Where is it?"

63

"Uh, a hotel in Santa Monica, I think."

"Wait, if you live near there, doesn't it make more sense for me to come to you?"

Esteban smiled. "Look at you, being practical. Okay, I can send a car then. Actually, I like that better. That way neither of us has to drive. I can have the driver pick you up and we can go from there."

"What kind of attire?"

"Coat and tie. Do you have a cocktail dress?"

"I can get one."

"Okay, it's settled." They smiled at each other and Marialena couldn't help but see him in a new light. He was taking her as his date. Could she really see herself with him, even just for one night? Yes. Absolutely. Sure, he was more than twenty years older, but he was kind and attractive. Although she wondered about his girlfriend, she didn't want to bring up it. She didn't know how.

They finished their dinner and she walked back to his car for her files.

"Where's your car now?" he asked.

"Oh, it's here, in my parking garage."

"Flat tire and all?"

"Yeah, unfortunately."

"The work of an ex-boyfriend?"

Marialena laughed. "My life isn't as exciting as you think. I found a nail."

"That'll do it. Do you know how to change a flat?"

Marialena shook her head. "Not in the slightest."

"Do you have a spare?"

She nodded. "Yeah, I do."

"Let me take a look at it. You can't drive very far with a spare, or too fast, but it should hold up when you take it to get a new tire."

"No, I couldn't let you do that."

"Why not?" he asked, leaning against his car.

She smiled. "Because, you're Esteban—"

"Yeah, I'm Esteban Gutierrez, I know." He laughed. "So what?"

"You'd ruin your nice clothes," she said.

"I could *wash* them, you know?"

"No, it's okay. I can drive it to the nearest gas station. It's fine," she said.

"Let's just take a look." He walked with her a block or so to her apartment and she acquiesced, not wanting their time to come to an end.

"How long have you known Patrick?" Marialena asked.

"Oh, I don't know that I know him. I've met him a few times over the last couple of years. He's a nice guy. How do like working with him?"

"Well, I just started, so I'm not sure yet. It's only temporary. I have a Monday through Friday job myself working in a temp agency. I help people find jobs."

"What's that like?"

"Just like any other job, I imagine. Some days it's rewarding and some days it's just frustrating."

They got to her condo and she let him in the front gate. When he saw her flat, he whistled.

"There's no way I am going to let you drive it in this condition. Marialena, this needs to be taken care of now."

Marialena nodded. "Okay, I could make a few phone calls, get it towed."

"I'm right here," he said kindly. She looked away. Esteban put a hand on her chin, bringing her face to his. "Let me do this for you." She looked into his eyes and nodded, finally relenting. He started to unbutton his white dress shirt. He was wearing a white t-shirt underneath. He took off his jacket and shirt and handed them to Marialena. They were warm to the touch. She resisted the urge to smell them.

"You're going to need to back out maybe two or three feet," he said, since there was a car right next to hers.

She placed the clothes in her lap and popped the trunk of her car for the spare.

She watched Esteban pull out the spare and the jack, admiring his strong arms. He was in great shape, very fit. He filled his t-shirt nicely. He looked even better in less clothing.

He used the jack to lift the car. Esteban worked silently, not bothering to announce what he was doing. Marialena enjoyed watching him. He worked without hesitation. He had obviously done this before. When he was finished, he put her old tire in the trunk.

"That does it," he said and closed her trunk.

"Thank you. Thank you so much," she said, pulling the car back into its spot.

"Can I wash my hands at your place?"

"Yes, of course."

She continued holding on to his clothes as she led the way to her condo. Esteban walked behind her, eyeing her body. She had amazing curves, and the skirt she wore left nothing to the imagination.

She opened the door to her place. Light beige walls, a bookcase, a blue sofa, a giant TV. Her condo wasn't overly feminine, and he liked it. A bit sporadic in its decoration, but it was clean and it felt homey. Her kitchen was on the far-right corner, and there was a balcony to the right. He saw two bedrooms and a bathroom down the hall to his left. The layout was very similar to his layout, though his space was much bigger.

"Nice place. Any roommates?" he asked.

"I live alone," she said. He was surprised. He didn't think a lot of people her age lived alone these days. The cost of living was too high. She led him into the kitchen and he washed his hands. Marialena was grateful she had done the dishes that morning before she left for work. Her sink was clean except for a coffee cup.

"Now, that wasn't so bad, was it?" Esteban asked, drying his hands. Marialena couldn't believe he was in her kitchen in his undershirt. He looked incredible underneath the bright kitchen light. His eyes were soft and warm. He took a step toward Marielena, and she held her breath. There was an electricity between them. He looked into her eyes and took another step closer. He studied her lips briefly and took a short intake of breath. She was sure he was going to kiss her, but he reached out for his dress shirt and jacket instead.

"Get your keys. We're going to get a tire," he said.

Marialena let out a breath and laughed. "No way. I can do that on my own. I was just going to change and take care of it, actually."

67

"So, change. I can wait. I'd have to sit in traffic on the way back right now, anyway," he said. It was true. It was half past six by now and traffic was at its worst.

"Okay, then. I can just go like this. It's fine."

"All right, let's go," he said, throwing on his jacket over his t-shirt, keeping the dress shirt in his hand.

When they got to the tire place, she told the cashier what she needed. He took a look at her car and returned a few minutes later.

"I'd recommend changing out both back tires, actually. The one on the passenger side has worn tread and it's not safe anymore. Both front tires are still okay, but I'd say you only have another six months on those. Or we could change them all out for you right now if you'd like. It would save you from coming back here."

"Um, I think just the two back tires for now," she answered.

Esteban leaned toward Marialena. "When was the last time you switched the front ones?"

"I haven't. The car is about five years old."

"You know what?" Esteban called out to the man behind the counter. "Let's change them all out. I'll take care of the tires." He leaned into Marialena. "I hope that's okay with you."

She pulled him away, toward the seating area. "What are you doing?" she asked.

"Look, I don't normally do this. I don't ask a lot of women out, I don't change their spares, and I don't buy them tires. So just let me feel like a decent human being," he said.

"A decent human being would turn this offer down," she said.

"No, a gracious person accepts the offer," he said. The matter was settled. Marialena nodded to the mechanic, indicating she'd have all four tires changed. Esteban picked out the brand and then walked over to where Marialena was sitting.

"You can just think of me when you're driving," he said as they sat down and waited.

"Oh, I think I'm going to be thinking about you more than when I'm driving."

"Is that a fact?" he asked, chuckling to himself.

"That's a fact," she said. Maybe he didn't have a girlfriend anymore. But what if he did? Marialena hated not knowing for sure, but couldn't help herself. She never got like this around men, and she liked how it felt.

When her car was ready, she drove them back to her place.

"Let's exchange info," he said. She took out her phone. He took it from her and added his phone number. For the contact name, he typed 'Favorite director.' She looked at it and smiled.

She took his phone and added her number. Under contact, she simply typed 'Marialena.' They said goodbye and he leaned into her ear when they hugged. "I look forward to Friday," he said in a whisper, his hands on her hips. She looked back at him, into his amazing hazel eyes, and felt herself getting hot. Yes, there was definitely something there. She walked up to her apartment, thinking about how it felt when he was close to her, wondering if she had misread the signals in her kitchen earlier, and if she hadn't misread them, why hadn't he? What would their date be like? Would she be daring enough to kiss him first? She wasn't sure and wondered

69

if it all hinged on whether or not he had a girlfriend. How was she supposed to find out for sure? She could ask Patrick, but didn't think it was appropriate. They were focused on his film. She'd have to wait to see where the date went.

As Esteban drove home, he was smiling all the way. When he got back, he put on some Bob Dylan, turned on his computer, and went to work. He had an idea for a premise and wanted to get his ideas down before they vanished. He didn't go to bed until two that morning. When he finally did, he felt better than he had in a long time.

Chapter Four

A car came to pick her up precisely when Esteban said it would. Marialena looked at herself in the mirror one last time before grabbing her coat and handbag. She had to admit, she looked the part. She wore her long hair down. It was full and flowing down her back. She had spent thirty minutes on her makeup, accentuating her eyes, perfecting that smoky-eye look. For her lipstick, she chose a dark red. She had spent a small fortune on the black cocktail dress, but it was worth it. She was going with Esteban Gutierrez after all. Her strapless dress was black and gold. It was very elegant. She didn't know where tonight would lead, but a few days earlier, she had thrown in his movie, "Paris in the Dark." When the love scene came on, she imagined being with Esteban. She had been turned on ever since...ever since she watched him change that spare tire, really.

Marialena got into the hired car and admired its interior. All black leather on the inside. The driver already knew where he was going, which was a good thing since Marialena didn't have Esteban's address. It was dark in the city, and she daydreamed about what the night had in store. When the car parked at a row of condos, she heard the driver say they had arrived.

She called Esteban's cell. He answered on the third ring, breathless.

"Hey, I'm just getting dressed. I'll be ready in about ten minutes. You can come up. I'll leave the door unlocked for you. Tell the driver not to go anywhere."

Marialena told the driver that they'd be coming right back down and not to leave. She left her coat in the car.

Marialena followed Esteban's directions once inside the building. He was on the third floor, third door on the right. When she arrived, she knocked to be polite, then opened the door. His condo was dark on the inside. She announced her presence.

"Hey, it's me."

"Okay, make yourself at home. Um, turn on a light if you need to. I'll be out in a few minutes."

She looked around for a light switch but didn't find one. Instead, she sat down on his dark brown couch. His living space was clean. He had a lot of dark furniture and it was all very masculine and very earthy. He had really good taste. There was a bookcase off to the side of the couch. In what she imaged was Esteban's little nook, he had a computer with the bookcase behind it. She liked it. She saw a record sleeve sitting on the coffee table and picked it up. It was an album she liked a lot. She remembered telling him about how much she had liked this band a few days ago. Marialena smiled to herself when she saw that the record was missing. He had probably been playing it. She studied the record sleeve and then heard him emerge from the bedroom, struggling with his tie. He hadn't looked at her yet and made a beeline to the light switch. His cell phone rang a few seconds later and he cursed under his breath. He had his back turned to her when he answered.

"Hey. Yeah. No, I'm running out of the door now. I can take a look at it tomorrow. Yeah, it's this fundraiser thing. Hey, no, listen I am actually running late. Yeah, you too."

He put his phone back in his pocket and turned to Marialena, who stood up as he walked toward her.

"Oh my god. Look at you." He put two hands on her waist and leaned in close to hug her. "You look absolutely stunning." He looked her square in the eyes, his hands still on her hips. She was elegant and sexy. Her dress was short, showing off her legs. Her waist looked impossibly small in her dress, her breasts heaving. "You still want to go as my date?" he asked, kissing her on the cheek.

"Yeah, of course. Why?" Esteban looked incredibly handsome, but was still half-dressed. His face had brushed up against hers as he had kissed her, and she had felt his stubble. He looked into her eyes, his hazel gaze making her stomach flip.

Esteban shrugged and pulled away, feeling the electricity. He walked to the mirror to finish his knot. "They'll probably take some pictures, you know, as we walk in."

"Oh, that's fine. I'm all in. You know, whatever," she said, trying to sound more casual than she felt.

"Let me just get this on." He finished his tie and looked at his reflection. "Not too bad," he said, squinting at his mirror image. He turned to look at her and held her gaze, feeling nervous. He wanted very much to kiss her, but the timing wasn't right. "Come here," he said. She walked over to him and he put a hand on her face. Marialena looked into his eyes in anticipation. He leaned in and kissed her on her jawline, opening his mouth ever so briefly, then he pulled her in closer and inhaled her scent, his mouth right by her ear. Both of their hearts were racing. Esteban felt himself getting aroused.

"You smell amazing." He pulled away to look at her again, feeling the sexual tension between them. This was really happening. He was going to take this young woman to the fundraiser as his date. He hoped he could keep up with her and found himself suddenly second guessing himself.

"Jesus," he said. "I don't want to drink or eat anything tonight for fear of getting the taste of you out of my mouth." Marialena gave him a small smile, but didn't say anything. "All right, well, give me just another minute or two. Otherwise, we'll never leave." He walked back into the bedroom to put his shoes and socks on. He sat down on the bed and tried to shake his nerves. It had been so long since he had taken anyone on a first date. He needed to relax.

Marialena found the rest of his records and flipped through some of the titles as she waited, still feeling his lips on her jawbone.

"I love that you have these records," she called out, still thinking about Esteban's soft kiss.

"Oh, yeah. I bet some of them are older than you are."

Marialena ignored the comment and continued looking, swooning over some of the titles. He had at least twenty Bob Dylan records. She hadn't even heard of half of them.

When he finally emerged, he looked every bit the part. He wore a black suit and black tie. Marialena felt butterflies in her stomach. "Okay, let's get this show started," he said.

They walked out together and he locked the door. They didn't say anything in the elevator, each lost in thought. She led him to the car he had rented for the night and the driver let them both in the back seat.

"So, will I recognize anyone there?" she asked.

"Yeah, maybe." He gave her a brief description of the location and the cause. "It's just dinner and drinks. There might be some dancing. I think we'll be a little late, but that's okay. No one is ever on time."

They talked about how their week had gone since the last time they met. Esteban admitted that he had been late getting ready because he had starting writing again.

"It could be nothing, but I might be on to something here. Might as well try to see where it goes." He left out the fact that he had gone straight to the computer and had worked for six hours the last time they were together. It was something he hadn't done in a very long time. He'd been writing since then.

They arrived at the fundraiser twenty-five minutes late.

"Hey, looks like we're here." He put a hand on her knee. "Nervous?"

Marialena shook her head. "No, not anymore."

"Oh, so you *were* nervous?" he asked playfully.

Marialena smiled. "I was nervous about seeing you, not about being here."

"Oh really? I made you nervous?" he asked. He smiled to himself.

"A good kind of nervous. I was looking forward to seeing you again," she said kindly.

Esteban nodded and waited for the driver to open the door. He took Marialena by the hand.

"When they take our pictures, someone will be standing by to take your coat. Unless you'll need it on the way out, I'd suggest leaving it with the driver."

"I might need it when we leave, yeah."

Esteban nodded. "Okay, we can check it when we get inside."

They walked on a red carpet and posed for pictures in front of a backdrop. Esteban held her hand for some of the shots and briefly put an arm around her waist for others. When they had finally made it through, he leaned in and whispered to her, "I've always hated that part, but I didn't mind it so much tonight." Marialena squeezed his hand in reply. They walked over to their seats. The tables were small, seating a total of six. He pointed to names at their table.

"Recognize any of these names?" he asked.

Marialena looked closely and nodded. She pointed to one name in particular. "I think he's in that new superhero movie. But I don't know anyone else."

"They probably don't know who I am, either," he said. Marialena gave him a playful shove. He leaned into her and gave her a kiss very close to her lips. He didn't want to ruin her lipstick or get any on himself. It was very dark and he wasn't used to being with a woman who wore a color like that. Laura, his ex, had usually worn light or nude colors. He broke his eye contact with Marialena, thinking about her lips for a moment longer, then pointed to a table. He cleared his throat. "I think that's us. Let's check your coat. Here, this way." He led her through the throng of guests and helped her take off her coat. He exchanged her coat for a ticket, which he put in his wallet. Marialena liked that he didn't give it to her, but held on to it instead.

"And the bar is that way. Care for a drink?"

"Sure, I'll take a wine."

"Red, white?"

"Red."

"Okay. Well here, let's walk to our table first. Then I'll get our drinks."

Music was playing from the speakers overhead, and it looked like a band was setting up. There were so many people mingling around them. Everyone was dressed to the nines. There were women in cocktail dresses similar to hers, some short, some longer, other women in pant suits. All the men wore suits, different colors, but black was the most popular. Esteban introduced her to people she had never heard of. He didn't label their date as anything, didn't refer to her by anything other than her name, Marialena Villanueva. She loved the way he pronounced it. She had never heard him pronounce his own until he was introduced to someone's wife. He had pronounced his name in proper Spanish, 'Estevan.' She noticed most people pronounced it with a B in the middle instead of a V.

When they finally made it to their table, Esteban dropped her off and gave her a kiss on the cheek before he left to get the drinks.

"I'll be right back."

No one else was at their table yet, but when Nick Ashton, a newcomer to Hollywood cast in the latest superhero movie, arrived a few minutes later, he introduced himself. He had arrived alone. When Esteban came back with their drinks, he put a protective arm around her. The two men began talking about business, while Marialena sat quietly, drinking her wine too quickly. Nick Ashton was quite a looker in person. He had a rather large frame, a masculine face with chiseled features, and light brown hair. Though the big bodybuilder look had never been her type, she had to admit, he was very attractive.

"You doing okay?" Esteban asked her by leaning in and caressing her shoulder with his hand.

Her body was already reacting to him, and she shuddered to think what would happen if they were left alone to explore.

"Yeah." She smiled back at him. Esteban turned back to the table. People were all over the place, mingling, saying hello. A few people had approached Esteban and he got dragged off for a few minutes in a conversation. Every now and then, Esteban's eyes would find Marialena and he would turn and smile to make sure she was okay.

A few other guests arrived at their table and Nick introduced them to her, taking Esteban's place so that she didn't have to introduce herself. "She's here with Esteban Gutierrez," Nick Ashton said. She smiled and shook everyone's hand. Nick leaned over the table when their guests walked away for drinks.

"Tell me, Marialena, what is it you do?" he asked.

"Well, I am working on a project right now with Patrick Denny."

"Patrick Denny? Really? Wow. That's a big name." He whistled under his breath. "Man, I'd love to work with that guy." Marialena smiled. She couldn't believe it either.

"Yeah, it's a pretty great experience so far. He's really been trusting me, so that's nice. We just got started a few weeks ago."

"When does shooting begin?"

"Very soon, actually. I think they're just trying to hammer out location details."

"Well, good luck. But I doubt you'll need it. Everything he touches turns to gold." Marialena knew what Nick said was true, but she wished he was saying it about Esteban and not Patrick Denny.

"Don't get me wrong, Esteban Gutierrez is pretty incredible, too," he said, reading her mind.

Was it that obvious? No, it couldn't have been. He must have just felt it subconsciously. "You sure do know how to pick them. I wish I was as lucky as you," he said.

"What are you talking about? You're going to be a household name in a few weeks. Every kid in America will want to be you."

Nick Ashton flashed a big smile. "Yeah, I guess I can't complain." He lifted his empty glass and motioned to hers. "Refill?"

"Yes, please."

"Same thing?"

"Yeah, thanks." She made a mental note to slow down. She hadn't had anything to eat in over four hours. She didn't want to get sloshed tonight and embarrass Esteban. Speaking of the devil, he returned and apologized for being gone for so long.

"Sorry, I haven't seen some of these people in a long time and they wouldn't let me off the hook."

"Oh no, it's okay. Nick was being totally charming while you were gone."

"Should I be jealous?" Esteban asked, smiling and finishing off his drink.

"Not in the slightest." Marialena wondered if he was serious or not. She didn't really know if he was the jealous type. She excused herself to use the restroom and snuck a glass of water. In the bathroom, she checked her reflection and was surprised by what she saw. She had forgotten how glamorous she looked. Marialena never thought she could fit in at a place like this, rubbing elbows with all of these people. It must be the confidence Esteban had given her. The way he looked at her alone made her feel like a million bucks. When she returned to her table, she found a full glass of red wine waiting for her, along with a full table. She sat down. Nick pointed to her and said to Esteban, "So, Patrick Denny, huh?"

"Yeah, I know. I should be asking for her autograph," Esteban replied.

Marialena took a small sip of her wine and thanked Nick. Esteban put a hand her knee as other guests around them found their tables. Someone jumped on a microphone on stage and gave a speech about the fundraiser and the cause. There was a round of applause and dinner was announced.

When dinner arrived, Marialena thanked her lucky stars that the waiters served water with dinner. She took a large sip and dove into dinner, making polite conversation with those at her table. She finished the glass of water before she finished her dinner, which was Poulet de Provencal. It was delicious, but she didn't have a big appetite. She took a sip of wine as she listened to the guests at her table talk about their time spent in France. Esteban shared his own memories about filming in France. He talked openly and told amazing stories, often making others laugh. He touched her often, putting a hand on her arm or resting his hand on her knee. Esteban wondered if he was coming on too strong, but it felt right for him to touch her. Each time he did, he wondered what it would be like to have her. He put a hand on her leg underneath the table and thought about taking her to his bedroom. Someone asked him something, and it snapped him out of his reverie.

"I don't know where my next picture will end up being filmed, but no, I don't plan on making another one in France," he said, keeping his hand on Marialena's leg.

Marialena smiled as he spoke, not really having her own opinions about visiting France since she had never been. Instead, she enjoyed listening. She felt Esteban's hand on her leg and loved that he was affectionate. She thought about returning the affection somehow, but she was too nervous while they were still sitting down in front of all these people.

After dinner, she walked to the bar with Esteban for another drink. It would be his third, but he seemed to be doing okay. They lingered off to the side for a few moments. She leaned back against a wall and he stood in front of her, blocking her view of the endless sea of people behind him. Everyone had gotten up from their tables and started to mingle again.

"Thanks so much for coming with me," he said.

"Thanks for inviting me," she said, searching for what kind of mood he was in. She loved the shade of his eyes. She could make out the green and longed to see how they looked in direct light.

"You look amazing tonight. Did I tell you that already?" he asked.

"You did. Thank you. So do you." She smiled. He held her gaze for a moment longer, but the moment faded when he moved next to her to watch the crowd from her viewpoint. Marialena put a hand on his arm and left it there. He looked at her and smiled, then someone tapped him on the shoulder and he broke away to greet the newcomer.

"Hey, great to see you." He embraced the tall man and the two exchanged pleasantries. Esteban introduced him to Marialena, who recognized the name but couldn't remember how she knew it. They got into a heavy discussion and Marialena excused herself and headed to the restroom. The band had starting playing during dinner and some people were now dancing, while others were talking loudly. When Marialena emerged, she lost track of Esteban, but Nick Ashton came to her rescue. He asked her if she wanted a drink, but she remembered that she had one at the table. She walked over to retrieve it, half expecting it to be gone. She saw Nick waiting for her a few feet away and she walked back to him.

"Hey, so congratulations on your film. It must have been a blast to work with that cast," she said.

"Oh yeah. It was loads of fun," he said.

Marialena felt tiny next to him. He was probably 6'3'' and looked like a superhero just standing next to her. He was certainly right for the part. She wondered how he managed to show up alone. There had to have been a line of ladies waiting to take her place by his side. She looked around the room and saw some people looking at them, then looking away whenever Marialena made eye contact.

The two talked for a few minutes about their favorite superhero movies growing up. When the music changed to a slow song, he asked her if she wanted to step outside with him for some fresh air.

"Oh no," she said, looking around for Esteban. He was looking at her and smiled. She gave Esteban a smile. "I really shouldn't," she said.

"So are you two like *together,* together?" he asked, noticing the look she shared with Esteban from across the room.

Marialena shrugged, unsure of what to say. "It's very new, Esteban and me, but yeah, I wouldn't mind something more serious," she said, surprised by her own honesty. She didn't mention anything about Esteban's girlfriend. She wasn't sure she was in the picture or what that meant for her if she was.

Nick chuckled. "Lucky man."

"I don't know, I kind of think I'm the lucky one," she said. "How about you? No date tonight?"

Nick laughed. "All the good ones are taken," he said, looking at her.

Marialena smiled, then shrugged. She didn't have a good response so she drank from her wine glass instead. They talked for a few more minutes, but then she politely excused herself and walked through the crowded room, closer to where Esteban's group was standing. She saw a couple of faces she was introduced to earlier, women

83

this time. She found herself in another conversation about comfortable heels. Marialena glanced down at her own shoes. She had decided to wear kitten heels so she wouldn't appear too much taller than Esteban. She heard Esteban's voice coming from the group next to hers, but he hadn't spotted her. She couldn't hear the other people he was talking to, but he seemed to be talking about something personal. She tried to make it look like she wasn't eavesdropping and turned her back to him as she laughed within her own group. Still, she managed to hear every word Esteban had spoken.

"Yeah, I was a wreck for a few months. It was awful. I had hit this all-time low. But I really couldn't stay with her after that. Seven years down the drain, just like that." Then someone said something she couldn't hear, but she heard Esteban's response. "No, it's okay. Thanks though. I'm kind of thanking my lucky stars for running into Marialena. The timing couldn't seem more right. She's a great girl...smart, beautiful."

So, there it was. He was single. It sounded like he had broken up with his girlfriend, and somewhat recently. She couldn't believe what he had said about her. *About her.* Marialena loved that he called her smart before he called her beautiful. She suddenly felt guilty for eavesdropping and tried to walk away unseen. A few minutes later, she approached Esteban's group from another angle so he could see her this time.

"Hey, look who it is. Marialena, let me introduce you to a couple of my very close friends," he said, placing an arm lightly around her lower back.

He introduced her to two men and the conversation drifted to a lighter topic. One of the men, Tom, had taken an interest in her. She drifted away from Esteban for a moment.

"You enjoying yourself?" Tom asked. He was an older man, maybe in his mid-fifties. Taller than her, but not by much. He had a friendly smile and it looked like he had already had a few too many drinks. But he seemed nice.

"Oh yeah, but I doubt I'll remember anyone's name after this."

Tom laughed a big hearty laugh. "No one ever does. But I doubt I'll forget yours. I hear you've made quite an impression on my friend here."

"Oh, I'm sure he has it backward," she said as Tom laughed again.

"She is a delight," he said to Esteban. Esteban turned to Marialena and smiled.

"Yeah, she's a handful all right. I imagine one day I'll be working for this one."

Marialena smiled and shook her head, embarrassed. She could tell that he was getting tipsy as well. He leaned into her, reading her mind.

"Hey, wanna get out of here soon?" he asked.

She nodded discreetly.

He took a deep sigh. "Yeah, I'm thinking it's about time. Hey guys, I gotta attend to the lady. Tom, call me. We'll get together soon. Sorry I was off the radar there for a while."

"Don't mention it. Yeah, we'll do dinner or something. Try and bring this one along," Tom said, nodding toward Marialena.

"Yeah, no problem," Esteban said.

"It was a pleasure meeting the both of you," Marialena said politely.

They didn't say goodbye to anyone else, which surprised Marialena. She thought they'd be there for at least another half hour, just trying to exit. It was still early, close to eleven, and there were still plenty of people.

Esteban led her to the coat check and helped her with her coat. Inside the car, he let out a loud sigh. "My god, I hate those things. Sorry I kept getting pulled away. It's almost like work, coming here. All these people are in the business. Thanks for coming with me. I feel guilty for abandoning you so much, but it was hard to free myself to get back to you."

Marialena laughed. "It's not a problem. But if you hate them so much, why did you come?"

"It's a charity," he said.

"So just donate. Who says you have to show up?" she asked, teasing him.

"How can I show you off if we don't go anywhere? Besides, I have to get out every once in a while. Remind people I'm still here. I'm just bad at it," he said. "Hey, so I saw you talking to that superhero guy. Nick?"

"Yeah?" she asked.

"What was that like?" he asked playfully.

"What do you mean?"

"Oh come on, you wouldn't have rather gone with him?" he asked.

"To the fundraiser? Are you serious? No way. Anyway, he's not my type."

"Admit it, he's all that and a bag of chips. I am literally half the man he is," Esteban said, laughing.

"You're all the man I need," she said, getting serious.

"You mean that, don't you?" he asked.

"Yeah, of course. I was thrilled to come with you."

"I thought for sure he was going to steal you away from me."

"What kind of person do you take me for?" she asked.

"A person whose taste in men is questionable right now. To think that you'd rather be with me than that guy," he said, laughing.

"Let me be the judge of my own taste in men, thank you very much," she said. "There are plenty of things to like about you." She spoke quietly, thankful the driver had some music playing. She wondered briefly if he was listening to the two of them.

"Oh yeah, like what?" he asked.

"You're the perfect height for kissing." Esteban laughed. "And your eyes are incredible. Did you know that? I could get lost in those eyes of yours."

"The perfect height for kissing? So, you've thought about it?" he asked, not able to help himself.

"Yeah, I've thought about it. Since you changed my tire the other night, I haven't been able to get it out of my mind. That white shirt? I have to admit, that was pretty hot."

Esteban laughed and looked out the window. "I don't know what to say."

"You know, I'm not an expert, but I don't think you're supposed to say anything. I'm pretty sure you're just kind of supposed to take action."

"Oh, I can take action," he said matter-of-factly.

Marialena laughed. "I wasn't so sure."

"What do you mean?" Esteban asked.

Marialena shrugged. "The other night when you were in my kitchen, I totally thought you were going to kiss me."

Esteban laughed. "You know, I thought I was too," he admitted.

"What happened?" Marialena asked, laughing.

"I don't know, I guess I got nervous."

"Nervous? You?"

"Yeah, why not? I'm not allowed to get nervous?" Marialena smiled.

"You're a beautiful woman, Marialena. Let me ask you something. How old are you?"

"I'm twenty-seven."

Esteban took a deep breath. "Twenty-seven. Wow."

"So?"

"I haven't been with a twenty-seven-year-old in about twenty years."

"Not much has changed," she said.

"Not on your end," he replied. "You know what, now that I'm thinking about it, maybe it's a good thing we haven't kissed. With all this buildup, it will only intensify it."

Marialena looked at him. "Yeah, I guess so. I'm surprised you said you were nervous. I thought that once you'd been around the block a few times, a first kiss lost its magic."

"No, I don't think that's true. I mean, it could depend on who you're with. But with a girl like you, I think that first kiss is going to be something special. Maybe I didn't kiss you because I knew I'd see you again, and being in a suit is much better than wearing a dirty white undershirt."

Marialena shook her head. "That white undershirt has been the thing of dreams for me. I haven't been able to get it out of my head."

Esteban laughed. He hadn't seen himself in that light for a very long time. He didn't think he had it anymore. His mind starting wandering, thinking about taking her upstairs.

"I can make arrangements for a white shirt," he said, smiling. He reached out for her hand and took it in his. She loved how warm his hands always were.

The driver arrived at Esteban's.

"*Quieres venir arriba*?" he asked, wanting to know if she'd come upstairs with him.

Marialena bit her lip and nodded. Of course she would. She wanted nothing more.

When they finally got upstairs, he closed the door behind her, pushed her up against the door, and took off her jacket. He threw it on the desk next to the door. Esteban took a step closer, pressing his body against hers, and whispered in her ear. "I've been thinking about this since I first met you." The concerns about her age were far from his mind.

"Me too," she said. He took a hand and placed it underneath her skirt and up her thigh. Then he buried his face in her chest, kissing her right above her breasts. Marialena swallowed and tilted her head up. Esteban's mouth rose to her collarbone and up to her ear. When he stopped, he looked into her eyes, his mouth inches away from hers. He put a hand on her face.

89

"Lucky for you, I'm wearing a white shirt underneath," he said softly. He took her by the hand and led her to the mirror by the kitchen. She stood by his side and watched him place his blazer on a dining room chair. He loosened his black tie and took it off, placing it around Marialena. He directed her to the mirror in front of him while he stood behind her. He unbuttoned his dress shirt and placed it on the chair behind him. When he came back to the mirror, Marialena saw that he was in his white undershirt, his arms filling out the shirt sleeves. He stood behind her and lifted up her long hair, draping it over her left shoulder. He kissed her back, and Marialena closed her eyes. He moved to her neck and kissed her from behind, his hands exploring her body. She opened her eyes, watching him in the mirror as he peeked from behind her, making eye contact in the reflection. His eyes looked hungry. He looked at her mouth in the reflection and turned her around. She draped her arms around his neck and they each dove into each other, kissing passionately. His mouth on hers was warm, and his hands held tightly as he kissed her.

Esteban pushed her back onto a small table and knocked off the books that were sitting on top of it. They fell to the floor and she sat on the table and wrapped her legs around his back. Esteban ran his hands up her legs, kissing on her the mouth. Marialena arched her back and Esteban responded by burying his face in her chest once more, pulling her dress down, exposing just a little bit of her breasts. He kissed her there and lifted up her skirt, placing his hands on her bottom. He lifted her up from the table, feeling the lace from her underwear.

"God, I want you," he said.

Marialena's body was squirming. She got up from the table and he followed her into the bedroom. He turned on a dim light and helped her unzip her dress. It slid down to the floor and she turned to face him. She was wearing a black strapless bra and black lacy underwear.

"You're absolutely perfect," he said in a whisper. She reached out for him and kissed him on the mouth, put her hands underneath his shirt and lifted it up over his head.

They made it to the bed and kissed for a few more minutes until neither of them could stand it anymore. Her hands ran all over him. He was on top of her, still in his pants, but he had kicked off his shoes. His mouth found hers and she wrapped her legs around him, his hands underneath her, both of them moaning. When he finally took off his pants and socks, he got back on top of her in his boxers. Esteban couldn't get enough of her and didn't know where he wanted to put his mouth; he wanted it all over her. He took off her bra and looked at her for a few seconds before putting his mouth on her breasts, spending time on each. Marialena arched her body underneath him, reaching down to touch him. He moaned hungrily and finally took off his boxers. Then he took off Marialena's underwear. She looked at him and smiled, feeling the excitement. He looked into her eyes as he entered her and she placed a hand on his face, letting herself go with the flow of his body. He was quick and hurried in the beginning, hungry. After a few minutes, Esteban slowed down, remembering his promise to wow her. In the end, he did just that as she lay breathless underneath him while he moaned to completion. They were both sweating profusely, but most of it was coming from Esteban. She kissed the sweat off of his body.

"I had forgotten it could be like that," he whispered out of breath.

"Yeah, me too."

He kissed her on the mouth. "Magical," he said.

Later, she could hear Esteban sleeping comfortably beside her, but she lay awake for a long time. She thought about him. There was a hunger to his lovemaking, and she could tell how excited he was. He had moaned and grunted throughout, like a starved man. Their lovemaking had been exciting and fast at first, then sweet and slow and passionate. He held her and touched her all over. He even stopped to look into her eyes, brushing hair from her face. He spent a few minutes kissing her and softly pushing himself into her. He was in great shape and he had been great in bed. She certainly felt 'wowed.' This was a man who didn't think he was entitled to sleep with her, like so many men before him. This was a man who enveloped her. The very thought made her nervous and excited and ready for more. But she wasn't sure where they were headed, if there would even be any more. The thought of never seeing him again, or of this being a one-time thing, made her sleep uneasily.

A few hours later, Esteban woke and reached for Marialena. His hand searched, but there wasn't anyone there. He sat up and surveyed the room, trying to recall if she had said anything to him about leaving. He got out of bed, threw on a clean pair of shorts, and took his bathrobe off of its hook.

He called her name into the darkness of his living room, but didn't hear a reply.

"Fuck." He walked over to his minibar and poured himself a whiskey. He had done something to fuck this up, he was sure of it. He thought about the sex, of how he had taken her to the mirror. Was that weird? Was it too much? He had wanted to do something different, something sensual. He had never done that before, but it was something he would have written for a movie, so he thought he'd try it. The sex started off hungrily, but he had been starved for it. He was worried that he might have left a bad impression on her. "You asshole," he said to himself. He took a drink, swallowed, and then refilled the glass. Of course she would leave, he thought to himself. Maybe she thought about what he had said. That fucking Nick Ashton. Asshole. And why wouldn't she have picked him? Or maybe, just maybe, he was overreacting. Maybe she was one of those girls who just didn't like to sleep in someone else's bed. He searched for a note. She looked like the type to leave a note. He went back into his room and scoured his phone for a message. There were a few he missed from other people, but none from her. He decided to get some fresh air on the terrace. He slid open the door and was startled to see Marialena staring at his view of Los Angeles. She turned when she heard the door and wiped her eyes.

"Hey, what are you doing out here? Jesus, I thought you had left." He sat down next to her on the oversized lounge chair.

"Oh. I'm sorry." She was wearing one of his shirts and she was wrapped in a blanket he kept on the couch in the living room. She squinted her eyes and looked at

93

him, tucking hair behind her ear. "Do you want me to go?"

"What? No, that's not what I meant. I was disappointed because I thought you had."

Marialena nodded. "This view is amazing, Esteban. Why do you keep the curtains closed?" she asked, sniffling.

"I don't always. I like it out here, too. Hey, is everything okay?"

"Yeah, I couldn't sleep." She looked out at the city, the wind blowing through her hair. She wrapped the blanket more tightly around her. "I feel a little like Cinderella at the ball," she said.

"Is that a good thing or a bad thing?" he asked. She turned back to look at him. He looked sober now. Not that he was completely drunk earlier, but she could tell that he was thinking more clearly.

Marialena shrugged. "A little bit of both, I guess."

"Yeah, but Cinderella has a happy ending, doesn't it? So why the long face?"

"Well, her story has a happy ending."

"I'm sorry, I don't have a glass shoe to offer you." Marialena wondered if there was a hidden meaning in that. He smiled when he noticed what specific shirt she was wearing.

"Nice shirt," he said.

"Yeah, sorry. I hope you don't mind. I found this one in the drawer. I didn't want to put on my dress."

"No, it's fine. I don't mind," he chuckled. "I bought that one in Paris, during the filming of the movie."

She smiled. They had yet to talk about his work. She was beginning to wonder if they ever would. It was strange to think that she had been so intimate with him, her favorite director, and she felt so close to him, but she hardly knew him.

"It looks better on you," he said.

Marialena smiled. They both stared out at the city for a few minutes.

Marialena cleared her throat and spoke. "It's just that I liked being there with you. Not mingling with all those fancy people, but there, just being with you. Is that weird? I hardly know you. But I felt like I belonged there, with you somehow. Maybe the sex has made me sentimental," she said.

"Hey, no, it's not weird. I had a good time too." He finally realized what she was getting at, and his heart broke for her. She was worried that this might have been a one-time thing. She looked down into her lap. He set his glass down on the floor and lifted up her chin to look into her eyes.

"I want to see you again," he said.

Marialena's heart raced. He had said it so seriously, she could tell that he meant it. She searched his eyes and he kissed her. She leaned back into the lounge chair, letting the blanket fall, exposing her panties. Esteban got on top of her and kissed her. She let her hands roam his back, underneath his robe. He was so warm.

She giggled in between his kisses. "Think anyone can see us?"

"I hope so," he said breathlessly. He continued to kiss her and he could feel her shivering underneath him.

"Come on, let's go back inside." Marialena nodded and picked up the blanket "Hey, so what are you doing for dinner later tonight?"

95

"Tonight, as in Saturday night?"

"Yeah, you should come over. Let me cook for you. I mean, stay through breakfast and all that. Stay all day if you want; I just have to get some work done later. I need about six or so hours to write, but you're free to stay. Or you could go home and come back."

"Dinner? You sure?" she asked, searching his eyes.

"Yes, I'm sure. I said I wanted to see you again, didn't I?"

"Yeah, I mean, I'd love to."

"Good, it's settled. Let me take you back to bed. I think I'm going to stay up and write for a bit."

She kept his shirt on as she climbed into his bed. He pulled up the covers for her and put a hand to her face.

"I'm so glad you didn't leave."

"Why would I have left?"

Esteban shrugged. "I'm just glad you didn't. Sleep well." He bent down and kissed her on the mouth.

He took his whiskey glass with him and sat at his computer. He didn't know how much time had passed when he heard her shuffling in the darkness. She walked up behind him and draped her arms around his chest as he typed. Esteban looked at the clock on his computer. The sun would be rising soon.

"Come back to bed," she whispered, kissing his ear.

"Yeah, okay. Just give me one minute."

She lingered there, her arms around his neck. He leaned back into her, enjoying her caress. He tilted his head to kiss her hand.

"What can I do when my muse is calling me back to bed but follow her siren into the bedroom?"

96

"So, come on already," she pleaded. She led him back into his room and lay on him, her body tangled with his, and they slept a peaceful sleep, each holding the other, content and carefree.

Chapter Five

It was Saturday morning, just past eleven, when Marialena left. Esteban sat back on his couch and took a deep breath. What was he getting himself into? When he had woken up, Marialena was at his side, sound asleep. He couldn't remember the last time there was another woman in his bed who wasn't Laura. In fact, he couldn't remember the last time he had woken up next to Laura. She didn't usually spend the night. Marialena looked impossibly young to him that morning, without any makeup on her face. Esteban was feeling a little foolish for having invited her to come back for dinner that night, but he was still drunk off the sex and she looked so sad out on the terrace. It broke his heart to see her like that.

He couldn't help but think of what they would be like if they moved forward. Laura's old complaints came back to haunt him. He knew Laura was ultimately at fault for cheating on him, but he also knew that he was responsible too. In part, anyway. She had faulted him for not going out more, for not having more fun, for sitting in front of his laptop when he was working, and for being so grumpy and down or quiet all the time. He knew that he hadn't been enough for Laura, and that made him feel terrible. Their relationship was a catch-22. He could see that now. But how could he be good enough for Marialena? She was twenty-seven and in the prime of her life. He didn't want to drag her down the same way he had with Laura, and he was feeling uncomfortable

98

about it. What made him most uncomfortable was that he *liked* Marialena. He yearned for her now he had tasted her, in more ways than one. But at what price? It wasn't fair to rob her of her youth. Still, he found himself looking forward to seeing her and had mixed feelings about whether they'd move forward. He felt incredibly guilty. When he got out of the shower that morning, he took a long look at himself in the mirror. Okay, so he didn't look forty-nine, but he felt it. His muscles were sore in places they hadn't been in so long. He looked at the lines around his eyes, the gray on his temples and sideburns. He exhaled loudly and turned out the light in the bathroom, frustrated.

Later that evening, Esteban was washing dishes when he heard the buzzer ring. He turned down the music and buzzed her in. Opening the door, Esteban was surprised to find Laura, not Marialena, on the other side.

"How could you?" she said, walking past him. Ugh, she groaned to herself. He was in a good mood. He always played music when he was in a good mood. He looked great, too. He was wearing an earthy green polo and a dark pair of jeans. She had always loved him in green.

"How could I what?" he asked, closing the door.

"You gave my ticket to some twenty-year-old slut, that's what. Esteban, I knew a lot of people there too. Now I'm this giant laughing stock," she said, her arms crossed in front of her.

Esteban walked to the kitchen. He knew he could handle Laura. She was pretty collected for the most part. He was surprised she had dropped by, but of course she knew he was home from the curtains he left open. She didn't look too bad, tired maybe. Her long, curly hair was down. She was wearing a white top and black yoga pants, with bright pink tennis shoes. The weekends were always long days for her. She taught yoga for a living, and the weekends were her busiest days.

"Excuse me? I'm pretty sure *I* was the laughing stock not that long ago. You cheated *on me*, remember? You slept with some guy behind my back for what, six months? It's no secret in our little circle of friends," he said, drying his hands.

"No, it's just that I had told everyone that we were working on this, on us." She sat down at the dining room table, deflated.

Esteban laughed, shaking his head. "Okay, that one is on you. We aren't working on us. I don't even know why you'd say something like that."

"But *I* want to work this out. I don't want to just throw away seven years because I screwed up once."

"First of all, it wasn't just one mistake. It was one mistake over and over again. Secondly, you know we were both unhappy. There's nothing to save. We were miserable for what...the last two years?"

"I still love you. We could start fresh," she said, as he poured himself a glass of wine. He offered her a glass and she accepted. She missed him, she missed their life together. Since he was in a good mood, maybe she could try to be civil. Seeing him made her heart ache, and he looked happy. Esteban sat down at the table with her.

"I don't know what to tell you, Laura."

"How was it, the fundraiser?"

"Same old thing."

"Did anyone ask where I was?"

"No, I mean I think mostly everyone knew. Plus, I don't think anyone wanted to be impolite to Marialena."

Laura nodded.

"How'd you find out about her, anyway?

"Joyce called me in between my classes. There's a picture of the two of you." She took her phone out to show Esteban. His name was listed. 'Esteban Gutierrez with date, Marialena Villaneuva.'

Esteban nodded. They looked pretty great together, but he didn't say that to Laura.

"Who is she, anyway? How'd you meet her?"

"Patrick Denny called me out of the blue and asked me to work with him on one of his new films. Anyway, he introduced me. She works with him."

Esteban knew Laura would be excited for him. His lack of creativity had also affected her and she was always glad to support him when possible.

"Patrick Denny? Wow. That's big. So, she works with him? I didn't think you'd get involved with anyone in the Hollywood scene."

"Well, she's not really. I think she's a friend or something, and he hired her temporarily."

"Friend of Patrick Denny's? You know what that means?"

"What?" he asked.

"Isn't he with a new girl every time he gets his picture taken? I bet she was one of those girls, once."

"Not that it matters, but between you and me, I think he tried and failed." He took a drink from his wine glass and looked at Laura. "She's not like that, Laura. She's not what you think. She's actually a nice girl."

"Yeah, and I'm sure the sex is terrible."

101

Esteban laughed. "Okay, I'm not going to talk to you about my sex life. Look, this is happening and I like her. Frankly, I don't owe you an explanation."

"This is so unlike you," she said.

Esteban nodded. "Yeah, it kind of is. I think I like it," he said, playfully.

"So, is it serious?" Laura asked, toying with her wine glass.

Esteban shook his head. "I don't know. I have no idea where this is going. We met this past week and I like her, but her age freaks me out a little bit."

"So, she's dumb and ditzy?" Laura asked.

"Nothing like that. I just, I don't know, I can't imagine what she sees in me, that's all," Esteban said, knowing he could be honest with Laura.

"Well, Jesus, Esteban, take some credit. You can be easy on the eyes when you want to be."

Esteban thought for a second. "You know, I've been thinking a lot about what you used to tell me—to be better at the whole relationship thing, go out more. Look, I know I was no picnic. I guess I'd hate to make someone go through that a second time."

"Esteban, I'm sorry. We were both going through some things."

"But you pointed that out to me from the beginning," Esteban said.

"I was harsh on you and I shouldn't have been," Laura said, feeling guilty. "I think about that now. How cruel I could be, and I am so sorry. I wish we could start over, Esteban. I liked our life together. I like what we had."

Esteban shook his head. "What we had? We were so distant, Laura."

"I mean that I liked our life together, but we got lost along the way. I want to start over. Really focus on the things that matter."

Esteban shook his head. "Look, I'm not trying to be rude here, but this thing with Marialena is so new, and it's early to be saying this, but honestly, Laura, it feels so different from what you and I had. I'm starting to kind of feel like you and I just weren't meant to be together. Yes, we loved each other, but we tried to force it." He looked away. "I don't think it's serious between us yet, but I like how she makes me feel."

"That's because it's new and exciting. It will wear out soon enough."

"I've thought about that too."

Suddenly a buzzer sounded and Esteban let Marialena in with his phone.

"Who's that?" Laura asked, sitting up straight.

Esteban looked at her. "Okay, if you would have called me to let me know you were coming over, I would have warned you."

"So wait, that's her? And you *let me stay*?" she asked, raising her voice.

"Hey, I've walked in on much worse," he said, having caught her in the middle of sex with another man. Esteban shrugged. "And I didn't know exactly when she'd be stopping by."

Laura only nodded. She had nothing to say.

"Are you staying or leaving?"

"I'll stay for a second. I have to see this in person," Laura said. Truthfully, she wanted to see the two of them together, to see if they really had any chemistry. Esteban was vulnerable right now, and it was possible that this would be a short-lived romance.

He could hear Marialena's footsteps walking toward his door.

"'If you do anything to cause a scene, I swear to god…" he said, leaving the last sentence unfinished. Laura waved a hand, insinuating that she would behave herself. He walked toward the door. Laura saw Esteban lean in…for a kiss or a hug, she couldn't tell.

Marialena held some of Esteban's clothes, folded in her hand. "I had time to wash these for you. Thanks for lending them to me." Marialena hadn't seen her yet, but Laura had seen enough. It was obvious that they had slept together. Laura felt her heart sink into her stomach.

Esteban took the clothes from her and set them down. "Hey, so I have some company. Marialena, this is Laura." Laura didn't stand up to get introduced, and she waved dismissively from where she was sitting. "But she'll be leaving in a little bit," Esteban said, making eye contact with Laura.

"Hi. Nice meet you," Marialena said, setting her purse down. Laura eyed her, giving her the once over. She was wearing jeans that were skin tight, with a blouse that showed off her body in all the right ways. For being young, she was quite busty, and her cup size was three times larger than Laura's own.

"Yeah, as I was saying, I have Marialena to thank for putting me together with Patrick Denny." Marialena wasn't entirely sure Laura was his ex-girlfriend, but she guessed that she was.

"And how is it that you got so chummy with someone like Patrick Denny?" Laura asked.

"Oh well, I'm not so sure I am. I barely know him, but I'm sure Patrick knows talent when he sees it. I had little to do with bringing the two of them together," Marialena said, trying to be neutral. It was true. She just told Patrick she admired Esteban. It was Patrick's idea to consult him.

Laura toyed with her glass, feeling like the third wheel. She downed her wine and put the glass in the sink. "Well, don't let me spoil your plans," she said. "It smells good in here. Esteban, what *is* it you're making for dinner? You know, he hardly cooks," she said to Marialena. Laura peeked into the oven, but made no comment. She couldn't gauge how close the two were, but they were sleeping together. Laura couldn't remember the last time she had spent the night with Esteban. Maybe he was right, maybe they *had* fizzled out a long time ago.

Esteban walked Laura to the door. They looked at each other, both saying the same thing without words—'I'm sorry.'

When Esteban closed the door, he apologized to Marialena. "Sorry about that. Uh, we have a little bit of history. We were in a relationship for a long time, and she just kind of showed up today."

"Is everything okay?"

"Yeah. She and I were supposed to go to that fundraiser together. We had gotten the tickets before we broke up. And she knew a few people there. I guess they told her I showed up with you."

"Oh, that can't be easy."

"Well, don't feel too bad. I don't want to get into it now, but it's okay. I don't care about how she took the news." Esteban sighed and walked over to her. "Hey, I'm happy to see you," he said, kissing her warmly on the lips.

"I am too." She smiled shyly.

"Forget about that. *That* is over. She's just upset."

Marialena nodded. She didn't look upset, but she had looked defeated. Laura was very pretty, early forties, with long curly hair. She was in great shape. But Marialena couldn't picture them happy together. They just looked like good friends.

Esteban sat down and stared at her across the table. "Hey, really. Don't worry about it."

Marialena nodded, feeling uncertain. Esteban read her mind.

"She had seen this picture of the two of us, me and you, that was posted on the Internet from the fundraiser. Someone had sent it to her. You were billed as my date. Is there anyone who is going to be upset by that on your end? Parents or anyone who might see that?"

Marialena shook her head. "No, I have nothing to worry about."

Esteban nodded, wondering what her parents thought about their daughter dating a man almost twice her age, but tried to put his thoughts away. "Hey, come here. Let's move to the couch. In a little while, we'll go out on the deck and I'll fire up the grill."

Marialena followed Esteban to the couch. He sat down next to her and kissed her passionately on the lips. Marialena put an arm around his neck and welcomed him. She leaned back into a lying position and he settled on top of her. She could hear him moaning. The music

106

was playing somewhere nearby, but it wasn't too loud. Esteban found his way between her legs, and she opened them up to welcome him.

"I've missed you today," he said, not able to help himself.

"Mmmm" was all she could muster as she pushed herself against his lips. A timer went off in the kitchen and Esteban groaned.

"I'll be right back," he said. "Don't go anywhere." Marialena ignored him and left to grab her glass of wine. She watched him in the kitchen as he prepared the food.

"I'm going to have to get this on the grill in a minute. You hungry?"

"Yeah, actually. Can I help you with anything?"

"No, I've got this. Come out with me?" he asked, taking the tray of meat with him.

"I didn't bring a jacket."

"I'll turn the heat lamps on."

Marialena followed him to the balcony and couldn't get over how beautiful it looked out there. Sure, she had seen it the night before, but she didn't think she could ever get tired of the view.

"So, I have to ask, do your parents know about me?" he asked, firing up the heat lamps.

"Well, they don't. Actually, they died about six years ago." Esteban sat down next to her, placing a hand on hers.

"I'm so sorry. I didn't mean to—"

"No, no. It's okay. You didn't know. But I probably would have told them. I don't think they would have minded."

"Do you want to talk about it?" he asked.

107

Marialena shook her head. "Not really." She shrugged. "They died in a car accident when I was twenty-one. I don't have any brothers or sisters, so it's just me now.

"Jesus, I'm so sorry." He put a protective arm around her. "I'm sorry you had to go through that."

"It's okay. I mean, it's not really okay, but I'm okay for the most part, I think. We don't have to talk about it."

Esteban nodded, getting the hint. He took her hand in his and lifted it to his lips. "They'd be extremely proud of you." His eyes met hers and she thanked him, without saying anything.

"Is it warm enough for you? I could run in and grab a sweater."

"I'm okay right now. Thanks."

"So, we have tri-tip on the menu tonight, with veggies and a casserole in the oven."

"You went all out, for someone who doesn't like to cook." She smiled coyly. She remembered what Laura had said a few moments earlier.

"Oh yeah." Esteban shook his head. "Don't mind her. I didn't cook around her very often. She kind of liked to take over most of the time and was very picky. After a while, I just stopped trying."

"You guys didn't live together?"

Esteban laughed. "Nooooo. No way. We tried once, years ago. It lasted a month. Our schedules were so different. She teaches yoga, and she's often up before the sun. And for a yoga instructor, she's not graceful at all. God, she could be so loud, especially in the mornings. We found that we liked each other better when we lived apart. We made time when we were able to, though. I

108

wrote during the day, and she worked. We'd often meet at night, but she always went home to her place. I could never write around her. She has this nervous energy. She's always been kind of antsy, the high-energy type."

"Well, you managed to write 'Paris in the Dark' during your relationship with her, right? It must have been good between the two of you once upon a time."

Esteban laughed. "The idea for 'Paris' came from something that happened a long time ago. When I came back to it, I wrote most of it while she was away in Europe. She was gone for two months."

"That must have been nice. Two months in Europe? And to come back to something like 'Paris in the Dark?'"

"Honestly, it created a little rift. I think that's when the real distancing started to happen. She was happy for me, sure. But it was tough. Laura didn't seem to take it too personally, but she knew it wasn't about us."

"Was it a former lover?" 'Paris in the Dark' was Marialena's favorite of his films. It captured a young and passionate love affair between two people in the world's most romantic city.

"No, honestly I think I wrote it about what I was missing."

"Esteban, why didn't you do anything about your relationship? I mean, that was years ago, right?" Marialena sat there, legs crossed, holding her wine glass. She loved just looking at Esteban and watched as he got up and headed towards the grill.

"Yeah, I don't know. I was younger then and more hopeful. I don't think I'll make that mistake twice, though. She cheated on me and part of it is because we were wrong for each other; I know I'm not perfect." He

109

paused and considered how that last sentence came out. "I don't mean I fooled around, I just mean I didn't make it hard for her to cheat. I'm not saying I blame myself entirely, but I'm not really interested in what she has to say. It's over between us and the sooner she realizes that, the easier it will get for her. To look back on it now, I just ignored all of the signs. I'd be working and she'd be waiting for me to be done, not really getting that I needed to lose myself in it. She kind of took it personally that I needed to work. As a writer, when it hits you, the need to write, you just have to go with it. I don't think she ever got that. I think she wanted me to just stop at a certain time."

Marialena nodded. "I feel bad now for making you come to bed this morning while you were writing. I should have just let you keep at it." He closed the grill and grabbed his glass of wine.

"No, don't. I *do* have to be saved from myself every once in a while. And to come back to bed, that's very sweet, and it was needed this morning, to be honest. But she was different. She used to talk on the phone, beg me to go shopping, make a racket just doing basic tasks. At first, I thought it was exciting because she had so much energy, but now I know better. I'd have this great idea and I'd be typing away, and she would literally pull me from my desk to ask me why I had two open milk containers in the fridge. That kind of thing."

"So, you're saying you're the relaxed type when it comes to milk?" Marialena asked, smiling. She wanted to stay out of it, but she wanted to let him talk about it if he needed to.

"Yeah, I think so," he said with a smile. He decided to drop it. He was getting annoyed just thinking about it.

They talked about her work with Patrick. She had one more week off from her regular job and was able to help with casting for the time being, but was encouraged to come to the set whenever she could.

"You've worked with Patrick Denny. You could quit your day job and work with anyone. You know that, right?"

"That's not entirely true. And I don't even know if I'm good yet. What if I fail?"

"You won't, I promise. Patrick wouldn't let you fail."

"Well, that's true I suppose. But I want to wait to see how it all comes together before I start chasing something I don't really know that I want."

Esteban nodded, understanding what she meant. This wasn't even her dream. She was just helping out a friend.

"Hey, do you want to eat out here or inside?"

"You know, I'd normally say out here, but it is getting cold. Is it okay if we go inside?"

"Yeah, why don't you get settled in there and I'll bring the food inside in a bit?"

"Are you sure you don't need help?"

Esteban looked at her, making her melt. He looked amazing in that shade of green, and Marialena was starting to wonder if he looked bad in anything.

She went inside and perused the books on his bookcase. She had read a lot of the same books and loved that he was so well read. She knew there was a reason she liked him.

111

When dinner was served, Marialena was surprised by how amazing the food was. He certainly knew his way around the kitchen.

"Esteban, this is incredible!"

"Thanks. I forgot how much fun it is. I haven't cooked like this in ages. I shouldn't have let Laura weigh me down. But I did. For so long. I feel like a different person now, so this is nice."

Marialena nodded. "People can do that to you, sometimes."

"You're right. I should have done something about it a long time ago; I shouldn't have let it last seven years. But yeah, it wasn't meant to be and I didn't do anything to change that." He took a sip of wine. "You know, let's talk about something else. I'm sick of me right now," he said.

"Okay, I have an idea. We ask each other a question, and we both have to answer it, but we can't go into details. We should ask each other five questions."

Esteban laughed, and Marialena felt her age in the moment, but she tried this once before and it had worked beautifully. "I know, it sounds immature, but trust me, it will get us out of our own heads."

"Okay," he said. "I'll go first I guess. What's your favorite color?" he asked.

"Blue. Yours?"

"Brown."

"Brown? No one ever says brown!"

"People say brown. What's wrong with brown?"

She laughed and shook her head. "No explanations. Okay, my turn. What's your favorite book?"

"The Count of Monte Cristo by Alexander Dumas. Yours?"

"The Adventures of Kavalier and Clay."

"I've heard of that one. Didn't it win the Pulitzer?"

"It did."

"What is your favorite food?" he asked.

"Hmmm, I really like pizza. Proper pizza. You can do anything with it. Meat, no meat, veggies, more meat, fruit, you name it. I like that there are so many options."

"Okay, I think this is mine," he said, pointing to the tri-tip. "Maybe just because it's tonight. I liked making it for us." Esteban smiled at her, feeling about ten years younger.

She smiled, touched by what he said. "My turn. What is your favorite season?" she asked.

"Winter, where it snows. I grew up in New York. It's so beautiful and peaceful and quiet. It's incredible."

"I've never been in the snow."

"Okay, you have to change that. Make it happen!" They ate for a few seconds, then he asked her what *her* favorite season was.

"Summer. Definitely summer."

"Okay, now it's my turn to judge your answer. You do realize that no one ever says summer?"

"Not true. I say summer. If you can pick brown, I can pick summer."

He laughed. "Okay, fine. We're even. What's your favorite sport?"

Marialena thought for a second. "No sport. But I love the Dodgers. Being so close to Dodger Stadium, we used to go pretty often."

Esteban nodded. "It's basketball for me."

113

"Okay, since the holidays are right around the corner, what's your favorite holiday?" she asked.

"I don't know that I really have one. I'm not a holiday kind of guy. You?" he asked.

"Halloween."

"Halloween? Really? Why?"

Marialena shrugged. "Everyone gets to be who they want to be for one day. It's fun and silly, and I don't know, kind of magical. It makes me happy."

"I can see that. Everyone usually says Christmas."

Marialena shrugged. "Christmas is hard for me, now anyway."

Esteban nodded. "Do you have other family?"

"Sure, but being with them is really tough. I'll go to my dad's brother's house for Thanksgiving, but Christmas is harder. I usually bail, and I think everyone knows why. They invite me every year, but they get it and no one gives me a hard time."

"So, what do you usually do?"

"I pretend it's a normal day. I have a small tree I put up, but usually I just lay low. I'll go for a run, buy a bottle of wine, that kind of thing. It's nice and quiet. Last year I watched 'Alone, Together.' It was nice." 'Alone, Together' was one of Esteban's early films. "What do you usually do for Christmas?" she asked.

Esteban shrugged. "I don't know. Laura always dragged me off somewhere." He hated the idea of Marialena being alone on a day that was supposed to be festive. "Hey, if you want, you can come here. I mean, I'm not doing anything. You can spend the night on Christmas Eve. We can make some dinner, watch a movie." He knew he was jumping ahead, but he couldn't

114

help it. She suddenly looked so sad and he wanted to cheer her up again.

"Yeah, that sounds nice," she said, warming to the idea.

"You can change your mind later, if you want. I just wanted to throw it out there. I have a guest bed. Whatever you want, no expectations," he said, trying not to lead her on.

"That sounds like fun. Can we watch one of your movies on Christmas Eve?" she asked, a smile on her face. She finished dinner. He had served her way too much, and there was still a lot left on her plate. Esteban refilled their glasses.

"No, we are definitely not going to watch one of my movies."

"Come on...why not?"

"I'm not you. I don't watch my movies all the time. It's too hard." He leaned back in his chair, his eyes lighting up. "I'll tell you what. You can watch my movies. I can watch you while you watch."

"Well, that's no fun," she said.

"No, it will be great for me. I get to watch your reactions."

"That just sounds weird."

"It's not weird. I'd love to see them through your eyes. Which movie would you pick?"

"Definitely 'Paris.'"

"'Paris' it is!" Esteban said cheerfully.

"Need me to bring a copy?" she asked, smiling. "I'm sure I have more than one."

Esteban laughed. "I think I have it somewhere."

115

"One last question," she said. "If you could have directed any film, which one would it be?"

"Ooh, interesting." Esteban thought for a minute, a little flushed from the entire bottle of wine they had finished. "You know what? I have to say, I'm really proud of my movies. I'm glad I directed them. Each one of them had its own battles, but I'm glad they're mine. So, I pick my own."

Marialena was glad she had asked him that question.

"You?"

"Oh, I'd pick yours, too. No doubt about it."

He nodded and smiled, thanking her with his eyes. "Well, I guess we have that in common."

"We have a lot of things in common, you know?" she said.

"Yeah, I guess we do." He bent down to kiss her on the forehead. "I now know more about myself than I ever did." He laughed. "Thanks for that. Let me clear these dishes, then we can relax."

"Let me help you." She followed him into the kitchen and rinsed the dishes while he put them in the dishwasher. A good song came on the radio and he lip synced as they tidied up. When they finished, Esteban opened up a second bottle of wine and brought it out to the couch.

"Want some more?"

Marialena thought for a second and then shook her head. "Maybe I shouldn't. I still have to drive home."

"You don't have to, you know?" He leaned into her and kissed her on the neck. Marialena took a deep breath and contemplated her options. She did want to stay, but

116

she didn't want to impose. Not two nights in a row. She elected to have a small glass of wine and decide later.

"I'll think about it," she replied.

Esteban kissed her on the mouth and ran his hand up her leg. She pulled him closer and put a hand underneath his shirt, his body reacting to her touch. Esteban closed the curtains to the terrace and they made love there on the couch. It was more relaxed this time, and Marialena reacted differently than she had the previous night. She arched her body more, moved with him a little more, and lost herself to him a little more. It was sweeter than it had been, but just as powerful. Esteban loved how her body looked underneath his. Her breasts were large and round. He could barely fit a hand over one of them, and he savored how they felt against his chest.

Afterward, they lay together. Esteban rested his head lightly on Marialena's and they already felt like two old souls who belonged together. He was surprised how comfortable he was with her, compared to Laura. Laura had often been fidgety after sex. After a while, Esteban just got used to it. But Marialena was so much more relaxed and at ease afterwards. He couldn't believe how different they were, and how much he had been missing, just cozying up to someone. He was a little worried that it was someone like Marialena. How far could their relationship go? She was so young. He didn't care what his friends or family had to say, but what if she was concerned? He didn't know how she felt about him and about his age. But for now, this was nice. Better than nice, this was heaven. Esteban noticed that she had fallen asleep beneath him, a victim to the wine. He had

117

never experienced that before, a lover falling asleep in his arms after sex. He turned ever so slightly to look at her. She seemed so peaceful lying there. But so terribly young. Esteban felt guilty again. He felt like he was taking something away from her.

He kissed her on the cheek and got up. He lifted the blanket to cover her body and checked his naked body again in the mirror. He looked fine. Still, something about them being together tugged at his heart. He threw on some clothes, turned on his laptop, and worked for about an hour. He could hear her stirring and looked up from his work. It was early still, not even eleven. Marialena wrapped the blanket around her naked body and walked over to him. He gave her his full attention.

"Hey." She sat down on his lap and kissed him on the mouth. She looked perfectly disheveled and also about five years younger than her age. She was so beautiful in this light, it took his breath away. He didn't know to how to keep from falling in love with her. She was so easy to love.

She placed both hands on his face and kissed him briefly on the mouth.

"Are you sure you don't mind if I stay?"

"No way. I would mind if you left, actually."

"I should have prepared for this, but I had no idea I'd stay again."

"It's okay. There are the clothes you brought back. I don't mind. I mean, they're practically yours at this point. Next time you come, bring some extra things, just in case." He chuckled softly, "I really don't mind. I like you here." He hated the mixed feelings he was having about her.

118

Marialena nodded, feeling their closeness. How had this happened so quickly?

"Did you mean what you said about coming for Christmas?" she asked, her hands in his short dark hair.

"Yeah, of course. I'd love to have you. The guest room is all yours if you want it. We don't have to..." he said, leaving the sentence unfinished. But he meant it. He wanted her there, but he still didn't know where they were going with this. He didn't want to lead her on, but he knew he wanted her there with him. He wanted to help her get through the holidays, and it would be nice for him too.

Marialena nodded and kept her arm around his neck. "Thank you. I'd really love to come," she said, searching his eyes.

"Then it's done. Hey, I'll get a tree." Marialena's eyes lit up and he laughed at how excited she looked.

"Thank you. It would mean the world to me, just to be here."

"You better not back out," he said.

"I'll be here."

She unlatched herself from him and put on her panties and his shirt and sweater from the night before. Esteban smiled at how cute she looked in his clothes.

"Are you going to keep working for a while?" she asked.

"Yeah, I think so. I have a few ideas I need to get down."

The music was still playing softly. She heard Nina Simone coming through his speakers. She sat down on his couch and listened to the lyrics. Marialena got lost in the song, and it felt like Nina was singing for the two of them. She noticed that Esteban was busy typing away, but what she didn't know was that he was also listening to the song and thinking about this budding romance, lost in serene contemplation.

Chapter Six

Marialena was meeting Patrick Denny for dinner, and she arrived a few minutes early. They had seen each other all day during the auditions, but he wanted to take her out, as a way of saying thank you. This would be her last week working with Patrick. It was only Tuesday, but she didn't know if she'd hear from Esteban anytime soon. He said he'd call, but they hadn't made any concrete plans.

Patrick arrived fifteen minutes late and apologized for the traffic. He ordered a bottle of champagne for the both of them, though Marialena wished he hadn't. She was in the mood for wine, but thought it impolite to say so.

He smiled, and she had to admit, he looked handsome. He was the type of man who looked great in just about anything, but Marialena didn't regret not sleeping with him that night. There was something too calm, too cool, and too collected about him, with his head of dark gray hair, his laughing blue eyes, and his great smile. Despite how she felt about him romantically, there was something electric about his presence. If you showed up with Patrick Denny anywhere, you knew people were going to be watching you, even if you didn't know Patrick Denny was a famous director. Maybe that's what turned her off, all that attention. Esteban was much more casual and laid back. She didn't feel like she had to be on her best behavior with him. She just felt like

121

herself. It was different with Patrick. He very much felt like her boss.

"That was one hell of a day, but we found our guy, didn't we?" he said.

"And our gal. And, God, that reading they had together!"

"I know, the sparks were already flying between those two."

"I'm just thrilled that we got so lucky. I hope we did, anyway. I guess we won't know until we actually start shooting."

"I think they'll be great." He straightened his tie. "Speaking of sparks flying, I heard about your date with Esteban Gutierrez last week. Did I have anything to do with that?" he asked, smiling.

Marialena blushed. She hadn't mentioned it to him, but wasn't surprised that he had found out.

"You might have. It was a great night. I have to apologize, though. At the fundraiser, I sort of mentioned I was working with you. I had nothing else to offer that crowd. I doubt they wanted to hear about my boring old nine-to-five."

"No, it's okay. Please, throw my name out there. Use me however you want," he said playfully.

"Everyone seemed to think I was more important than I actually was. It was a strange feeling. I felt like a fraud, but it was nice to be there with Esteban. He was wonderful about the whole thing."

"You're no fraud. And trust me, it looks good for the both of us. I'm glad you mentioned me. It's always a good thing when people are interested in what you're doing. With you being out there, it's like free promotion."

Marialena nodded. The waiter dropped off the bottle and made a big to-do when it was uncorked. Patrick Denny raised his glass.

"To our project."

"Cheers," she said along with him. They clinked glasses and Patrick perused the menu. Marialena had already glanced at it and knew what she was going to order. Patrick put down his menu a few minutes later.

"So, will you be seeing him again?" he asked.

Marialena didn't tell him that she already had. "Oh, I don't know. I'd like to see him again, but I'm not sure."

"You know," Patrick sighed, "I don't think he has a long line of exes. He seems to stay with his lovers for a while. I'd be careful if I were you."

"He and I seem to have that in common," she admitted.

"Oh, is that so?"

Marialena shrugged. "I've never been great at dating casually."

Patrick laughed. "Is that why I was so unlucky with you?"

Marialena smiled. "Probably."

"I'd like to think that I'll settle down one day."

"Me too."

"I was close once. We were married briefly. I thought the world revolved around her and I was sure she thought the same of me."

"What happened?"

"I was unfaithful. Often. Too many temptations."

"How long ago was this?"

"Ages ago. I was around your age. How about you, were you ever close to getting married, ever close to finding 'the one?'"

"Me? No, never." Marialena laughed. "I have a very short, very boring history. I've never been close. All my previous boyfriends were far from the one. But I guess they were fun while they lasted."

"What was your longest relationship?"

"Ten months."

"Not bad. I'd say he was a lucky man."

Marialena shrugged. "Someone should have told him." They both laughed and the waiter came by to take their order.

"So, what happened?"

Marialena looked at the tables around her as she searched for an answer. "He lived farther away, in Manhattan Beach. We were attracted to each other, but it was the only thing we had in common. He was kind and attentive and all that stuff, but we didn't have too much to talk about once we actually got to hanging out. We'd be sitting at a dinner table and his eyes would wander, or he'd be preoccupied with something on his phone. He was an avid reader—news, articles, you name it. There was a physical spark, but not one that comes from the heart, if you know what I mean?"

"Who ended it?"

Marialena took a sip of wine and smiled. "I did. He didn't take it well, which had surprised me. I thought that he felt the same way I did. Why waste time? Especially since we lived so far apart?"

"Hmm, so he was hurt because he didn't realize there was anything wrong with the relationship. I bet he was content, having you there while he Googled stuff on his phone."

"Maybe. But there was no chemistry."

"You mentioned there was a physical spark. Sometimes for a man, that's all you need."

"I disagree. I think for the long term, you need all the other stuff, too."

"Such as?"

"Being able to make each other laugh, being honed in, attentive. Respect, just getting it, you know?"

When dinner finally arrived, the conversation drifted back to their project, the film. He was sorry that Marialena was going to have to go back to work, but he understood.

"I'm going to miss seeing that face every day," he said, as they finished up the last of their champagne. They hadn't gone through the entire bottle. Marialena still had to drive home.

"I still want to come by after I leave. See how the whole thing works. Have you figured out which high school you're going to use?"

"Grant. It's on Coldwater and Oxnard, in Van Nuys." Marialena nodded, she knew the area.

"That reminds me. I need to call Esteban. I want to ask his opinion on the scene when Rosa figures out about Julian's sexuality. It's the most important scene in the film and I'd like his expertise." Marialena nodded, listening. "I think I'll call him tomorrow, and when we start shooting that scene, I'd like him there. You could come too."

Marialena thought about it, curious to see the two men at work together.

"Thank you for dinner," she said, looking at the time. She promised her cousin, Roxanne, that she'd call her since she hadn't been able to talk to her all weekend. They had a lot to talk about, but it was already late in Nashville.

She said goodbye to Patrick and they hugged warmly. When she got back to her car, she realized how close she was to Esteban's place, and she thought about dropping by after calling her cousin. Was that too much, too soon? She had just seen him on Saturday.

Marialena decided not to drive off yet, but called her cousin from the parking lot. She locked her doors and waited for her cousin to pick up.

"Hey!" Roxanne said excitedly.

"I'm sorry it's so late there."

"It's fine. How was dinner?"

"Amazing. I'm still here. It's probably a good thing. I had two glasses of champagne."

"You're still at the restaurant?"

"I'm in the parking lot."

"Okay, okay. So, what happened this weekend? I can't believe you spent two nights there!"

"I know, I don't know where to start. He's great."

"I've been looking at his pictures all night. He's cute. Not super crazy cute, but he's cute."

"Trust me, he's super crazy *handsome*."

"How was the sex?"

"It was sweet. He's very sweet about the whole thing."

"Sweet? Who wants sweet?"

Marialena laughed.

"Oh, that's right. You do. So, do you think you'll be seeing him again?"

"I don't know. I'm so close to his place right now. Driving back to Los Feliz feels wrong somehow."

"So, you like him. *Like him,* like him?"

"Yeah, I do," Marialena replied. Roxanne could hear the happiness in her cousin's voice.

"Listen, just be careful, okay? He might just be using you to make his ex-girlfriend jealous."

"It doesn't feel like that, Rox. It's too soon to say what it does feel like, but it doesn't feel like he's just using me."

"Well, that's good."

"I think I am going to drive home; I'll keep you on the line with me."

"You okay to drive?"

"Yeah, I'm fine."

"Because your new man lives around the corner. Get off the phone with me and call him! Tell him you're just calling to say hi. See what he says."

"You think so?"

"What do you have to lose?"

"I don't want to come off as needy."

"You're not. If you like him as much as you say you do, you're not being needy. You're just interested."

"Okay, okay. I'll call him."

"And if he thinks you're being needy, fuck it. He doesn't deserve you. Now go call him. Love you."

"Love you, more," Marialena said and got off the phone. She called Esteban, her heart racing. She had yet to speak to him on the phone, except for when she had arrived at his place. He picked up after the third ring.

127

"Hey," he said, seeing her name pop on up his phone. He sounded relaxed and casual.

"Hi."

"Thank god you called me. You knew right when I needed to be saved."

"Everything okay?"

"Yeah," he sighed. "I've just been at it all day. My body feels cramped. I should probably go for a walk. How about you, how was your day?"

"Oh, I'm good. I just had dinner with Patrick Denny."

"You trying to make me jealous?"

Marialena laughed. "No, no. It was all business."

"Where'd you two go?"

"This restaurant on Wilshire called "Ricardo's.""

"Ricardo's? Really? I've been. Good food, great coffee. That's about ten minutes from me. You should have called, I could have met you when you were done."

"Yeah, I'm still here actually. Waiting for the champagne to wear off."

"Do you want me to meet you?" he asked. Marialena smiled, thankful that he couldn't see it.

"No, I'm fine. It's getting late and I should probably head home soon. You gonna go for a walk?"

"Eh, maybe. I might just get something to eat and catch the game or something. I need a break." He sighed on the other end, clearly tired. "God, I missed you last night and this morning. I've already gotten so used to you in this short amount of time. You're dangerous, you know that?"

Marialena laughed. "Dangerous? Hardly."

"When can I see you again?" he asked.

Marialena looked out the window at the people going to their cars. "Name the time and place."

"I like you here, that way I can have you all to myself," he said, getting aroused.

Marialena could feel herself blushing. "Okay, I could come by sometime during the week."

"Sure, let me know."

"I can come by tomorrow evening? I'll even bring some groceries," she said, unsure of herself.

"You're gonna cook for me?"

"Yeah. I'd like to, if that's okay."

"Of course. Listen, bring a change of clothes. Spend the night."

"I'll have to go to work early on Wednesday."

"Yeah, but at least you can leave from here instead of from your place. It makes more sense."

Marialena thought about it. "Okay, why not."

"See you tomorrow," he said, his voice husky.

"See you then." She hung up. Things were definitely going somewhere. With Esteban Gutierrez. She couldn't believe it and smiled the entire way home.

129

Chapter Seven

It was a Tuesday morning and Esteban was out for a run. When he was writing, he loved going out for long walks, running, or even just driving. It gave him time to think about the storyline and the dialogue, and to hammer out some details. Sometimes that was easier to do when he was away from the computer.

When he got home, he saw that he had a voicemail. He sat down on his couch and returned Patrick Denny's missed phone call. Patrick answered right away.

"Esteban, hello. Thank you for calling me back."

"How are you?" he asked politely.

"I am well. Better now that you called. I have this scene. It's the most important scene in the film, and I'd like to see if we could find time to walk through it together, and you could tell me what you think."

"Yeah, sure. Whatever you need."

"Since you're doing me a favor, any time you could swing by would be fine. A day this week would be preferable."

Esteban looked at his watch. "I'm not doing anything until later," he said. It was still early and Marialena was coming over some time later in the evening. "I could stop over around lunchtime."

"Sure, that sounds great. I can order in. There's a great Italian place that delivers. We can eat here, if that's okay. It will be easier, since everything is here."

"That's fine."

Esteban worked on his writing, made some coffee, and then put on some nicer clothes. A pair of good jeans and a navy-blue dress shirt. He threw on his brown sports jacket over the shirt and left.

When he got to Patrick's office, he was shown in right away. Patrick had been expecting him.

"Hey, thanks so much for coming by on short notice," he said, sticking out his hand.

"No problem. I know how these things work."

"I appreciate it, nonetheless," Patrick said, sitting down.

"So, what's the scene?"

Patrick held up a finger. "One second. Let me get the menu for you. We could order first," he said, opening up a drawer and handing the delivery menu to Esteban.

"Oh, thanks." He wasn't terribly hungry and wanted to have an appetite when Marialena came over later that evening. He decided to go with a salad and a slice of pizza, since they offered individual slices. He smiled to himself when he remembered that it was what Marialena's favorite food.

Patrick sat back in his chair as Esteban took a sip of hot coffee that had been offered to him.

"The scene in question is the one where Rosa, the female lead, figures out that Julian, the male lead, is gay. We have a location at Grant High School. They have this bridge there," he said and showed Esteban a picture of the brick bridge. It was on the second level of the high school, connecting two buildings.

Esteban took the picture and glanced at it. "I imagined these two kids sitting on the bridge after school. Not many people are around. Here's the script

131

and photographs of the actors." Esteban read it silently, then looked at the pictures. When he was done, he placed them in front of him and sat back, thinking.

"How are you going to shoot it?"

"The space only allows for a handheld. They're facing each other, sitting cross-legged maybe. I was going to try to get different angles."

"Sure." Esteban thought for a second. "You know, I don't think they should be sitting facing each other. You should take it in one shot, with both actors possibly sitting against the cement, no coverage. They could face forward, and the camera would zoom in on his face, then pan over to hers during the moment when she realizes he's gay."

Patrick nodded.

"It will help the audience feel like they're part of the conversation." Esteban was getting excited. "Do you want him to feel vulnerable in this scene?"

"Very much so, yes."

"Okay, this is what I'm thinking. Give her a jacket, make her look like she's warm and cozy. Get makeup to add some color to his cheeks, and get a fan out there to blow some wind around. Let him be under-dressed a little. Use some stock footage of the school on a cold day, overcast sky, that kind of thing. It's a small thing, but audiences might feel bad for him if he looks cold."

"In addition to feeling bad because he seems lost."

"Yes."

"One shot. I like that. I thought about that for a second myself, but I hadn't thought of them sitting against the wall."

"Yeah, they're casual, kind of bored. Tired maybe. Instead of her searching his eyes as he talks, they're both staring out into space as they talk. It gives him the confidence to start talking about it, since she's not looking at him. He kind of peeks over to her and she turns to look at him, just slightly so that we can still see her face. You could zoom in there, or leave it on both of their faces."

"What do you think his reaction is when she figures it out?"

Esteban sat back and thought for a second. "Let's see. He's lost, you said?"

"Yes. He's struggling with it."

"Okay, so she figures it out and what's the line?" He picks up the script again. "She says, 'Julian, I didn't know,' and so he might chuckle to himself, you know, self-deprecating, and turns away from the camera. He might shake his head. And that's when he says, 'You know, I don't know either.'"

"And you think one shot?"

"Sure, he turns away from her, and he can turn away from us, too. You can end it with her taking his hand, and that's when she says, 'We can figure it out. I can help you,'" he said, reading from the script.

"Okay, I like where you're going with this."

"I mean, that's how I would do it."

Patrick nodded. "It's good. I like how the cold weather can be a factor. It's subtle, but it could be effective."

"It's one of those things that *could* be, or maybe not."

133

"Yeah, I could see that. So subtle, it's lost on the audience."

"Exactly."

"It's worth a shot."

"It's a hell of a scene. Kudos, man. It's going to be great. And it's a powerful message. We need a picture like this."

"Yes, I think so too. Thanks for coming aboard and lending a hand. I really appreciate it."

"No, thanks for thinking of me."

"Marialena was right about you. When I met her, she had this sparkle in her eyes when she talked about your work. That's powerful. I can't say that I've received that kind of affection about my work."

"Your work is different. It inspires a different kind of feeling."

"It doesn't move people the way your work does."

"I disagree. Your work is thought-provoking. That's powerful too."

"Thank you."

"What else do we have? Any other scenes you want me to take a look at?"

"Well, that's the big one. I think the rest of the film really revolves around that one scene. The timing, the heart of it all, how you feel about the characters. It all depends on how we capture this one scene."

"Yeah, I know that feeling."

"I keep wondering if he should cry or not."

Esteban nodded. "You know, what I've learned about crying is that it depends on the actor. In my experience, crying can hurt you as much as help you, but it all depends on how good or bad the actor is."

"Okay, if you could see him crying, how would you picture it?"

"Maybe like he's trying not to."

Patrick nodded. "That's what I picture, too."

"Are you going to go with that?"

Patrick shook his head. "I don't know. It's not written, but I kept wondering if it should be. I honestly don't know if it's necessary. And again, it sets the tone for the rest of the film."

Esteban nodded. "Shoot it, see if it works. Shoot different versions. Maybe the Rosa character can cry too."

"Yeah," Patrick replied.

"I think the audio is really important here. You've got to capture them breathing. Hearing the weight of their words, and even their lack of words. Capture their silences. Make their silences loud. Make it a little uncomfortable for the audience."

"That's interesting."

"You've got to make the audience understand how lost he feels, right? How uncomfortable he feels?"

"I kind of thought in this scene, he'd finally start to embrace the idea."

"I mean, it's your picture, but if it were me, the embracing of it comes after this scene."

The food arrived and both men dove in silently, each lost in their own thoughts about the scene. Esteban took a bite of his pizza and finally broke the silence.

"I mean, if he's uncomfortable with it, he's not going to embrace it the minute someone else finds out. It takes a little bit of time to sink in, doesn't it? If he himself doesn't know?"

135

"Yeah, maybe. It's such a short scene to try and convey so much."

"So, make it longer. Ask the actors if they have anything they could add. You never know. I mean, this guy who's playing Julian, he might already be in the right mindset. He's already trying to get into the character's head. He might add something useful."

"Yeah, I've done that in the past."

"Sure, we all have."

"So, you'll come by that day?" Patrick asked.

"Yeah, I'll be there."

Patrick nodded. "How rude of me, I haven't even asked how you are, how work is for you these days."

Esteban shook his head. "You weren't being rude. I didn't give you a chance to ask. I kind of dove into the matter at hand. But it's going. It took a while, but I'm happy to report that I'm back at it. It's too soon to tell if anything will come of it, but it's an idea. So far, it's going well."

Patrick wiped his mouth with a napkin and sat back. "It's good to have you back. This world needs your films."

Esteban laughed. "Thanks. I appreciate that."

"No, I'm serious. If you ever need a favor, please don't hesitate. I mean that."

Esteban nodded. "Well, you introduced me to Marialena. I think we're even. In fact, I'm probably still in your debt. She's great."

Patrick smiled. "I'm glad you think so. There's an innocence to her, isn't there? It's kind of rare in this day and age, for a woman like her anyway."

"Yeah, I know what you mean."

"Well, I know it's early, but good luck. With Marialena, with your next project. All of it, you deserve it."

"Oh, I don't know about that, but thank you," Esteban said, unable to finish his salad. He went for his coffee instead and took a sip.

Patrick wanted to ask him if he was going to continue to see Marialena, but he didn't want to be impolite. He knew he could talk about it with Marialena, but he hardly knew Esteban outside of work. He didn't want to cross a line if there was one, so he kept quiet. Instead, he closed his food container and talked more about his film. He brought up a few more scenes, and Esteban offered his two cents, feeling comfortable enough with the script to be able to advise Patrick on the scenes in question. The subject matter didn't need a whole lot of explanation. It was easy to see why Patrick wanted to make a film like this, and it was the first movie he had ever written himself. Naturally, he was closer to this than the others he had worked on.

"Well, I think that about does it for now. If I can think of anything else, I'll let you know. Thanks so much for stopping by. I'll give you a call when we're ready to shoot the bridge scene in a couple of weeks. I'd really like for you to be there. I can't thank you enough for finding the time to stop by and go over some of this with me."

"Any time."

Patrick walked Esteban out. "Listen, again, if you ever need anything in return, I am at your disposal."

Esteban smiled and shook his hand. "Thanks for lunch."

137

Patrick nodded and walked back to his office, thinking about everything they had discussed. Esteban certainly had a knack for understanding the characters and getting the audience to feel close to them. Most directors could do that, but Esteban was able to bridge the gap more easily than he's ever seen, and without hesitation. He was a hell of a director and Patrick wondered why he didn't have more films under his belt. Four films was not a lot for his level of talent, and he wondered what was holding him back.

Chapter Eight

It was a cold Saturday morning, and Esteban and Marialena were getting coffee at a local café. As they were headed out, someone called Esteban's name.

"Hey, Esteban. How are you, man?"

"Oh, hey Eric. How's it going?" Eric was a little taller than Marialena, in his fifties. He was a little round in the middle and had a cheery smile. He was bundled up, with a scarf around his neck and a warm jacket.

"Just doing some Christmas shopping today. Man, it's cold." Eric looked at Marialena, waiting for an introduction.

"Eric, this is my, uh—" Esteban stalled for a second before Marialena chimed in and stuck out her hand.

"Marialena Villaneuva. Nice to meet you."

Eric nodded. "Pleasure is all mine. Hey, listen, Esteban, we're having this get-together on a Friday night in a couple of weeks. We'd love it if you could come by."

"Oh yeah, thanks. Keep me posted. You have my number?"

"Yeah, we'll let you know as it gets closer. It's sort of a Christmas thing. You know how Marta gets about the holidays." Esteban nodded and patted him on the arm.

"Sounds good. It was good to see you, man."

"You too."

When Esteban and Marialena were out of earshot, he turned to her and apologized. "He and his wife are friends of Laura's and mine. I don't know how

139

appropriate it would be to go. Anyway, I'm sorry. I kind of froze. I didn't want to label us, and I wasn't sure what you would have preferred I said."

"No, it's okay." She held her warm cup of coffee in both hands.

"We should probably figure that out," he said with an embarrassed laugh.

"Do we? I thought we were just enjoying this." They had been out for a walk, had ended with coffee, and were now headed back up to his condo.

"No, I think we need to talk," Esteban said. They had been seeing each other for a month, and Esteban needed to know what Marialena thought about him. Marialena didn't like how serious he looked. They walked to his condo in silence, each lost in their own thoughts. The coffee was starting to make Marialena's stomach turn. She was getting nervous.

They walked into his condo and Marialena made a beeline for his couch, took off her shoes, and sat with her legs underneath her.

Esteban put a loving hand on her knee.

"I don't know where to start." He ran a hand through his short hair, clearly frustrated. Marialena sat there quietly, her eyes wide.

"How do you feel about where this is going?" he asked her.

Marialena shrugged. "I thought it was going great. Why? What do you think?"

Esteban sighed. "I don't know. I'm going to be fifty next month and I'm kind of freaking out. I never thought I'd be the kind of person to freak out, but maybe it's just your presence in my life." He looked at Marialena, not

140

wanting to hurt her. She gave no reaction and just sat listening.

"You're so young. I just want to kind of settle down with someone, Marialena. This is great. You're absolutely right. But what we have, I feel like maybe—" he stalled, trying to find the right words. "You should be with someone your own age. You shouldn't have gotten caught up with me."

"What are you saying?"

"I don't know. I mean, we don't have to decide anything right now. We're just talking."

"All of this because you introduced me to someone?" Marialena asked, feeling hurt.

"We needed to talk about this. It's been on my mind. Haven't you been thinking about it?"

"The only thing I've been thinking about is how wonderful this is."

"I've been thinking about that too, but I don't know, with my birthday around the corner, it's putting me in a dark mood I guess. I just want you to think about this. *Us*, how this is really going to work. Can you really see us, *this*, two or three years from now? I mean, do you really want to be with someone like me?"

Marialena smiled sadly into her coffee cup. "No, I don't want to be with someone *like* you. I want to be with *you*. And yes, I can see myself with you two or three years from now."

Esteban paced. Marialena stayed seated, unmoving.

"Marialena, you don't know what this feels like."

"Then tell me," she said.

"You can't possibly want this."

"Why wouldn't I want this? My god, you're going to turn fifty and you're acting like you're eighty," she said, setting down her coffee. She was going to say that she'd still love him, but they hadn't used that word yet and this wasn't the right time to test it out.

"You can have any guy you want. Anyone. Why me?" he asked, ignoring her last comment.

"If I can have any guy I want, why can't I have the one I actually want? Which is you, Esteban. I want this." He sat back down next to her and took her hands in his. "What is it you want?" she asked him. "Fuck our age difference. That doesn't matter. What do *you* want?"

"It doesn't matter *to you* because you're young."

"Did I embarrass you when we were spotted together? Is that it?"

"What?! No. That's not it. I don't know. When he asked me to come to that party, I thought of the two of us there. You and I. And there'd be a bunch of people my age. You'd stick out like a sore thumb. Wouldn't you be uncomfortable? Shouldn't you be with people, I don't know, your own age?"

"I can't believe you right now, Esteban. I can't believe you'd think I'd need that," she said.

"Look, I don't know what you want or need. That's why we're talking about this. You know, Laura used to complain all the time about me not going out enough, or that I wasn't making enough time for her. I would hate to make you feel that way."

"Listen to me, Esteban. I am not Laura. And maybe you didn't want to make time for her, because in your heart you didn't want to. Think about it. Maybe it was a subconscious thing. And you know what, you're right.

142

Two or three years with you? I don't know, Esteban. I'm not sure I want that."

"See!" Esteban said. "That's why we're talking about this."

"No, Esteban, I'm talking about more than that. Why stop at two or three years?"

Esteban exhaled loudly, listening to what she was saying.

"What about you, Esteban?" she asked. "I know I want you. Do you want me?" she said this so softly, he wasn't sure if her heard her.

He looked into her eyes and smiled. "Yeah, I do."

"What's there to be worried about? We are great together, don't you think so?"

"Yeah, I do. Trust me, you don't have to sell it to me. I guess I'm just getting older, and I don't know...I don't want to waste any of your time or mine. *Wasting* is the wrong word. I guess I'm just ready to find the right one and settle down or something. Fuck, I don't know."

"Well, look. She could be right here."

Esteban nodded. "I just want you to be sure about what you're getting into."

"I'm pretty sure."

"Don't you miss people your own age?"

"What? No, it's not like that, Esteban. This has been so rewarding. I love being with you."

"I don't want you to miss out on anything. It's been bothering me since we met. This is supposed to be a great time for people your age."

"Esteban, I love this. I've had a better time with you than anyone else I can think of."

143

"And what if some young guy comes into the picture and tries to take you away?"

"He won't."

"Oh, he'll try. They always try."

"Esteban, please stop." She leaned into him, pushed him back into the sofa, and cuddled up with him.

"You really want this?" he asked her, kissing her hair.

"I do," she whispered back.

After a few minutes of silence, Esteban brought up children.

"Did you ever want kids?" he asked her.

Marialena stayed in his arms and didn't look at him. She thought for a minute. "Sure, you?"

"I haven't thought about kids in a very long time. I don't know."

"Well..." She untangled herself from his arms. "We're really talking about this, aren't we?"

"I know. I mean, we've only been seeing each other for a month."

"I'm not even your girlfriend or anything."

Esteban smiled at her and put a hand on hers. He took a deep breath. "If we say we want this, it's all the way, isn't it? It would be real. You *would* be my girlfriend. How do you feel about that?"

"I'd feel pretty great about it, actually." He pulled her closer to his body.

"I'm just scared, Lena." It was the first time he had shortened her name. She loved how it sounded from his lips. She put a loving arm around his waist.

"What are you scared of?" she asked.

"That I won't be enough, that you'll cheat on me or something. I don't know. I hit rock bottom when I found out Laura did, and we were already falling apart. This would be different, somehow. If you cheated on me, I don't know. And the sad thing is, why wouldn't you? Look at us."

"Hey," she pulled away from him. "What's wrong with you? Stop comparing me to Laura. I'm not her. I've never cheated on anyone before. Not only that, Esteban, if something happened between us, I'd talk to you about it. We'd work on it. I mean, I can't sit here and tell you it would be perfect. No relationship is perfect, even if I was with someone my own age. I can't guarantee anything, but I know I'm not Laura."

"I'm still not convinced that you'd be happy with this," he said.

Marialena laughed. "You're being ridiculous and I find you extremely handsome. I love waking up to you, kissing you, making love to you."

"But for how long?" he asked seriously.

"What do you want from me? I can't prove it to you, Esteban."

"I know." He caressed her and they were both silent for a few minutes. "Hey," he said, sitting up. "Why don't you stay with me through the holidays? You can stay here, bring whatever you need."

"Are you serious? Why?" she asked, sitting up to face him better. She tucked a loose strand of hair behind her ear.

"Remember when I told you that Laura and I moved in together for a month? I knew immediately it wasn't going to work out."

145

"That's the worst reason I could possibly think for me to move in. Plus, you should have realized then that you guys were wrong for each other."

"I know, that's why I want to do this. Look, obviously it would be different with you and me. Plus, it's the holidays. It could be awesome. After a month, we'd know if we were compatible. I mean, really compatible."

"Esteban, that sounds like a really bad idea."

"Why?"

"First of all, it takes a lot longer than a month. Secondly, our relationship is way too young for that."

"I don't think it's a bad idea. Look, you'll really know if you want to be with me or not. Come on, think about it."

"I don't think one month will make a difference. Even living with you."

"No, but we'll go to those parties. You'll be in the thick of it."

"I could still go to those parties with you. I don't have to live here to go with you."

"Yeah, but, Lena, you'll be here, seeing me at my best, my worst. I can get grumpy. I'm terrible around the holidays, a real grinch."

"What am I going to do about my place? I just can't abandon it for a month."

"Okay, we can stay at your place a few times a week. I know this is a crazy idea, but I kind of love how crazy it is, don't you? And don't you think you'd be that much more sure about me by the end of it?"

"No, honestly I don't think it will change my mind. I adore you already. But if this is what you need for me to prove it to you, then sure. I'll think about it."

146

They both sat back, lost in their thoughts.

"What if, after a month, you change your mind about me?" she asked.

"What do you mean?"

"Right now, you think you might be too old for me or whatever, but what if you think I'm too young for you?"

"Then we'll figure it out. Let's see, today is December 1st. Let's have dinner together on January 2nd. Don't make any plans that day. We can have another discussion then."

"So, that's like decision day?"

"I guess."

"So, if we live together now, what does that make us? Roomies?" she asked playfully.

He turned to her and looked her in the eyes; her heart skipped a beat.

"It makes us lovers."

Marialena looked off into the distance, testing the word. "Lovers." Then she turned to him and laughed. "This is Esteban Gutierrez, my lover." He laughed with her. "It doesn't have that ring to it, does it?" she asked.

Esteban cleared his throat. "How does, 'this is my girlfriend, Marialena,' sound?'"

Marialena nodded. "That sounds good. So, for a month, for all intents and purposes, you have a girlfriend and I have a boyfriend."

"I guess so."

Marialena looked into his eyes. "My boyfriend, my lover," she whispered. Her stomach turned over and over. Esteban kissed her on the lips and she moaned softly. He tasted like coffee, delicious and warm.

147

Marialena took his sweater off and loved how warm his skin was. They got lost in each other's embrace, lips locked, with the sun shining into the living room.

They could get used to this.

Chapter Nine

It was seven p.m. on a Saturday night at Esteban's when Marialena's phone rang.

"Hi, Roxy. So, I'm moved in."

"Can I just tell you right now that this is weird?" Roxanne asked.

"I don't know. I've kind of gotten used to the idea. It's not weird."

"It's fucking weird and you know it. I just don't like that no one's met him, and no one knows what his intentions are. He could be a mass murderer for crying out loud."

Marialena laughed. "Look, he's not going to kill me. Besides, he's well-known. I doubt he's a murderer."

"Directors are capable of killing, sweetheart. Anyway, I'm kidding. But still Mar, I'm not a hundred percent comfortable with this."

"Who I am supposed to introduce him to? It's not like anyone gives a shit anyway. Oh wait, hold on..." Marialena looked out the door of the guest room she was keeping her things in.

"Everything okay?"

"Yeah, I think he just went into the restroom. Shit," Marialena said quietly.

"So what?"

"Well, I don't know. He might have heard. The restroom is right next door and my door was slightly open."

"Okay, well at least he knows we're on to him."

"Oh, come on. Stop messing around. He's been so sweet."

"I know, I'm just worried, lovely."

"Don't be. I'm fine." A few seconds later there was a knock on her door. "Oh wait, hold on for a second." Marialena opened the door to find Esteban raising an eyebrow. "My cousin," she said to Esteban. "She's in Nashville and is apparently worried about my well-being."

Esteban nodded and held out his hand for the phone. "May I?"

Marialena handed him her phone, feeling like she was fifteen years old instead of twenty-seven.

"Hi, this is Esteban Guiterrez. I understand that this is Marialena's cousin? Listen, do you have FaceTime on your phone? Mind if I call you back on my line for a little bit?" He handed Marialena's phone back to her.

"What are you doing?" she asked, smiling.

"I heard what you said about me," he said and winked at her. "I want to set the record straight. Read me her number, will you?"

Marialena gave him her number and he dialed the FaceTime video call. Her cousin answered right away. Despite the late hour in Nashville, Roxanne hadn't gotten ready for bed yet and was still wide awake. Her long curly hair was up in a ponytail and she was wearing a scarf, but that was all Esteban and Marialena could really see. Esteban looked for some resemblance between the two women, but couldn't see any. Marialena's skin tone was dark brown, and Roxanne looked almost pale. Esteban was even more olive-toned that Roxanne was. The two girls showed no similarities.

"Okay, so I was walking by when I overheard Marialena say that maybe you thought she could be in danger. I can assure you she is not. And you now have my number and I have yours, in case I need to reach you if, god forbid, there was an emergency. Now, I'll text you my address. I don't mind. In fact, I'm relieved someone is looking out for her the way you are. But now that I have you on the phone, I wanted to ask you something. You were the one who thought I was Patrick Denny, right?" Esteban was smiling now.

Roxanne smiled, embarrassed. "Maybe." She started to laugh. "Sorry about that."

"No, it's okay. I am in your debt. If it wasn't for you, I might not have met this wonderful young lady." He turned and tried to get Marialena in the frame; he kissed her head.

"Okay, so you might not be a mass murderer. My apologies. Still, one can never be too sure these days. I appreciate the phone call. It's nice to meet you."

"Nice to meet you too." He passed the phone to Marialena and said off frame, "Talk as long as you need to." He waved goodbye to Roxanne and closed the door behind him.

"Oh shit," Marialena said. "I feel like a teenager who got caught."

Roxanne laughed. "That was pretty amazing. You're right. He seemed sweet about the whole thing. You were right, though. He heard you."

"I am dying right now," Marialena said, clearly embarrassed.

151

"It's okay, don't worry about it. He seemed fine with it."

The girls talked for twenty more minutes. Marialena walked back out to find Esteban typing away at his computer. She handed him his phone.

"Here you go. Thanks for that. I'm so sorry." She sat down backward on the sofa so that she could face him. Esteban smiled.

"It's okay. I mean, she was worried. It's normal," he said kindly.

"I am going to take a shower and forget this ever happened," she said. Esteban laughed, but looked at his phone as she was walking away. When he heard the shower start, he called Roxanne back, feeling like a kid himself.

"Hey, so this is Esteban again. Sorry. I was wondering. Do you have a sec? Marialena is in the shower, and I don't know, there was something else I wanted to add. Let me ask you something. You think this is a bad idea, her and me. I can sense it. Why?" He heard Roxanne sigh on the other end. "Be totally honest," he added.

"Okay, you want honesty? What's this 'decision' day? It sounds terrible. I mean, might as well call it D-Day. What the fuck?"

"Oh, we didn't mean to call it that, it kind of just happened. But I can explain."

"Okay, please do. Because, yeah, I think this whole fucking idea is weird, no offense. Look, I don't know if Marialena mentioned this to you or not, but the holidays are not a good time for her. And if you're going to break her heart, I mean like right after the holidays, that doesn't sit well with me. I tried to tell her, and she thinks she's strong enough to take it, but between you and me, I don't think she is."

"Okay, that's fair. But listen, I don't plan on breaking her heart. If anything, I'm sort of hoping she breaks mine."

"What? Why?"

Esteban was silent for a second. He took a deep breath. "I'm crazy about her. Absolutely crazy. She's amazing. But here's the thing, I need to know if she feels the same way. I'm worried that if I tell her that I'm falling for her, she'll stay with me out of politeness. I just came out of a seven-year relationship because we were both too polite to do anything about it."

"So Marialena is paying for your old mistakes?" Roxanne asked. Esteban had to admit, he liked Roxanne's honesty.

"I know it sounds crazy, but you have to believe me. I just want her to be sure about me."

"One month isn't enough time."

"I know, and she said that too. I don't disagree. But she will be that much more sure of me. Look, I'm going to be fifty soon, and I want Marialena to be the one. I'm sure of it. I have never felt this way about anyone before and it's not just that she's young and beautiful. She's amazing, pure and simple. I love how full my place is when she's here. I love how warm she feels when I'm around her. But what if she's just dating me because I'm her favorite director? I know how people can get. They get blinded by the fame of it all. Not that I think she's like that, but I want to be sure. Roxanne, I have to be sure that she really and truly wants me back."

153

"You said it wasn't that she's super young and super hot? I kind of thought older guys dug that shit. I thought you guys all got off on the fact that if you're crazy successful and crazy famous, you could have any girl you want, the younger the better."

"Well, yeah. Sure, I know other guys like that. But Roxanne, that's not me."

"Okay. I believe you. Still, it's just been a month. If you ask me, you guys are going from zero to sixty."

"What I am afraid of is going fifteen miles for the next five years. Zero to sixty sounds great, if I could just get her to meet me at sixty. Besides, that's the dream, isn't it?"

"To live life at sixty miles to per hour? I mean, I guess. When you put it like that."

"I'm crazy about her, Roxanne."

"I know. I think she's crazy about you too."

"I just need to feel it, to really feel it. I know, you're right. It *is* crazy. But I need to try something."

"Okay," she said simply.

"So, you're saying you're okay with this?"

"I am saying that I get it. I don't like it, but I get it."

"Listen, please don't tell her how I feel about her. We haven't really gotten there yet. I want to feel her out a little bit. I don't want her feelings to be the least bit effected by mine."

"So, this is like the real deal and shit?"

"I don't know. I mean, it is for me."

"And you know this after one month?"

"Sometimes you just know."

"Listen, I won't say anything to her. For what's it worth, I'm pretty sure she feels the same way."

"It sounds like she's done in the shower. Can I count on you not saying anything to her?"

"I won't. I get it."

"If you want to come by and visit, as long as Marialena is staying here, you're welcome to my place."

"Yeah, I don't think I'm going to get any time off this month, but I appreciate it. And I appreciate the heart to heart."

"Yeah, thanks for listening. One more thing. There's another reason I asked her to stay," he said, listening for Marialena, in case she came out of the restroom. "I didn't want her to be alone for the holidays. I know what that's like and what it can do to people. I didn't want her to go through that."

"She's used to it now, I think," Roxanne yawned. "But that's sweet. I'm glad she won't be alone this year. Just don't fuck it up."

Esteban laughed. "Good talking to you. Call me if you need anything."

"Okay, will do. Have a good night."

"Goodnight, Roxanne."

Chapter Ten

It was the middle of the week, on a breezy Wednesday afternoon, when Esteban received a phone call from Patrick Denny.

"Hello, Esteban. Listen, I wanted to call to remind you that we'd be shooting this Saturday at Grant High School in the valley. We'll be there at eight a.m., so I think we'll have our marine layer working for us in the morning. Can you make it?"

"Yeah, man. I'll be there." Esteban took down the address and had a general idea where it was. It wouldn't be too far of a drive. "I'll see you then."

When he hung up with Patrick, he set the address aside and took a deep breath. He shut down his laptop and stared at the blank screen. He and Marialena had been invited to a second holiday party on the night before the shoot, one that Laura wouldn't be at this time, and he was debating whether or not they should go. Esteban decided to go out for a walk and maybe get a bite to eat somewhere nearby. He collected his keys and wallet and left for an afternoon to himself to ponder his plans.

When Marialena arrived later that night, he told her of both plans. He hadn't really been out socially with Marialena, and while she was able to hold her own at the fundraiser, this would be a completely different setting. He wondered if she'd feel uncomfortable in any way, but he knew she'd say that she'd be fine.

Marialena listened to him explain who his friends were, as she changed out of her work clothes into something more comfortable. He sat on the bed, watching her.

"So, this party starts at nine? If we go, we can have a drink or two, mingle for a bit. Then we come home like two old early birds around eleven. Are you worried that you won't be on your A-game at eight the next morning?"

"Not really. The party will probably go really late, and honestly, I can't remember the last time I was somewhere as early as eight in the morning. It might just be easier for me to stay up the whole night."

Marialena looked at him, surprised. "I can't imagine *wanting* to stay up all night. I used to have terrible insomnia right after my parents died," she said, sitting down with him on the bed. "It was awful. Why put yourself through that willingly?"

Esteban shrugged and placed a hand on her leg lovingly. "I'm kind of used to it, staying up late. It's getting up early that might be the hard part."

"Well, I can help wake you up in the morning."

"Hey, Patrick wanted you to come, you know?" he said, lying down on the bed.

"I thought about it. As curious as I am to see two legends at work, I'd probably only get in the way."

Esteban smiled, putting an arm around her as she lay on top of him.

"Two legends? You're not talking about me, are you?"

"Sure, I am."

157

"I don't think anyone has ever called me a legend before," he said with a self-deprecating laugh.

Marialena got on top of him and kissed him on the mouth. "And I think you need to re-watch one of your own films again," she said, reaching down to touch him. His body responded as he placed a hand on her back, underneath her shirt, finding her bra and unsnapping it with one hand.

Forty minutes later, they lay in each other's arms.

Later that week, when Marialena got back to Esteban's place, she shuffled up the steps with little energy. She entered Esteban's condo still wearing her sunglasses.

Esteban looked up from his laptop. He stood up to kiss her on the cheek and lifted the sunglasses from her face, noticing that something was off. She had uttered a weak 'hey.'

"Is everything okay?"

"I have a massive headache," she said, squinting into his eyes.

"For how long?"

Marialena collapsed onto the couch and kicked her shoes off. "A couple of hours."

"Have you taken anything for it?"

"Yeah, I took something at work as soon as I felt it, and it helped a little. I think I'm just going to lie down for a little while. Hopefully, with some rest it will go away and I'll feel well enough to go to the party tonight. But as of right now, I'm not up for it."

"Yeah, get some rest. I'll close the blinds in the bedroom. Let me know if you need anything else." Marialena followed him, stripped down to her camisole

158

and underwear, and got into bed. Esteban had to admit, she didn't look too hot and wondered if she got these kinds of headaches frequently.

He pulled the covers over her and bent down to kiss her forehead. "Just close your eyes," he said.

Marialena did just that. She drifted in and out of a restless sleep, willing herself to feel better for the party. After an hour and a half, Esteban peeked into the bedroom and she felt him sit on the bed beside her. "Feeling better?" he asked.

Marialena turned to face him. "Honestly, no. You might have to fly solo," she said, her voice raspy and tired.

"I could stay here," he said.

"No, you should go. You haven't been out in a while. It's okay."

Esteban shrugged. "I could stay and keep you company."

Marialena shook her head. "I'm just going to be in bed. C'mon, go. And if I start to feel better, I could meet you there."

"Can I get you anything?"

"No, I don't want to overdo it on the medicine, not yet. Thanks," she said, and put her hand underneath her pillow for better head support.

"Okay. I'll check on you in a bit."

"Mmmkay." Marialena closed her eyes again. Esteban left the room and turned on the television. He probably should go the party. He hadn't seen his friends from this particular group in more than three months. It would be good for him to go. He watched the basketball game for a little while, then he walked back into the

159

bedroom and sat back down on the bed to check on Marialena. She opened her eyes as soon as he came in.

"Hey, how do you feel?"

"Like shit," she said.

"Have you been able to sleep?"

"Not really."

"Are you sure you don't need me to stay?"

"I'm positive. Go and have fun. I'm sorry I got sick."

"Nonsense. It happens. Feel better and get some rest. It's only a few miles away, so if you need to me to come back home for whatever reason, just call me."

"Okay."

"I just need to change."

Marialena got back on her side and closed her eyes while he got dressed. He was was careful not to make too much noise, which Marialena was grateful for. He kept the lights off and was able to get ready in the dark. He bent down to kiss Marialena on the forehead before he left and Marialena turned to look at him. He was wearing his brown sports jacket and a white dress shirt and jeans, the outfit he wore when she had first met him. Marialena smiled at him despite how she was feeling.

"You look so handsome. Maybe you should stay," she said.

Esteban smiled. "Thanks. You know, I will if you want me to."

"No, I'm only kidding. But I am going to try to force myself to get better. I'd love nothing more than to be on your arm tonight," she said.

"Next time. Do you need anything before I leave? Medicine, water?"

"No, thanks. I might get up in a little bit and take a hot shower."

"I could stay for that," he said, smiling.

Marialena laughed. "I'm sure you could." She pushed him away gently. "Go and have fun."

"Okay, I'm only a phone call away," he said and kissed her on the lips. She welcomed him as she put her arms around him and didn't let him go right away. Then, after a moment of holding him close to her, she released him and he got up, adjusted his shirt, and looked down at her. "Get some rest."

"Okay, bye." She listened to him walk out the door. She stayed in bed for a little while longer, then forced herself to get out of bed, her head throbbing. She removed her clothes, threw them in the hamper, and walked to the bathroom naked. She turned around and saw that Esteban had left the living room light on for her. When she got into the shower, the pressure in her back and neck lessened and she titled her head up, loving how the hot water felt against her skin. She stayed in the shower for a few minutes longer than she normally did and started to feel a little less dizzy. She wrapped a towel around herself and walked into the kitchen to make a cup of tea. She glanced at the time and noticed it was already almost ten. She lost a whole evening to this headache and she really wanted to attend this party with Esteban. It was a shame, the way this headache had crept up on her. She used to get headaches all the time right after her parents died. She thought it was attributed to her constant lack of sleep, but she continued to get them every once in a while. This headache started in her neck and crept its way up, making her head throb, and her eyes were sensitive to light. She took another pill and walked into the bedroom to change. She was feeling a little better when she decided to sit on the couch and watch some TV, trying to figure out if she was well enough to get ready for this party. She knew she wouldn't be able to muster enough willpower to actually go. She tried to imagine herself on Esteban's arm as they wandered from person to person. What would people think when they escaped to a corner to whisper sweet nothings into each other's ears. She wondered if they'd be kind to her. Esteban didn't strike her as the type of guy who had unkind friends.

She flipped channels and stumbled onto an old Clint Eastwood movie. She had never seen this one before, but left it on because she admired the lighting. She watched as Clint Eastwood stood in the hot sun, somewhere in Italy probably. She texted Esteban as she watched.

"Watching a Clint Eastwood spaghetti western, feeling a little better, but probably won't be able to join you tonight."

She heard back from him a few minutes later. "Glad you're feeling better. I'll probably be here another hour or two, lots of people I haven't seen."

"Sure. Have fun."

"Get some more rest. I'll try to be quiet when I come in."

"Thanks. I'm pretty tired. I'll probably try to catch some zzz's soon. This headache knocked me out."

Back at the party, Esteban put his phone in his pocket and walked toward the group. Michael, his friend and host, was his age. Esteban had met him at another party, and the two immediately hit it off when they discovered their similar tastes in movie soundtracks. Michael nodded toward Esteban.

"Your new lady friend checking in on you?"

Esteban laughed. "She's under the weather, but sends her best."

"So, is this thing serious between the two of you?"

Esteban looked around at the other guests as he thought of an answer. "It's going pretty well. It's probably leaning toward something serious, but we're still trying to figure it out," he said, giving the political answer.

"You said she's staying with you for a while?"

"Yeah, through the holidays. It's easier, without all that traffic going back and forth from her place to mine, or visa versa."

"So what's going to happen after the holidays?" Michael asked, curious.

Esteban exhaled. "Who knows, man? I like her, we like each other, but I just don't know if she's the right fit."

Michael laughed. "The right fit? What are you, shopping for shoes? If you like her, just go for it."

Esteban's smile faded and he looked into his drink. "Well, I didn't tell you this before, and you would have found out if she had come, but she's a little younger than I am."

Michael nodded, then laughed. "Okay, when you say it like that, I have a feeling she's more than just a little younger. How young?"

"She's twenty-seven."

"Twenty-seven? Okay, well, that's not too bad. She could be twenty-one. So why are you tripping? That sounds to me like a beautiful thing."

163

Esteban smiled and nodded at someone across the room, then looked back at Michael. "I don't know. I guess I never thought I'd be the kind of guy who'd date someone like her."

"You mean, because she's young?"

"Yeah."

"Let me ask you something. Why her? Why do you like her? Aside from her age, I mean."

"Actually, it's her age I don't like. Everything else about her is great."

"So, her age gets in the way somehow?"

Esteban bit his lip. "No, it's not even that. It's mostly in my head. She's great. Everything about her is great."

"Oh man, then you *are* tripping. Who the hell cares how old she is? If it works, it works. That's all there is to it. How does she feel about you?"

Esteban shrugged, then smiled, looking directly at Michael. "She likes me."

Michael patted him on the shoulder. "You're all right, you know that?" He laughed boisterously. "You're the only man I know who'd be worried about a problem like that."

"Am I?"

"You think I'd have a problem dating a twenty-seven-year-old? Hell no."

Esteban laughed. "Well, Sasha might have a problem with that," he said, referring to Michael's long-time girlfriend.

"Sure. But come on, man, what are you worried about? It sounds like everything is peachy keen on your end."

"I don't know. I couldn't tell you. Maybe I just don't want to be a stereotypical Hollywood guy."

"Oh come on, that's bullshit. If you like her, fuck that stereotype crap. Who the fuck cares? Live your life according to your own rules. For love? Why not?"

Esteban sighed. "So, you'd do it?"

Michael chuckled to himself. "I'd do it in a heartbeat."

Esteban looked at his friend and exhaled. "You know, when we first decided to give this a shot, she asked me if I was worried about what anyone else might think, and my first reaction was 'no, of course not,' but now it's as clear as day. I am worried. And you're right. It's my fucking life. And I do like her. I should go for it, shouldn't I?"

"Well, sure. If that's what you want. But she's moved in with you. I mean, that's going for it as far as I'm concerned."

"Yeah, but we're just feeling each other out. She knows that. It's just temporary."

Michael nodded. "How'd you feel if she moved out tomorrow?"

"I'd fucking miss her, man."

"There it is. Move on that," he said, taking a sip of his drink. "Let her know, pour out your heart, all that shit. You're the fucking writer, you know what I'm talking about."

Esteban laughed. "Real life is harder."

"Real life is more important. What the fuck you waiting for?"

"Okay, I hear you."

"I wanna meet this girl. You better bring her by in the new year."

"All right. I'll work on it."

"You better not disappoint. I'm counting on you," Michael said and laughed.

"Oh, come on, when have I ever disappointed you?"

"Well, don't start," he said, putting a hand on Esteban's arm. "Give me a minute here," Michael said, looking at Sasha from across the room. "The lady needs me."

"All right."

"You better not leave without saying goodbye. I'm not through with you."

Esteban held up both hands in the air. "Don't worry. Message received loud and clear."

"You're all right." Michael said.

Esteban smiled and looked down into his drink. Michael was right. What did Esteban have to be so worried about? Why was her age such a problem? It shouldn't be, and it didn't seem to get in the way in the slightest. But then a light bulb went on over his head. It was never really about her age, it was about his. He failed to mention that to Michael. It wasn't so much about her being so young, it was about Esteban being older. Maybe he really did need that follow-up conversation with Michael after all. He was curious what Michael had to say about the matter. Esteban finished his drink, mad at himself for putting the blame on Marialena's age rather than his own.

He stepped onto the balcony, where a few other guests had lingered. Michael didn't have a view like Esteban's, but he had a nice balcony, with similar patio furniture and a fire-pit where a circle of people had gathered. A woman he had met earlier approached him.

"It's not too cold tonight," she said, letting the shawl she was wearing fall from her shoulders. Kristina was a nice looking woman, thin and as tall as Esteban. She wore a long black skirt and a blouse that fell off her shoulders, exposing a nice tan. Esteban thought she might be of Greek descent.

Esteban smiled politely. "No, it's nice out for December."

"The fire-pit helps," she said, drinking a glass of wine. "So, how do you know Michael?" the woman asked. She was in her forties and she had seen Esteban arrive alone. She had asked Sasha about him and her interest was piqued when Sasha told her he was a movie director. But she hadn't seen the movies mentioned. She asked if he was seeing anyone, and Sasha had told her that he was out of a long-term relationship. And that's when Sasha had introduced Esteban to Kristina. They chatted for a minute or two but went their separate ways when Michael had approached.

"Oh, we're old friends. I met him at a party when I first moved out to Los Angeles."

"Where from?"

"Then? From Temecula, but I am originally from New York," he said, swirling the alcohol around in his glass.

"I'm from Ohio myself."

"What brought you to Los Angeles?" he asked.

"I have family here. Well, my ex-husband did. We moved about fifteen years ago, then I made a life here. You know how that goes."

"Sure. Ever plan on going back to Ohio?"

"I don't think so. My kids are settled here, so this is home now."

Esteban swirled his drink around a little more, feeling like this Kristina woman might be interested in him. He smiled, trying to figure out a way to be polite about the situation. But Kristina had made it easy when she asked her next question.

"I couldn't help notice that you arrived alone."

"Oh, yeah. My girlfriend is at home trying to fight a migraine. I actually feel a little guilty being here tonight, so I might leave soon."

Kristina nodded, understanding. So, he *did* have a girlfriend.

"Well, it was nice to meet you, Esteban."

"Yeah, you too." He held his drink in the air before walking back inside. "Merry Christmas," he said.

"Merry Christmas."

Esteban made his rounds with the few people that he knew. He refilled his glass with a bit more whiskey and found Michael putting more ice in the ice bucket.

"Can I ask you something when you're done with that? I'll probably be leaving here in a minute, but I want your advice about something."

"Yeah, why don't I walk you out?"

"Sure. Let me say goodbye to a few folks. I'll come back in a sec."

"Sounds good."

"Thanks for the invite, man. It's a great party," Esteban said. It took him about fifteen minutes to make his rounds. He gave Sasha a big hug and he and Michael stepped into the elevator.

"So, what's up?"

"You know, Marialena…it's not about her age. It's about mine. I'm getting older, man. I don't really have that much in the way of an exciting life to offer someone who is so young and vibrant. I'm just a boring old writer." They stepped out of the elevator.

"You don't think you're good enough for her?"

"Long term, I don't know if I'll be enough for her."

Michael shrugged. "Does that really have to do with age? Maybe it's all in your head because of the past year you've had."

They stopped at Esteban's car. "Everything Laura said to me, all of my shortcomings, what if they effect Marialena the same way?"

"The complaints Laura had might not be the same for your new lady. You're overthinking this, in my opinion. It should be simple, and I think Laura just fucked you up a little bit. If you like her and she likes you, that's all you need to know for now. The relationship will settle and you can ask yourself if you want more. Relax, enjoy her. Let her enjoy you."

Esteban nodded. "Okay, thanks. I think I *am* overthinking it."

"You know, if it doesn't work out, I think Sasha's friend Kristina likes you," Michael said with a big smile.

"Yeah, I caught on to that."

"Well, we can blame Sasha for that one. She didn't know you were seeing someone."

"Tell her I appreciate it. I didn't know I still had it, to be honest with you."

"You're a good-looking and successful director. You know women flock to those kinds of things."

169

"Successful? You know, I thought I was done for this past year? I thought it was the end of me."

"Shoot, you just came out of a dry spell. You were probably in a rut and this is probably a new beginning."

Esteban shrugged. "Yeah, I know you're right now. Then I wasn't so sure," he said, getting his keys out of his pocket. He embraced Michael in a quick hug. "Thanks for tonight."

"Merry Christmas. Get out of that head of yours every once in a while. It will do you good."

"Yeah, I will. Have a good night."

"Drive safely," Michael said and walked away.

When Esteban got home, he threw his jacket on the sofa and un-buttoned his shirt. He walked into the bedroom and saw that Marialena was sitting up in bed, reading a book.

"Hey," he said, expecting her to be asleep. It was past one a.m., and she had worked early that morning. "How are you feeling?"

She set down her book. "I'm feeling a little better, but I couldn't sleep," she said, watching him as he got undressed.

Esteban sat on the bed in his shorts and pulled her toward him.

"Is everything okay?" he asked. "Are you feeling stressed at work?"

Marialena curled up into his arms. "I think it's probably the time of year. I used to have terrible insomnia, but it's gone away for the most part. Maybe it's just a one-time kind of thing. I think I'll be okay, now that you're home. How was the party?"

170

"Oh, it was good. It was kind of nice to see some old friends. You would have loved my friend Michael. It was at his place. It's too bad you missed out, but I'm glad I'm home now."

"I'm glad you went."

Esteban held her for a moment longer, loving how she felt next to him. He thought about what Michael had said, and he tried getting out of his own head.

"Hey, let me brush my teeth and I'll come right back, okay?"

Marialena double-checked her alarm to make sure it was set for early the next morning, when Esteban would meet Patrick Denny on location. Esteban came back in a few minutes later, turned out the lights, and climbed into bed. He pulled her in close.

"Come here," he said softly. She threw an arm around him and curled up next to him, his body warm.

After a few minutes, Esteban broke the silence. "Hey, I'm really happy you're here for the holidays. I love coming home to you." He turned to look at her, but she didn't respond. She was already out.

The next morning, they both woke at the sound of Marialena's alarm. He had decided last night that he didn't want to stay up and work all night long and was pretty beat when he came home.

"How do you feel this morning?" he asked.

"Good," she replied. "How about you? Get enough sleep?"

"Eh, it's nothing coffee can't fix," he said.

"I'll get up and make some while you shower."

"Thanks. You sure you don't want to come?"

171

"I'm sure. But you can tell me all about it when you get back. I wonder how long it will take."

"I think I'm just going to stay for the one scene. I don't know if he'll ask me to hang there for the whole day. He might," he said, getting up and checking the weather outside. It was overcast, which would be good for filming. Of course, the weather in the valley was sometimes different even though it was just a few miles away.

Marialena got out of bed, feeling more tired than usual, but her head wasn't throbbing anymore. Esteban put a hand on her face. "Hey, are you going to be okay? I was a little worried about you last night. You fell right asleep as soon as I got into bed. Is everything okay?"

Marialena looked into his eyes as he spoke, then turned away when she replied. "Yeah, I think so. It's just my past, I think. I'll be okay."

He took her hand. "Hey, it's okay," he said and pulled her close to him. "If you ever want to talk, I'm right here."

She let herself be held for a moment. "I know, I'm just afraid that if I talk about it, the whole insomnia thing might start up again. Let me just try to figure this out for now."

"Okay. Just know that you can talk to me whenever you want. It might help."

"Yeah, okay. I know. I just want to get past the holidays. It will be easier then, okay?"

He nodded. "I understand." He kissed her on the cheek. "I'm going to jump in the shower."

Marialena gave him a tight-lipped smile and resumed making the bed.

A half hour later, Esteban had a quick breakfast with Marialena and headed toward the valley.

After he parked and gave his name to the guard, he walked in and looked for the action. It was easy to find. He saw Patrick Denny talking to someone and made a beeline toward him.

"Hey, thanks for making it," Patrick Denny said and stuck out his hand.

"No problem," Esteban said, taking off his sunglasses and squinting in the bright light. It was still overcast, but it was bright outside.

"Please, help yourself to some coffee and something to eat."

"I'm good, thanks." He had finished the coffee that Marialena had made for him on his way there. He was starting to feel excited now that he was on the set.

"All right, so we have our weather. We went took your recommendation about making it seem colder than it is."

Esteban nodded and smiled, seeing the extras in layers of clothes and scarves.

"Yeah, looks good. That's the bridge, I'm assuming? Mind if I run up ahead?"

"No, be my guest."

Esteban wandered into the building and saw the stairs right away. He made his way up to the second level and took a look around. He tried to take in all the angles, walking the bridge back and forth, and exploring with his director's eyes. There wasn't much to work with. It would be a raw scene, which was good. He recognized the actors from the pictures he had seen at Patrick's office— actors that his girlfriend had cast. She had a good eye.

They looked right for the part. The male lead was tall and baby-faced. He had just the right rolled-out-of-bed look. The female lead was also young, but petite and sweet. The ends of her hair were a dark pink, and he wondered if that was the actor or if it was the costume designer's idea. It was good, either way.

Patrick came up from the other side, where most of the equipment was set.

"What do you think?"

"I like it. It feels right for the scene."

A little while later, they got started. It was the most important scene in the film. The two characters were just getting out of their theater class where they had to deliver monologues. Julian went last and moved everyone by his performance. Class ended and Julian ducked out, but Rosa caught his arm. They went to the bridge, and they sat against the wall to talk.

The shot that morning started with them on the bridge. Patrick filmed a few takes. Both directors exchanged more ideas and opinions after each take. The actor who played Julian ended up crying in the second take, when the Rosa character understood that he was trying to say that he was gay. She teared up with him, and you could tell that the two actors shared something. They had excellent on-screen chemistry. At the end of the take, she took his hand and kissed it. He looked away from the camera, and when he turned back, he was still crying. He wiped his face quickly, not wanting anyone to see. At that moment, a couple of girls walked by and the scene ended with Rosa standing up to ask Julian to call her that evening.

"Don't text. Actually call."

"What time?"

"Whenever you want," she said. "I have to go, but it's going to be okay. We'll figure it out."

"Yeah," he said.

"And cut," Patrick said. "That last one was great." Then he turned to Esteban. "When the two of them were in frame together, it was really something else. Thanks for that recommendation."

"Let's see the playback," Esteban suggested.

The playback was set up and a few people gathered around to watch. "Look at that color on his cheeks. It really stands out and makes him look that much more vulnerable," Patrick whispered.

Patrick felt goosebumps when the actors cried together. He turned to Esteban and smiled. "That's it. That's our scene."

"It works."

"The close-ups are beautiful."

"Yeah, they really are."

"Thank you for coming and being a part of this, Esteban."

"Did you want me to stick around for more?"

"No, I don't think so. Unless you want to. You're welcome to stay."

"Yeah, I might hang out for a bit longer. I'll come find you before I leave." Esteban hung out for a couple more scenes. He wanted to see how Patrick shot and if there was anything he could take back to his next film. He watched them do three different scenes in the classroom and had to wait for wardrobe each time. When he glanced at his watch, it was already almost three. Patrick looked busy and he didn't want to interrupt, so he waited

175

for him to make eye contact. Esteban gave him a head nod. Patrick held up a finger and asked Esteban to wait just a second.

Patrick excused himself from the brief conversation and walked over to Esteban.

"Have you picked up on anything else? I'm all ears."

"Yeah, I'm kind of mulling it all over for now. It's funny, all of us directors do the exact same thing, but we each have our unique styles."

"Yeah, we do, don't we?"

"There was one small thing, something that I've never really tried before. Scenes where the kids are on stage, during monologues, try to get them to look in the camera. Make the audience feel like they're students in that classroom. You know, when they're looking from face to face?"

"You think the camera should be one of those faces?"

"I think you should try it...and get more close-ups. The audience should pick up on how nervous these kids are, and no one should be better than Julian. Tell them to tone it down a bit."

"Okay, wow, you're right."

Esteban nodded. "I have to get going, but you got this man. It's looking great so far."

"I am in your debt. I mean that."

Esteban waved him off and Patrick patted his arm.

Esteban walked back to catering and grabbed a bag of chips. The afternoon was bright and clear, and the marine layer had burned off. When Esteban walked in, he found Marialena on the phone chatting to Roxanne, he guessed. She held up one finger, letting him know that she'd get off the phone in a minute. Esteban nodded and walked into the kitchen to make some tea. She was smiling and talking into the phone when she realized Esteban was watching her. They made eye contact and both smiled.

He gave her some privacy and prepped the tea. He remembered that she liked a little bit of sugar with hers and handed it to her when it was ready.

She smiled and he took his tea with him to the computer. A few minutes later, Marialena hung up the phone.

"Hey, thanks for the tea. It's delicious. What kind is this? It tastes like heaven."

"Vanilla caramel."

"It's like Christmas in a cup. I like it. So how was it?" she asked, taking her tea with her to the sofa.

He smiled. "It was good. Different, but it was good. I'm glad I went. He has a different style from me, that's for sure."

"How so?"

"Well, I know it's early in the shooting schedule, but he seems very distant from his cast. He doesn't seem to get down to their level. He's great at directing them, but it's not warm direction, which is strange because he's a warm man."

"He can be warm, sure, but he's also extraordinarily intimidating."

"*Intimidating*. Yes, that's exactly it. And I picked up on that. The actors are great, but there's something missing. When I direct, I don't mind getting up close and personal with my cast, from day one. And yeah, maybe

177

he'll warm up to them, or they to him. But that warmth is missing."

Marialena nodded. "Well, each director has a different style. His style might work for him."

"Sure. And he's been successful. It's just weird seeing the different style. I couldn't work that way. But aside from that, it was good. I gave him some small ideas, and a few ways he could shoot differently. He was receptive. I imagined he would get defensive or justify why he was shooting it a certain way. I might have gotten defensive if someone suggested something like that to me, but he was good about listening and took my advice without a problem."

"And how were the actors?"

"Oh, they were great. Marialena, you did a great job of finding those two. I love the freckles on the Rosa character. They're absolutely right for the part, no doubt about that."

Marialena gave him a big smile. "I can't wait to see those two on the big screen."

"I know. So, are you feeling better?"

"Oh yes. I'm a little tired, but my headache is gone."

"Did you get some more sleep after I left this morning?"

"I did, but the headache from last night wore me out a little bit. The day after always makes me feel a little off."

"Well, take it easy today. Why don't we get delivery later, and maybe watch a movie and just cozy up on the couch?"

Marialena nodded. "Yeah, sounds good."

"All right, I have a lot of positive energy flowing from that shoot. Mind if I get some ideas down for a few hours?"

"No, of course not."

He got up from his chair and leaned over to kiss her on the mouth. He moaned softly. "You taste delicious," he said.

She smiled. "So do you."

He pulled away and sat down while Marialena grabbed her laptop and streamed her favorite show with headphones on the couch, feeling relaxed.

Chapter Eleven

Marialena got home from work and found Esteban on the terrace drinking a beer.

"That beer sounds like a good idea. I think I am going to join you."

She grabbed a beer from the fridge and came back outside.

"I love to come out during this time of day. You missed the most beautiful sunset."

"I saw it on my way home, actually."

Esteban sat back on the sofa he had outside. "How was work?"

"It was a good day...long, but good." She was back at the temp agency and her life felt more or less normal. "But I got a call from Patrick Denny earlier. He wants to meet with me for dinner. He said he had something he wanted to share with me."

"Oh yeah? What do you think it could be?"

"I have no idea. But if you think it's weird, then I won't go."

Esteban took a drink from his beer. "No, I don't think it's weird. Should I?"

"No, I don't think so. I don't know, actually. You and I haven't been together long enough for me to know if something like that would bother you," she admitted.

Esteban shrugged. "I've never really been the jealous type. I've only been joking those other times. But I guess I could be if I had reason to be."

"You don't have anything to worry about on my end," she said, placing a loving hand on his leg. "But I have to admit, I'm curious to find out what he wants."

"Go if you want to go. I won't hold you back."

Marialena nodded. "Okay, I'll call him back later."

After she and Esteban had dinner, he went back to work and she stepped into the guest room to call Patrick. They made dinner plans for Thursday. The restaurant he chose was one that Marialena had never heard of before, but she promised she would be there.

Later that week, she arrived at the restaurant after stopping at Esteban's to change. Esteban had watched her getting ready, applying makeup more appropriate for an evening out than she was used to wearing.

"Okay, so now I am starting to worry a little bit," Esteban said as she kissed him to leave. "You look amazing tonight." He looked at her as if seeing her for the first time.

"Don't worry. My heart is yours," she said before she left, seeing the intensity in his eyes. Those had been the most intimate words the two had exchanged at this point, but both of them had been thinking about expressing more.

Marlialena got to the restaurant and saw Patrick already sitting at the table. She was about ten minutes late and hadn't realized it would take three times as long from where she was staying with Esteban. Living on this side of the city was still taking some getting used to.

"Sorry I'm late. My god, traffic was terrible."

"Really? I got here from the valley just fine." He stood up to kiss her on the cheek. He got a good look at her before they sat down. "Marialena, you look lovely."

181

"Thank you," she smiled. She was wearing a dark blue dress, accentuating her figure. It was new, and truthfully she had bought it in anticipation of going to the holiday party. Thankfully, he was dressed to match and she didn't feel too out of place. One look at him made her think of Esteban, and how she wished he would dress like that every once in a while. Marialena left the house feeling guilty that she didn't get dressed up for him, but they never went anywhere that called for it. She sat down, but didn't look at the menu right away. Instead, she tried to put those thoughts away. She knew it wasn't fair to Esteban. He was who he was, and she liked him for it. No, she loved him for who he was. She knew that much. It made her feel more confident to utter the next sentence.

"I wasn't coming from Los Feliz, actually. I was staying at Esteban's, but I had miscalculated the traffic."

"Oh really? So you two are—" He let question hang in midair.

Marialena shrugged happily, a little smile giving it away.

Patrick laughed. "Well, I had hoped the two of you would hit it off."

She gave him a look of mock-shock. "Patrick, you don't mean that you planned this. Wait, did you put him up to giving me a ride home that night?"

Patrick laughed and ordered a bottle of wine for the two of them. When the waiter left, he put two hands in the air, not wanting to take credit for it.

"Trust me, that was all Esteban. But I must admit, when he told me he was no longer with his girlfriend, the idea of the two of you did cross my mind. I just thought

182

I'd have to try a little harder to set you up. Turns out, I didn't have to try at all."

The wine arrived and the waiter poured two glasses.

"Cheers, to new love. I really do hope the two of you are happy." They raised their glasses and each took a sip.

"Thank you for introducing us. I mean, you did bring us together, after all. And it's been pretty great. He has been wonderful."

"So, you're happy?"

Marialena searched the restaurant, not wanting to sound as excited as she felt. "Yes. It's still new, but yeah, he's great."

"Okay. Well, I don't mind taking some of the credit," he said.

Marialena looked down at the menu, then took in her surroundings. The place was dark, private, and very quiet.

"Patrick, this place is incredible. It's like a hidden gem. How'd you find out about it?"

"It's one of my favorites. I like it because it's quiet."

"This is a place people go for complete privacy, isn't it?"

"Yeah, it's mysterious. I like that about it. It's almost as if no one else is here except for us."

"So why are we here?" she asked, forgetting about the menu.

Patrick laughed. "My goodness. Look at you. Ready to attack. Relax, enjoy the wine. Aren't you going to ask me about the film?"

Marialena sat back and smiled. He was right. She was tense, not to mention embarrassed that she hadn't asked him about the film.

183

"Of course. You're right. I'm sorry. I'm a little on edge."

"Why's that?"

"Oh, I guess just being here with another man...a man with a secret. I'm not good at this, remember?"

Patrick laughed again. "Maybe that's what I love about you. You must be a terrible poker player."

She scoffed. "What makes you say that?"

"You wear your heart on your sleeve."

"That's a bad thing?"

"Just for poker. Otherwise, it's charming. And rare, I might add."

Marialena smiled shyly. "How *is* the film?" she asked, changing the subject.

"It's moving along wonderfully. Everything is running smoothly, and it was nice to have Esteban on set when he came out a few weeks ago."

"I'm glad. I must say, having such a big part in casting and then just walking away wasn't easy. I feel like I've abandoned a child."

"You're welcome to drop by as often as you'd like."

Marialena shrugged. "I'd just get in the way."

"I think the opposite is true. But more on that later. What looks good to you tonight?"

Marialena studied the menu. "It all looks great. But this vegetarian option is calling my name."

"You're not a vegetarian, are you?"

"No, but it looks delicious."

Patrick looked at her and could also name a few things that looked delicious...about her, but he didn't say anything.

184

"I am going to balance this situation by ordering the steak. We need some meat at this table." Marialena laughed.

Patrick poured more wine for the both of them, filling their glasses. He decided to cut to the chase.

"Marialena, I wanted you to come out here tonight because I'd like to ask you to come work for me."

She looked at him, surprised. "What do you mean?"

"I need a personal assistant. I liked having you on the set. I like your eye, your vision, and your professionalism."

"Personal assistant? What about Rebecca?" she asked, referring to his secretary.

"Rebecca works for the studio."

"Patrick, I'm flattered."

"You said yourself, you felt as if you were leaving a child behind," he added.

She looked into his eyes. "Why are you so kind to me?"

Patrick held his glass for a second before putting it to his lips. "Darling, it's not about being kind. I've gotten to this point in my life by surrounding myself with people who are successful and who are being good at what they do. And there's something about you, I see things differently when you're around."

Marialena nodded, thinking.

"You don't need to give me an answer right away. Just think about it. I'd like it if you jumped back on board for the rest of the shoot, but take your time to think about it."

"Sure. I'll give it some thought. I guess I just have a few questions. Is this temporary, just for the duration of the filming?"

"No, it would be permanent."

"You're not always working on a film."

"But I *am* always working."

"Health benefits?"

"You won't have to worry about that. We'll make sure we get the best plan for you. And obviously, you'd be paid generously for your work."

"What does the job entail?"

"Well, for now, you'd be on set, as my right hand. Rebecca will be there too, so you can learn from her. I'll also need you for some after-hours functions. Business dinners, business parties."

"Really?"

"Yes. I've been thinking about it and I need someone to help keep me focused at these things. So often, I've gotten distracted by some woman there and missed my opportunity at mingling with the right people. I haven't been here very long, and I want to start doing this right. It's all been getting to my head."

"Okay, that makes sense."

"I need to do this for myself. But Marialena, the list of people I wanted for this starts and ends with you."

"What if I say no?"

"Then I'll have to hire a stranger." He smiled. "You're playing hard to get."

Marialena scoffed as the food arrived. "I'm not, I was just curious. Honestly, I don't have an answer right now. I need to think about it."

"Of course."

186

"Does this mean you're moving to Los Angeles?"

"I thought I had already moved here," he said, confused.

"Your place in New York, I mean."

"Oh well, I go back there once a while. I imagine I'll go back for a week when the shooting is done. I miss the air there."

"No one says that about New York."

They both laughed. She asked him what it meant for her when he went to New York.

"You're welcome to come with me. In fact, there are a few occasions when I'd like to have you. We can figure out arrangements later, but I don't think I'll need you the entire week when I go, so for you it could be a weekend trip."

Marialena nodded and took a bite of her vegetarian pasta.

"Delicious," she said.

"The food here is outstanding."

"I need to remember this place."

"Oh, I don't know. You're meant for a well-lit place, where everyone can see you."

"Then why did you bring me here?" she teased.

"I didn't want you to see the look on my face in case you turned me down." She was unsure if he was serious or not. "No, I like it here, honestly. The food, the atmosphere. I am serious about my offer and I didn't want any interruptions or photographers." He thought back to the first time he had been there. "I had a date here once. Met her for drinks. She was married I think, which is why she decided we meet here."

187

Marialena looked around. It was the perfect place to come if someone were having an affair. She noticed that she hadn't seen anyone come in or out. The door was in the back, and the carpet was rich and thick. Every table had its own speaker, playing classical music. It really did seem like they were the only ones here. "This restaurant has a whole new meaning for me now."

"Yeah, be careful if someone mentions this place to you."

Marialena smiled warmly. The rest of the night, the conversation returned to the film. She couldn't wait to get back home to Esteban. She was curious how she felt about Patrick's job offer. She had always liked that she had a stable job, steady income. She was worried that working with Patrick might mean she wouldn't have the same kind of job security.

Dinner was coming to an end. He was on his third glass of wine, and she had less than two, so she knew she'd be able to make it home okay. Patrick ordered dessert and he offered her some, but she was stuffed. The food had been marvelous and she had finished most of it.

"So, think it over. Give me a call before Christmas, or really any time you want."

Marialena nodded.

"Are you okay to drive home?" he asked her.

"Yeah, I'm going back to Esteban's. Are you?"

"I'm fine. I'll get a driver. So, is it serious between you and Gutierrez?"

"It's too soon to say, honestly. But for the record, I'm crazy about him."

Patrick nodded and smiled warmly. She certainly had that glow when she talked about him. She offered him a lift home, but he refused. "No, I'll be fine. Thank you, though."

They said goodbye and he watched her leave. He stayed to pick up the check and she drove home to find Esteban washing dishes. He must have just had dinner. She kissed him on the cheek and he offered her a glass of wine, which she turned down.

He set the dishes down and forgot about cleaning for a second. He had had dinner late since he'd been busy calling the bank, and then he called his brother and made plans to see him in Temecula the following evening.

"How was dinner?" he asked, hand-drying the last of the dishes. Marialena took off her shoes and he sat with her on the sofa.

"So, he wants me to come work for him, as his personal assistant."

"Wow, so what did you say?"

"Well, I didn't. I mean, I thanked him for the offer, but I needed time to think about it. Plus, I kind of wanted to talk about it with you."

Esteban nodded. "How do you feel?"

Marialena shrugged. "It sounds scary."

"Scary? How do you mean?"

She shrugged again. "I can think of a million reasons. His success has been short-lived. Last year, he won the Oscar. What if he has a dry spell? What if no one remembers him two years from now, or three? I could be out of a job. What if he winds up getting a girlfriend? What if she hates me and has me fired? What if he does

189

something stupid that taints his name or reputation somehow. I could be affected by that."

"Okay, yes, those could all happen. The last one seems unlikely. If you're out there as his personal assistant, people would be able to differentiate between you and the man you work for."

"You think so?"

"You watch too many movies. You have an overactive imagination."

"It's my job I'm putting on the line, though."

"Wouldn't you be able to get back into what you do?"

"Maybe."

"All those companies you find people for? I mean, you would be the last person I'd imagine who would need help looking for a job. If you're as good as I think you are, wouldn't someone from those companies hire you in a heartbeat?"

She exhaled loudly. "Yeah, I mean, I guess I could reach out to them if I had to. I don't know, I'm just worried that—" she looked at him, afraid to admit it. "What if he just wants to hire me because he wanted to sleep with me that night?"

Esteban nodded and leaned back onto the couch. "I don't know, I think anywhere you go you're going to run into that. I think someone somewhere will always feel that way about you. It shouldn't hold you back from something you might want to pursue. You seem capable of putting your foot down."

Marialena closed her eyes and tilted her head back. "I just don't know what to do. The money would be nice, but I love my job security."

"Make him sign an agreement that if he lets you go, you'll get a severance package of some kind."

"That's a good idea. Except I don't have a lawyer."

"I bet he does."

"How do you feel about it, though?" she asked him.

Esteban shrugged. "I don't know. I can't honestly say. This is your decision."

"It sounds to me like I would be a sort of office wife. What is that term? Work wife? I'd have to go out with him to functions and what not. He actually admitted that he couldn't keep his dick in his pants long enough to separate business from pleasure. And I'd serve as a sort of cock-blocker or something."

She blushed at her terminology. Esteban smiled. "Wow," he said, running a hand through his hair. "Is that what Oscar status gets you?"

Marialena smiled. "If it does, maybe I should ask you not to make any more movies."

Esteban laughed. "Or just aim low." She laughed along with him.

"You don't have to worry about that. I think it's just about who you are, anyway."

"No, I know."

"Would it help you if I took this job? I mean, is there any way it would benefit your career?"

Esteban sat up, surprised. "Wait, do you think my career needs help?"

"No, that's not what I meant. I just know how hard it is to get a movie made sometimes. I don't know, I just wondered if it would be easier for you, like, if I knew the same kind of people he knew?"

191

"No. Honestly, Lena, don't let your decision be influenced by what it might mean for me or us. I can't help you decide this. This is for you. It's all about what you want, what you need."

"So, you would be okay with me out there? Living the big life, going to Hollywood parties, being on someone else's set. Working on someone else's film?"

Esteban shrugged. "Of course I'd be fine with it. You have to make this decision for yourself. This is kind of a life changer for you. I won't stand in the way and I won't tell you what you should decide."

"I wouldn't want it to impact our relationship. That much I know."

"Is that what you're worried about?"

"I mean, you made a good point about me being able to get back on my own two feet if it doesn't work out for him and me. But then, what if it works out and I end up working for him and it's a successful business venture. I'd have to go to New York every once in a while. I'd have to go out to parties with him. I'd hate for you to be upset by that."

"You're sweet for thinking of me," he said, placing a hand on her lap, "but don't worry about how I'd feel. I'm a grown man and I can fend for myself. Are you asking me if I trust you? Is that what this is all about? Because I'm going to have to ask you, do you trust yourself?"

She was smart enough to know that it was still early and that things always looked good in the beginning, but she was confident that she wouldn't be tempted by Hollywood. She had never been one to be won over by luxury or how rich someone might be. She had dated that type enough to know that it wasn't always what it seemed, not to mention she hadn't fallen for Patrick and probably never would. She was confident that it wasn't what she was worried about. She was worried about upsetting Esteban.

She took his hand in hers. "I'm not worried about me. I'm sort of worried about Patrick a little, but I'm not worried about me. Honestly, and I mean this with all my heart, I wouldn't want anything to damage this, what we have going for us. I know it's still early, but I like us together. We are still feeling each other out and I understand that. We're still a little ways away from 'decision' day. But if there is a future for us, I'd like to protect it."

Esteban sat back. He knew he had made the right decision tonight by calling the family lawyer and his brother. It was time they knew about Marialena.

"Lena, don't worry about us. Or how I'd feel if you took this. If you want it, go for it. If you don't, then turn him down. It's that simple."

Marialena had a thoughtful look on her face. "Okay," she said.

"It's all you, kid. Which way are you leaning? Do you at least know that?"

"I have no idea. I had no idea that this kind of life was even possible for me. Not just me and you, but I mean all of it. A month and a half ago, I was alone in my condo. And now, my entire life could be different and all I have to do is say 'yes.' I have never wanted the Hollywood life, I have no idea what to do with it."

"Well, maybe the fact that you haven't bought into it is what makes you so valuable to Patrick. That isn't easy to find here."

193

"Maybe," she said wistfully.

"You should make a list."

"Pros and cons?"

"Sure."

She nodded. "Okay, I will." He got up and handed her a piece of paper from his printer. She set it down on the coffee table.

"I'm going to get out of these clothes."

When she returned, she was wearing her own pajamas. A set in light pink. Esteban watched her intently, wondering what she was thinking. He pictured her sitting there, for years to come, as someone more serious to him, someone like his wife. Could she really be a wife, one or two years from now? He knew the answer in that moment, watching her sitting crossed legged on his couch. She caught him watching her.

"What?" she asked curiously. "Why are you looking at me like that?"

"I was just wondering if you were cold. Do you want the heater on?" he replied, lying.

"No, I'm okay. Thanks."

She went back to work on her list while Esteban worked on his screenplay. She didn't want to admit it to him, but she had a feeling that if she took this job, it could help him. She thought of their future, if they had one, and how much better she'd be at being his girlfriend if she met people in the business who could help him. She would be working for Patrick, but surely people would find out that she belonged to Esteban, and there would be a buzz around Esteban, just because of her association with Patrick. But what if there wasn't a future for her with Esteban? What if he ended things? It was a possibility. Working for Patrick meant more money, and she wouldn't have to worry about finances. She'd be able to take that trip to Flagstaff and the Grand Canyon. She'd even get to go to New York. Still, as appealing as that looked to her, she hated the idea of her life without Esteban. It was so early in their relationship. How had she gotten so hung on up him, and why was this decision so hard to make? Her thoughts were interrupted briefly when Esteban announced his plans for the next day.

"Hey, so I forget to tell you. I made dinner plans with my brother tomorrow. I'm going to drive out to Temecula, but I'll be back before midnight, probably."

"That sounds like fun," she said, taking her eyes off her list.

"You'll be okay?"

"Yeah, I'll probably just go home then, to Los Feliz. I need to do some laundry."

Esteban nodded.

She noticed how he hadn't asked her to meet his brother, or to come back to his condo so that she'd be in his bed when he arrived. Tomorrow was Friday, so she could have gotten out of work in time to drive down with him. She shook the idea out of her head. Maybe he wanted to give her some space. What she didn't know, what she couldn't have known, is that Esteban needed the time to think. He was sure about his decision, but one night apart might give him the time necessary to reflect on his decision and to reach out to his family. He knew it wouldn't be an easy conversation with his brother. While he knew he wouldn't be swayed by his brother's opinion, he knew that it was a big decision and he needed time to sit with it. To weigh everything. He'd meet with his

195

brother and then go to the bank on Saturday morning. It was good that Marialena would be at her own place.

Chapter Twelve

Esteban drove to Temecula the next evening. He had told his brother he wanted to try some place different, with a little more privacy.

When he arrived, his brother was already there, chumming it up with a bartender he seemed to know. It seemed that Henry knew everyone in the business. When Henry saw his brother, he smiled and leaned in for a hug. Henry stood five inches taller than Esteban, despite the fact that he was ten years younger. He needed to shave, but otherwise looked great. He had a smile that drove women nuts, and he always dressed very well, since he had the body for it. Tall and slim. He had gotten all the good genes, Esteban had often said.

"Hey, so what's with the cloak and dagger?" Henry asked, referring to the fact that Esteban had asked him to pick a different restaurant from the one they owned together.

"Never mind that. It's good to see you, Henry," Esteban said, patting his brother's arm.

"Yeah, good to see you too, man. Two weeks after Thanksgiving, no less. To what do I owe the pleasure?" Henry asked. The two of them had spent Thanksgiving at Henry's, with a few of Henry's inner circle of friends and whatever woman he was seeing at the time.

They got a table and they both sat down and ordered beers and burgers.

"How's the restaurant?" Esteban asked, not wanting to dive in with the reason he was really there.

Henry shrugged. "Oh, you know, it's same as the last time I saw you. We're busy now, with the holidays and all that, but January will definitely slow down."

"I should come out more often. I haven't been back for a while."

"Yeah, it would be good of you to come. We've changed some things around, but it's still the same." Henry was concerned with Quarter 1 results for the new year. Esteban listened intently, but gave no advice. This was his brother's business. Sure, he owned half of it, but that was only on paper. He trusted his brother to make the right business decisions, and he hadn't been disappointed.

The food came and Henry changed the conversation. "Okay, enough about business. How's your love life? You're still seeing that woman?" The last time they were together, Esteban had told Henry about Marialena. He had been vague and left some details out, her age being one of them.

"Yeah, she actually moved in a few weeks ago," Esteban said and couldn't help smiling.

"No shit," he said, noticing how happy Esteban looked. "Wow. You do move quickly."

"Well, it's just temporary. Just for the holidays, really. But listen, there's no point in beating around the bush. I love her, man. I've been thinking about it, and I'm sure about this. I'm sure about her."

"Really? How long have you known her again?" Henry asked, amused.

"A month and a half. But when you know, you just know."

Henry shrugged. "Did you ever know with Laura?"

Esteban shook his head. "Not like this. This is different. I always felt this disconnect with Laura. Marialena is unique. *She's the one.*"

"*The one*? Really?"

"That's why I'm here. I thought you should know. I want to give her Mom's ring."

"You want to give her Mom's ring after only knowing her for a month and a half?"

Esteban nodded. "I'm not here to ask for your permission."

Henry shook his hand, leaned back into his chair, and laughed.

"Well, I'm in no hurry to get engaged. Take it. I thought you'd give it to Laura eventually, anyway. I never really thought of it as mine." Their mom had left the ring in her will, for whoever got engaged first. She had left Esteban in charge as executor, and he had it in a deposit box in a nearby bank.

"I never once thought about giving it to Laura. Isn't that sad? I really should have ended that a long time ago."

"God, and remember how mom hated her?" Henry asked, laughing.

"She didn't hate her," Esteban said, but he was smiling. He knew what Henry was talking about.

"She did and you know it. That one Thanksgiving we all flew over there, and Laura had made those mashed potatoes...poorly, I'm assuming. What was the story?"

199

"Mom came into the kitchen. Laura was out in the living room by this point, reading a magazine or something."

"That's right. She was on the phone with a friend from L.A., and the way she worded it, she said she was 'stuck in New York' for the holidays."

"Yeah, I remember that. I think it was a customer of hers."

"While we're all sitting there. God, what a bitch. Anyway, go on."

"So, Mom and I were in the kitchen, and you know how she was with mashed potatoes."

"Oh, it's her favorite."

"Right, so she had to get a taste. And she tried it—" Esteban stopped telling the story because he started laughing, "The face she made. You would have thought Laura used sour milk or something. Anyway, that's what I thought. But I guess Laura didn't add any butter or salt or anything like that."

"Just potatoes and milk?"

"I guess so. So, Mom got out the butter and added a heaping spoonful to the potatoes. And I'm talking about serving spoon size, none of this tablespoon type shit," Esteban said, holding up his own unused spoon.

"Yeah, Mom knew what she was doing," Henry said, smiling.

"Right. And she added salt, pepper, all that. Anyway, we were all sitting around the table—"

"Okay, yes. I remember this part. Laura tried the mashed potatoes and she's like, 'Whose are these? These aren't the ones I made.' She was all uppity and shit."

200

"Right. So, I took the blame. I was like, 'Oh yeah, I thought they could use some extra butter.'"

"Oh yeah, and then she was like 'Esteban, are you kidding me? They didn't need butter. Jesus, why does everything have to include butter on Thanksgiving? Some of us are trying to be healthy,'" he said, laughing.

"Yeah, that sounds about right. And Mom looked at me, stifling a giggle, and I lost my shit. Laura was so fucking mad that I was laughing."

"Oh man, Mom was the best," Henry said, reminiscing.

"Yeah, she was."

"And Laura, what the fuck? Who wants to be healthy on Thanksgiving?"

Esteban shrugged. "She did, apparently."

"I'm so glad you got out of that relationship."

"Yeah, me too. Marialena is totally different. It's amazing, actually."

"So, this is really happening?"

"Yeah, it is," Esteban said, beaming.

"Do you have the ring yet?" Henry asked. He wanted to see it again.

"No, I'm going to pick it up tomorrow morning."

"When are you planning on popping the big question?"

"I haven't figured that out yet. Soon, I think."

"Holy shit, my brother is going to get married."

"Well, she sort of has to say 'yes' first."

"Well, she's going to say 'yes,' right? Don't you propose when you know she's going to say 'yes?' Hey, do me a favor, will you? The ring means a lot to me. Don't give it away if you're not sure. I mean, I'm not planning

201

on asking anyone, but dude, it's Mom's ring. If it falls through, could you figure out a way to get it back or something?"

"Like a prenup?"

"Yeah, I don't know. Something like that."

Esteban sat back in his chair. He knew Henry was closer to his mom than he was, but he was surprised he had asked.

"Yeah, sure man. If it means that much to you, of course. I'll make arrangements to meet with my lawyer."

"Al Robinson?"

"Yeah, who else?"

"He got me out of that speeding ticket when I was in Los Angeles that one time. I'm in debt to that guy. Anyway, what's her name again?"

"Marialena Villanueva."

"Cool name. Not for long, I guess," Henry said with a smile. "I want to meet her. What are you doing for New Year's Eve?"

Esteban shrugged. "No plans yet. We can meet for dinner or something."

"Sounds good. Yeah, staying out there for a party or something could be cool."

"Look, there's something I haven't told you about her. If you're going to meet her, you should probably know ahead of time."

"What's that?"

"She's younger than I am."

Henry sat back and laughed. "That's it? I thought you were going to say that she was previously married with ten kids."

Esteban smiled. "No, no previous marriages. Just younger."

"Okay, I have to ask. How old is she?"

"She's uh...twenty-seven."

Henry looked at his brother to see if he was kidding or not, but it was clear that he was wasn't. "Well, no wonder you want to marry her," Henry said smiling.

"It's not like that. She's great."

"Yeah, I bet."

"No, really. She's amazing."

"Wait, how you did you meet a twenty-seven-year-old?"

"I told you, she worked with a director and he introduced us. We hit it off."

"Dude, a twenty-seven-year-old? You're going to propose to a twenty-seven-year-old with mom's ring?" Henry shook his head, smiling. "I don't know about this, man."

"Look, it's not like that. She's a nice girl. You'll see when you meet her."

"How do you know she's not using you or something?"

"She's not. I know you don't believe me, but you have to trust me on this one. I love her, man. We're crazy about each other. And Mom trusted me with her ring. This is what I want to do. I have thought about this."

"You're sure?"

"I am. A hundred percent," Esteban said without hesitation.

"Well, it must mean something that you didn't give it to Laura after all those years. But I really hope it's not

203

just because she's great in bed, Steven," Henry said, using his nickname for his brother.

"It's not. I promise you. I've never been in a relationship like this before. She's amazing. She fills my place up when she's there, and she makes me happy in a way I haven't been before. She's not into the whole Hollywood scene either. She's grounded. She's kind and loving, and just a real genuine person. She's great."

"Okay, I'm sorry. If it's as great as you say it is, I'm happy for you. I'm sorry if that's not coming through."

"No, it's okay."

They finished dinner and hugged before Esteban left. "I'm really sorry about questioning it, man. It's just sudden."

"It's okay. I would have too, honestly. But I'll get that prenup if it will put your mind at ease."

"It's just that it was Mom's ring, that's all."

"I know, it's okay. I should." Henry walked his brother to his car and Esteban drove home to his condo in Los Angeles.

When he was in bed later that night, he received a text from Marialena, who was back at her own place.

"Hope you get back safely."

Esteban texted her back. "Got back an hour ago. In bed now."

Thirty minutes later, he had fallen asleep but woke up when Marialena crawled into his bed.

"I hope you don't mind that I came back," she said. He turned around sleepily.

"Everything okay?" he asked.

"I had trouble sleeping," Marialena said, remembering her past and how she used to have restless

204

nights after her parents died. She had gone home that night, to her empty apartment, and felt out of place there. She hadn't bothered to decorate it for the holidays. Being in the condo felt lonely and she couldn't help but think of her parents. So she couldn't sleep and even though it was midnight, she longed for Esteban.

"It's totally fine that you're here," he said and put a loving arm around her. "I have to run some errands tomorrow, so I'll be up early. But yeah, it's fine."

Marialena wiped a tear from her eye, hoping Esteban hadn't noticed. He had felt a tear fall on his arm and heard her sniffle, but he didn't say anything. He wondered if it had to do with her past, remembering Roxanne's warning about how things were hard for her around this time of year. She drifted into sleep a few minutes later.

Chapter Thirteen

Marialena was on her way home from work when she called Patrick. She was feeling brave and had given her boss her notice earlier that day, before even telling Patrick that she had accepted. Still, she was confident she was making the right decision. When she put in her notice, her boss assumed that one of their clients had stolen her, but Marialena set her straight.

"No, I did some work when I was off last month for a movie, and the director wants to hire me full-time."

"Hollywood has taken another soul, huh?"

Her boss had always liked Marialena, in more ways than one, and trusted her when she wasn't there to run the office.

Marialena smiled. "Thanks for everything. I'll always value my time here." Her boss smiled and pulled her in for a warm hug.

"We'll miss you. Good luck out there."

When she had gotten in her car, she dialed Patrick and he answered on the fourth ring.

"Marialena, hello. I hope you have some good news for me," he said bluntly.

"Well, I wanted to talk about that. I have a few conditions," she said, glad he couldn't see her biting her lip.

"Of course. Shoot."

"I want a severance package in case you have to let me go for whatever reason."

206

"Why on Earth would I want to let you go?"

"Who knows? I just thought it would be a good idea."

"Okay, sure. I can get my guy to set up something."

"Sick time, vacation time?"

"Sure. Sick time, of course. As long as it's not abused. But I trust that you're not the type who would. Vacation time? Please, I'm not a workhorse, Marialena. I know that you have a personal life outside of this."

"Just making sure we're on the same page. You can't blame me for that," she said with authority.

"Listen to you! Makes me all the more glad to have you by my side."

"Okay, then yes. I'm in. But I want to see the severance package before I start."

"Not a problem. When *can* you start?"

"In the New Year. How is January 4th?" Marialena asked, knowing that she and Esteban had a big discussion coming up on the 2nd. She'd need time to recover if she'd be facing bad news, yet really hoped that wouldn't be the case.

"January 4th sounds great. Listen, I'm having a New Year's Eve party. Why don't you come? Bring Esteban. I can have all the legal documents you need by then."

"Okay, sure. That sounds nice."

"Marialena?" he asked.

"Yes?"

"Welcome aboard. You're doing me a huge favor. I won't let you down."

"Thanks for the opportunity, Patrick. I won't let you down, either," she said.

207

After she hung up the phone, she called Roxanne to tell her that it was official.

"You're going to be working in Hollywood. Oh my god, that's so awesome. You know, I wasn't sure you were going to say yes."

"I know. But I did. Time to move on. I've had that temp agency job long enough."

"Wow, I'm so proud of you, you know that?"

"Thanks. Hey, listen. He approved vacation time, so hopefully you and I can go somewhere next year. I'll be making extra money, so I'm thinking we can meet somewhere, maybe in the middle."

"That sounds fun. I don't know about meeting in the middle, though. I was thinking I could take you to see New York."

"We can do that, though Patrick has a place there and I might be going sooner than you think. Anyway, let's plan something for the summer or the fall next year."

"Okay, but I want to see you before then."

"Me too."

"We'll figure it out."

"Hey, I need to stop and get gas. But I just wanted to call and tell you the good news."

"I'm so happy for you."

"Thanks, love. And thanks for all of your support, and all that fuzzy stuff."

"No problem. Love you!"

"Love you back!" Marialena hung up the phone and decided to go shopping. She needed some extra clothes if she was going to be working with Patrick.

Chapter Fourteen

It was the week before Christmas, and unbeknownst to Esteban, Marialena had just quit her job. He was at his computer when he received a phone call from Laura.

"Hello?" he answered.

"Hey. How are you?"

"Good, good. Just writing. So, you got my text?"

"Yeah. I can come over to pick it up this afternoon. Around one okay?"

"Sure. I'll be here."

Laura had asked Esteban if she could have a package delivered to his place. It was an expensive piece of jewelry she was having fixed up for her mother, and she was never home, so she wouldn't be able to sign for it. Laura knew Esteban would be home far more than she was, and his condo was more secure than her house. Esteban said that he wouldn't mind, and the package had arrived that morning.

When Laura got there, they hugged briefly, not having seen each other since the day after the fundraiser.

"Coffee?"

"Love some. Thanks."

He handed her the small package. She immediately opened it and gasped at the ring. She set it on the table and watched him prepare coffee. She noticed a small Christmas tree, which surprised her. He never put up a tree. She wondered if he had a party.

"How's everything?" she asked, when he came back with the two coffees. "Have you lost weight? You look different. Leaner."

"Yeah, I've been going to the gym more frequently. But everything's great."

"Wow. It suits you. Hey, you mentioned you were writing earlier. That's great."

"I know. God, for a while there I thought I wouldn't be able to again. I thought I was done."

"I always knew that wasn't the case. It always comes back to you."

"How are you?" he asked, feeling a little uncomfortable.

"I'm okay. Always busy around this time of year. Parties, classes, shopping. What's with the Christmas tree?" she asked.

"Oh, yeah. Marialena did it. She's gonna be around for the holidays, so we needed a tree," he said, kind of dismissively. She noticed his use of 'we.'

"So, you guys are still seeing each other?" she asked with a raised eyebrow.

"Yeah," Esteban said, not wanting to elaborate. He didn't want to tell her that she had been living there for three weeks, that he was the happiest he had ever been, or that he was going to propose to her.

Laura looked around his condo. She started to notice little things. A pink water bottle in the kitchen. A woman's cardigan on the sofa. A pair of women's shoes by the closet.

"My god, Esteban, is she actually living here?"

Esteban sighed, knowing it was coming. Sooner or later, Laura would find out. Might as well tell her now.

"Jesus Christ," Laura said, sighing. "You're not helping her out financially, are you?" she asked before he could say anything.

"She's just staying with me through the holidays. She has a place of her own. This was my idea."

Laura nodded, taking it in. She sat back in her chair and held the coffee in her hands.

"Do you love her?" she finally asked.

Esteban shook his head. He got up and turned his back to her while he refilled his coffee cup. When Esteban sat back down, he looked worried.

"What is it?" she asked.

"I do love her," he said simply. Laura nodded. "I'm sorry. I know that this is probably something you didn't want to hear. But you asked."

"Esteban, listen to me. Just be careful. I mean, she moved in here, what, after a month? That's just crazy! This whole thing seems crazy. Are you sure this is what you want? Think about it."

"I have thought about it. It's not perfect. There's the obvious age difference, but there's something else. Something pulling me toward her. I can't explain it."

"Are you sure it's not just her tits?" Esteban looked at her. "Even I have to admit, they're pretty fucking spectacular."

Esteban took a deep breath. "Look, I should probably tell you. I wouldn't want you to hear it from someone somewhere down the road." He searched her eyes. "I'm going to propose."

Laura stood up, surprised at the news. "Are you kidding? Esteban, you've known her for two months!"

211

Esteban stood up but didn't raise his voice. "I am really sorry. I'm sorry I didn't feel this way about us. I am sorry for so many things," he said softly.

She sat back down at the edge of her seat.

"Esteban, when I cheated on you, when you found out, I felt like I broke your spirit. And it killed me. It still kills me. What if you're just still going through something? Maybe you're still vulnerable."

Esteban sat down with her, eyes searching the table. "I don't think so. It's weird. It's like I know she's right for me. And I just feel terrible about us, me and you. I just never felt this way."

"Is it your mom's ring?"

"Yeah," Esteban said, feeling sad for Laura.

"How does she feel about you?"

"The same way, I think."

"I think you should wait. Esteban, please wait. It's way, and I mean way, too soon."

"I know, but it feels right, Laura. I can't explain it." Esteban looked at her, and Laura hated to admit it, but he looked very much in love. He had a passion in his eyes that had been lacking in their relationship.

"Christ, I can't believe we're having this discussion."

"You have to believe that I am sorry for everything that we both did wrong."

Laura nodded. She believed him. She believed that he was sorry, and he was taking the blame for it as well. When Laura had seen Marialena for the first time, she knew she could never compete with her. She realized that Marialena had done something to lift Esteban's spirts, something she could never do. And she knew then that she had to come to terms with losing Esteban for

212

good. She was glad that he was happy, but she was worried about him too.

She placed her hand on his. "You have to remember, she's very young. Maybe she doesn't know love from sex. And maybe you're caught up in that."

Esteban nodded, but he knew better. Marialena was young, but she wasn't stupid. Still, he was nervous. He had gotten the ring a couple of days earlier and it was hidden behind a book on the bookcase. Since he had brought it home, he had a kind of nervous energy when he was around Marialena. He caught himself staring at her, imaging what her reaction would be. He wasn't sure when he was going to give it to her, but he wanted to do it soon. He was totally and completely in love with her. But he just didn't know how she'd react. Their one month of living together would be coming to an end soon, so it was either break up or move forward. He didn't think she wanted to break up with him, he knew that much. So it was time to move forward, and he wanted to give her the ring. Esteban felt sick just thinking about it. He had never felt this way about someone before. He was going to turn fifty soon; it was time to settle down. He just hoped Marialena felt the same way.

"Hey, thanks for listening. Again, I'm sorry. For everything." They were still holding hands. Both were caught off guard when they heard the front door being unlocked.

Esteban stood up quickly and wiped his hands on his pants. He exchanged a worried look with Laura.

Marialena saw the both of them.

"You're home early," Esteban said, feeling like he had gotten caught.

"Yeah, hi." She smiled curtly at Laura, but didn't ask for an explanation. "I was gonna surprise you with some news." Marialena looked at both of them, trying to gauge was what going on. "Hey, you guys look like you're in the middle of something. Sorry, Esteban, I should have called to let you know. I think I'm just going to walk to the café. Would either of you like anything?"

"There's coffee here," Esteban said, not wanting her to go.

"No. It's okay. A walk would be great, actually." Esteban went over to Marialena. He put a hand on her face and kissed her softly, lingering just long enough to make Laura uncomfortable. "I'll explain later," he whispered. She looked at him with worried eyes and turned to leave. Esteban took her hand, holding on to her fingers as she walked away.

"Hey, let me meet you there," he said.

Laura stood up. "No, this is silly. I was just leaving." She took the ring box from the table. "Thanks for this." Esteban gave her a menacing stare as he walked Laura to the door, realizing what it might look like to Marialena.

"I wanted to help you out, but do you know what this must look like to her?" he asked.

"It will keep things interesting," Laura whispered back, feeling rebellious.

Esteban scoffed, "Yeah."

"Hey, I'm sorry," she finally said. "I wasn't thinking. Esteban, good luck with...good luck with everything. And Merry Christmas." They hugged each other coldly and he came back in to find Marialena looking at the packaging that the ring came in. Laura had left it on the table. The 'ship to' name and address belonged to Esteban. Laura

214

had also left the slip, showing that the estimated value for the ring was over three thousand dollars.

"What the hell is this?" Marialena asked, wondering if they were having an affair. He sat down on the dining room table and explained the whole thing to her. She listened, but he wasn't sure if she believed him.

"If you still have feelings for her, we can talk about this."

Esteban laughed. "I can assure you, I do not have feelings for *that* woman. Not anymore," he said, a little more seriously. "I was doing her a favor."

"Why didn't you tell me that she had reached out to you?"

"Look, I thought you'd be at work. Honestly, I didn't really think about it."

Marialena was unsure whether he was telling the truth or not. He had been acting strangely all week. Esteban scooted his chair over, closer to hers, and took both of her hands in his own.

Marialena looked into his eyes. "Look, I don't blame you for being upset. I really don't. I know what it must look like. But trust me, there isn't anything going on. I promise."

"Would you tell me if there was, or would you wait until 'decision' day?" she asked.

"You want to know the truth? I have no idea. I haven't thought about it because there's nothing to think about. She asked me to sign for her package, and I did. That's it. That's all there is to it."

Marialena nodded, but looked down at her hands instead of at him.

Esteban laughed to himself and turned his head unable to face her. "Fuck!" he said loudly and stood up. "Marialena, trust me. There is nothing going on. I promise. You have to believe me. I do one fucking favor for her and it leads to all of this. Damn it!"

"Well, it's just that you seemed pretty guilty when I came in," she said, her voice rising to match his. "I saw that."

"That's because I was telling her about us, about how we moved in together. That's all. I was apologizing for all the wrongs I had made when I was with her," he said, his voice calm and soft.

Marialena walked over to him. "Okay." She looked into his eyes and nodded. "It just looked weird, but I believe you." He put his arms around her.

Esteban exhaled and held her in front of him. "Let's take a walk, maybe get some lunch," he said.

"Yeah, okay." Marialena nodded. "I'm sorry if I overreacted."

"You didn't. I get it. She's my ex and we have history and it looked weird. I don't blame you one bit for not believing me. But I will never, ever go back to her."

"God, when I saw the packing slip for the ring, I almost died. I assumed the worst."

"I'm sorry." He was going to propose to Marialena and he wanted it to be a total surprise, but she was thinking the opposite was true. He didn't want to tell her that he loved her, because he was afraid that it would all spill out. His engagement plans, all of it. And he didn't want to jump into it, not like this. So instead, he took her hand and they walked to the café, trying to forget what had happened.

216

Chapter Fifteen

Christmas Eve had finally arrived and both Esteban and Marialena devoted the day entirely to each other. Both of them slept in, came back to bed after coffee, and made love under the covers. It had been a romantic, sleepy morning. When they were finally up and ready, it was already noon.

They skipped breakfast, but made lunch together. Marialena begged Esteban to play Christmas music while they ate.

"Hey, you invited me to spend the holidays with you. This was *your* doing," she said with a laugh.

"I didn't realize you were going to torture me," he said as he smiled then took a huge bite out of his sandwich.

After lunch, they cleaned up the kitchen, and Marialena parked herself in front of his movie collection.

"I hope these aren't in order." She said as she moved them around.

"Well, it doesn't look like they are anymore."

"Oh shit, I'm sorry."

He laughed and came to kneel beside her. "I'm only kidding." He pulled out two stacks. "Aha!" he said triumphantly. Marialena reached out for it, but he held it out of reach.

"It's not like I don't have my very own copy," she said.

"I'm not ready to watch it yet. Tonight?"

217

"Well, I figured as much. I just wanted to see it."

"Okay. I think I am going to dress in something warmer. I'm kind of cold."

"The coffee should be ready soon."

"I don't think I want any more, actually. Thanks, though."

Marialena entered Esteban's room and sat down on the bed. Their month together was coming to an end soon. She lay down, got under the covers, and inhaled the scent from his side of the bed. She threw her arms around his pillow and closed her eyes. She didn't want to leave...not next week, not ever.

When Esteban came in to check on her, she was still on his side of the bed. He stood in the doorway and looked at her for a second before climbing in with her. She shifted her body and let him wrap his arms around her.

"I'm going to miss this," she said.

Esteban didn't say anything. Instead, his heart started racing. It was happening. He could see it. She was falling for him. He kept going back and forth and wasn't sure if he was going to give her the ring that night or not. But if she kept doing things like this, he didn't think he'd be able to stop himself. Even now, he was bursting with excitement. They still hadn't used any deep words toward each other. Esteban was close, but he was still holding back, waiting to see how Marialena felt.

Marialena lay in his arms, her hands underneath his clothes, snuggling against his cream-colored sweater, loving how it felt against her arms. He was so warm. Marialena couldn't help herself. Tears came flooding down her cheeks. Esteban cupped her face.

"Hey, what's wrong?"

Marialena smiled sadly and shook her head. "I don't know. I'm fine. I think it's just everything. Probably just a mix of emotions today. I'm okay." He kissed her tears and she stopped crying, willing herself to look forward to the rest of the day. Esteban comforted her and she lay in his arms, peaceful for a few more minutes.

"Okay, I am going to get up, put on some more layers, and then I'm thinking about taking a walk around the neighborhood. I need some fresh air."

"Yeah, that sounds good. I think I'll come."

"What about your coffee?"

"I'll take it with me. Sure you don't want any?"

"You know what? I want to make hot chocolate."

Esteban laughed. "I can't think of a time before you when I actually had hot chocolate in my cabinets."

"Yeah, your cabinets are thanking me now. Their life is so much sweeter." They got out of bed and she made a beeline to the kitchen to put some milk on the stove.

He held her from behind as they waited for the milk to heat up. He nuzzled her neck. "I'm feeling warmer already," she said.

Esteban laughed. "That's because I turned up the heater about twenty minutes ago."

He kissed her passionately on the mouth. "I can enjoy hot chocolate this way," he said, surprising himself. He never used to be this romantic. Marialena was bringing it out of him.

Marialena put on some boots and wore a warm jacket over her light sweater.

"You sure you're going to be warm enough?" he asked sarcastically.

Marialena smiled and took his hand as they walked out the door. "But it's cold outside."

"It's fifty-five degrees," he said.

She nudged Esteban and they walked around their neighborhood quietly, neither of them saying much. It was nice to be at peace like this with each another. Neither of them had to say anything, and it was still enjoyable. She just loved being around him. She looked at him and smiled. She didn't notice his age anymore. He didn't even look older to her. Sure, he had some small lines and his face was weathered, but he was still incredibly handsome. She loved the gray that showed up on his temples and sideburns. She loved how protective his hands felt when they were on her. She loved the wisdom behind his eyes, his thoughtfulness that showed in his face while he was thinking. He was always working on his writing, even when he wasn't writing. She imagined him there now. She still didn't know what it was about. He didn't want to discuss it yet. He had told her that he wanted to be further along before he allowed himself to talk about it, and she didn't press him. He didn't always work from home either, sometimes he took his laptop to the café down the street. Sometimes he took it to her place while she did her laundry or caught up on errands and bills. She had liked seeing him there, even if he seemed out of place. Her condo was colorful and bright, and his was dark and mostly decorated in brown hues. Even her books in her bookcase had more color than his.

When they got back to his place, Esteban started to prep the roast to cook a little later. They both agreed to have an early dinner. When he saw her eyeing his bookcase, he came trotting over. He had hidden her ring on the top shelf, behind a copy of 'Don Quixote' which had also been his mother's.

"Gonna read a book?" he asked.

"Yeah," she said, eyeing him suspiciously.

"Which one are you leaning toward?" he asked, trying to sound casual.

"I'm not sure. Are some of these off limits?" she asked, not sure why he seemed so interested.

"No, not necessarily. Would you like a recommendation?"

"Sure."

He pulled out a copy of 'The Dreams of a Painter.' "Just read the first two chapters and you'll find yourself transported. It's amazing."

She took the book in her hands and she flipped through its pages.

"Maybe." She looked at the top shelf of the bookcase, then back to the meat he had been prepping, still wondering why he had come running over as soon as she had shown interest in his books. Esteban took his phone out of his pocket and tried to text Roxanne as quickly as possible, without Marialena noticing.

"Help. Call Lena on her phone. Act casual."

A few seconds later, Marialena's cell phone rang and she took the copy of 'The Dreams of a Painter' with her. She answered the phone, walked into the guest room, and closed the door behind her.

Esteban quickly pocketed the ring, then sent a thank you text to Roxanne.

"Thanks. I hid her engagement ring in my bookcase, and she was starting to look for a book." He had called

221

Roxanne the day he got the ring from the deposit box and told her what he had been planning. She had been thrilled, and they talked for thirty minutes. He was honest and told her he wasn't sure when he was going to ask Marialena, and Roxanne promised she'd keep her mouth shut.

"You hid her ring in the bookcase? That's like hiding a piece of cheese from a mouse in an open cookie jar." Roxanne texted back. Esteban smiled at her phrasing.

"She had never shown interest before."

"Seriously, she's never looked at your books?"

"Yeah, like only one of the first few times she came over."

"That's weird."

"We've been busy," Esteban texted with a smile on his face.

"New relationship. How could I forget?"

He let Roxanne get back to the conversation with Marialena, who was in the middle of complaining how strange Esteban was acting.

"I mean, does he not trust me with his books?"

"Maybe he was really excited you were showing interest," Roxanne said, defending him.

"He has never been that excited. It felt like he didn't trust me over there."

"You're overreacting. I'm sure it's nothing. How has he been otherwise?"

"Great. Off, but great."

"Off?" Roxanne asked.

"I don't know. He just seems off. Something's going on with him. Not today so much, but other times."

"You said he's turning fifty soon. It could be that. Honey, it's Christmas Eve. Go out there and enjoy your man. Don't worry so much about how he's been acting." Roxanne was true to her word, she wasn't going to spill the beans.

"I know, it's just that this month is coming to an end, and it's been so nice. I actually got onto his side of the bed this morning, just to breathe it all in. I thought I was just walking into his room to change, but instead I went back to bed; it was so overwhelming, just lying there in his covers. I don't want this to end. And it's not just that, I'm thinking about my mom and dad too."

"Aww sweetie, I know. But what makes you think it's going to end?"

"I don't know. What if he realizes I'm too young for him? Every time I feel like we're on the right track, I do something stupid, like drink hot chocolate and pout because he won't let me look at his books."

"Seriously, you're overreacting. Older people drink hot chocolate. What's wrong with you?"

"I just wish I was classier sometimes. It's all those little things I do. What if he's been paying attention to all those things and now they're adding up?"

Roxanne bit her lip. She desperately wanted to tell her that he was crazy about her, but she promised him she wouldn't. "Talk to him," she said.

"I don't want to ruin the mood." Marialena laughed to herself. "The holidays can really suck, can't they?"

"They sure can. But Marialena, look at the bright side. You guys are together. He's making you a roast! He's your favorite director and you're going to watch his

223

movie together...*your favorite movie of all time!* You really can't complain."

Marialena laughed and wiped her eyes. "God, I love you. Thanks for listening to all my bullshit all the time. I'm sorry I keep bugging you about all of this stuff."

"It's okay. I know you don't have a lot of people you can really talk to about this. And I love you too. Now get out there and have a good time. Talk to him later, will you?"

"Okay, we'll see. I'll go out there in a second. How are you? Are you still going to Jason and Trisha's?" Marialena had never met them, but Trisha was Roxanne's best friend in Nashville. Jason and Trisha were engaged, and they were having a small Christmas Eve dinner party.

"Yeah, I'm making a Cobb salad. Marcy had to help me with the bacon."

"Because you can't make it without burning it or undercooking it?"

"You know it. It came out good this time though, thanks to Marcy. And the whole apartment smells amazing."

"Are you spending the night?"

"I might, but I'm not sure. They like to keep it cold as balls there."

"You're not acclimated to Nashville weather yet?"

"Shut up. You wouldn't be either."

"That's true. I'm pretty frozen today."

"Tell that director of yours to turn the heat up."

Marialena laughed. "He did already."

"You know, someone as semi-famous as him ought to be partying on Christmas Eve."

224

"Well, I'm pretty sure he got invited to a few places, but he's kind of low-key."

"God, you guys are perfect for each other."

"Tell *him* that," Marialena joked.

"*You* tell him."

"Touche."

"Okay, I've gotta run in a minute. Try not to freak out over every little thing over there. I'll keep my cell close, just in case. Put me on the phone with your man. I want to wish him a Merry Christmas quickly."

"Okay. I love you so much. Merry Christmas."

"Love you too. Merry Christmas. Call me tomorrow, okay?" Roxanne waited to hear Esteban on the other end. "Hey, Merry Christmas."

"Thank you. Merry Christmas," he said, eyeing Marialena, who sat down on the couch with his book recommendation.

"Hey, so *FYI*, she's a little touchy these days. I don't know if she told you or not, but the anniversary of her parents' death is in three days. They died on the twenty-seventh. That's why the holidays are so rough on her."

"Okay, thanks. I wasn't sure."

"She just gets a little sensitive this time of year."

"Mmmhmmm," he said, trying to sound casual.

"She's right there, isn't she?"

"Yeah," he said.

"Okay, so I won't keep you. Are you planning on her asking soon?"

"Not sure. Probably. Maybe later," he said, warming to the idea.

"Aaaahhhhh!" Roxanne exclaimed.

Esteban laughed. "I'm still thinking about it. But I kind of like the idea. Anyway, thank you. I hope you have a great Christmas."

"You too. I've gotta run. Good luck."

"Talk to you soon."

Marialena turned around, half listening to them. "What was that about?"

Esteban shrugged. "Christmas presents," he said, and left it at that.

"Oh, you got someone to help you?"

"Something like that," he said and smiled. Esteban sat down next to Marialena, and he turned on the TV to watch the game. The ring was burning a hole in his pocket and he was sure Marialena would feel it when she curled up next to him, but he was just being paranoid.

He put his arm around her and kissed her head. She wrapped them in a blanket and continued to read.

"I'll get dinner started in about an hour."

"Need help with anything?"

Esteban had a thought. "Yeah, could you help me with the mashed potatoes?" he said, thinking of his mom.

"I'd love to!"

Later, she peeled the potatoes and took the butter and the milk out of the fridge. Esteban watched from the corner of his eye, channeling his mom. He was smiling, but trying to hide it. Thankfully, Marialena was focused on the task at hand.

She took the milk and stirred it into the potatoes. Next was butter. She took a spoon and heaped two spoonfuls, then stirred.

"You know you want it," she said into the pot.

Esteban started to laugh. "Are you actually talking to your food?"

Marialena shrugged. "I love mashed potatoes and mashed potatoes love butter. It's the perfect relationship," she said. Esteban smiled. He knew then that he would ask tonight. "I'm not making that much, since potatoes don't reheat very well. I'll just make more when we have tamales tomorrow."

"Tamales and mashed potatoes?"

"Tamales and everything. They go with breakfast, lunch, and dinner," she said, excited that she was able to bring some, since it was a family tradition to have them around the holidays. They usually ate them on Christmas Eve, but she didn't want to downplay Esteban's roast.

When it was finally time for dinner, they talked about the book he had lent her. Dreams were the topic of the book, so they discussed their own dreams.

"I've woken up a few times, and I've had to write some of my dreams down," Esteban said.

"Did they ever amount to anything?"

"Sure. The love scene in 'Paris' was from a dream. I was around your age; I had gone to some bar one night to see this band play. I'll never forget it. There was a couple in front of me. The place was swarming with people. It was hot inside. Maybe the air conditioner was broken, because I remember everyone was sweating."

"This is the dream?" she asked, unsure.

"No, this really happened. I was really at the bar. I remember I went alone and I was drinking all this beer. There was this couple in front of me, and they clung to each other. My god, the way they were swaying to the music. I kept looking at them in front of me, his hand on

227

her ass, and I remember thinking that I'd a) never have to the balls to do that in public and b) how in sync they were. So that night, I went home and there was a message on my answering machine about a last-minute party at my friend's house down the street. It was late, around midnight, but I decided to walk there and I remember I was starving. So I ate all this party food, dips, chips, hors d'oeuvres, you name it. I didn't get wasted, but I walked back home and I fell asleep in my clothes. That night, I had the most amazing dream. It was a sex dream, and I was with this woman, not exactly the same woman at the bar, but someone else. She didn't have a face, just a body. You know how dreams are. And anyway, we made love and it was exquisite. I remember waking up with this massive hard-on. But instead of doing anything about it, I wrote everything down. I knew that I didn't want to forget it, and you know, years later, I was able to try to recapture that same love scene in 'Paris.'"

"Oh my god, that was from a dream you had?"

"Yeah, isn't that crazy? Inspired by midnight party food, booze, and a random couple in front of me at a bar."

"Jesus, that's incredible. Was the woman from the bar black? Like the character in your movie?"

"No. I have no idea who the woman was. It's funny, isn't it? I think of that couple every now and again. I never saw their faces, but they inspired one of my movies."

Marialena sat back. "Wow."

"I know. I mean, it wasn't until years later that I wrote the film, but that moment in my life, that dream,

228

stayed with me. I knew I wanted to write a story that revolved around that."

"And so, why Paris?"

"You mean, why does it take place there?"

Marialena nodded. Esteban shrugged, then laughed. "Honestly, it was because of the hors d'oeuvres I had that night."

"You're kidding me."

Esteban laughed harder. "No, I swear."

"It's the most romantic city in the world, and you shot there because you were inspired by party food?"

"No, it was a great city to film in, but it was really just the exterior shots that were filmed there."

"Okay, I don't want to hear anymore." She held up a hand, stopping him. He continued laughing.

"Yeah, I should probably hold off on the director's commentary until we've watched the film. Am I ruining it for you?" he asked.

"Hors d'oeuvres? Really?"

"I wouldn't have shot there if it wasn't an incredible city," he said, getting serious. "I was in awe, and I kept thinking how lucky I was to be able to do what I wanted to do in such an inspiring place. But we won't talk about it." He smiled at her. "I have to admit, I'm getting a little nervous."

"How come?"

"I don't know. I mean, I haven't watched this movie since it first came out."

"You're joking? Just stop. Just stop right there." They both laughed. Marialena decided to change the subject. "This roast... Oh my god, so good. It's so nice on a day like today."

229

"Yeah, and thanks for the mashed potatoes. They're excellent. They used to be my mom's favorite. She'd love you right now," he said and smiled. "The roast is my mom's recipe. I thought it would be appropriate," he said, though he didn't tell her why. "I actually haven't had this in years on Christmas Eve. I believe I was forty-four when I went back to her place for Christmas Eve and she made it. I had helped her make it, then later that night she had written down the recipe for me. She didn't always make it. Sometimes she made *sopa de galets,* which my brother liked a lot. It was a tradition in her family, but I preferred this."

"*Sopa de galets?* I've never heard of that."

"It's pretty good. Maybe I could find a place that serves it. I like it, and it's served with bread, but I liked this more and my mom knew it, so she'd alternate making this for me and *sopa de galets* for Henry."

"That's sweet of her. When did she pass?"

"Oh, I don't know. Four years now?"

"I'm so sorry."

"It's okay. We all have our losses," he said.

"She got to see some of your success."

"Yeah, she did. But I think she was more worried about my personal life."

"I bet. Unmarried successful man, a mother's worst nightmare."

Esteban laughed. "She didn't approve of any of my girlfriends."

Marialena smiled with him. "Why not?"

"Honestly, probably because she didn't really get to meet them, and it irked her. Any time I flew down there, I usually went alone."

230

"Your previous girlfriends never wanted to come?"

"It's not that. Laura came once. But everyone was usually busy around the holidays. I guess I always gravitated toward the successful, busy independent type. It was sexy. And it gave me time to write. I didn't want to feel guilty for not spending much time with them, but there was always this weird gap in the relationship. I was never terribly close to them. Now I realize that I was after the wrong type of woman."

"Are you saying I'm unsuccessful?" Marialena asked. She wondered if there was some truth to what he was saying.

"No way. Are you kidding me? You're incredibly driven. But you find passion in other things besides work. You find beauty in the small things, in the intimate things. The women I dated before didn't. You hold on to life where others take it for granted."

"Maybe it's because I've realized how little time we have."

"Yeah, maybe. But more than that, you seem to find happiness despite your past. I wasn't so lucky. When Laura cheated on me, it's like I almost gave up. You actually got Patrick Denny to work with you based on what? The way you see people? That's incredible. Instead of losing hope, it's like you looked harder to find it and hold on to it."

"You give me too much credit. I was a mess when my parents died. For a long time. In fact, if you talked to Roxanne, she'd give you a very different version of me. Besides, Patrick Denny was interested in my looks before he was interested in anything else."

231

"Sure. But he hired you for other reasons. So, why'd you turn him down that night you met him?"

She thought for a second. "I don't know why I turned him down. Once I found out he wasn't you, I saw him for what he was. Yeah, he won an Oscar, but I loved you for your vision. For the way *you saw* people, and that's inspiring to me. Your movies give me hope. His are art, but yours are hope. And as soon as he told me he wasn't you, that hope was gone. It was totally different. It's like the magic disappeared."

"What if he let you believe he was me? Would you have slept with him?"

Marialena shifted in her seat and took a large sip of wine while she thought of a way to answer that. She thought back to that night, the way they were flirting, and she blushed, embarrassed about how she had acted when she thought he was Esteban.

"I honestly don't know. I found out early on that he wasn't you. So, I didn't have to entertain the idea for long. It made more sense when I met you though. You seemed to fit the part in a way that he didn't. I remember looking into your eyes that first day, and I saw something." She shrugged. "I saw you, Esteban Gutierrez," she said, her heart somersaulting in her chest.

"I was so down for so long. I was still going through some shit when we met."

"No, I didn't see you that way. I saw something like hope. Patrick was different. He was charming, sure. And he wanted sex, yes. But, I don't know. It wasn't the same as when I met you. The more I talked to you that first day, the more your eyes lit up. It was nice."

232

"It's like you saw right through me."

"Not through you. I just saw you. I saw *you*, Esteban."

Esteban smiled into his almost empty dinner plate. "My mom would have really liked you."

They finished, cleared the dishes, and settled on the couch with the rest of the wine. Esteban rearranged the sofa, so that he could sit on the corner with his back to the terrace.

"You're not going to sit next to me?"

"Nope, I am sitting right here. I told you, I was going to watch *you*."

"Don't you want to watch this masterpiece?"

He laughed. "I've seen it before. In fact, I believe I was there. Besides, you're a masterpiece in your own right. I'd rather watch you."

She smiled at him. "Okay, fine."

He popped in the DVD and they both settled in. She clapped quietly when his name was on the screen.

"Written and Directed by Esteban Gutierrez."

"You're such a nerd," he whispered to her. Marialena shushed him and he threw a piece of napkin at her. She picked it up distractedly and put it on the coffee table. They continued to watch and every once in a while, a piece of his napkin would land on her, or somewhere near her. She picked them up and started a little collection, but she didn't pay him any attention. The movie was about a power outage in the city of Paris, as the sun is setting in the middle of winter. There are different scenes within the movie, scenes where people respond terribly to the power outages. Some people were rude. Scenes in busy restaurants, scenes in the

233

streets, scenes that show how important technology is in people's lives, and even how technology pushes them further away from one another. There was a scene that took place on a bus where a young person is scrolling through a dating app, yet doesn't look at the beautiful young woman in front of him. Both are quiet and staring at their phones instead of starting a conversation. The film revolves around a young man, an American, who had just arrived in the city and is moving into an apartment when the power goes out. He goes next door to see if his new neighbor has a flashlight or if they have a candle he can borrow. He explains that he needs to finish unpacking, but the young woman, a beautiful black French woman, his neighbor, is alone. And her apartment is lit with candles. She gives him a few only to find this his hands are freezing, so he stays for tea. She rigged up the tea pot, with lit candles underneath, and she explains why she has so many candles. They're left over from a wedding. He asks if it was hers, and she laughs. 'A friend's,' she says in her beautiful French accent. The two of them stay in the apartment for some time, exchanging fascinating and intellectual conversations. She takes him to see the Eiffel Tower. As more scenes unfold, people deal with the outage. Some are making the best of it, some the worst. The American and the French girl make their way through the city. They stumble over broken cobblestones, and when they return to her apartment, he helps her light all the candles again. The American is shivering in her apartment and explains he is from Southern California, where it never gets cold. She makes fun of him, but moves closer to him to warm him up. More tea, with whiskey this time.

234

There's a musician with a guitar on the sidewalk and the French girl opens up the window, despite the cold, to hear the guitarist better. She lights more candles.

Esteban watched Marialena as she fell for his characters. He fell in love with her all over again, the way she leaned back in the sofa when his young lovers met for the first time, during the power outage. The way she curled up inside of the blanket when they touched for the first time. The way her face looked when the candles were lit on the screen, reflecting in her face, her eyes dancing with the flames. Towards the end, when the love scene came on, he watched her as her body tensed with the lovemaking. The sounds from the screen were quiet then, and they could hear the lovers breathing, with minimal music. He watched Marialena, who turned to look at him only once with a look on her had never seen before. He wanted to pick her up and carry her to his room, or take her right there on the couch, but he resisted. The second half of the movie was shot in the dark, with only enough light to show the actors. He watched her as she sighed with their orgasms during the lovemaking, Marialena's hand on her heart. He continued watching her as the characters in the film fell asleep in each other's arms as the sun rose the next morning, each candle slowly fading into nothing, one by one. It was a magical scene, he knew it and could see it reflected in Marialena's eyes. The movie ended with the couple reuniting the next evening, power restored. In that scene, the American returned to her apartment, and he turned off all the lights as she relit the candles. The credits rolled to the sound of the street musician playing a French song.

235

Neither of them moved.

"My God, Esteban."

"Yeah, I'm a little bit of a romantic. Who knew?" Marialena got up and sat down next to him.

"That was incredible."

"It was pretty incredible watching it from your perspective. Thanks for that," he said, running a hand through his hair. Marialena looked at him in the darkness. He seemed ten years younger and relaxed. At peace. She put a hand on his shoulder for leverage and climbed on top of him. There were no sounds then, except for the two of them. The TV had faded to black and the only light came from the Christmas tree in the corner. They made love there on the couch, both sweaty and wet, clinging to each other.

Aterward, Marialena collapsed into his arms. "My God," she said. "Best viewing ever."

Esteban laughed. "It's a little strange, a director being turned on by his own movie."

"It was inspired by your own dream though."

"Yeah, but I mean, it was really you I was turned on by. You brought that dream to life," he said, his hand on her naked backside. "Just now."

Marialena rested her head on his shoulder. "I love you," she said.

He let those words sink in.

"I love you," she said again, her voice sounding more emotional.

He kissed her hair and got up from underneath her, searching for his clothes on the floor. He made sure the ring was still in the pocket of his pants. He put his boxers back on and sat up on the couch, handing Marialena the blanket. He set his pants down and pulled Marialena close to him on the left, her hair perfectly draped around her face. She kissed his naked chest. Esteban closed his eyes.

"Lena," he said into the darkness. He put an arm around her and pulled her in closer. "Lena, there's something I want to say."

Marialena looked at him in the darkness, her eyes big. She sat up straighter and pulled herself away from him, covering herself up in the blanket. Why hadn't he said 'I love you' back?

"What?" she asked softly.

"Well, it's about you and me."

"Now? We're still a week away from 'decision' day.'"

"I don't think this can wait until then."

Her mind started to race. She thought of the presents under the Christmas tree that she had wrapped for him, presents that would go unopened. She thought about driving back to her condo in the darkness, a condo that screamed out to her in its loneliness. She didn't want to go back, but she had no choice, she had agreed to this after all. She wiped the tears from her eyes.

"I don't want to lose you," she said, sniffling into his bare arms.

He held her closer. "Marialena. It's okay," he said.

"It's just that I've fallen so in love with you. So much more than I thought I ever could. I don't want this to end," she said.

"I don't want it to end either." He unlocked himself from her arms.

237

He picked up her clothes from the floor and handed them to her. "Here, you should probably put these on," he said, running a hand through his hair. He was getting nervous. It seemed like she was getting the wrong idea and he needed to fix it fast.

Each of them put on their clothes. She was slower than he was. She didn't want to move too quickly, and she didn't want him to say the words she was dreading to hear.

"So, I've been thinking about this a lot," Esteban started, deciding to just go with it. "Look, Marialena, this relationship has been so different for me. I've never experienced anything as incredible as this before and I have a question I've been meaning to ask you." She watched him as he took something out of his pocket and got down on one knee. He held out the ring box in his hand and opened it.

"Will you marry me?"

Marialena put a hand to her mouth, stifling a gasp. She looked at the ring, then into his hazel eyes. He looked so sweet, hopeful, and in love.

"Marialena, I am in love with you. And I want to spend the rest of my life with you. Will you marry me?" he asked again.

Marialena froze. Tears started to stream down her face and she hid it in her hands as she started to cry.

"Hey, ssshh," he said. "It's okay. Don't cry. Why are you crying?"

She fell into his arms and cried softly into his shoulder.

"I think I need a minute," she said a little while afterward. She walked to the bathroom and dried her tears. She looked into the mirror, feeling shitty. She had ruined his engagement, but she couldn't help it. She was so overcome with emotion and had no idea this was coming. She splashed cold water on her face and when she came out, she turned to Esteban. "I think I just need some fresh air." She walked out to the terrace. Esteban put the ring back into his pocket and sighed heavily. This was not going well at all. After a minute, he followed her out there. She had been staring out into the city. She saw a couple on the sidewalk, each holding presents in their arms. Esteban came up behind her and placed a hand on her shoulder.

"You okay?" he asked.

"I thought you were going to break up with me," she said. The night was quiet. The breeze was chilly, but she wasn't cold.

"Why would you think that?" he asked, still behind her.

She shrugged. "I don't know. I'm so sorry I've ruined the night."

He pulled her into his arms. "You didn't ruin anything."

"It's just that I love you so much," she said, her voice muffled.

"I love you too." It was the first time he had said it.

Marialena broke away from him. She looked into his eyes. He looked a little disheveled, a little tired. Scruffy, even.

"I'm a mess," she said, wiping her eyes, still crying. "I had no idea you wanted to ask me to marry you. You've been acting strangely all week."

239

Esteban smiled and looked at the city. She took her place behind him.

"I've had the ring for about a week. That's probably why. I was getting excited."

Marialena laughed. "That explains it. My god, I thought you were thinking about how to break it off with me. I totally misread the whole thing."

"The ring was my mom's. She left it when she passed, and I wanted to give it to you."

She nodded as she looked into his eyes. "It's a beautiful ring."

"What are you thinking, Marialena? What is going on in that head of yours?"

She shrugged and smiled. "I'm thinking that I wish we could start over. I wish you could ask me again," she said, wiping a tear from her eye.

"I think I can arrange that." He took the ring back out of his pocket and got down on one knee. Marialena couldn't keep the tears from falling.

"Marialena Villanueva, you've made happier that I've ever thought possible and I would like it very much if you'd become my wife. I love you. Will you marry me?"

Marialena nodded as she looked into his eyes. "Yes, I'd love to." He placed the ring on her finger.

"We might need to resize it," he said as he slid it on. "Wow, look at that. It's the perfect fit."

Marialena admired it on her hand. "Oh Esteban, it's beautiful. This was really your mom's?"

Esteban nodded. "Yeah, it was." The ring was beautiful, with a sapphire in the middle and five swirls of diamonds around the outside. There were twenty-five diamonds in total. Esteban's mom had always said that it wasn't meant to be an engagement ring, but that she had fallen in love with it in the window when she and his father were dating. She liked the shape of it because it reminded her of the spiral arms of the Milky Way galaxy. She was very surprised when Esteban's father had proposed. It was perfect.

"It is perfect," Marialena said. "I don't think we even need to have it resized."

He smiled at her. "It was meant to be."

She smiled and threw her arms around his neck. He kissed her passionately.

"I love you so much."

"I love you, Esteban."

"Come on, let's go back inside." She nodded. He poured each of them a glass of wine and they sat back on the couch and talked about his movie until she was yawning from the alcohol. Marialena smiled at Esteban. He looked so happy. She couldn't believe this was really happening. She glanced down at her ring. It was so beautiful. She leaned in to kiss Esteban on the lips.

"Thank you for my ring. It's beautiful. I've never seen anything like it."

"My mom had liked it for a while, and my Dad couldn't remember where they had seen it. When my dad finally found it, he was so thrilled that he asked my mom to marry him *that day*. She couldn't believe he had remembered that she had liked that ring. But she said it was fate because she kept thinking about it, but had no reason to make such an extravagant purchase for herself."

"That's a really sweet story," Marialena replied, coming back inside and sitting on the sofa with Esteban.

241

"I cannot believe you asked me to marry you. We're actually going to get married." Marialena shook her head and wiped tears from her eyes. "This is so unreal."

Esteban put an arm around her shoulders. "I know. I've been really excited just thinking about it."

"You were very good at keeping it from me."

"Yeah, but you thought we were going to break up." He ran his left hand through his hair. "That's not what I was going for."

"I know. I thought everything was fine, but something just seemed off.

"I think it's good to talk about the relationship and what we needed out of it and each other, but scheduling a 'decision' day might have been a bad idea, especially the way I did it. I honestly needed to make sure that you wanted this, and it was starting to feel like you *really* did. So I just had all this pent-up excitement."

Esteban drained the rest of his wine. He remembered the note in his DVD case and fished out the case from where he had stuck it underneath a stack of books on the coffee table. "Open it," he said.

She took the DVD case and opened it. A note slipped out, and she picked it up and unfolded it. In cursive writing, the note said, "If I had to do this over, I would have dedicated it to you, Marialena. You alone are the bright light that shines within my heart, even in the darkest hour. I hope I can be the same for you."

Tears fell as she read it. She took the note and held it to her heart.

"Thank you, Esteban. For all of this, for everything."

She fell into his arms and rested her head on his chest. "I love you."

"I love you too."

"We're going to get married."

"Yeah, I know."

"You're going to be my husband one day."

"I know," he said, feeling proud.

"How did I get so lucky?"

"I ask myself that every day."

Marialena took a deep sigh. "I feel like I should be running around and jumping for joy, but all that wine made me super sleepy. I think I need to hit the hay soon."

"I think I'll join you. Hey, Merry Christmas," he said.

"Merry Christmas," she said and smiled through a happy and tearful sniffle.

Chapter Sixteen

It was Decemeber twenty-seventh and Marialena woke up early. She was careful not to disturb Esteban as she took a shower, and she was grateful that her clothes were kept in another room. She got dressed in the guest room, quietly brewed some coffee, and was ready forty-five minutes later.

She got into the car, pulled into the closest florist, picked up several bouquets of flowers, and drove to the cemetery where her parents were buried. She took a blanket out of the trunk. When she got to where they were buried, she folded it three times, since the grass was damp and cold underneath her. She placed the flowers down and held back tears as she looked at the items others had left for her parents. She assumed her uncle had stopped there recently. He left a cigar box and a mini bottle of tequila, which was strange since she never saw her dad drink tequila. He was more of a beer man when he was alive.

Marialena rearranged everything on their grave as she added the flowers and sat down for about thirty minutes. She didn't talk and she didn't cry. She just sat there and thought of them. She thought about Esteban with her dad. They were only a couple of years apart. She wondered how they would have gotten along. It would have been uncomfortable, but she would have been able to convince her dad that she loved him. She wondered what they'd talk about. Sports? Cars? Her dad would

244

have gotten a kick out of Esteban's Maserati. But her dad didn't watch a whole lot of movies and didn't have an eye for that kind of thing.

And how would her mom have gotten along with Esteban? She figured she would have worried at first, would have said the same things that Esteban had said when they first met, but Marialena knew that she would have eventually been able to win her mom over. She toyed with one of the rose petals. When it was time to leave, she placed a hand on the grass above them and whispered, "I love you." She got up, picked up the blanket, and walked to her car, her hair flying in the breeze. She sat in the car and wept into her hands, finally breaking down. She missed them so much. It had only been six years and it already felt like a lifetime without them.

Marialena collected herself and called her aunt's cell phone. Her Tia Teresa answered on the third ring.

"Hi Tia," Marialena said, using the Spanish word for aunt. "It's Marialena. I went to the cemetery today. Thanks so much for stopping by to see them."

"Of course. You don't have to thank us. How was your Christmas?"

"Good. I am, I uh, have some good news. I wanted to tell you, I got engaged on Christmas Eve."

"Oh honey, congratulations. Who is the lucky man?"

Marialena smiled and wiped the last of the tears from her eyes.

"His name is Esteban Gutierrez."

"Oh sweetie, I am so happy for you. You should bring him by so we can all meet him."

"I will, Tia. Listen, is Tio Lalo around?"

245

"No, he's not home right now. But I will tell him you called, and I'll tell him about your engagement. Honey, your parents would be proud," her aunt said kindly.

"Thank you, Tia." It was a short conversation. She had never been close to her dad's side of the family. Her dad and his brother never saw eye to eye on family matters, and both of them were stubborn. It caused a lot of friction between them. She remembered her uncle being strict with her older cousins when she came over, making it uncomfortable for Marialena, whose own dad was kind and loving.

When Marialena was driving home from the cemetery she received a phone call from Roxanne.

"Hey, sweetie. How are you holding up?" She knew Marialena visited the cemetery early every year.

"Good. I decided to go early. Tio Lalo had been there recently too. He left some stuff."

Roxanne exhaled loudly. "Did you go with Esteban?"

"No, I left him at home sleeping."

"You've got to talk to him."

"I know. I will. It's just that it feels different this year. Is it because I am in love and getting engaged? I can't talk about it with him today. I can't. I will some other time though, I promise."

"Why not today? You'll feel so much better. Honestly, you're probably feeling this way because you're finally living your life."

"I just miss them so much, Rox," Marialena said, tears falling from her eyes.

"I know, love. It's okay." She could tell that Marialena had started to cry. "Are you driving?"

"Yeah, I'm driving back to Esteban's."

"Why don't you pull over?"

"I'm on the 101."

"So, get off at one of the exits." Roxanne didn't want Marialena to drive while crying.

"No, it's okay. I'm fine. Look, I just feel like if I tell him today, I'll lose it a little. We just got engaged, and I don't want him to see me like this. I know, it's stupid. But I really want to wait to tell him. Next month sometime, okay?"

"I know it's hard, sweetie," Roxanne said. She had already told Esteban today was the anniversary of their death. She assumed that Marialena would have talked about it by now, but she hadn't. "You have to do it sooner or later. But if you want to do it later, that's your call."

"I know. I called my dad's brother. Well, he wasn't home, but I talked to my Tia."

"Your Tia Teresa?" Roxanne had met them, but wasn't related to them, since she was related to Marielana through their mothers.

"Yeah, I told her I was engaged. They want to meet him."

"Well, yeah, I can imagine. When?"

"I don't know. Not any time soon, I don't think. I mean, I have to tell Esteban first, and then I have to get him to understand that my uncle is nothing like my dad. God, I wish he could meet your parents instead."

"So, fly down here or something."

"I know. I should. At least your mom and my mom were more alike than my dad and his brother."

"They were, weren't they?"

247

"It would have been so different if your parents hadn't moved away." She knew that Roxanne's parents would have taken her in as their own.

"I know. Remember, I tried to get them to move back when it happened?"

"It almost worked," Marialena said, remembering that Roxanne had threatened not to come back. She was old enough then. Instead, they offered Marialena a home with them in Nashville, which she couldn't dream of doing. She didn't want to leave Los Feliz or her parents behind, even though they had already died. Marialena felt that if she moved to Nashville, she wouldn't be able to grieve properly. So, Roxanne told her parents she'd stay with Marialena, and managed to get away with it for a while. When Roxanne's parents flew back out a few months after the funeral, they helped Marialena sell her parents' house and find her a condo. It was then that they had convinced Roxanne to come back with them, with heavy hearts.

"I'm sorry things didn't work out," Roxanne said. "But look on the bright side, you're engaged to a wonderful man and he loves you so much."

"It's weird to think that everything happens for a reason, but I feel so guilty at the same time. I feel like I had to give up my parents to gain this kind of happiness."

"You know that's not true," Roxanne said.

"It just feels like it, sometimes. If they had still been alive, I probably wouldn't have met Esteban. I would have been dating some random guy, I bet."

"No, I still would have come out to visit when I did and we would have gone to that same restaurant; I would have made that same mistake, thinking Patrick was Esteban."

"You think so?" Marialena asked, her cousin's hopefulness giving her a reason to smile.

"Yep, you can always count on my dumb ass for something like that to happen."

"Hey, that dumb ass is the reason I'm engaged."

"All I did was make a silly mistake. You got yourself engaged. I had nothing to do with that."

"Well, who knows what would have happened if they were still alive?"

"Yeah, who knows? But I'm glad you're not alone anymore."

"Me too," Marialena said with a deep sigh. "I'm almost home."

"Okay, what are you going to do today?" Roxanne asked.

"I don't know. Esteban is probably going to write. I'll get out the house, go shopping maybe. I still need to find some clothes for my new job."

"Okay, sweetie, I love you. Call me later if you need to."

"Okay, thanks. Love you."

"Love you more," Roxanne said.

Marialena took the headphones out of her ears and set her phone aside. She pulled into her parking space at Esteban's and looked in the mirror. She tried to shake off what she had just gone through, but she wasn't sure if she was going to be convincing enough for Esteban.

When she got up to his place, she saw him at the dining room table with a cup of coffee and the morning

249

paper. He set it aside as she walked in. She gave him a kiss.

"Hey, sorry about running off this morning. I had something I needed to take care of," she said, avoiding his eyes.

"Everything okay?" he asked, even though he already had a feeling she had gone to the cemetery.

"Yeah, thanks."

"So I was thinking, with it being Sunday, why don't we go to Santa Barbara or something? I haven't been to a winery in ages."

"What about your writing?"

Esteban shrugged. She had been crying, he could tell. It pained him to see her like that. He wished she could talk about it with him, but he wouldn't force it.

"I can take a day off from writing. I feel kind of guilty, actually. I've been at it nonstop since we've known each other."

"No, it's okay. I like it. I am curious, though. I want to know what it's about."

Esteban laughed. "Not yet, but soon. I promise." He didn't like to talk about his work until he was further along. He didn't want to jinx it. He had always been like that with his writing. It remained a secret until most of it was complete, at least in his head.

Marialena shrugged. "You took Christmas and Christmas Eve off. Are you sure you want to take today off too?"

"Yeah, I'm sure. I can bounce back. It's just that you have all this time off from work now, why don't we take advantage of it?" He reached out for her hand. "Let me take you out, wherever you want to go. We don't have

250

to do Santa Barbara. We can go to Temecula, or we can stay here and go to the movies and to dinner. Or whatever."

She lit up at the idea of going to the movies. She hadn't gone with him yet. "The movies sounds nice. Maybe we can go to Guapo's." That was the Mexican restaurant near her condo, where they had gone the first time they met.

"Yeah, that sounds good." He looked through the paper and handed her the movie section. "Anything look good to you?"

"Wait, you're the professional. What looks good to you?"

Esteban shrugged. "There are a few good ones out there. This is a great time of year for movies, since the Oscars are right around the corner."

They settled on a film and Marialena dumped the remainder of her coffee into the sink. Her stomach was a little uneasy. She kept her head down, letting her hair fall into her face. "I went to visit my parents at the cemetery this morning. Today is the six-year anniversary of their death."

Esteban put a hand on her arm. "I would have come with you. Why didn't you ask me? Or tell me?"

Marialena shrugged, unable to face him. "I know you would have come, but honestly I wanted to go alone. I'm not ready yet. I feel guilty. I'm so happy in my life right now and they're dead and I can't do anything about it," she said, tears falling from her eyes.

"Hey, it's okay. You don't have to feel guilty, Marialena. It's okay to want to be happy. Six years is a

251

long time. Do not feel guilty. It's okay to want to live your life."

"I know, but they're gone and I really wish you could have met them."

He pulled Marialena close to him. "I know, sweetie. I'm so sorry," he said, as she cried into his arms.

She pulled away after a few minutes and wiped her tears away. "I want to talk about it with you, trust me I do, but I don't think today is the day for that. I know it sounds cruel to say this, but honestly, I'd like some distractions," she said, feeling guilty.

"No, it's not cruel. Marialena, your parents would want you to be happy."

"I know they would have. Honestly, I want to just go to bed and stay there, and trust me, I've done that plenty of times. But it might be nice to just go out. A movie was a good idea."

Esteban nodded. "Okay, we'll do that for sure. Marialena, I love you. Please know that you can talk about this with me whenever you want, okay?"

"I know. Just please, not today," she said and looked down at her ring. She had so much to be happy about.

"So, are you feeling like a movie *tonight*, or would you rather go during the day? Before dinner, I mean?"

He looked great in the emerald green knit sweater she had gotten him for Christmas. It was so *him*. "Tonight, definitely tonight. My god, it's going to feel like a bona fide date," she said, wiping the last of the tears from her eyes.

"Yeah. I've been so busy with all the writing, I haven't really taken you out anywhere. I'm so sorry."

"No, it's okay. I'm glad you're writing. It makes me happy."

Esteban shook his head. "I need to make more time for us. We'll go out more. Movies, dinner, romantic getaways, wineries, you name it," he said, with a fire in his eyes. "We'll do it all."

"Okay, I like the sound of that."

"I'm sorry it's taken me this long to come around."

"You're busy. This is what you do for a living. I get it."

"No, I want to make you a part of my living."

Marialena smiled. "Okay. We'll do it all."

"Let's start with a winery that's not too far away. It's in Malibu, right on PCH. You can see the ocean from there."

"Ooh, that sounds nice."

"I think it opens at noon. Let's plan to have a few glasses of wine, and from there we'll check out some new music. I was thinking about getting some albums on vinyl. Then we'll have dinner and go to a movie. Is there anything you needed to do, anywhere you wanted to go?"

"I sort of wanted to go shopping. I need a few clothes for New Year's Eve and for my new job with Patrick."

"Okay, we can leave whenever you want. I don't mind going shopping with you."

"Shopping for women's clothes?" she asked, not really picturing it.

Esteban smiled. "Yeah, sure. Why not?"

Marialena sat back on the couch. She'd be doing five things with Esteban that day. With her future husband.

253

She leaned her head back on the couch and smiled a big smile.

"You do realize we haven't done this much in one day, right?"

"I know, it's my fault."

"No, that's not what I mean. I'm excited, that's all. You're going to be my husband and I get to show you off to the world."

Esteban chuckled. "I thought it was me who was getting to show you off."

"No, it's me," she said with a big smile. "Let me get ready, put some makeup on. We can leave soon," she said, pulling away.

He drove to a mall in Beverly Hills and they walked, hand in hand. Marialena saw a dress she liked. It was gold and sparkled like a diamond, perfect for New Year's. They walked into the store together and he waited by the dressing room as she tried it on. She looked at herself in the mirror inside the dressing room and she had to admit, the dress was absolutely stunning. It fit her like a glove, tight and short in all the right places. She stepped out of the dressing room to show Esteban. "I think this might be good for New Year's."

He looked at her when she stepped out and couldn't take his eyes off of her. "That's it. We're buying that dress. New Year's or not. Hell, you can wear that to bed tonight."

Marialena giggled. "Sold!"

She went back into the dressing room and Esteban followed her in. He put his hands on her waist. "Marialena, you in that dress. Oh my god," he whispered as he kissed her. "It's perfect on you."

"You're perfect on me," she said, flirting back. He kissed her mouth, then her neck, with his hands on her butt. She moaned softly.

"God, I want you," he whispered and groaned. But he kept his cool and collected himself before he stepped out of the dressing room.

Marialena smiled at her reflection when he was gone.

She poked around in a few more stores, bought a couple more dresses for her new job with Patrick, but didn't spend too much more time in the mall.

From the mall, he decided to drive to Malibu. "We'll get some records on the way back from dinner. We don't even have to do it today."

"Yeah, maybe we can squeeze it in after dinner or before the movies or something," she said. "I'm getting a tiny bit hungry. Do they have food at the winery?"

"No, but there's a food truck that comes by several times a day. Otherwise, I think they might have some cheese and crackers, that kind a thing."

"I think I just need something."

When Esteban got to the Pacific Coast Highway, Marialena felt herself relax by the ocean. It looked so dark and cold, since it was still overcast. But it was beautiful, and Marialena was glad that they'd be spending some time near the ocean that afternoon.

When they got to the winery, Esteban ordered two glasses of Cabernet Sauvignon while Marialena grabbed some food from the food truck. She came back with tacos and she and Esteban sat outside while they ate.

"I'm glad I was able to find a dress for New Year's. I'm kind of nervous, going to Patrick's party. I've never been to a New Year's party of that caliber before."

"I have. A ton of people, loud music, drinks everywhere you turn. Don't be nervous, you'll do fine. You did pretty well at the fundraiser. You can hold your own."

"I know, but this is going to be my new world. Rubbing elbows with all of his people. Sometimes I wonder what I got myself into."

"Nah, you'll do fine. Plus, I'll be there. I've got your back. I doubt I'll know any of his guests, so I won't get pulled away as much as I did at the fundraiser. I still feel bad about that actually, but I hadn't seen some of those people in so long, I felt like I owed them some time."

"Oh, the fundraiser was fine. I'm not really worried about that. I almost feel like a fraud. Here I am, working for someone like Patrick Denny and it's all because of chance. I have no experience or background in this line of work."

"You will. Don't worry. You'll pick it up in no time. Besides Lena, it's just a party. Try not to worry about it. Just think of how awesome you'll look in that dress. Plus, we're meeting up with my brother before the party."

"Yeah, should I be nervous about that?"

Esteban shook his head. "No, he's a likable guy."

"Are you two anything alike?"

"Not even a little bit. He's lighter than I am, and he's taller. About five or six inches, I think."

"Oh, that's interesting."

"He's fun to be around, though. The life of the party, you know? He's got that kind of personality."

"You could be the life of the party if you wanted to. You're easy to talk to."

Esteban shook his head. "I do okay. I wouldn't consider myself a shut-in or anything like that. I don't know, being a writer is hard sometimes. Don't get me wrong, I love it. But when I'm out, I feel like I should be at home writing, and when I'm writing, sometimes I feel like I should be out living, or even just getting ideas for my writing." He paused to take the last bite of his taco. "These were good. Thanks."

"They *were* good. Want a second? I could go back."

"No, I'm okay. That was plenty. Anyway, I'm one of those types of people who always has a better answer or a better line moments after I've answered. I guess that's why I'm a writer," he said as an afterthought.

Marialena nodded. "I've never tried writing for anything other than school. I wonder how I'd do."

"It depends. Are you a dreamer?"

Marialena thought for a second. "Sometimes. A little bit, I guess. I like to get lost in movies or books."

"What about in your own thoughts?"

"Sure, but mostly I feel like my thoughts are just random and scattered."

"Well, who knows? Maybe there are different types of writers out there. Maybe your stories would be very different from mine."

"Oh, I'm sure they would be."

"You know, I tend to write best when I'm in my own little world, I get to meditate on the characters. That's when they really start talking to me. When I'm sitting in traffic or taking a long walk is when I think of the best lines or storylines."

257

"When you're on the 405?"

"It's true. The 405 is my inspiration. I wouldn't be who I am without that dreadful traffic."

"I can't believe that! But I bet you're not the only one. I bet half the movies and screenplays written in this town are born on the 405…or the 101. God, that taco was just what I needed. Having food out here is an excellent idea. You know what? You're missing out on this view. Come over here and sit next to me."

"I happen to like my view very much, thank you," he replied, looking directly at her.

"Come on. Get over here and keep me warm. It's too beautiful for you to miss."

"Okay, will do. It's so nice here. Would you ever want to live near the ocean?"

Marialena stared into the sea for a moment before she answered. "You know, I don't know. Maybe if I didn't have to get up and go to work, or if I could do what you did."

"Are you saying I don't work?" he asked, teasing her.

"No, but you set your own schedule. You can get up and go to sleep whenever you want."

"Yeah, I often stay up late to write."

"I noticed that. No, I don't think I could live here. I'd miss the sun too much. It's often too overcast by the beach."

Esteban nodded. "We could have heat lamps on the deck like we do now."

"Are you saying you want to move to the beach?"

"It could be nice. Instead of a view of the city, we could have a view of the water."

"I feel like if I were this close to the water all the time, I may never want to wake up. I'd stay in bed all day and just listen to the waves crashing. I kind of like the hustle and bustle of the city."

"So, deep down you're a dreamer and you're fighting it!" he said.

"Or, deep down I'm not and that's why I'm more comfortable in the city. Don't get me wrong, this is nice. I like this, but I also like the distractions of the city."

"Okay, if you could move anywhere in Los Angeles, where would you move?"

"You know, I really like your place. I love the view and easy parking. I love your home, the layout. It's perfect. What about you?"

"I like where I am too. Now that you're there, it gives home a new meaning."

They stayed at the winery for another hour, each of them having a second glass of wine. When they finally left, it was early enough to swing by the record store, then to the restaurant for dinner, and then a movie. They had had plenty of time do to everything, even with all the Los Angeles traffic.

At the record store, Marialena browsed the DVD department like she always did, even before she dated Esteban. She looked for his movies. She found a new copy of "Paris in the Dark" and she stuck it in the front of the P's, like she always did when she found one of his movies. Esteban walked into the DVD section with her and he smirked when he noticed his film in front of the P's. He picked it up and smiled.

"Did you do this?"

"I always do that. Every time."

"You're so sweet."

"What albums did you pick up?" she asked, looking at the three or four albums he held.

"Oh, check this out. So, I got the newest Bob Dylan. It just came out a couple of days ago. I also got a Springsteen album I don't have, and then I saw this one. Frank Turner. Another singer songwriter, but I've been hearing his stuff on the radio and I like it. Did you want to check out the records? We could get a few for you?"

"Maybe next time. I'm not sure if I want to start a record collection, you know? I like yours just fine. You have a lot of albums I like, anyway."

Esteban nodded. Marialena and Laura were so different. Laura wore yoga pants and t-shirts and tennis shoes as much as possible, but Marialena was always dressed up like she was going somewhere nice. She was always professional. Even now, she was casual but nice casual. She was wearing a pair of tight jeans and a beige sweater with dark brown knee-high boots. He thought about how much money went into a wardrobe like hers. He knew she made her own money and it didn't seem to him like she was a big spender, but it made Esteban want to provide more for her. He wasn't a millionaire, and he hadn't come out with a movie in over two years. His bank accounts were still healthy, but it was time to start working again. Really working. Now that it looked like his writer's block had ended, he was anxious to get going.

"I don't think I want anything from here, though. But thanks," she added.

"No problem. Ready to get something to eat?"

"Yeah, that sounds good."

"Since we're going to be in the area, do you need to stop by your place for anything?"

Marialena thought for a second, then shook her head. "No, I don't think so. Everything I need is at your place." After a pause, she added, "I can't believe this was where we had our first date. It feels like a lifetime ago."

"It's been almost two months," he said as they walked inside.

Marialena sat down and opened up the menu. She decided to go with enchiladas, one of her favorites, while Esteban ordered a chile relleno.

They talked and ate, side by side. The dinner was amazing, and their conversation flowed. Marialena wasn't used to spending this much time with Esteban, but she didn't have anything to worry about. He was easy to talk to and educated in all topics. They talked about their favorite movie theater experiences and what he liked about watching a movie with an audience.

After dinner, he drove them back to their side of town, to his local movie theater. He purchased the tickets and handed one to Marialena.

"This feels so official now."

"What? Me and you?"

"Yeah, this is like a proper date," she said.

"Let me get this straight. You moved in with me and I proposed to you and you accepted, but it only feels official when I take you to the movies?"

"Sure. It was like we were living in our own little world, but now we are out in society. It feels different."

Esteban nodded. "Ah. So, am I a shut in?"

261

"No, just busy. I mean, we've gone out. But this is official stuff here. A movie date with a movie director. This is the stuff that dreams are made of."

Esteban led her to the popcorn line. "I want to get some candy. Want anything?"

"Candy? No thanks, I'm good."

When they got seated, the trailers were just about to start. Marialena leaned in and whispered, "Thanks so much for this, Esteban. I really appreciate it. I love you."

"I love you too." She kissed him on the mouth and loved how he tasted like candy.

The movie was finished two hours later, and Esteban wanted to stay throughout the closing credits. When the movie let out, Esteban handed her some of his left over Reese's Pieces with a twinkle in his eye.

"You didn't finish them?"

"Nah, I was saving some for you."

"God, these are good. I am so glad we don't do this more often. Tacos, wine, enchiladas, candy. You're dangerous, Mr. Gutierrez."

He pushed her up against his car softly. "Dangerous? No, just think of all the workout sex we could have."

Marialena laughed and kissed him on the lips. "That's one way to look at it," she said.

In the car, they talked about the film the whole way back with smiles on their faces. She seemed okay now, better than she had that morning. Esteban was glad he was able to help.

Chapter Seventeen

It was New Year's Eve. Marialena and Esteban arrived at a restaurant in Bel-Air to meet Henry. On the way, Esteban described his relationship with his brother. He told her he how he had felt bad for leaving Henry when he was just a kid, and that he should have been around more often. He explained that Henry had a restaurant in Temecula, but he didn't tell her he owned half of it.

"Ten years is a big gap between brothers. But it's cool he runs a place there. How did he end up in Temecula, though? Both of you are from New York, right?"

"I had a small place there when I moved here for the first time. When our mom died, he decided he wanted to come out here to be closer to family. He took over the lease and I moved here."

"Was he close to your mom?" she asked, toying with the engagement ring on her finger.

"We both were, but he spent the most time with her. He stayed in New York until the end."

"Wow. That's sweet of him." Marialena was quiet for a minute. "Gosh, New York is so different than California."

"We lived in a small town outside of New York, and he liked Temecula when he came out to visit, so he stayed."

"And he's never been married?"

Esteban laughed. "I don't think he's the marrying type. I think he likes his single life a little too much."

Marialena nodded and wondered what he'd be like.

When they arrived at the restaurant, Henry was already there with a table in the back. He liked to arrive to new places early, check out the place, menu, feel the vibe. When they got to his table, he hugged Esteban, but didn't take his eyes off Marialena.

"And you must be Marialena," he said, pronouncing her name correctly. He didn't take his eyes off of her as he shook her hand.

"It's nice to meet you. I'm just going to run to the restroom," Marialena said. She was surprised when she met Henry. She thought he'd look more like Esteban, even though Esteban had said they were nothing alike. Still, she expected some resemblance. He was a lot taller and they had completely different features. Henry had brown eyes with a longer face than Esteban's, a bigger smile with large dimples. His eyes weren't as round as Esteban's, or as warm. Still, Henry was handsome in his own right. Both men were good looking, they just didn't look anything alike. They didn't even have the same build. Esteban was stockier with a wider frame, whereas Henry was tall and thin.

When she was out of earshot, Henry immediately spoke. "Jesus, Esteban. That's the woman you want to propose to?"

"That's the woman I *did* propose to, actually. Last week," Esteban said with a confident smile.

"Holy shit. Congratulations. I assume she said yes?"

"You assume correctly. Anyway, why?" Esteban asked.

"Dude, have you seen her? That woman is quite a looker. I had no idea you meant you were marrying someone like that. She might be out of your league, man."

Esteban shook his head, his smile fading.

"She's not out of my league. She's not what you think, actually."

"She certainly looks the part."

"Will you stop? I get it, she's young, she's gorgeous. You think I don't know that?"

Henry shrugged. "You said she's twenty-seven?"

Esteban nodded.

Henry continued, "Are you sure you're not in over your head? I know women like her. She might be too much for you, man."

Esteban shook his head. "Stop. Just get to know her, and you'll see what I'm talking about."

"All right, but I'm glad you're getting the prenup, that's all I'm saying."

"What the hell is wrong with you, man? Would you just fucking cool it, already?" Henry looked at Marialena walking toward them. When she arrived at the table, she sensed that they were discussing her. The table was tense.

"Everything okay?" she asked, looking at Esteban first and then at Henry as she sat down next to Esteban.

Henry laughed under his breath. "Yeah, please, sit down. I hear congratulations are in order. Let's see it." Marialena smiled, but Esteban didn't look too happy. "Wow. Mom's ring. It looks amazing. You do it justice." Henry held her hand a moment to look, and Marialena resisted the urge to take it away. It was his mother's ring,

265

after all. Finally, he let go. "Did you have to get it resized?"

"No, actually. It fits perfectly."

"How about that. Esteban, you didn't resize it?"

"No, it was meant to be," Esteban said, still a little upset.

"Let's get a bottle of champagne to celebrate. It's New Year's Eve after all," Henry said. Esteban shrugged, but Marialena smiled warmly.

"Sure, let's do it."

When the champagne arrived, Henry raised his glass to his brother and Marialena. "To you both. Congratulations...and to the New Year."

They clinked glasses and Henry asked Marialena and Esteban what their plans were for the night.

"My boss is having a party," Marialena said, wondering if she should extend the invitation to Henry.

"Oh yeah, Esteban mentioned that you took a job with the director guy."

"Yes, Patrick Denny. I'm his new assistant, though I haven't really started yet."

"That's a pretty impressive boss you have there. He won the Oscar last year, if I recall correctly."

"He did," she replied.

"And what sort of things would an assistant do for a man like that? I know you haven't started yet, but you must know what you've gotten yourself into. Anyway, I'm curious."

Esteban looked at his brother. "Henry, come on man. Stop with the grilling."

"Hey, I'm just asking questions here. Marialena, you don't mind, do you?"

She did mind, and she didn't like what he was insinuating. Or maybe she was just imagining it. "Honestly, I don't really know yet. I think I'll be screening his calls and taking notes, that kind of thing. He's working on a film now, so we're going to be pretty busy for a while. As soon as I know more, I'll fill you in," she said firmly. "What about you? Esteban tells me you run a restaurant in Temecula?"

"My business. Of course you'd be interested in that, seeing as how it's going to be half yours," he said, testing her.

Marialena gave Esteban a confused look. Esteban decided to speak up.

"Knock it off, why are you being such an asshole?"

Henry shrugged. "Am I? I'm sorry." He took a deep breath. "You're right." Henry took his empty glass and refilled it. "Marialena, my apologies. I'm sorry."

"It's okay," she said, trying to be civil.

"Oh, so the business. Normally I wouldn't confess this, but you're practically family. The business isn't doing so well. Honestly, Temecula is getting younger and younger. More and more hipsters are coming out on the weekends. I think it's time to mix things up, change the menu, the décor. I've been putting it off for a year or so, but I think this is the year to finally do something about it."

"I imagine it can get pretty crazy out there during the summer, with the wine festivals and all," Marialena said.

"The wine festival is just one weekend, but honestly, it's growing out there. There's always a wedding, always some kind of event. Craft beer is in and rail drinks are out.

So, I've been thinking about adding more of a beer selection, adding some more local wines, maybe a wine tasting night. I don't know. There are so many directions I could go, but I just don't know if I want to invest in it. I'm kind of wondering if I should sell the place, take the money, and go a different way. I'm still undecided."

Marialena nodded, trying to forget the awkwardness from a few minutes earlier. It was obvious Henry felt threatened, but she didn't know why.

"Anyway, this guy owns half of it. What do you think, Steven?" Henry asked his brother.

Esteban sat back in his chair. "Oh, I don't know. Craft beers sound like a good idea. Organic food, some kind of crazy hamburger. Kids nowadays seem to go for that kind of thing."

"I didn't know you owned half," Marialena said, turning to her fiancé. "That's so cool,"

"It's just on paper. He runs the thing. It's all him. I've been trying to give him my half for a while now, but he's stubborn."

"I like having you on paper. It keeps me grounded, and it also keeps me from doing anything too crazy. Anyway, Marialena, you should come check it out. Have a look around. Dinner would be on the house."

Henry started to relax. He looked at Marialena, who was sitting up straight and attentive. She wore a black dress and a black blazer. He couldn't see her body too well, but when she had walked to the bathroom, he had gotten a good look at her ass. She was stunning, and his first reaction was that he felt a little jealous, something he had never felt toward his brother before.

268

"Oh yeah, sounds like fun," she said and smiled at Henry, who was looking directly at her.

"Make it a nice little weekend getaway. We have a lot of wineries down there."

She was gorgeous. And someone like her was marrying his brother. Esteban must have been right. Maybe she was different. Sudddenly, Henry wanted to know more about her, but didn't know where to start.

"Yeah, I've been to Temecula, actually. Where is the restaurant located?" Marialena asked.

"In Old Town."

"Oh, I've never been to Old Town."

"Why on Earth would you pass up Old Town?" Henry asked, smiling.

Marialena shrugged. "I don't know. I guess I didn't know what I was missing."

The rest of the dinner seemed to go smoother, and Esteban finally started to feel more at ease.

"Well, I'm glad you got me out here," Henry said, getting up. "I have a couple of parties lined up tonight. You two have fun. Marialena, it was nice to meet you. Take care of my brother, will you?" He hugged her quickly, and then he hugged Esteban, towering over him. "Hey, I love you, man," Henry said and looked into his older brother's eyes to make sure they were cool. He gave Marialena a smile. He wanted to learn more about her, but the evening was over. He'd have to figure her out another time.

Esteban nodded. "Love you too. Be safe out there tonight."

When they got in the car, Esteban did not hesitate to apologize for his brother's behavior.

"It's okay. It's not your fault. He wasn't that bad," she said.

"It's not okay, he was being an ass," he replied.

"Look, it wasn't perfect and I am not sure if he likes me or not, but it doesn't really matter to me. Does it matter to you?"

"Of course it matters. He's my brother."

"Okay, so he's family. He'll come around. Maybe my age was a shock. Did you tell him beforehand?"

"I did. He didn't like it at first. Still, that's no reason to be disrespectful."

Marialena put her hand on Esteban's knee. "It's okay. We'll get through it. Maybe it won't be so bad next time we see him. But it's New Year's Eve, let's try to have a good night."

Henry had come off a little rough around the edges, and she had no idea why. Esteban had described him as being the life of the party, but he hadn't seemed that way. He seemed bitter and upset, and Marialena wasn't sure why. She tried to put thoughts of their dinner away as she glanced at her phone. The party at Patrick's was supposed to start at ten. They needed to get home to change.

When they got back, Esteban lay in bed in his boxers. He watched Marialena as she put on her new dress.

He sat up, shirtless and rock hard. "My god, you're a vision." She walked toward him and sat on top of him, hitching up the skirt so that she could wrap her legs around him. He kissed her hard on the mouth and started to pull the zipper.

"I don't know if I want you with the dress or without."

She put her hands on the back on his head, rustling his short hair, and smiled. "Your choice," she said.

"This is tough," he said, and pulled her dress down past her breasts.

"Careful," she said.

"I think it needs to come off." She got off of him and turned around as he finished unzipping it. When both of their clothes were off, he left the lights on and climbed on top of her hungrily.

Marialena laughed underneath him. "We're already late."

"No one is ever on time," Esteban said and dove into her mouth. He entered her and moaned loudly. He kissed her all over and was able to finish quickly.

Marialena brushed hair away from her face. "Wow, that might have been the quickest sex I've ever had," she said, feeling very relaxed.

Esteban lay on his back, his hands behind his head. "Man, that dress is dangerous."

"Think you'll be able to keep your hands off of me long enough for me to put it on again?"

Esteban laughed and moved next to her, putting an arm around her naked body. "I'm good for a while, but I can't make any promises when we get to the party."

"I love you," she said, never getting tired of saying it to him.

"I love you too."

She stayed in bed with him for a few minutes, not wanting to get up. She looked in the mirror in his bedroom and noticed how disheveled her hair had

271

gotten during sex, but it looked appropriate for the evening. It was just enough out of place that it looked like she tried to make it look that way.

She retouched her makeup and watched Esteban in the reflection behind her. He was going to wear one of his suits. She moved to give him more space and kissed the very back of his neck, careful not to get any makeup on his collar. She peeked at him in the reflection, remembering the first time he had done that with her when they came home from the fundraiser. "That was amazing," he said, looking at her. "I am one lucky man."

"We're both lucky." Marialena smiled at him in the reflection, then stepped aside to let him finish tying his tie. She put on her jewelry and he dropped his blazer on the bed while he tied his shoes. They left a few minutes later.

Marialena was getting nervous as Esteban drove to Patrick's, who lived deep within the hills in Bel-Air. She was going to have to drive this same route, through the winding hills, and hated the idea of it, but this is what she signed up for.

"Am I ever going to get used to driving through all this?"

"Sure. Once you do it enough, you'll get used to it," he said.

It was almost eleven p.m. and the party was buzzing. Esteban held her hand as they walked through the crowd. A waiter walked by with a glass of champagne. They each grabbed one.

"Hey, that's Patrick over there." He was laughing with a group of people, and Marialena waved. He excused himself and walked over. He shook Esteban's hand, then hugged and kissed Marialena on the cheek. He was careful not to say anything about how Marialena looked in front of Esteban. She was going to work for him now, so he had to be a gentleman.

"Marialena, Esteban, thanks for coming."

"Your house is amazing," Marialena said.

"Thank you. It's home for now. As you know, you'll probably be working out of here some of the time. Listen, I have those documents for you. We can step away to somewhere quieter. Esteban, if you don't mind."

Marialena looked at Esteban and he said he'd find a drink by the bar and stay close. Marialena followed Patrick into his office, which was really more of a library with a desk. Marialena gushed at all the books he owned.

"I had no idea you were a reader."

Patrick laughed. He watched as Marialena glanced at some of the titles. She crossed her arms, feeling a little cold in this room. That's when Patrick noticed what looked like an unorthodox engagement ring on her left hand.

Patrick had a file sitting on top of his desk. He sat down and handed it to Marialena. She opened it and read it carefully.

"Wait, this says you're going to pay me sixteen thousand dollars if you have to let me go. Is that right?"

Patrick nodded. "A small sum as a token of my gratitude. But don't get too excited. I don't plan on firing you." He smiled warmly. "And of course, it doesn't count if you do something to get yourself fired."

"No, I get that. Thank you. That's a generous package."

273

"There's a check attached to the back. It's a beginner's bonus. You might have to find a dress in a pinch in case we have to go out somewhere on a moment's notice. My advice, take two-thirds of that and go shopping. Save the other thousand in case you need it later."

"Jesus, Patrick, this is too much. I don't need all of this."

Patrick shrugged. "You do this well enough on your own, but I want people to see you and think success. I want you to not only act the part, but to look the part. This is just going to help. Take it, please. I insist."

Marialena smiled and closed the file. "Thank you so much. I hope I'm worth it."

"You are. And I'm not the only one who thinks so," he said and held out his hand to look at her ring. "Is this what I think it is?"

"Yeah, we're engaged," she said shyly.

"Congratulations. That's wonderful. Wow. It's a beautiful ring."

"It was his mom's ring. She wanted to keep it in the family."

She looked absolutely radiant, but she was shy and he didn't know why.

"Are you happy?"

"Yes. Very happy."

He searched her eyes, and she knew she was giving off a vibe that maybe she wasn't happy, so she came clean.

"We met with his brother today and broke the news to him. He was less than thrilled. I thought he'd be happy for his brother, but honestly, I just felt kind of cheap. Like my age made me less than worthy."

Patrick went to Marialena's side and put an arm around her. "Listen, don't let anyone get in the way of your happiness. Honestly, you're going to run into that from time to time. And you know what? Fuck them. It's not their lives. This is your life, your moment, and your time to shine in the sun," he said warmly. "Now, his brother is a different matter and I get it. He's just looking out for Esteban. But Marialena, please don't ever let me hear you say that someone made you feel cheap again. You should know better than to let that get to you."

"I know you're right. I'll get over it. It'll pass."

"I don't want you to be the least bit upset tonight. Not here, under my roof on New Year's Eve. Aside from that, you two are happy?"

Marialena smiled at him, the twinkle coming back. "Yeah, we are. This has been amazing and I couldn't be happier. Esteban means the world to me."

"Good. I'm glad. Congratulations again. Look, I was planning on making an announcement and introducing you to everyone officially. May I also announce your engagement? We have some press here, so it might get out. I won't do it if you don't want me to, but it could be good publicity for Esteban."

"I don't mind, but I have to run it by him first."

"Of course. I'd like to introduce you either way, but we don't have to mention the engagement."

"Okay." Marialena looked at the time. "It's going to be midnight soon. When were you planning the announcement?"

"Soon...before midnight. Come find me when you're done talking it over with Esteban."

Marialena folded up the check and documents and put them inside her clutch.

Patrick walked out with Marialena and she made a beeline for the bar. She found Esteban right away.

"Patrick is going to announce my new position to the party. He wanted to acknowledge our engagement as well. What do you think?"

She looked at Esteban for his reaction, and she could tell he was unsure. Then he looked into her eyes and nodded.

"Sure, why not?" he said, bracing himself for what was to come.

"He said the press is here."

Esteban nodded. "Okay, that's fine." Esteban's heart started beating a little faster, but he was excited. Marialena found Patrick across the room and nodded at him. He nodded back and motioned for them to follow him.

Marialena took Esteban's hand and followed Patrick up the stairs. They stood on the second floor, which was closed off to the party. Patrick stood against the railing and the music died down.

"Ladies and gentleman. Thank you for coming tonight. I'm pleased you could be here, and there's a reason I wanted to gather all of my friends and family under one roof. Many of you who know me on a personal level know that I'm not the best at keeping my appointments or returning phone calls." There was laughter in the crowd. "The truth is, I've been incredibly lucky in this business and a lot of it is thanks to all of you.

I could not have gotten to where I am now without you. Unfortunately, it comes with a price, and that price is not being able to give each and every one of you the time that you deserve. Keeping up with appointments, meetings, and phone calls has been difficult for me, mostly because I can't read my own handwriting." More laughter from the crowd. "Also, because I forget to charge my phone. And you deserve better than that. I need some help in my life and so I threw this party in honor of a wonderful young lady who is going to be my right hand. I'd like you all to meet Marialena Villanueva." He reached out for her hand and she let him. She stood next to him and smiled.

"Marialena is going to be my personal assistant for the foreseeable future. She starts in a few days, so if you need anything from me, please wait until January 4th, when she officially starts." More laughter. "She's a fantastic woman, and yes, she does take bribes in the form of coffee." Marialena laughed and nodded to the crowd.

"Anyway, I'm not the only lucky man in this room. I have one more announcement. Ladies and gentleman, it has come to my attention that we are graced by the presence of Esteban Gutierrez. He's a director whose work is very close to my heart." He waved Esteban over and he took his place next to Marialena. She noticed a few pictures being taken of the three of them.

"Now, I was just informed that I am going to have to share Marialena with this man. Please join me in congratulating these two on their engagement. May they find love and happiness in the upcoming new year, and forever thereafter."

Esteban smiled and held Marialena close while everyone clapped. She whispered into his ear, "I can't believe this is happening."

They walked down the steps and got bombarded right away, now that the guests knew who he was. Marialena heard 'congratulations' coming from every direction. Some people tapped her on the shoulder, some asked to see her ring, and some confronted Esteban and introduced themselves. Producers, directors, actors. When midnight struck, they each had a glass of champagne in hand and Esteban took her in his arms and kissed her, long and hard. Marialena could hear people cheering around them.

"I love you," he said, not turning around to look at anyone else.

"I love you back."

"Happy New Year."

"Happy New Year to you." She looked around and people where hugging and kissing. Some reached out for her or for Esteban, and they hugged people around them. A woman put her arms around Esteban's neck. Esteban laughed and played along, but it was uncomfortable for him. Marialena could tell, so she took his hand and led him into the kitchen, where the staff was enjoying champagne too.

They hung out in the kitchen for a few minutes, laughing. He put his arms around her. "So how did that feel, up there in front of all those people?"

Marialena smiled. "I was so nervous."

"You were perfect."

"How'd you feel?" she asked, her eyes dancing.

"Like the luckiest man alive," he said.

278

She smiled as they waited for the noise to die down a little bit.

"How much longer do you want to stay?" she asked.

"Do you feel like you have to stay and mingle?"

"Maybe for a little bit, actually."

"All right. Just say when. Give me a signal or something, and we'll be on our way."

"Okay."

"You ready?" he asked her, and she nodded. They continued to hold hands in between meeting people. Sometimes he would let go, or sometimes she would, to talk to someone, but they always reached out for each other. They felt very close to one another that night.

Chapter Eighteen

It was mid-morning and Marialena was sitting cross-legged on the couch, watching TV, when she heard the buzzer at the front door. She wondered if Esteban had forgotten his keys when he left for his morning run. She unlocked the door and noticed that Esteban's keys were missing from the key dish. She wondered who could be on their way up and stayed close to the front door.

She looked through the peephole and saw Henry on the other side. He looked disheveled and was still in the same clothes from the night before, but he had lost his dress shirt and was in a plain white t-shirt. *Brothers*, she thought to herself. He smiled sheepishly as she let him in.

"Sorry, Esteban's not here right now. He's out running. He should be back soon, if you want to wait," she said, leading him inside. She felt a little nervous and wasn't sure what to expect.

"Good morning. Really, I just wanted to come over to apologize." He looked at Marialena, who was wearing a pair of leggings and an oversized sweater. Her hair was in up in a ponytail and she wasn't wearing any makeup, making her look younger than she had the night before. "I was an ass last night and I'm really sorry."

She set her hand on the back of the chair and Henry placed his hand on top of her left hand, feeling his mom's ring underneath.

"Hey, you want something to drink? Water? Coffee?" she asked, abruptly taking her hand away from his.

"Jesus, Marialena, I'm not going to hurt you," he said.

"Well, I'd like some water," she said, her back to him. "Sure I can't get you anything?"

"Fine, I'll take a glass of water," he said, taking a deep breath. "We got off on the wrong foot last night. Let me make it up to you and take you out to lunch. Is that café still around the corner?"

"I don't know if that's a good idea. I think Esteban will be home soon."

"You're not allowed to go to lunch?"

"It's not that," Marialena said, unable to make eye contact.

They heard keys jingling. Esteban came inside, drenched in sweat. He saw his brother and Marialena in the kitchen and they didn't look like they were having a casual conversation. Marialena gave him her glass of water.

"Thanks, babe. Hey, what's going on?"

"I came over to apologize. I'm sorry for being such a dick last night. I wanted to ask Marialena out to lunch, make it up to her, one on one."

Marialena looked at Esteban, but he didn't say anything. He took a large gulp of water instead.

"Marialena, what do you say?" Henry asked.

"I'm not really up for it," Marialena said, feeling guilty for saying no.

"Esteban, would you just tell her I'm not a bad guy. I feel terrible for the way I acted." He turned back to

281

Marialena. "Marialena, come on. Who knows when I'm going to see you guys again?"

Marialena was quiet for a moment. "Okay, fine," she said and put an arm around Esteban's sweaty neck. Henry did not look away. "Is that okay?"

"Yeah, of course," Esteban replied.

Marialena put on some shoes and grabbed a scarf and her purse from the guest room.

"You didn't sleep last night, did you?" she asked him as they walked outside.

"I slept for a few hours this morning at a friend's house. I'll be fine."

They were silent for a few minutes. It was a cold morning, but thankfully it was a short walk.

"How was the party?" Marialena asked.

"Oh, it was a blast. You guys?"

"Our engagement was announced to everyone. So I guess it's official in the eyes of Hollywood."

They sat down; the place was surprisingly crowded. Neither of them needed a menu. Marielana ordered a coffee. Henry gave her a look. "No food?"

"I'm not hungry."

"Coffee, and I'll have a hamburger, extra fries." This time Marialena looked at Henry. "So you could have some," he said. Henry looked at her. "Okay, I have to ask one question, and then I promise I'll stop. Are you pregnant?"

"What? You saw me drink all that champagne last night. No, I'm not. But congratulations, you're the first to ask," she said.

"Look, I know you're going to marry my brother and all, but he *has* been my older brother for thirty-nine years. I love the guy too."

Marialena gave him a small smile. "Okay, that's fair."

Henry continued. "So, it's official in the eyes of Hollywood? Tell me, how do your parents feel about it?"

"Well, my parents died six years ago."

"I'm so sorry," he said.

"Thank you." Their coffee arrived and she smiled a little. "And you can spare me all of that daddy complex bullshit. It doesn't apply to me. I loved both of my parents very much, and we had a great relationship. When my parents were alive, I was nineteen years old and dated a twenty-eight-year-old for like six months. And they didn't mind, as long as he was nice. He *was* nice, but it didn't work out for other reasons."

"So, you think you just like older men?" he asked, taking a sip of his coffee and sitting back in the booth.

"I guess so. I just wish it wasn't a big deal. Who cares if there's an age difference?"

"Well, I think people care because they don't believe in love. Maybe people assume you're after his money or fame, and he's after the sex, because they don't see anything else."

"Do you believe in love?" she asked.

Henry shook his head. "No, I don't. I think that you can love someone, but true love? That's only for stories, movies. Esteban makes a lot of money making people fall for that shit."

"I don't agree with that."

"Before my brother, did you believe in love?"

283

"Sure. I believed it existed. I had never found it until now, but I believed it was out there." Marialena shrugged, then smiled. "I don't know. Guys my age aren't easy to fall in love with, for me anyway. The last guy I dated wasn't really into the same things. He liked going to bars, karaoke, video games, action movies, that kind of thing. Oh, and the worst, music festivals. I hate music festivals!" she said, laughing.

Henry laughed with her. "You hate music festivals?"

"Burning Man, Iron Man, whatever it's called."

"Coachella?"

"Yes! They're the worst. It's so much nicer to just sit at home, drink a glass of wine or two, light a fire or something, and just listen to the album."

"Hate to break it to you kid, but Esteban's favorite thing is Coachella. Every year. He hasn't mentioned it to you?"

Marialena laughed. "It is not."

"I'm surprised it hasn't come up. Yeah, he has this weird appreciation for desert festivals."

Henry turned his plate around so she had easy access to his fries. "Help me with this, please."

She leaned in and grabbed a french fry. "You're nicer than I am. I don't let anyone steal my fries."

"Why do I think I ordered extra?"

"Thanks for getting me to come out. I have to ask though, what was going on last night?"

"You mean, why was I being such an asshole?"

"Okay, your words not mine," she said, not wanting to be impolite.

Henry thought for a second and took a deep breath. "You know, when Esteban told me the news that he was

284

getting married to someone your age, I was doubtful. But as soon as I saw you, as soon as I saw the ring, something in me shifted. I panicked. It's weird. I don't know why it happened, but for some reason, I felt like I wanted what he had. I wished I were sitting across from my brother telling him I'm getting engaged. And I sort of took it out on you. I'm sorry."

Marialena nodded, taking it all in.

He continued, "I couldn't get it out of my head last night. Basically, I got jealous." He took another sip of his coffee. "I don't believe in signs, but what if it's a sign that I should get my life together?"

"You don't have your life together?"

"I don't know, I kind of thought I did. I guess I feel like I'm missing something. Or I'm freaking out that I should be feeling that I'm missing something. I don't know, I'm still trying to figure out what exactly *I am* feeling."

"What are you looking for?" she asked.

"I have no idea. I haven't been looking."

"I wasn't looking either, and I found Esteban. You never know what fate has in store."

"Fate? Come on," he said dismissively.

"No, I'm serious. Maybe seeing the ring *was* a sign, and maybe you're finally ready to deal with it."

"I guess we'll find out," he said, not wanting to be too rude. He liked her, and he didn't know why. It was something about her eyes, something about the way she looked at him.

"Another coffee for the lady and the check, please. Oh fuck it, I'll take another coffee as well," he said. He turned to her and smiled. "I can't tell if a second coffee right now is a good idea or a bad idea."

"So where was this party you went to?"

"A friend's house in Venice. She has a place near the canals. It was a bitch to find parking, but otherwise it was fun."

"A woman friend? And you slept on the couch, so not a lover?"

"Former lover. We're just friends now," he said, blushing a little bit.

"Are you seeing anyone back in Temecula?"

"That depends," he said, showing his dimples. "Are you asking me out?"

"My guess is no," she said, not answering his question. "Otherwise, you would have spent New Year's there."

"You guess correctly," he said.

On the way back to Esteban's condo, Marialena asked him if he was okay for the drive back to Temecula.

"Maybe you should just sleep in the guest room for a few hours. You don't look too hot."

"Gee, thanks," he said and smiled at her. "But yeah, maybe I will. Thanks for taking a chance on me. I'm sorry again. I was rude, and you didn't deserve it. And you know, if things don't work out with you and Esteban, you could keep me in mind. We can keep the ring in the family," he said playfully.

"I thought you were picky."

"Oh, I am being picky. He's a lucky man. I'm really happy for the both of you."

They walked into the condo and Esteban was on his laptop.

"So, we made up. Everything is fine. This family will stay together," Henry announced.

"Is it okay if your brother stays to sleep for a few hours? I don't think he should be driving home right now."

"Yeah. You need to catch some zzz's?"

"I probably should," Henry said. They shared a look. "You've got a great lady there," Henry pointed out, apologizing to his brother with his eyes.

"Thanks, I think so, too. But yeah, you should find whatever you need in the guest room. Sleep as much as you need to, we're not going anywhere."

"All right, see you guys in a few hours." He thanked Marialena and headed toward the guest room.

A few hours later, Marialena was getting cold and wanted to throw on a warmer pair of pants and some socks. But her clothes were in the guest room where Henry was sleeping. She knocked on the bedroom door softly, but Henry was sound asleep in the bed. She made a beeline to the drawers, but heard him stirring when she rummaged through her clothes.

"Hey," he said groggily.

She turned around. "Sorry, I was just looking for something warmer," she said, seeing him in bed.

"No, it's okay. I'm invading your space," he said.

"Got them. Sorry to wake you."

"Hey, come here for a second," he said, into the darkness. Marialena didn't move. "Come here, I'm not going to bite." Marialena walked towards him uneasily.

"Thanks for this afternoon. That was pretty great. Again, I'm sorry," he said and sat up, the comforter falling down and exposing his naked chest. He had tattoos on

287

his arms, but she didn't look long enough to see what they were. He watched her tense up. She looked so vulnerable. He wanted nothing more than to kiss her. He laughed instead. "Are you ever going to feel comfortable around me?"

Marialena shrugged. "You should get some more rest," she said, not unkindly. She left him in the room, ignoring his question, unsure about his intentions. She told Esteban she was going for a walk. He asked her if she needed company, but she held out her phone.

"I want to wish Roxanne a Happy New Year."

"Okay, be careful."

"Happy New Year!" she yelled into her phone, when Roxanne answered.

"Wow, you're excited." Roxanne said, not matching Marialena's energy. "Happy New Year."

"How was your party?" Marialena asked.

"Not as exciting as yours, I bet."

"Patrick announced that Esteban and I are engaged. It was so sweet."

"Some job you have. So dull," Roxanne said sarcastically.

"Okay, all joking aside, I have a serious dilemma."

"Spill it."

"As you know, I met Esteban's brother last night. I'm picking up on some heavy flirtation. And this is so weird. Nothing like this ever happened to me before. It's like, I find one man, and now they decide to all come running. What the hell?"

"It's because you never went out before and now you're meeting all these interesting people."

"But his own brother? Isn't that weird?"

288

"You said he was ten years younger?"

"Yeah."

"Thirty-nine to your twenty-seven?"

"Okay, so?"

"So, are you attracted to him?"

"What?"

"I mean, are you attracted to him? What does he look like? Is he hot?"

"He's different from Esteban. I don't know."

"Answer the question. Marialena, it's simple. Do you find him attractive?"

"I am engaged to his brother. *Hello*."

"Okay, so you won't answer, which means he probably is. And let's be fair here, you've only known Esteban for what, two months? What if Esteban wasn't in the picture? Would you be attracted to Henry?"

"No, I mean, he reminds me of Patrick. Like all he needs to do is sleep with me and the spell would be broken. Maybe this is some kind of test. It's just seems so unfair. Why is this happening all at once? I was single for so long, and nothing."

Roxanne laughed.

"What?" Marialena said, half annoyed, half amused.

"Oh, life isn't really as hard as you're making it out to be, that's all."

"I know, but I can sense something with Henry. Not so much on my end, but on his. I swear, I think he likes me."

"So what?"

"So, what do I do about it?"

"He lives in Temecula, right? So you don't do anything. Let him deal with that shit. So, he thinks you're

289

hot? Marialena, you *are* hot. Get used to it. Jesus Christ, it's not the end of the world."

"No one else in the past five years has looked at me the way he does."

"Henry?"

"And Esteban. And Patrick."

"That's because you finally let them see you."

"I don't know. I guess it all revolves around Esteban, doesn't it? I let my wall for him down when I thought he was Patrick, and of course I laid it down for Henry, who's his brother."

"There you go, it sounds like it was really Esteban all along."

"I mean, I know that, but it feels like they're waiting for me to change my mind." Marialena sighed. "I miss you."

"I miss you too."

When Marialena walked back into the condo, she found Henry in a fresh set of clothes, ones that she didn't recognize.

"Nice wardrobe change. You're looking less dodgy this evening," Marialena said and smiled.

"Yeah, I keep spare clothes in the car."

"You're such a bachelor," she said.

"Hey, it's always good to be prepared. You never know when you're going to spend the night at your brother's on New Year's Day."

Esteban was in the kitchen grabbing a couple of beers. "Yeah, I convinced him to stay for dinner."

"Don't go all out, man. Let's just order a couple of pizzas or something. Stay in, watch some college football."

290

"Pizza? You know, I have no idea where to even order pizza around here," Esteban admitted. "I'm not the ordering in kind of guy. I'm always cooped up in here, so sometimes going out to get food is my only chance to escape."

Henry took out his phone. "Lucia's. There, easy."

"Well, sure. I've *been* there," Esteban said.

"What shall we get? One pepperoni, one sausage?"

"Yeah, that's fine. I probably won't have any, so order whatever you want," Marialena said.

"No pizza? What on earth is wrong with you?" Henry asked.

"I love pizza. But if they have salad, order me one. All this eating out is too much for me."

"Why do you pick all the weird ones?" he asked, thinking of Laura.

Esteban threw a pillow at him.

Marialena brought her glass of wine and sat next to Esteban. She scooted close to him as he put an arm around her. Henry looked at them out of the corner of his eye and couldn't remember the last time he felt comfortable with someone that same way. Every relationship Henry had been in the past five years started and ended with sex. There had been nothing else. And for the first time in his life, he felt he was missing something. Esteban and Marialena looked so happy and at peace with each other. Henry turned his thoughts back to the game and brought the beer bottle to his lips. A little while later, Marialena announced that she was going to take a nap and excused herself to Esteban's room, leaving the two brothers together.

"Hey, so what do you think about me selling the restaurant?" Henry asked his brother.

"That's your project. If you want to do it, just do it."

"I know. I'm just worried about dropping all this money on a makeover. I've been kind of mulling it over. What if I come out here?"

"You'd want to move here?"

"Sure, being closer to family might be nice," Henry said, thinking about Marialena.

"Now that I'm getting married and all, it would be nice to have family closer. I worry about Marialena. She doesn't have anyone out here."

"Yeah, she told me about her parents' death. She didn't really go into too much detail, but man, that's rough."

"I've talked to her cousin Roxanne about her parents' death, but only briefly. I haven't been able to get too much out of Marialena either, but I think she might have some...trouble with it."

"What kind of trouble?"

"I don't think she sleeps much when I'm not around. I can't say for sure, but what if I have to go away to shoot? I could be gone for a few months. I'd hate to leave her here, all alone."

"Dude, whatever you need, I can be here. For you, for her."

The two brothers sat in silence for a few minutes.

"So, you think I should sell?" Henry asked. "Move closer?"

"If you want to, I think you should."

"It might be a good idea to stay here for a week, feel out the market. Maybe I should. January is super slow. I could take some time off."

"Sure. You can stay here if you want."

"You know what I just realized? We haven't slept under the same roof since Mom died."

Esteban sighed. "Yeah, I guess we haven't."

"It's like she's bringing us together through Marialena."

Esteban looked at him. "You think so?"

"I don't know. Maybe I'm just getting sentimental," he said.

"Maybe. Hey, you said January was a slow month for you? How's February?"

"Much of the same. Why?"

"Well, I sort of have plans coming up that would take me out of Los Angeles for a little while. Rob Anderson, a good producer friend of mine asked me to join him at his cabin in the mountains. He's letting me use his place on my own, which is great for me as a writer. But he's going to be there the first couple of days with me. It's at the beginning of February. He, uh, might have some financial pull on the next project of mine. I agreed to it before Marialena and I got serious. Anyway, I was thinking about canceling my trip because I didn't want to leave her, but if you could find a reason to come out here the week I'd be gone, that would be great."

"Why can't you just take her with you?"

"If she's working for Patrick, he's going to need her that week, with the Oscars and all."

"He's going?"

293

"I'm sure he will. He won the Oscar for best picture last year."

"What makes you think she'd stay here and not at her own place?"

Esteban shrugged. "I could say that I want her to make sure you don't use my place as a bachelor pad."

Henry laughed. "I'm not that bad, am I?"

Esteban smiled. "I think she'd buy it."

"What kind of problems are we talking about here, with Marialena I mean?"

"I'm not really sure. It could be nothing. But I don't want to leave her without knowing for sure. From what I can tell, her parents' death has hit her hard."

"I can imagine. But yeah, I could come by. Sure."

Esteban nodded and looked at his brother. "So, I'll take this trip and you're okay to stay here?"

"Yeah, of course. It's totally fine."

"All right, thanks, man."

Marialena came out to join them for the second half of the game.

"I don't know what's wrong with me. I'm so tired today."

Marialena curled up with Esteban on the sofa. She put her head in his lap while he placed an arm on her hips. The guys were cheering and hollering, yelling at the TV. Marialena fell asleep again and in no time she was knocked out. Henry saw Esteban's hand moving around her body, underneath the blanket.

"She's burning up. I should turn down the electric blanket," Esteban said in a whisper.

Henry got up and looked for the heat control, his hand brushing up against her ankle. She was so warm, and Henry realized he was getting cold too.

He took some of the blanket that was bunched up by Marielana's feet and he covered himself with what was left. Marialena woke up when he sat down and she made more room for him. But then she felt uncomfortable with Henry so close to her, so she sat up, feeling a little warm.

"Hey, we just turned it down," Esteban said.

"Oh, thanks."

"You missed one hell of a game."

"It's okay, I'm not into sports," she said, stretching. She decided to take off her sweater. She was wearing one of Esteban's t-shirts underneath. Henry tried not to look, but he noticed that she wasn't wearing a bra. As if reading his mind, Marialena brought up the blanket to her chin and sat there for a few minutes with the guys before she decided to go off to bed again.

Marialena woke up the next morning before the guys and made breakfast. Eggs, bacon, toast, jam, and coffee.

Henry was the first one out of bed. He sat down at the table while Marialena finished the bacon.

"So, I was talking to my brother and I want to make sure it's totally cool with you, but I think I'm going to come out for maybe a week in February. I'll probably stay here," he said, not mentioning anything about Esteban's trip.

"Yeah, it's Esteban's place, so it's really up to him."

"He's fine with it, but you live here too. I just thought I'd run it by you. Esteban will probably talk to

295

you about it. We just discussed it last night while you were sleeping."

"Yeah, sure," Marialena said, shrugging. "It's fine."

When Esteban woke up, he joined them in the kitchen and they all had breakfast together. Afterwards, Henry thanked both of them for their hospitality.

"All right, sounds like I'll be seeing you soon. I gave Marialena a heads-up about coming back in February."

Esteban nodded. He looked at Marialena and she smiled.

"Get home safe, brother."

When he left, Esteban turned to Marialena. "Hey, so you're comfortable with him coming up next month?"

"Yeah, sure. I mean, he's family right?"

Esteban sighed. "I have this trip planned for when he's coming."

"Oh, you do?" she asked quietly.

"Yeah, I didn't mention it before because honestly, I wasn't sure if I was going. But I think I should. It's a five-day trip to the Colorado Rockies. Anyway, my friend is going to be there for a couple of days, then he's leaving the place to me for the remainder of the trip, which would be great for my writing. He's going to help bring in money for my next picture, and I don't want to waste this opportunity, so I'm thinking I should go. I agreed to the trip right after I met you, and honestly, I was going to cancel it, but I don't know Marialena, I think I should go," he said.

"No, you should go. When in February?"

"Oscars week."

"Well, that's okay. I'm sure I'll be plenty busy. But why don't we just let Henry stay here alone? I could stay at my place."

"Marialena, I'd like it if you were under my roof. I'd feel better about you not being alone," he said, not using the excuse that he didn't trust Henry. "I wouldn't worry so much," he said, putting a hand on her face.

"Being here with your brother alone? Are you sure that's a good idea? I barely know him."

"He's a good guy. Trust me. But I would never ask you to do something you're uncomfortable with. Think about it."

She nodded. "Okay, I'll think about it."

Later that night, it was time for dinner. Marialena was wearing a new red dress that she bought for the occasion. Red, the color of love. She thought it would be perfect.

"I'd hate to sell my place or rent it out," she said. "I paid for it with the money from selling my parents' house. I don't know if I can get rid of it. And I don't like the idea of some stranger living there either. That's just too weird for me. I guess I'd want to hang on to it for a few months. See how I feel about it."

"It's paid in full?"

"Yeah, it is."

"Wow, okay. Sure, hold on to it for a while. And you don't have to move in with me right away if you don't want to. Take your time if you need it."

Marialena shook her head. "I want to be with you."

"There's room in the guest room to add a bookshelf, and we can buy a bigger place eventually. I'd hate for you to get rid of your things."

297

"I don't need those things. So much of that is from my past. I want to move on. I want to move on with you. It's all just stuff. I don't need it. I just don't want to let go of the condo. I just don't want to say goodbye to the space yet."

"Okay, so you want to officially move in?"

Marialena nodded. "Yes, I'd like that very much."

"Okay, so that's settled."

She smiled, feeling excited.

"I kind of love your space right now. I love being here. It's honestly good for me. It's helping me move on. Maybe we can make it our own over time, but not with the stuff at my place. New stuff. I think that's best."

"Okay, so let's talk about a wedding. We haven't really talked about it. What kind of wedding do you want?"

"God, I have no idea. I've never been the kind of girl who had that whole wedding thing mapped out. I can't imagine having a big wedding. How about you?"

"I can't say I've imagined a wedding for myself, either. This is new to me."

"Whatever kind of wedding it is, I would like for it to be small and intimate. But I definitely want a white wedding dress." Marialena looked across the table at him and smiled. "Wow, so we're officially living together."

"I know. I think we need to get a dresser for the room. For your clothes. I don't want you living out of the guest room."

Esteban took Marialena's hand across the dinner table.

"Lena, I'm so happy we're doing this," he said.

"Me too. It just feels right," she said.

Chapter Nineteen

It was a Tuesday morning and bitterly cold for Los Angeles. Marialena didn't want to get out of bed. She gently forced her arm in between Esteban's torso and arm, and he sleepily obliged.

"Happy birthday," Marialena said in a whisper.

Esteban stirred. "Mmmhm."

Marialena kissed his face. "Happy birthday," she said again.

"Thanks," Esteban said without opening his eyes.

Marialena gently pushed Esteban on his back, brought up the covers, and climbed on top of him, reaching for his groin.

"Okay, I'm up," he said with a small smile.

She took off her shirt and tried to fight the cold air in the bedroom. Esteban took one of her breasts in his mouth and turned her gently on her back.

Marialena giggled. "It's too cold," she said.

"I'll keep you warm," he said lustfully.

"You look amazing," she said.

"Not bad for a fifty-year-old?"

"Not bad at all," she said. "I want you."

Esteban kissed her forehead. Her skin was like satin. He pushed himself inside of her. Marialena tilted her head toward the wall behind her and let out a small sigh.

When he came, he held her body tightly and collapsed on top of her. Marialena smiled and ran a hand across his back.

"Was that my birthday present?" he asked. "Because I don't need anything else for the rest of my life."

Marialena lay in bed with him for a few more minutes. "I have to get up soon. I should be out by four or five tonight. You said we're meeting your brother at seven, right?"

Esteban rolled onto his back. "Yeah, we're meeting him there. A friend of his runs the place, but I've never been. The food is supposed to be amazing."

"Oh good, I need a few restaurant recommendations for my job with Patrick."

"Yeah, talk to Henry. That's his scene."

"Maybe I will. Okay, I'm jumping in the shower."

"Hey, mind if I jump in there with you?" Esteban asked.

Marialena nodded. "Yeah, but let me have a head start first."

He nodded, and a few minutes later, he joined Marialena in the steamy shower. He loved how she looked with her hair wet, water dripping down her face. He kissed her underneath the shower head, holding her body close to his.

When they came out of the shower, Marialena began to rush. "Sorry. I wanted to cook you breakfast, but I don't think I'll have time."

"I definitely prefer that shower to a breakfast," Esteban said, a towel around his face.

"I can't wait to do this with you for the rest of my life," she said, looking into his eyes.

"Me neither," he said.

Marialena was working out of Patrick Denny's office location. They sat in the cutting room going over scenes with the editor and editing assistants. The movie was coming out pretty well and Marialena was taking notes. They'd have to cut some scenes, but they kept in the fact that Julian, the main character, had a plain white room with no personality. Rosa questions it, but Julian kind of shrugs and admits that he feels like he has no personality, that's he lost and trying to figure out who he wants to be.

She sat next to Patrick on the couch. He made sure to ask the editors what they thought before making a final decision, but he always listened to what Marialena had to say when she spoke up. This made Marialena uncomfortable, but she kept reminding herself that Patrick had hired her for a reason and she had to have more confidence.

It was a busy day and she was exhausted when she came back from work. She felt a bit distracted. But as soon as she came home to Esteban, her work worries drifted away. She decided to give him his gifts before dinner because she just couldn't wait.

She had bought him a few gifts, some new sweaters, a wine delivery package, and a beer delivery package. She also got him a first edition of a book he really liked. She had everything wrapped and hidden in the guest room.

"Lena, these are great. I love this one," he said.

She looked at him in his new sweater. "I have to admit, I'm coming around to the color brown. It's very becoming on you."

"Why do you think I like it so much?" he asked with a smile.

"I also like greys on you too," she said, admiring him. "Well, there are more presents. No more clothes, unfortunately. I can't say I've pinpointed your style yet."

"That's probably because I don't have one," Esteban laughed.

Marialena handed him a gift bag.

"It's heavy," he said, opening it to find a six-pack of beer inside. He read the label and smiled. "Hey, what's this?"

"So, I'm going to have a different kind of beer mailed to you every month."

"Nice. I've never done anything like that before."

"Well, you're good for a full year."

"Thanks, love," Esteban said and kissed her.

"Here is the last one," she said and handed him the first edition book. He opened it and was elated.

"Where'd you get this?"

"I did some digging."

"I love this," he said, flipping the pages.

"I knew you would. I also know that you already have it."

"Yeah, but I don't have the first edition. Marialena, I love it. Thank you."

"Happy birthday, Esteban."

She realized it was time she got ready for dinner. She purchased something special for the occasion, a long black high-waisted airy skirt. She wore that with a low-neck leotard, exposing her cleavage.

When they arrived, Henry was already at the bar with another man. He introduced his friend as Sergio, who was the manager. She wondered if Sergio and Henry got into trouble together. They gave off that daredevil vibe.

"Nice to meet you both," Sergio said politely.

Henry watched Marialena as she shook hands with Sergio. She looked amazing in black and he wanted to focus on her chest, but he smiled into her eyes instead. He hugged his brother, and Sergio showed them to their table.

The place was classy, but warm. "So, fifty, huh?" Henry asked.

Esteban shook his head and smiled. "I know. It's crazy."

"Time sure does fly."

"And you still have ten years to catch up, you lucky bastard," Esteban said. The men ordered whiskeys, Marialena stuck to wine.

"To my brother Esteban, and to your new love. May I be as lucky when I'm your age."

Esteban smiled and took a drink from his whiskey glass. "That does mean you'd actually have to settle down one day, you know?" Esteban said with a laugh.

"My lack of a relationship always comes up," Henry said, looking at Marialena. "Do you believe this guy?"

"Hey, I'm your older brother. I'm supposed to look out for you. If I don't, who will?"

Henry shrugged, liking the attention. "I do well enough on my own."

"You're too skinny," Esteban said, laughing.

"Nah, it's all muscle."

"So Henry," Marialena said, "I need some places like this to recommend. Do you have any others up your sleeve?"

"What are you looking for? Food recommendations? Good atmosphere? Five star, dives?"

"A little bit of everything, actually. Part of my job will be setting up meetings and appointments at restaurants. Anything you can give me will be helpful."

"Yeah, I can compile a list. Check them out before you recommend them though; make sure they still exist. Places out here change owners and names or close down frequently. But I can come up with some. Give me your email later."

Marialena nodded. "Thanks."

"Henry, are you coming back to spend the night?" Esteban asked.

"Well, I might want to head out tonight, but yeah, I'd like to come back a little later."

"Oh, where you planning on going?" Marialena asked just to be polite.

"I don't know yet. The night is wide open," he replied, smiling his flashy smile. Marialena smiled with him; she couldn't help it. It was contagious.

"So, what are your big plans for the big five-oh?" Henry asked Esteban. "Besides the obvious," he said, motioning toward Marialena. "Anything different you want to try? Cross something off the old bucket list?"

Esteban thought for a second. "Well, you know, I definitely want to be healthier. I'm working out a little more." He sat back. "As for bucket lists? I don't know that I ever really had a list. Honestly, I wish I had made more movies by this age. But now that I am incredibly happy in

304

my personal life, I feel guilty, sort of. I want to spend as much time with Lena as possible, but I also have this story that I want to tell and it just sucks, the timing of it all.

"Maybe you're writing more *because* you're happy," Henry suggested.

"Yeah, could be. Catch-22."

"All that typing doesn't drive you crazy?" Henry asked Marialena.

Marialena laughed. "He doesn't use a typewriter, for crying out loud. I barely even hear it. Honestly, I like knowing that he's there, in his little writer's nook with that bookcase behind him. I always know where to find him."

Esteban smiled a guilty smile. Henry laughed. "It sounds like a waste of a damn fine relationship to me; no offense, brother."

Marialena scoffed at Henry, but was smiling.

"Hey man, I still find time for her," Esteban said with a laugh.

The food arrived, and the conversation turned to what Marialena and Henry would like to have accomplished by fifty. Marialena wanted a library, like Patrick's.

"I want a place I can just lose myself, tune out the world. No phones, no computer. Just books and all the adventures that await me there. A blanket, a comfy sofa, hot chocolate, and Esteban by my side."

Henry said that when he turned fifty, he wanted to rent a sports car, something flashy, and drive along the Pacific Coast Highway, go to the beach, and just lie in the sand, a beer or two by his side.

"To hear the sound of the waves as the sun goes down, reflecting in the ocean. Music coming from somewhere in the background. A beautiful woman by my side." Henry dared to look at Marialena for the last sentence. She looked away and blushed.

"Well, those all sound pretty good," Esteban said.

"And yet, you're stuck here with us," Henry said with a smile. "Way to dream big, Steven."

Esteban laughed. "Are you kidding? I'm with my two favorite people on the planet. This is good."

"Would you have wanted a big party? I have to admit, I can't really picture that for you," Henry asked Esteban.

Esteban shook his head. "Yeah, I'm not really the party type, actually. Marialena, this is perfect. This is all I want."

The check arrived, and Henry picked it up before Marialena could. "Allow me, please," he said warmly. Marialena thanked him.

Esteban and Marialena lingered around Henry as he said goodbye to Sergio.

"Hey, wait. It's your birthday, right?" Sergio asked Esteban. "Here, allow me to get a round for you guys. On the house."

"Okay, yeah, sure. You're only fifty once, right? Why the hell not?" Esteban said.

Henry ordered three whiskeys for them, instead of shots. Marialena found a round pub table for three near the bar area. This place was pretty cool, and the food had been amazing. She made a mental note to bring Patrick here.

Henry sat down next to Marialena, with Esteban on the other side.

"You like whiskey?" Henry asked.

"Not sure. I've never tried it."

"My bad. Want something else?"

Marialena shook her head. "No, this is fine. There's a first time for everything, right?"

"Oh shit," Henry whispered, seeing someone he recognized across the room. "The problem with being in the restaurant business is running into people you don't want to see. This guy, Jim, can be a total dick sometimes. I know him from Temecula. He owns a restaurant there, near mine."

The man in question approached the three of them. He was in his mid-forties, dressed nicely in a pair of slacks and a sports jacket. He was tall, like Henry.

"Hey Henry, coming out to try some decent food for a change?" Jim asked.

"I know the manager. What's your excuse?"

Jim laughed and turned his attention to Esteban briefly, but his eyes lingered on Marialena. "So, who's your company?" he asked, sizing her up in a way that made Marialena feel uncomfortable.

"This is my brother, Esteban. Esteban, this is Jim. He owns a place near me in Temecula."

"Hi, Jim. Nice to meet you."

"And this is my girlfriend, Marialena." Marialena stuck out her hand, but looked at Henry questioningly. "Er, fiancée. I mean she's my bro—" Henry said, realizing his mistake. But Jim didn't hear him try to clear it up and instead interrupted him.

307

"Fiancée ? Is that so?" he asked, laughing. He took Marialena's hand. "You don't mean to tell me that you're engaged to his imbecile of a man?" Jim asked. Marialena took her hand back and sat down, but didn't say anything. She looked at Esteban, who was smiling at the whole exchange.

"I'm surprised," Jim continued. "Henry, where have you been hiding this one? My god, if I had a woman like you, I'd be bragging all over town about it," he said, not taking his eyes off of her.

"Well, I guess it's a good thing I'm not marrying someone like you," Marialena said cooly. She said it with a smile on her face and took a sip of her whiskey.

"Ouch." Jim turned his attention back to Henry, who was still standing. Henry put an arm on the back of Marialena's chair for effect, deciding to go with it, since neither Esteban nor Marialena had said anything to clear up his mistake.

"I'll catch you around, though, yeah?"

"Yeah, I'm just finishing up here myself, but we're doing the whole coffee thing back at my table. The food really was great, though. See you around," Jim said and waved goodbye to the table. Esteban let out a big laugh as he left.

"Marialena, I am so sorry about that. Honest mistake," Henry said.

"It's okay. He was kind of a jerk. How do you know him, again?"

Henry took a large sip of his whiskey. "He's sort of like my competition. He owns a place similar to mine, on the same street, and we talk shit to each other all the time. But if I need something for the restaurant, I can usually rely on him to help me out. And vice versa."

"So, it's a love/hate relationship?" Esteban asked.

"Yeah, I guess. Anyway, I'm sorry, man. I didn't mean to—"

"Dude, don't even mention it. It's fine. It was funny as hell, though."

"Yeah, but I didn't like the way he looked at Marialena."

"I couldn't tell if that was at my expense or yours," Marialena admitted.

"I think he's just a dick in general."

Marialena nodded and tried the whiskey again.

"So, do you like the whiskey?" Esteban asked.

"It's not really my thing."

"Want me to finish it?" Henry asked. Marialena nodded and handed her glass to him.

"Slow down there, you still have to drive home," Esteban said to his brother.

Marialena watched him as he drank and she agreed with Esteban. "What kind of car do you drive? I could drive it back to Esteban's and make some coffee before you go back out."

"It's an automatic," he said. "Yeah, that's fine." He didn't really care anymore about going back out. They stayed for twenty more minutes.

"You guys about ready?" Esteban asked.

"Yeah, I think so," Henry said after downing one more whiskey before leaving.

They walked out into the breezy night and gave their tickets to the valet. Jim came out at the same time with his group of friends. The valet pulled up with Esteban's car and Esteban gave Marialena a quick hug. "Hey, I'll see you in a little bit," he said, whispering in her ear. He chuckled and said, "Put an arm around Henry; give this Jim guy a show."

Marialena smiled at Esteban, who was clearly enjoying this and didn't seem to mind. Esteban paid the valet, got into his car, and drove off.

Jim detached himself from his friends. Marialena reached for Henry's hand, who gave it to her without hesitation.

"Hey, so are you still planning on selling the restaurant?" Jim asked.

"Yeah, I've actually been in touch with a guy out here. I think he's interested."

"Anyone I know?"

Henry shook his head. "I don't think so." Henry's car pulled up. "Hey, so that's me."

Jim took one last look at Marialena, who stood there as Henry paid. Henry put his arm around Marielana's shoulders, and Marialena wrapped her arm around his waist.

"Where are you guys headed, anyway?" Jim asked.

"Out, not sure yet," Henry said.

"I was kind of hoping we could stay in. I've missed you," she said quietly to Henry, but loud enough for Jim to hear.

Henry shrugged, then smiled at Jim. "Well, what can you do?"

"Well, it was nice to meet you," Jim said, sticking out his hand. "You should bring her to Temecula sometime."

"In your dreams," Henry said, laughing.

Marialena got in the driver's seat. "Was that too much?" she asked, pulling away.

"No, that was just right," he said, looking at her. "Thank you."

"Is he going to find out that I'm marrying your brother? I'd hate for him to figure out the truth."

"That guy? No way. He doesn't know anything about my personal life and I doubt he'll find out."

"He seemed okay at the end, but I didn't like him. He gave me the creeps when we were at the bar."

"Yeah, he's an asshole. He just gives off this vibe that he and his place are better than me and mine. And when I told him I was selling, he laughed. He actually laughed."

"Instead of staying and re-modeling?"

"It's risky if I stay, and I'm not comfortable with anything that's risky. If I sell, I'll have all this capital and I could help out other restaurants. Plus, I kind of feel like everything is starting to fall into place at exactly the right time. With you and Esteban getting together, I realize that I want to be closer to him. I haven't been in so long. I know we were kidding inside when Esteban said that he needed to look out for me, but he does have this way of keeping me grounded. I went pretty wild in Temecula there for a while."

"Won't Los Angeles be more of a temptation?" she asked, not sure what he meant by wild.

"You'd think so. But not if I'm close to you guys." Henry looked out of the window. "Hey, do you want to stop somewhere before we go back?"

"I think you had enough to drink."

311

"See, that's what I mean. You're watching out for me," he said. "Besides, I didn't mean for a drink. Coffee, dessert, a walk around the beach or something?"

"I'd take you up on that, except it's Esteban's birthday."

"Fuck, that's right."

"I'll make the coffee when we get back. We can take it out on the terrace."

"Yeah, that sounds good actually."

"You still going out later?"

Henry laughed. "If I recall correctly, you said something about staying in because you missed me."

Marialena laughed.

"I'm kidding. Thanks for that, though." Henry leaned back and closed his eyes. "I wish someone somewhere were saying that about me."

Marialena felt sad for him in that moment. "One day, someone will."

He opened up one eye and looked at her. "You have too much faith in me." Henry exhaled loudly. "I don't think I'm going out tonight, actually. I'm getting tired. I'm turning into an old man."

"Let's see how you feel after some caffeine."

"Yeah, maybe. It might be kind of nice to stay in, though. See what it's like to live like Steven."

"It's not so bad," Marialena said, smiling. "You might like it." As she drove the short distance back to Esteban's, they sat quietly in the car, comfortable in their own silence.

Chapter Twenty

It was five days before the Oscars, and Marialena's job with Patrick was in full swing. She had been working for him for about five weeks and loved it. He was a great boss. They spent a lot of time on set, but filming was officially done, so Marialena worked out of his offices at the studio. This week, things were a little more exciting. There was so much to keep up with, even though Patrick would only be presenting an award.

She needed to make sure he had a limo, his tuxedo, and dinner beforehand. Marialena would go with him to the rehearsal, but she wouldn't be there for the actual night. It was expected that he'd take a date, and she needed to make sure his date had kept her own schedule of appointments. She had never been on the phone so much and she was actually glad she wasn't going. *Preparing* for the Oscars was hard enough. There weren't as many parties as she'd originally imagined. Patrick Denny was an A-list celebrity, so he'd be going to the best ones.

Esteban had left for his trip, and Henry wouldn't be coming out until the following night, so she decided to stay at her own place. At five, she finally fell into a fitful sleep and had to wake up three hours later to be at Patrick's by ten. He didn't really have to employ her five days a week and sometimes he just needed her to run errands, but she didn't mind. The editing of the film would be a lengthy process and she helped him with that, but he hated being cooped up, so they would go for walks or out to lunch.

She had managed to make it through the busy day, and had lots more coffee than she was used to. When it was time to call it a day, she texted Henry to see if he was at Esteban's yet.

"Yeah, got in about thirty minutes ago. Come on over; we can order a pizza and watch a movie."

When she got to Esteban's, she greeted Henry, who had mentioned that pizza was on the way, with a salad for her in case she wanted that instead.

"Hey, is everything okay? Rough day at work?" he asked, noticing that she looked drained.

"Well, it's Oscars week and yeah, it's been crazy. I'll be okay though. I'm just tired." She sat down on the couch and curled up with a blanket while he picked a movie for them to watch. She had fallen asleep before the food had even arrived and she didn't wake up once it had.

He wasn't sure if he should wake her or not. He ate while watching the movie on the couch near her. He put the uneaten food in the fridge, deciding to let her sleep.

"Hey, the movie is over," he whispered. "Marialena?"

She stirred.

"The movie ended. You slept right through it," he said.

"Oh, I'm sorry."

"It's okay. There's some pizza and a salad in the fridge. Are you hungry?"

"I'm too tired," she said.

"Are you feeling okay?"

314

Marialena nodded. "Yeah, I just couldn't sleep last night."

"I think you should try to eat before you go to bed."

"Okay, sure. Just let me try and wake up a little."

He watched her as she fell right back to sleep. He draped some of the blanket over his lap, feeling her toes on the left side of his leg. He walked to Esteban's room and turned down the blankets for her. Then he went back out and picked her up in his arms.

"I'm taking you to bed," he said. He set her down as gently as possible and covered her up with blankets. He sat there on the bed with her in the darkness and waited about twenty minutes. He finally walked into his room and fell asleep with her on his mind, wondering if she'd be okay.

The next morning, Marialena found herself in bed, still in a pair of jeans and her long-sleeved shirt. She hadn't remembered going to bed, but was thankful she had ended up there. She took a shower and got ready for work as quietly as possible. Before leaving, she left a note that simply said 'thank you' and posted it on the mirror in the bathroom, where she was sure he'd see it.

Work with Patrick was another busy day. He had made her laugh a lot that day while he told her story after story about the Oscars in-between phone calls.

"If you want to come next year, I can make arrangements. Hell, I can make arrangements this year. I'm sure I can find someone who owes me a favor."

"No, I'm good. I want to wait until Esteban gets nominated or presents or something," she said.

"You two lovebirds. How is everything by the way?"

"Great, he's away right now. But it's great."

"Has a wedding date been set?"

"No, not yet. We aren't in a hurry. I think it's going to be a small wedding."

"Good choice. Small is the way to go these days."

"I agree."

Later, when she got to Esteban's that night, the place was empty, but Henry arrived half an hour after she did.

"How was your day?" she asked.

"Great. I think this restaurant deal is actually going to go through. Now I just have to look for a place to live."

Marialena was in the kitchen, thawing some chicken.

"That's great. I'm making dinner."

"Yeah? What are you going to make?"

"Lemon roasted chicken, veggies, and pasta on the side. Probably the salad you ordered last night too."

"Yeah, that sounds great."

"Sorry about falling asleep on you last night. I just didn't get much sleep the night before. I felt like a zombie as soon as I got here."

Henry leaned against the counter, looking professional and handsome. Marialena couldn't help but notice how tall he looked right now, in Esteban's kitchen, or how attentive he was.

Henry sat down to dinner. "If you don't mind me asking, why are you having trouble sleeping? Everything okay at work?"

"I used to have really bad insomnia after my parents died. Really bad. It was awful. Right after they died, I couldn't sleep, I couldn't eat. I got my own place, but it didn't help," she said, rushing through the words. "When

I did manage to sleep, I would wake up with terrible nightmares. It lasted more than a year or so, but somehow, little by little, it went away. I don't think I was ever really okay, but I was okay enough to support myself. I was able to focus at work and everything, but as soon as I got home... I don't know. I felt empty. That was my life for a long time. And I'm so happy with Esteban, but for some reason, when we're apart at night, the old hauntings come back."

"Maybe you've allowed yourself to love again, and you're worried something is going to happen to him," he said, taking a bite of food.

"It sounds crazy, but yeah, that's probably what's happening in my mind."

"You know, when you got here, you went right to sleep?" he asked, trying not to make a big deal out it. "Maybe you don't need *him* here. You just need someone," he said.

Marialena shook her head. "I have no idea. God, this is so embarrassing. I feel like I'm five years old," she admitted.

Marialena took her plate to the counter and wrapped up the rest for leftovers.

"So, do you want to try another movie tonight?" he asked.

Marialena nodded. "Okay, yeah. Although, I'm surprised. You're in Los Angeles, and what is this, two nights in a row with no date?"

"Oh, I'm not here to date," he said, thinking of her. "I have all this business to take care of."

"So, you really think the deal is going to go through?" she asked.

317

"Yeah, I'm meeting him tomorrow afternoon."

"What's going to happen to your staff?"

"They'll lose their jobs. That's the hard part. It's why I put off doing this for so long."

Henry moved over to the couch with his wine and continued watching the game until she was ready to join him.

They picked out a thriller to watch together, both underneath the same blanket. When the movie was over, they talked about it for a few minutes, then Henry got up and stretched.

"So, what's the plan for tonight?" he asked.

"Well, I guess I'm just going to try to sleep in bed tonight," she said.

"Okay, but what if you can't fall asleep? What can I do?"

"If I can't fall asleep, that's my problem."

"Yeah, but—" He sat down on the edge of the sofa. "Why don't I come in and check on you in the middle of the night."

"I appreciate everything you're doing for me, I do. But honestly, I don't know if I'm comfortable with that."

"Why not? We're all adults. I'm not going to try anything."

"No, it's not that. What if Esteban comes home and finds us in there? He could come home unexpectedly and assume the worst. Henry, I can't chance it. I don't want him to get the wrong idea."

"He's not going to come home early. Look, we'll play it by ear. Besides, I won't stay the whole night. Only long enough for you to fall asleep. It worked last night." He watched her fidget. "Hey, it's not a big deal. I don't mind."

Marialena had to admit, he really looked like he didn't mind. He seemed genuinely concerned and she wondered if this was what it was like to have an older brother look out for you. She started to see him then in a new light.

Marialena could feel her eyes water, feeling his concern for her. "I'm sorry. I'm just not good at dealing with this. I think I'm going to read for a bit before I try to sleep."

She stood up to leave but Henry took her hand. "Hey, don't worry, okay? We'll figure this out. I'm not going anywhere. I'll come check on you in a few hours. Say around midnight?"

Marialena nodded. She was giving in and it was a comforting thought knowing he'd be there.

Marialena went to bed with a book, but couldn't focus. She was thinking about giving Henry her condo, wondering if he'd even consider taking it. She liked the idea, because it meant that she wouldn't have to get rid of it right away, and she trusted him. He was family, after all. Not officially family, but close enough.

An hour later, she heard Henry walking around the living room. She heard him turn off the TV, then go the restroom to brush his teeth and go to bed. She lay there thinking about her parents and about Esteban. She lay in the darkness and the thoughts haunted her, like they always used to. She imagined her phone ringing, over and over. She remembered how she ignored the phone call, reliving the guilt she had felt. She wasn't sure what time it was when she heard Henry walk into the bedroom.

He knelt down on the bed beside her. "Hey, want me to stay here for a while?"

She looked at him in the darkness, coming back to reality. She was terrified of reliving her past, of losing Esteban the same way she had lost her parents. She felt tears slowly fall down her face.

"I thought I was past this," she said, sniffling.

"Hey, it's okay. Whatever you need, I'm here. I promise, Esteban is going to come back and I'll be here until he does," he said, knowing what she was scared of. He put an arm around her.

"My parents died about six years ago, on December 27th," she said, the tears still falling. "They were on their way home from a holiday party. The other driver had fallen asleep and was going a hundred miles an hour or something crazy like that. They died instantly, and the worst part is that I slept through the entire thing. I remember being woken up that night by a phone call and just letting it go to voicemail." She paused, her voice hoarse from the memories. "The next morning, I saw the missed calls, but I thought my parents were sleeping the whole time. It wasn't until someone called the house that I found out. I felt so terribly guilty, like I should have known something had happened." Tears started to fall freely and she put her face in her hands. Henry lifted up the covers so he could hold her. She put her arms around his neck and sobbed into his chest.

"Marialena, *I'm so sorry* you had to go through that."

He wasn't sure what he should do next, but he went with his gut and climbed under the covers. He pulled her down with him and she let herself be comforted, resting her head on his chest, his arm around her.

After about five minutes, she stopped crying. "Thank you so much for helping out, but we probably shouldn't do this," she said quietly.

"Marialena, it's okay. We're not doing anything wrong."

"What if Esteban comes home early and finds us this way? I can't risk losing him, Henry."

Henry sighed. "Look, Marialena, he didn't want you to be alone, so he asked me to come out here for the week. So, it's okay. He knows."

Marialena shimmied her way out of his arms and looked up at Henry, who turned his body to face her.

"Esteban knows?"

"He didn't know for sure. But he had a strong feeling."

She put two hands on her face, embarrassed.

"Hey, I am happy to be here. Plus, I was able to get the ball rolling on the restaurant, so you're doing me a favor."

Marialena gave him a small, sad smile.

"Look, I'll wait until you fall asleep. And I'll go back to my room. Okay?"

"Okay." Marialena nodded. "Thank you so much, Henry."

"No problem. Try to get some sleep, okay?"

She lay down on her side of the bed and was able to sleep without too much trouble.

Marialena woke up before her alarm the next morning. She looked over and saw Henry still in bed with her.

"Hey, Henry, wake up." She put a hand on the covers by his chest and pulled them down a little bit.

Henry stirred and looked around sleepily. "Oh fuck. I must have fallen asleep. Shit, Lena, I'm sorry." Marialena noticed his use of Esteban's nickname for her.

"It's okay. Thanks for last night. But we probably shouldn't do this again."

"Hey," he got up as she started to walk out of the room. "Does Esteban know about what happened, with your mom and dad? The details?"

"No, we started to talk about it on the anniversary of their passing, but I just couldn't bring myself to do it. I'll make some time when he gets back. He needs to know."

"I'm sorry you have to go through that. We won't talk about it anymore. Come here," he said and pulled her into a big hug. Marialena put her arms around him. "All right, have a good day at work," he said and walked into the guest room.

Before leaving, she left the keys to her condo in Los Feliz with a note that read, "Good luck with the deal. I know you're looking for a place; here's a spot you could check out in the meantime. $800 a month. Just lock up when you leave." She attached the address and the gate code with her garage door opener and left the note in the bathroom.

He texted her later that afternoon. "Nice place you got here. I think you have yourself a new tenant. Also, I

322

sold the restaurant about two hours ago, so we're going out to celebrate."

"Congratulations!" she texted back, smiling from ear to ear.

Patrick walked into his office.

"Good day?" he asked.

"Everything just seems like it's going to work out. Everything in my life just feels right, for the first time in a long time," she said.

Patrick smiled and sat down across from her. "I'd like to think I had something to do with that, albeit in a very small way."

"You did, in a very *big* way. Thank you. Hey, so on Sunday, do you need me with you, or do you want me to stay with Tina?" she asked, referring to his date.

"I'll run it by Tina, if she needs you, go to her. I'll ask her tonight when I see her."

Patrick told her she could leave early on Friday, because they'd have so much to prepare for on Sunday.

Marialena heard Henry come home when she was getting dressed in Esteban's room.

"Honey, I'm home," he called out. Marialena smiled. He sounded like he was in a good mood.

When she came out, he had a bottle of wine in his hand, with two glasses. He looked amazing, in a tailored gray dress shirt and a really nice black pair of slacks. And he had shaved.

"Wow, look at you," she said, feeling more comfortable around him.

"I clean up nicely, don't I?" he asked with a big smile. "You're home early. Wanna have some wine with me?"

"Yes. Hey, so congratulations on selling," she said.

"Thanks, I have some mixed feelings right now. I'm thrilled that the restaurant is no longer mine, but I have to go back on Monday and tell the staff. That's going to be the hardest thing I've ever had to do."

Marialena took the glass he offered her and brought it with her to the couch.

"Hey, sooner or later it was going to happen, right? If not now, then years from now. You can't escape it, you still would have been in this same position."

"It's just that they're all great people. I hate that I have to do it."

"What are you going to do now? After Monday, I mean?" she asked.

"I need to stay out in Temecula for a little while, until the restaurant officially closes. But Lena, that condo of yours is great. Eight hundred dollars is crazy. Now, I checked around. It should be at least twice that."

"It goes for about fourteen. But it's okay. I wasn't going to rent it out. You're family. I'm making the best money I've ever made, and I'm going to be staying here with your brother. I feel guilty charging you anything, to be honest. Do we need some legal stuff prepared? Do I need to get you to sign a lease or something?"

"Yeah. I can call Al Robinson. He's our family lawyer. We can have him draw something up."

"I'm glad it's going to help you. And you've already helped me so much."

He smiled kindly. "So, when are you moving in here?"

"I guess I kind of already did. I just need some furniture pieces to match his stuff."

"Want to go tomorrow, see what we can find? For your new place and mine?"

"Yeah, sure. Sounds like fun. Henry, I need to make a phone call. When were you thinking of going out?"

"How's seven?"

"Seven sounds great. Make yourself at home, please." She drank the last of her wine and called her cousin from Esteban's room, lying down.

"Hey."

"Hey, how are you?" Roxanne asked.

"Good. He's going to take the condo." Marialena had told her earlier that morning that she had offered it to him.

"Great. That's awesome. Eight hundred a month is a great deal, for out there I mean."

"I know. It's going to be nice with him close by; he's been great. He wants to go out tonight; it's nice to have the company."

"You don't think that's weird, do you?"

"No, it's not weird. He's going to be family. Trust me, Esteban has my heart."

"Okay, just making sure."

"It's fine. Anyway, how about you? What are you doing tonight?"

Roxanne sighed on the other end. "It's cold as balls out tonight. But I have that date with Tony." She had met Tony at a Christmas party. "I hate wearing layers, and I can't pull off sexy when I'm wearing so many damn clothes. It's much easier to be sexy in Los Angeles."

Marialena laughed. "Just tell Tony that he'll need to warm you up."

"Dating sucks. Maybe it's a good thing you didn't have to deal with it. I tried to get you to go out there and date, and you struck gold without even trying. I shouldn't have been so hard on you."

"It's okay. I knew you were looking out for me. I kind of feel like I'm making up for lost time now."

"Only without all the draw backs. Without all the waiting and the wondering."

"Yeah, but then again, dating has never been my thing."

"God, even when we were young, I had to twist your arm. Remember when we were teenagers? I talked my mom into letting us go to that party? Two guys asked us out and you didn't want to go."

"Hey, but I did go."

"Double date. In & Out and the movies at Citywalk. You remember?"

"Yes, and it was awful. You two went one way, and Carlos and I went another. We had nothing in common!"

"You remember his name? Oh my God, you are too much. I didn't have anything in common with my guy either. Who cares? But you were an old lady on the inside when you were sixteen, anyway. It's no wonder you had nothing in common with him," Roxanne said, laughing.

"Oh, I wasn't that bad."

"You read poetry for fun!"

"I was a romantic!"

"You were a snob!"

Marialena laughed. "I was into the arts."

Roxanne laughed with her. "Hey, hate to run, but I really should get moving. It's going to take a while to get all these damn clothes on. Hopefully it won't take as long for Tony to get them off." They laughed and said goodbye.

Marialena wished she lived closer. She would have loved for her to meet Esteban and Henry. She wondered if Roxanne would ever be into Henry.

She stretched out in bed and stayed there for half an hour, thinking of Esteban. She missed how warm he always was. He was always wearing some kind of knit sweater and he looked so inviting. Esteban in a knit sweater was practically an open invitation for her to end up in his arms.

She wondered, circumstances being different, if she could have fallen for someone like Henry? They had chemistry, but it was mostly due to the fact that he was Esteban's brother. She didn't feel any romantic feelings toward him. Her feelings for Esteban were just too strong. Esteban felt like home, and Henry felt like a good time. She was looking forward to their night, without an ounce of romance in her heart or between her legs. She was going to marry Esteban and nothing made her happier.

327

Chapter Twenty-one

Marialena emerged from the bedroom ready to go. She felt good, deciding on a pencil skirt and black blouse with ankle boots. Not too sexy, not too cold, just right for the evening, though she wasn't sure where they were going.

Henry whistled when she walked into the living room. "Jesus, Marialena, you look amazing. You sure you don't want to dump my brother? I'll let you keep the ring. I mean, I might even marry you myself."

Marialena smiled, but ignored his comment. "Is this okay for tonight? I don't know where we're going."

"Well, I have a tie and a blazer with me. I was going to put them on a minute."

"Where are we going exactly?"

"It's a surprise."

"And you're wearing a suit?"

"Yeah, I wanted to try some place fancy. Reservations are for seven-thirty."

Marialena looked at her watch. She had just enough time for a wardrobe change. "If you're going to wear a suit, I should probably change," she said, gauging Henry's reaction.

"Just go like that. Who cares?"

Marialena shrugged. "I don't know, I don't want to feel out of place. Can't you just tell me where we're going?" she asked.

"I said it was a surprise. But fine, change if you want. I'm going to get my tie on," he said.

"Can you give me a minute? My clothes are in your room. I just need to grab a dress."

"Sure," he said and finished off his wine.

Marialena walked into the guestroom. She saw Henry's blazer and tie hanging on the door. It was a light gray suit, so she decided to go with a cream-colored dress. It was a little snug but it would work. She took the dress with her, with matching heels, and walked back to Esteban's room where she changed. She looked in the mirror, deciding to leave her hair up. The dress was a little sexier than she wanted it to be, but she had no choice now than to leave it on. When she came back out, Henry was in the guest room. Marialena made a beeline towards the coat closet by the front door and put on a light beige pea coat.

Henry walked out of the guest room and gave her a once over, her coat covering her dress. "Very elegant," he said, wondering what she was wearing underneath.

She looked at him and smiled. "Thanks."

"You're not going to return the compliment? It's not very often I get dolled up," he said, teasing her.

"You look very nice," she said quietly.

"Okay, so the car should be here any minute."

"We're not driving?"

"Nope," Henry said, a hand on his tie, loosening it a little. He received a notification on his phone. "Look at that, right on time," he said. "Ready?"

Marialena nodded. She grabbed her purse and they were out the door. They didn't say anything in the

329

elevator on the way down, but she could smell his cologne and, she had to admit, he smelled great.

"Where are we going?"

"Will you stop? You'll find out when we get there," he said, his eyes smiling.

Marialena smiled. "Okay, just as long as we don't end up in Beverly Hills. I made reservations for my boss tonight at a restaurant there. I don't want to run into him tonight."

"We aren't going to Beverly Hills, so you're safe."

"It's too bad Esteban couldn't be here tonight," she said wistfully.

"Yeah, it's too bad. You really love him, don't you?" Henry asked, his tone pensive.

Marialena looked at him and smiled. "Yeah, I do."

"Why him?" Henry asked.

Marialena laughed. "Are you kidding me?"

"No, I'm serious, actually. Why Esteban?" Henry looked out the window and smiled. "I just mean, he's my brother. I've known the man for thirty-nine years."

"I like everything. I love who he is, what he does."

"You like that he's a stay-at-home writer?"

"It's his job, and he happens to be very good at it. So, he doesn't go out a lot. That's fine, I don't either."

"You're here now," he said.

"Only because you invited me. I'd totally be at home watching a movie or reading a book."

"That's a damn shame."

Marialena laughed. "You need to meet my cousin, Roxanne. God, I swear the two of you have joined forces or something. I like staying home. I like movies. I like *Esteban's* movies. Going out is nice too, sure. But I've

330

always loved movies. And I love that that's what Esteban does for a living. It's inspiring."

Henry nodded. "So, you're into the artist type?"

Marialena shrugged. "I don't know if I'd say that. I'm into Esteban, that's all I know. He's amazing and makes me happy. We feel right together. I feel like I'm on the right path with him. It's an incredible feeling, Henry. I hope you get to find out what that's like one day."

"I feel like I'm light-years away from all that."

"A few months ago, I wouldn't have pictured it for myself either. But he's changed all that. Kids, marriage, the whole thing. I want it all."

"Kids? I don't mean to burst your bubble or anything Lena, but what about his age? Have you taken that into consideration? I mean, have you guys talked about it?"

Marialena sat back in her seat. "Well, I know he's older, but it's not impossible. I mean, it's harder for a woman, but I'm still young," she said quietly. "And you? You've never thought about being a Dad?"

"Nope."

"There was never a scare? With all the women you've dated over the years?"

"Jesus, Marialena. What kind of guy do you take me for?" he asked, smiling.

Marialena laughed. "A promiscuous one."

"Hey, I like to get laid as much as everyone else," Henry said.

"No, but you get around, don't you?"

Henry gave her a disapproving look, but he smiled to let her know he was only teasing. "I guess once upon a time I did," he said, trying to be honest. "But I was always super cautious."

331

"Any regrets?" she asked.

Oh, only that Esteban met you before I did, he said to himself. Out loud, he said, "Not really. Maybe one or two. Let's not go down that path." The conversation had drifted into serious territory and he really didn't want to continue that conversation. "Hey, so we're almost there."

"It's so beautiful, isn't it?" she said, looking up at the skyscrapers. "Does it remind you of New York?"

"Honestly, not really. Have you ever been there?"

"No. Patrick has a place there and I think he plans on going soon. But I think I'd rather see it for the first time with Esteban, or Roxanne."

"What about Los Angeles? Do you like living here?"

"Of course. It's home. I've been here all my life; I love it here. Esteban might want to move one day, but me? I like it."

"You'd give it all up for him?" he asked.

"Sure. Isn't that what you do for love?"

"What about compromise?"

"Well, yeah, sure. But I don't know, I can see Esteban and me out in the country somewhere. God, he mentioned snow, though." Marialena laughed. "I don't know if I could get used to that."

"Well, don't move away so soon. I haven't even moved here yet." Henry said. The driver was coming to a stop. Henry looked out the window. "Looks like we're here."

"The Bonaventure? Is this where we're going?"

"Yeah, ever been?"

"No," she said, surprised. "Henry, it's a Friday night, the weekend before the Oscars. How did you get these reservations?"

"I know a guy," Henry said, smiling.

Marialena gave him a side look. "Oh my god. I've always wanted to come here. I almost came here with my cousin Roxanne. How did you know to bring me here?"

"It's one the best views in the city. Lucky guess," he said.

"Have *you* ever been here?" she asked in a whisper.

Henry laughed. "One time. I'll tell you about it upstairs."

When they got into the elevator, Marialena gave him an excited look. He looked down at the floor and smiled, resisting the urge to take her in his arms and to kiss her. He took a deep breath.

"I've always hated elevators," he lied.

She smiled and patted his arm. "We're almost there."

"So, who's this connection you have?" she asked when they were seated. He watched her take off her coat and place it on the back of her chair. She looked absolutely exquisite in her dress. It was the best he had ever seen her look. That dress hugged her body in all the right places. She wore a cream colored dress with a high neck and lacy sleeves. It was so elegant on her, yet it didn't leave anything to the imagination. The dress was almost like a second skin on her.

333

Henry cleared his throat before answering. "An old manager. He doesn't work here anymore but still has some ties. I told him I sold my restaurant and wanted to celebrate by bringing a beautiful young lady to dinner. I didn't tell him the young lady was my brother's fiancée, but you know, you do what you have to."

"Henry, this is incredible," she said. The restaurant offered a 360-degree view of downtown Los Angeles, and they had a table right by the wall-to-wall windows. "It's so beautifiul," she said, looking out at the city. "You said you'd tell me about the other time you'd been here," she reminded him when the waitress left.

"Ah yes. There has been one other time."

"Okay, who was she?"

Henry leaned back in his chair. "So, I came out to Los Angeles occasionally, to see Esteban. Back then, we were a little closer. I drove up to see him once and I met a woman. She was great. We ended up seeing each other for four incredible months. Anyway, I brought her here."

"What was she like?"

"Smart, beautiful, great sense of humor. She was your age then, maybe a little older." The waitress came back with the wine and Henry let her pour it. He took a glass when she left and held it to his mouth. "She was pretty amazing, actually. I remember thinking she and I could really work out."

"So, what happened?"

Henry shrugged. "It was good for a while; I didn't mind driving here to see her. But, I guess I wasn't around often enough. She found someone else."

"She dumped you?"

"Well, we weren't serious about each other. It was kind of casual. I could have been serious about her, but I never really said anything."

"Were you broken-hearted?" Marialena asked.

Henry laughed. "What? No, I wasn't. I just moved on."

"Henry, that makes me so sad. When you like someone, you're supposed to do something about it."

"Oh, I showed it. I just didn't, you know, go the extra mile. I didn't ask her to be my girlfriend or anything."

"Henry, you've got to start acting on that kind of thing. If you like someone, go for it. And if it's not meant to be, at least you would have found out for sure."

"Take the jump, huh? That kind of thing?" he asked, leaning in.

"Yeah. That's what life is all about. Otherwise, you're just playing it safe, and that's no fun. This whole relationship with Esteban is one giant leap. I feel like everyone is telling me not to, and here I am, jumping. Trust me, I know when to jump."

When the food finally arrived, the conversation dipped into some serious topics, then switched over to light-hearted banter. It wasn't what Henry had aimed for that night, but he knew that if it stayed serious, he'd be less tempted to flirt. It was keeping him grounded. He didn't want to make her uncomfortable, or make things awkward. Still, he had to bite his lip a few times to keep from saying anything that would cross the line. He had nothing to gain from Marialena except her friendship. It was nice. It wasn't easy, but it was nice. She was going to marry his brother. She was wearing his mom's ring on her finger. He had to respect that. She needed a family, and he wanted to be that for her.

"So, there's one more place I want to take you after this," he said when dinner was starting to wind down.

"Is it a secret, or are you going to tell me this time?" she asked, picking the last piece of steak from her salad.

"Have you ever been to the Skybar on Sunset?"

"Henry, it's a Friday night. There's no way we can get in."

"Oh, we're getting in."

"Wow, I'm impressed. You've got some mad skills." Marialena leaned back in her chair. "Henry, I'm glad you're moving here. This is nice, I have to admit. You just being out here is nice. I like having someone around to just hang out with. Someone who I can count on not to...you know?"

Henry nodded, understanding what she meant. "Yeah, I could be like the brother you never had."

Marialena smiled. "I like that."

Henry poured the last of the wine and held his glass to hers. "To family," he said.

"To family."

Chapter Twenty-two

Before Henry had paid for dinner, he had made arrangements for another driver to pick them up and take them to their next destination. Henry and Marialena walked out onto the drop-off area and waited.

"Are you cold?" he asked her.

"No, I'm okay actually. You? You're not wearing a proper jacket."

"I grew up in New York; this is warm enough."

"Do you miss the cold weather in New York?"

"Sometimes."

"Why?" she asked, not liking the cold herself.

"Okay, imagine this. You're at home, maybe watching one of your movies, and you have a fire going and the snow starts to fall outside. You peek out the window and it starts to cover everything in a beautiful white blanket. It's a quiet kind of cold. One that you can almost taste. And it wakes up every part of your body. It's incredible. You know what? Screw Skybar, we're getting on a plane right now," he said.

Marialena laughed as their driver pulled up.

"Let's do it. Let's all go one day. Roxanne, you, me and Steven," he said excitedly.

"You know, Roxanne and I have been talking about it, but what the hell, you and Esteban could tag along. Why not?"

"Tag along? Excuse me, who's going to show you around?"

"Roxanne. She's been there before."

"Oh, no way. You have to experience it with a local."

"Okay, sure. I like the idea of all of us being there. That sounds nice."

"So, this cousin of yours? You two close?"

"Yeah. She grew up here and is two years older than me. We were pretty inseparable growing up."

"And she's your only family?"

"No, I have family here too. But they're not close like her family was. We used to go on a lot of trips together, both of our families. Camping, vacations, you name it. What about you, did you and Esteban go vacationing as a family?"

"Well, not too often. We're too far apart in age. But we did take Mom out to Spain before she got sick. It was a good time. My mom loved it. That's where I got the idea to open up a restaurant. The food was so good there."

"That sounds like a nice trip."

"It was. Esteban wrote a lot of 'Alone Together' there."

"Really, on vacation?"

"Well, I don't know how much of it he wrote, but yeah, he'd find a corner at some restaurant or stay back at the hotel. I mean, he'd come around to take my mom out and all that. But it was a fun time."

When they finally got to the door at Skybar, Henry gave his name, and sure enough, he was on the list. He gave Marialena a knowing smile. It was dark and crowded. The lights outside were kept dim, and she couldn't make out anyone's face. Surprisingly, they found an empty couch in a dark corner facing the swimming pool. She sat down, took off her coat, thankful for the heat lamps everywhere. Henry said he'd get a couple of drinks and he was gone for about ten minutes.

The place was amazing. The crowd here was young, but it wasn't terribly rowdy. It was more classy than anything else. There was music playing, and each group had their own little private seating area around the pool or in different places around the bar.

"I've driven by the place so many times, it's hard to believe that this was on the roof the entire time."

"Yeah, it's like a different world up here, but I mean that in a good way. I guess I didn't realize it would be like this, though. It feels a little secluded. I don't know if that's the right word."

"No, I know what you mean," she said. "It's intimate."

"There you go, that's the word I was looking for. Hey, we don't have to stay if it's weird."

"No, it's okay. Besides, it will only be weird if we make it weird," she said.

He nodded, liking her logic.

"Did you go to places like this when you were younger, in New York I mean?"

"Places like this? No way. I went to dives. I played in a band, and we played at some really rough places."

"Shut up. You were?"

Henry laughed. "Yeah, I played guitar."

"What kind of band?"

"Rock, as if I'd be in any other kind of band."

"Did you sing too?"

"No way. But I wrote a lot of the songs."

"Lyrics?"

"No, just the music."

339

"Do you still play?"

"I have two guitars at home, but I don't play anymore."

"Henry! Why not?"

He laughed. "I don't have the time."

"*Make* time," she said. "Bring your guitars to Los Angeles when you move. I'd love to see them at my condo."

"You mean my condo."

She nudged him. "I'd love to hear you play."

"We have no one to sing."

Marialena shrugged. "I could sing."

"You sing?"

"I mean, I'm not great, but I'm not terrible either."

Henry laughed. Marialena excused herself to use the ladies' room. When she came out of the stall to check herself in the mirror, she noticed another woman looking at her. She was a black woman, drop dead gorgeous, but Marialena couldn't place her.

"I know you from somewhere," the woman said to Marialena's reflection. And that's when Marialena recognized her voice, her French accent. She was the star from Esteban's movie, 'Paris in the Dark.'"

Marialena's eyes widened and she smiled, turning to face the woman. "No, but I know you. You're in 'Paris in the Dark.'" Marialena said, feeling star-struck.

"I *do* know you. You're engaged to Esteban Gutierrez. I'm sorry, I don't know your name."

Marialena nodded, stepping aside to make room for the other ladies who needed the mirror. "It's Marialena Villanueva. How'd you know I was engaged to Esteban?"

The actress laughed. "A friend of mine was at the party. Patrick Denny's party, no?" God, her French accent was divine.

Marialena nodded. "Yeah, that's crazy. It's such a small world."

The actress laughed. "My friend sent me a picture of the two of you that night. He let me down gently. I had a tiny crush on your fiancé while we were filming." Marialena wondered if she was a little tipsy or if she was just naturally amiable.

"Oh," Marialena said, unsure how to respond.

"Don't worry. It was harmless. Congratulations on your engagement. Is he here, Esteban?" the actress asked, her arm linked in Marialena's. They stopped again when they were out of the restroom.

Marialena shook her head. "No, he's out of town. He's working on a new project, actually."

The actress brought her hands together in anticipation. "This is great."

"Yeah, I'm actually here with Esteban's brother. He just sold his restaurant, so we're here celebrating."

"Ah, he has a brother I did not know about?" She laughed. She looked at Marialena, feeling positively happy to have bumped into her. "Listen, what are you and Esteban doing on Sunday? We're going to this party after the Oscars. You two should come."

"Oh no, I couldn't. Plus, Esteban will still be out of town."

"Bring the brother, no?"

Marialena shook her head. "I'm afraid I'll have my hands full that night."

The actress waited for clarification, so Marialena continued. "I work for Patrick Denny, so I'll be running around with him that day."

"Ah, Patrick Denny. Are you an actress also?"

Marialena smiled, flattered. "No, I'm afraid not."

"You could be, with that figure of yours," the actress said, looking at Marialena's body. "It's what the men like. Not my skin and bones," she said, tugging at her dress. "It's no wonder Esteban proposed. I was surprised. He had a girlfriend for a long time, no?"

"He did."

"And you came right in and boom, an engagement. Esteban has great taste in women if he chose you."

"Listen, it was nice to meet you. I should get back," she said, motioning toward Henry.

"Ah, the brother," the actress said, standing next to Marialena to take a peek at Henry. He was sitting down looking at his phone. "He's tall, not like Esteban." She tugged on Marialena's arm. "You must let Esteban know that we ran into each other. And give him my love, please? He was one of my favorite directors." She gave Marialena's arm a squeeze. "Give me your number. We should get together, just you and me. I would love a chance to get to know the woman who captured his heart." Marialena smiled and gave her the number to the cell phone she used for Patrick.

"You'll never believe who that was." Marialena Googled the movie for her name.

"Who?" Henry asked.

"Floriane Marchal! She was the lead actress in 'Paris in the Dark.'"

"Wow, she looked different."

"She confessed that she had a tiny crush on him while they were filming."

Henry laughed. "Okay, what is it about that guy? What am I not seeing?"

Marialena smiled. "Face it, he's sexy and you're jealous."

"He *is not* sexy."

"Well, she apparently thought so, too. Did you see her? She's gorgeous. I mean, he cast her in his movie. He had to have thought so, too. And she wants to hang out."

"So, what's the big deal?"

"She has a crush on my fiancé."

"You have nothing to worry about. Esteban loves you. Christ, he started writing again the day he met you."

"What do you mean?"

"Esteban didn't tell you?"

"Tell me what?"

"Last year was an all-time low for him. He was going through some pretty heavy shit."

"I know that he had writer's block for a little while."

"Marialena, it was really hard on him. And he started to write again the day he met you." Marialena smiled. "Trust me, you have nothing to worry about. That man loves you. He wouldn't do anything to jeopardize what you have."

Little did they know that those words would come back to haunt them both in a matter of days.

They continued talking when Floriane Marchal approached them.

"Sorry for interrupting. I had to come over to meet Esteban's brother. You're a tall drink of water, aren't you?"

343

Henry shrugged. "He got the eyes and the talent. I got the height. I'd say we're even."

"And the smile," she said flirtatiously. "I won't keep you, but please give my love to Esteban. Marialena, I'll call you. I want to get together." She waved goodbye and they sat back down.

Marialena laughed when she was out of earshot. "Holy shit, Henry, you might actually have a chance at her."

"No, I don't think so. She's way out of my league. Hey, I think I might go for one more. You want another wine?"

"Oh no, I'm good. I think I probably need to stop."

Henry was gone for a few minutes at the bar while Marialena thought about the night and how strange it had been. The restaurant, running into Floriane, Floriane admitting she liked Esteban.

When Henry returned, he sat down close to Marialena. "So, we'll leave after I'm done with this one."

"It's fine, I just got cold suddenly."

"Thanks for coming out here with me tonight," he said and took out his phone to arrange for a car.

"It was fun. I love that you were a musician. God, I've always wanted to pick up a guitar."

"It's not hard. I could show you."

"Do you have an acoustic?"

"I do. My first and only love," he said and laughed. He told her how bad he was when he was just starting out, different songs he learned while he finished his last drink.

"Okay, I'm about done with this." He looked at his phone. There was a driver a couple of blocks away. "You ready?"

Marialena nodded. She linked an arm in his as they walked, feeling sentimental.

"Thanks for this, Henry. For all of it. I had a really nice time."

"No problem." He loved how she felt on his arm.

Henry put a hand on her hand. When they got to the curb, Marialena rested her head on Henry's shoulder, something she wouldn't be able to do with Esteban, since he was a little shorter than she was.

Henry was singing softly on the way to Esteban's condo, feeling the effects of the alcohol. When she unlocked the door, Henry made a beeline to the restroom. When he came out, his tie and his blazer were in his hand. He threw them on the bed in the guest room, watching Marialena put away her shoes. Ten minutes later, she came out of the bathroom to find Henry asleep on Esteban's side of the bed. He was still wearing his dress shirt and pants.

When Marialena got into bed, she slid over to Henry's side, nudging him gently.

"Henry, you need to get out of those clothes," she said. He stirred but didn't wake up. "Henry, come on."

She lifted his shirt, sliding her hand on his chest, trying to help him out of his clothes. She felt Henry take a deep breath. He placed an arm on her back lazily, sliding his hand down and stopping when he got to her butt. His fingers barely came into contact with her skin underneath her pajama shorts. She slid away quickly.

"Hey, what are you doing?" she asked.

345

Henry looked at her and put a hand on his forehead. "Jesus, I was asleep. What were you doing?" he asked sleepily.

"I was helping you out of your clothes."

"Oh. I didn't realize it was you. Sorry," he said with a guilty smile.

"Wait, why are you smiling?"

"I totally didn't realize it was you, until my hand was on your, uh."

"My butt?"

"Yeah," he said with a chuckle. "And then I knew it was you and these alarm bells went off in my head. The word 'abort' came to mind," he said, laughing a little.

"So, my big butt gave me away?" Marialena threw her pillow at him. "You're terrible," she said, smiling.

He opened one eye and confiscated her pillow. "Hey, a woman tries to take my clothes off while I'm sleeping, I'm going to reach out for her. It's a natural reaction."

"Yeah. I bet it is for you," she said.

"Sorry. I think I had too much to drink."

Marialena got out of bed. When she came back, she had two glasses of water in her hand and gave him one. Henry sat up in bed and took off his dress shirt, setting it in his lap to hide his erection. Marialena sat down next to him on the edge of the bed.

He looked at her and set his glass down on the end table beside him. "Hey, Marialena, listen...I'm sorry for reaching out for you."

"No, it's okay. It's my fault," she said and set her glass next to his. She took his shirt from his lap and

346

placed it on top of the dresser, but didn't notice his erection.

"I'm sorry we have to do this," she said as he got into bed. "I hope this isn't too awkward."

"Well, you need to sleep, right?"

Marialena felt guilty. She slid over to him, brought her arm out from underneath her covers, and kissed him on the corner of his mouth. "Thank you," she said. "Thanks for everything. For keeping me company at night, for tonight, for just being here."

He turned to look at her. She was so incredibly young without her makeup.

"No problem," he said with a tight-lipped smile. But there was a problem. He was starting to fall for her and he wouldn't be able to do anything about it. "Get some sleep," he said, ignoring his aching body.

"Goodnight, Henry."

In the morning, Henry watched Marialena as she slept. He took a deep breath and stayed in bed, not wanting to get up just yet. He studied her for a few minutes. He thought about Esteban. This was going to be his view every morning for the rest of his life. Henry closed his eyes and got onto his back.

"Fuck," he said to himself. He walked back to the guest room and tried to fall asleep there instead.

Marialena woke up a few hours later. She noticed that Henry was gone and she said a silent thank you to whoever was listening. She hated needing him for this, to sleep. She felt like she was using him. But was Henry the kind of guy who would feel used? She admitted to herself that while he'd probably like to have sex with her, he wasn't the type to catch feelings.

347

When she got out of bed, she got ready for the day, took a shower, and left him a note to tell him she was going out for a little while. She put her thoughts away and walked to a coffee shop. She liked watching people as they came and went, seeing young couples, old couples. She thought of herself and Esteban.

Marialena glanced at her phone. It was time to start heading back. She stopped by the diner and ordered Henry some eggs, bacon, and toast.

When she got back to the condo, Henry was in front of the TV. He looked relaxed in a flannel and jeans. "I brought you some breakfast. I would have made it myself, but we're out of bacon."

"Hey, thanks," he said, following her into the kitchen. He scratched the back of his head. "About last night, I'm sorry."

Marialena waved her hand in the air dismissively. "Don't worry about it. It's okay." She handed him his food and grabbed some silverware from the drawer.

"No, really. I'm sorry. I had too much to drink."

"It's fine, Henry."

"I have a little bit of a hangover. I think I just want to stay in and enjoy the rain we're supposed to have tonight from in here."

"Okay, well, I am going to get some groceries and do some light shopping. Need me to bring you back anything?"

"No, thanks. I have everything I need."

Marialena didn't come back home until it was already dark and rainy outside. She wanted to give Henry some privacy, so she went to the mall and to a bookstore, then got groceries, trying to kill some time. Henry paused the movie and tried to help with the groceries, but she shooed him away. When she sat down with a glass of wine, they heard the buzzer go off at the front door.

"Expecting anyone?"

Marialena shook her head. "No. I wonder who it could be."

Henry went to the buzzer. "Hello?" he asked into the speaker.

A female voice replied, "Esteban, it's Laura. Can you let me in? I have a small emergency."

Henry buzzed without correcting her. He exchanged a look with Marialena. "What the hell does she want?"

Marialena shrugged. "She said it was an emergency. I hope everything is okay."

Chapter Twenty-three

Laura walked in. She was holding herself, shivering and wet, wearing shorts and a black shirt.

"Jesus, Laura, what happened?" Henry asked. Marialena quickly walked to the kitchen to put some hot water on the stove and grabbed a blanket for Laura.

"Look, I am so sorry. But I don't have my wallet and I called a cab. He's waiting downstairs. I promised him I would return with some money."

Henry nodded, walked to the guest room, and grabbed his wallet. "I'll take care of it." Laura walked out with him and Marialena prepped some tea.

When they got back, Laura explained the situation to Henry and Marialena.

"The stupidest thing. I got home from work, took out the trash, and locked myself out. I don't have my phone, I don't have my wallet, I have nothing. So, I walked to the nearest gas station and they let me call Esteban. But there was no answer. It went straight to voicemail."

"He's away on a trip," Henry answered.

"Fuck," Laura said. She looked past Henry at Marialena. "He has a key to my apartment. Do you know where it is? He used to keep it in the dish with the rest of his keys, but it's not there."

Marialena shook her head. "No, I haven't seen extra keys anywhere."

"It was just one, on a single keychain."

"I'm sorry, I haven't seen anything like that."

"I know this might seem weird, but is it okay if I look through some of the drawers?"

"Um, yeah, sure. Let me help you." Marialena walked into Esteban's room and rummaged through his drawers. Laura checked the kitchen while Henry searched the guest room, blushing when he came across Marialena's underwear.

They regrouped into the living room. "Nothing," Henry said.

Laura exhaled and sat down on the couch with her head in her hands, then sat up again and realized she was still wet. The tea kettle went off in the kitchen.

"Shit," Laura said to no one in particular.

"Your landlord doesn't have an extra key?" Henry asked.

"I live in a house. The owner lives in Florida."

"Roommates?" he asked.

"In Vegas for the weekend. Both of them. They left yesterday."

Marialena prepared the tea for Laura, who came into the kitchen and accepted graciously.

"Can I get you a change of clothes, a sweater?" Marialena asked.

Laura looked into her tea cup. She looked miserable. But Henry was quick on his feet and he grabbed one of his flannels for Laura. She thanked him and excused herself to change out of her damp shirt.

Laura came out of the bathroom, the shirt big on her. Still, she preferred Henry's clothes to Marialena's. She took the tea cup in her hands and sat down.

"Where is Esteban?" she asked them.

351

"The Colorado Rockies. He went for the week and doesn't have cell service."

"Of course, something like this would happen to me when he doesn't have cell service," she said bitterly.

"You tried the windows?" Henry asked.

Laura nodded. "For half an hour. Actually, if I could use the computer, I just need to find the number of a locksmith."

"Yeah, of course," Marialena answered, turning on Esteban's computer.

"Let me know if you need some cash," Henry offered.

"If I get a locksmith to come, my wallet is inside my place. As soon as they let me in, I'd be able to pay them. Let me just see what I can figure out." She held her teacup in the air. "What about you, why are you here?" she asked, being nosy.

Henry shrugged. "I had some business in the area. I sold the restaurant yesterday. Esteban had the guest room, so I stayed here."

"You sold the restaurant? How come?"

"It needed a makeover and I didn't want to put in the time or money," Henry said simply.

"That's too bad. I liked that place."

"Well, I did too. For a long time," Henry said wistfully.

Laura jumped on the computer, found a number, and borrowed Henry's phone to make the call. Henry and Marialena turned their attention to her as she handed the cell phone back to Henry.

"There's a two-hour window for the locksmith, but they said it would most likely be two hours from now."

Marialena cleared her throat. "Okay, so you'll stay here. It's fine. We can get some food."

Laura was genuinely touched by her offer. "I'd hate to put you guys out."

Marilena shook her head. "It's fine, honestly."

Laura allowed herself to look at Marialena's left hand. And there it was, the engagement ring. She took a quick look. She had already known they were engaged, but seeing it in person was a little different. "Okay, thanks," she said quietly to Marialena.

Henry lingered in the kitchen and texted Marialena.

"Okay, so do you want me to go pick up some food then? Maybe take some one-on-one girl time with her?"

"I don't know, actually. This is weird," she replied in text.

"I know. Just give me the sign. I can run out and get some stuff."

"Maybe you should."

"On it."

Henry served two glasses of wine. "Look, why don't I run out and get us something to eat? You ladies can stay and chat, and I'll be back with the food in a little bit. Laura, you hungry?"

"Yeah, food sounds great actually."

"Chinese?"

"Sure. Beef and broccoli."

"You got it. Marialena?"

"Vegetables and white rice."

"Okay, you're weird, but okay. See you two in a bit."

As soon as he walked out of the door, she congratulated Marialena. "Congratulations. I'm sorry I didn't say that sooner. I was a little preoccupied."

"Oh no, it's okay. Thanks."

"How is he?"

"Oh, he's great."

"Still working on his next great masterpiece?"

"He's still at it."

Laura sat back in her chair with her wine glass. "You know, I could never figure out if I liked him better when he was writing or when he wasn't."

"Really? He seems so happy when he's writing."

"Yeah, but he's impossibly distracted. It used to drive me crazy."

"I guess it hasn't bothered me too much."

"Not yet," Laura replied. She smiled with her eyes.

"I like that he finds happiness in his writing. Not to mention, it's his work, you know? It's how he supports himself. And when he's done, he gets to share it with the world. I love that."

"But what do you do all day when he's working?" Laura asked.

Marialena shrugged. "I read, I go out, I find things to do. I've been kind of a loner myself, so I'm okay. It really hasn't been something I've had to adjust to."

"Don't take this the wrong way, honestly I am happy for you and for Esteban, but honey, you're so young. You have your whole life ahead of you. Why him? Why Esteban? I'm just curious," she said, trying to say it as kindly as possible.

Marialena looked at her; she didn't like the question. From Henry it was okay, but from Esteban's ex-girlfriend?

Laura read her mind and saw the look on Marialena's face. "Look, I'm sorry. I'm not trying to pry or break the two of you up or anything. I just know what he's like."

"I can't explain it, *we just work*. The age difference doesn't bother me. His work, and the fact that he's been working nonstop since I've met him doesn't bother me either. I get it, he's a writer. It's what they do. And he's actually been great at making time for me. It's been a non-issue. I get that it might not always be like that, but I love him and I am willing to figure it out when we get there."

"Yeah, I hear you. I think I told myself that in the beginning, but I must have gotten lost along the way," Laura said.

Marialena held her wine glass to her lips. "With all due respect, Laura, you and I are not the same person."

"No, but Esteban is," Laura said kindly. "Well, look, thank you for your hospitality. I am grateful, and I know that you don't have to be nice to me. And I appreciate it. I'm just bringing it up because I don't want you to fall into the same pattern that I did. I loved him too. You know, I never thought I'd be the kind of person who cheats," Laura admitted into the silence.

"How did Esteban find out?"

Laura placed two hands on her glass, not looking up at Marialena. "He surprised me with coffee one afternoon right after my class. I had complained to him earlier that morning that I was tired and I wouldn't be coming over, so he just decided to bring me coffee. He walked into the studio through the back door, which I stupidly hadn't locked that night, and he heard us having sex in the office. He didn't see us, but he left two coffees by the door. The name on the cups were his, so I knew it was him. And I remember thinking two things at once when I saw those coffee cups." Laura paused and Marialena nodded, listening intently, feeling terrible for Esteban.

"I remember feeling this terrible guilt. I bent down to clean up the coffee that had spilled when I accidentally knocked them over. I asked the other guy to leave. I told him that my boyfriend had found out about us, and he left without a word. I sat there on the floor and I cried my eyes out. I hated that he caught us that way. I thought he'd take me back and that we'd talk about it. He's so passive aggressive, and I really thought that he just needed a few days to cool off and that we'd talk and work things out. I was shocked when he wouldn't see me or talk to me."

"And so how did you get back to speaking terms?"

"We didn't, really. He wouldn't return my phone calls. After a few days, I came home to find a box of my stuff in the living room. One of my roommates said he dropped it off."

"I'm so sorry you both had to go through something so terrible. What happened to the guy?" Marialena asked, pouring more wine for each of them.

"Well, I learned later that he was married. The fact that Esteban found out was a sign for him or something, so the next week he decided to break it off. He didn't want to get caught the same way I had."

"Did you know he was married?"

"I didn't. And I guess that's why I am trying to warn you. Marialena, I'm just a boring yoga instructor and I had one temptation and I ran with it. But you, I mean,

356

look at you. You are probably fighting them off from all sides."

"Yes and no. For some reason, the guys that hit on me, or think they have a chance, always seem to have this sense of entitlement. And sure, I get hit on by all types of men, but the nice ones are clingy, and the hot ones are assholes, and I never really found anyone I was happy with. For a long time I stopped trying, but Esteban was different. He was nervous. I mean, he was *actually* nervous, and I thought that was so sweet. I thought the world of him, and I thought he was so handsome and just great, and *he* was nervous. That was endearing." She looked at Laura, unsure about whether or not to go on. Laura prodded her, so Marialena continued. "When he took me to the fundraiser, he actually gave me the option of going as his date or as a friend. I can't tell you how refreshing that was. And I know that might not scream confidence on his part, but honestly, some of the guys I have dated were so overly macho. Esteban was just nice, polite, you know? And things just got better from there."

"So, what about Henry? Why is he here?" Laura asked, wanting all the juicy details.

"Oh, well, he's moving here and I think he's just trying to get a feel for it."

"Does Esteban know he's here?"

Marialena was taken aback by her question. "Of course he does. It was his idea."

"Well, I just know how Henry can get."

"He's been great, actually."

"Has he?"

"Yeah. Why, where are you going with this?" Marialena asked as politely as she could.

357

"Nowhere, I was just curious. He hasn't made a pass at you, has he?"

"No. Why? Did he with you?"

"No," Laura laughed. "I think he hates my guts. Sure, he can be nice, but I know how he really feels about me. We never got along, but I know him well enough not to trust him around someone like you."

"Oh no, he's been fine."

"Maybe he's turned over a new leaf," Laura said.

"Or maybe he just knows that I am incredibly in love with Esteban and that nothing will come between us," Marialena said matter-of-factly.

"Listen, I'm sorry to come off so rough around the edges. Don't mind me, I don't mean to put all these thoughts in your head. I'm sorry if I'm making you second guess anything."

"You're not. It's okay. You have a history with them, I get that," Marialena said, trying to sound more civil than she felt.

"I appreciate all of this. I'm sorry, I'm just having a bad day," Laura admitted.

"It's okay. Hey, I just have a question though. How did you and Esteban become friends after all that?"

"Oh, I wouldn't say we're friends."

"Well, you know what I mean," Marialena said.

"Yeah. Well, after he dropped off the box, I came over here and sort of tried to talk to him. He let me in and he was civil, admitting that he felt better after dropping off my stuff, that he was in a better place. I actually did most of the talking. I told him I didn't want to lose him, our life together. But he didn't want me back. He was done, and you could *just tell*. But I thought he needed more time, and occasionally I would text him; I tried to keep him in my life. Hell, even after you were around. But the last time I saw him, he told me that he wanted to marry you, and I knew we were done. It's strange to think that seven months ago he and I were dating, and now he's marrying someone else," Laura said, her face hard to read.

"Honestly, I think about that all the time," Marialena said, admitting it out loud. "But you know what? I'm not scared at all. This feels right, and I know Esteban feels the same way."

Thankfully, they both heard Henry come back with the food at the perfect time.

Marialena rushed to help him with the food. She took it to the kitchen and set out plates for the three of them. Henry shared a look with Marialena, wondering if everything had gone okay, and she gave him a small smile and nodded. They were at a stage now where they could read each other without speaking.

"Man, it was pouring out there for a little while," Henry said.

"Really? We didn't really hear it in here. I hope it will be okay for the Oscars tomorrow," Marialena said, thinking of Patrick.

"You going?" Laura asked, confused.

"No, but I'm helping prep for it. My boss is presenting, and I have to help get him ready, at least for part of it."

"Who's your boss?"

"Patrick Denny."

"I thought you worked with him, not for him."

Marialena nodded. "I did, then he hired me to work with him, full-time."

"What's he like?" Laura asked.

Marialena shrugged, sticking a vegetable in her mouth. "He's a nice man, spends a lot, laughs a lot."

"I'd be laughing a lot if I had his kind of money. Spending a lot too," Henry replied.

"He's just naturally happy. He doesn't seem to worry about anything. And he's incredibly driven. He's so positive about everything. It's nice."

"Yeah, I hate people like that. Maybe it's the New York in me," Henry said.

"He's from New York," Marialena said.

"Maybe he has a place there, but I doubt he's from there," Henry replied, pulling out his phone. "Okay, let's see. It says here he was born in Ireland, but his family moved to New York when he was a teenager."

"That's probably why he talks the way he does."

"How?" Laura asked.

"Distinguished."

"No, the word you're looking for is pretentious," Henry said.

"He can be charming though," Marialena replied.

"His charm didn't work on you?" Laura asked.

"Oh no. He's not really my type."

"Wait, so you do have a type?" Henry asked.

"Sure. I did," Marialena admitted.

"I bet fifty-year-old-writer/director isn't what you had in mind," Henry said.

Marialena smiled. "You know, it might have been."

"Oh stop, it was not," Henry said, laughing.

"No, I mean it, I think there's something sexy about that," Marialena said, not caring what she said in front of Laura at this point in time.

"Oh, that doesn't surprise me. Look at Esteban. He's great on set. Focused, determined, and he still gives his actors some freedom. I used to tell him he should just direct, stop writing for a while. Especially this last year when he had writer's block, but he really likes using his own material," Laura said.

"Sure. But his writing is so good. It's so close to the soul. I'm glad he's writing so much lately. I hope this next one will be as good as all the others."

Marialena looked at her phone, checking for messages. God, she missed him. Why hadn't he sent anything to her? She was starting to worry. "I haven't heard anything from Esteban," she said, hating that she sounded like she was pouting.

"Maybe he lost his charger," Henry said.

Laura sighed. "He can kind of tune out sometimes. Lose touch with reality." She reached over and placed a hand on Marialena's. "Hey, I'm sorry. It's not easy," Laura said and gave her a knowing look. That's when Marialena realized what Laura was trying to say to her earlier...that it wouldn't be easy.

Marialena excused herself for a few minutes and went to the restroom to splash some cold water on her face. When she emerged, Henry was on the phone. The locksmith was on his way to Laura's. Laura shot up from her chair and placed her plate in the sink.

"Thank you both for your hospitality." Marialena had a plate in her hand but set it on the counter when she noticed Laura approach her. "It would mean a lot to me if we could all see one another someday. I know Esteban was invited to all those parties and declined, but I think we'll always have the same circle of friends and I do hope I see the two of you. No hard feelings?"

Marialena shook her head and smiled. "No hard feelings."

"I wish the best for the both of you. I really do," Laura said warmly.

Marialena nodded. "Thanks."

Marialena said goodnight and went into Esteban's room to lie down, thinking about everything Laura had said to her. When Laura and Henry got into his car, Laura gave him her address as he waited for the inevitable question. He didn't have to wait long.

"Hey, so what do you think about her?" Laura asked.

Henry stared at the red light ahead of him. "She's Esteban's fiancée. My opinion doesn't matter. He's the one who's going to marry her."

"Oh, come on. What do you really think?"

"She's cool," he said, casually.

"That's it?"

"What do you want me to say, Laura? They love each other," he said.

"And, so you approve?"

Henry laughed. "Yeah, they *love* each other, Laura. You should see them together. It's something else. Hell, it inspires me."

"They really love each other?" Laura asked.

"They *really* do. I mean, no offense or anything, but it's not like when the two of you were together. They're different. She wears his sweaters to bed for crying out loud. And Esteban, he's *over* the moon."

"So, it's not just the sex?"

"I don't think so. I don't get that vibe. Look, this is me saying this, so that has to give it some value, but I think this is the real thing."

"Coming from you, that *is* saying something."

"Anyway, was everything cool while I was gone? No catfights?"

Laura laughed. "I might have come off a little headstrong, but I think she'll do all right." Laura sat back in her seat. "You know, she's not what I thought. I kind of like her."

"Yeah, she's not bad."

"Oh, come one, you've got to do better than that. Hell, I have a crush on her."

"She's attractive, sure."

Laura looked at Henry, waiting for more.

"What?" Henry asked. He could feel her staring at him.

"Don't make me ask," Laura said. She leaned in closer to the driver's side. "Do you like her?" she whispered.

"Yeah, she's a nice girl," Henry said automatically.

"You know that's not what I mean."

"She's hung up on my brother. That's not exactly the dream for a guy like me. If you're asking me if I think she's good-looking, I already said she was. But I'm not trying to go after her because she's not mine for the taking. And the fact that she has stars in her eyes for Esteban isn't exactly a turn-on."

"Look at you, being all respectable," Laura said with a twinkle in her eye.

Henry shrugged. "When the time calls for it, I know when to be a decent human being."

Henry kept his eyes ahead of him, focusing on driving and trying to listen to the instructions the navigation system was giving him.

"Hey, so did they tell you where they were coming from, the locksmiths, I mean?"

"No, but they told me they'd be about twenty minutes."

"All right, we'll wait in the car. Anyway, I'm sorry. I don't really have an umbrella."

"It's okay. I'll just take a hot shower as soon as I get back inside."

Henry parked the car in Laura's driveway while they waited for the locksmith, who showed up a couple of minutes later. Laura thanked Henry before she got out of the car.

"Hey, don't mention it. And keep the flannel. It's fine," he said, not really wanting it back at this point.

Laura nodded. "I don't know if I'll ever see you again, Henry. But I won't forget what you've done for me tonight. Thanks again."

Henry nodded. He waited until he saw Laura get back inside, grab her wallet to pay, and didn't drive away until Laura closed the door behind her. He was a little worried on his drive back to Marialena's. What if Laura had told Marialena about his past? He hadn't cared before, but now that Marialena was in his life, he didn't want her to know about his philandering. Sure, he could be honest about some things, but she was starting to come around to him. They were finally trusting themselves around each other, and he didn't want to take another step back.

When he got to the condo, Marialena was in bed.

"She got in okay?" Marialena asked when Henry poked his head in her bedroom.

"Yeah. Hey, you all right?" Henry asked, searching for any change of behavior in her, in case Laura had told her.

"I miss him, Henry. He's only been gone for less than a week, but I thought I'd hear from him. I'm worried and a little upset, actually."

Henry knelt down beside her. "Hey, I'm sorry. Don't worry. I'm sure he's fine. As for being pissed, well I can't help you with that. Laura's right, though. He tends to check out from time to time."

"She warned me about that. But I never noticed it while we were living together. Maybe it was different for them, since they lived apart. I just don't like feeling like this."

Henry sat down on the bed with her. She made room for him.

"Just one more day and he'll be home, and everything will be back to normal."

"I know, but he hasn't called. What if something is wrong?"

"Nothing is wrong. Have you checked the weather there? Maybe he's snowed in."

"I have. It is snowing, but I can't tell if it's bad. Think he's okay?"

"Look, he's fine. Is that all you're worried about?"

"Well, I just thought he'd call," Marialena said, being honest.

Henry sighed. "Yeah, I would have if I were him, but who knows what goes through his brain when he's writing? He loves you. I know that much. Tomorrow, when you get home from work, we'll watch the stupid Oscars and you can let me make fun of your boss. How does that sound?"

"It sounds like a plan." Marialena got out of bed. "I'm going to take a shower tonight. If it's okay with you, do you mind if I try sleeping alone? I want to see if I can do it."

"Well, I'll come check on you later, okay?" He knew she wouldn't be able to fall asleep, but he wanted to give her a chance to try.

"Okay, goodnight," she said.

"Goodnight, Lena," he said and walked out to turn on the TV in the living room. He wasn't sure what she had talked about with Laura, and Marialena seemed preoccupied with Esteban right now. He didn't think that he had anything to worry about, so he tried to focus on the last quarter of the basketball game instead.

Chapter Twenty-four

Marialena looked up at the sky as she got back into her car after stopping at a café for two lattes. The sky looked ominous, but the weather reports said it would clear by noon.

Before she left the cafe, she sent Henry a quick text. He had come in to the room late last night and sat still as a rock until she fell into a restful sleep. She wondered what he thought about as he sat next to her in the darkness of the bedroom. She loved listening to the sound of his breathing as she fell asleep. When she had woken up, he was gone, and she wanted to thank him.

"Sorry I'm so stubborn. Thanks for last night. I needed it," the text read.

"Let's skip the waiting and let me just join you tonight. It will be easier and I'll be asleep sooner that way."

"Okay, sounds good."

When she arrived at Patrick's house, the housekeeper let her in. She found Patrick sitting on his couch, reading the paper.

"Jesus, you look relaxed for a man going to the Oscars," she said, handing him his latte.

"Oh, thanks for this. You read my mind." He put the paper down and motioned for her to shit. "Well, it's still early."

"How's Tina doing?"

"She's upstairs, sleeping."

Marialena looked at the time. It was ten. She wondered how much longer Tina would be asleep. There was still a lot to do.

"Oh, we'll wake her up soon. How about you, how's your morning?"

"Good so far."

"And how's Esteban liking the snow in Colorado?"

"Good," Marialena said, lying.

Patrick nodded, not taking the time to read her. He sat back and drank his latte.

"So, is Tina going to get ready here?" Marialena asked.

"Yes, her dress is here, upstairs."

They both heard Tina coming down the stairs. She was wearing a white satin robe and slippers. "Good morning," Marialena said cheerfully.

"Good morning, lovely. You sleep well?" Patrick asked.

Tina nodded. Marialena couldn't tell how old Tina was, but guessed that they were around the same age. That was about the only thing they had in common. Tina had that classic southern California look. She was tall, rail thin, tan, with light brown hair and green eyes to make a man's heart skip a beat. She had pouty lips and long eyelashes that Marialena would have killed for once upon a time. Tina looked great by Patrick's side, but she couldn't gauge if they were serious or not. Patrick didn't talk about her too often. Marialena thought that maybe Tina was just a little hobby for now, a new toy.

"Honey, Marialena is going to be available to you, should you need assistance this afternoon."

Tina slumped into the chair and nodded at Marialena. "Yeah, okay. Thanks," she said sleepily. "Sorry, I feel a little sluggish this morning from the sleeping pill I took."

Marialena nodded, understanding. She remembered how she felt the next morning when she had taken them. She went to the kitchen and started some coffee for Tina. The housekeeper found Marialena in the kitchen and tried to shoo her away, but Marialena insisted.

"It's okay. I don't mind," she said politely. Marialena peeked into the cupboard and looked for the cinnamon sticks she kept at Patrick's. She broke up a stick and stuck some in the coffee grounds, the way she usually did when she made coffee. It was something she had learned from her mom, and she always loved how it smelled while it brewed.

"This smells heavenly. Thank you," Tina said.

"Patrick said the dress is upstairs?"

Tina nodded. "Yeah."

"Okay, we have a nail appointment in one hour. Tina, can you be ready by then?"

"Yeah, I'll probably eat something in a bit. Then I just need to shower and I should be ready to go."

"Don't bother with makeup or hair. They're going to do all that stuff later."

Tina nodded. "This must be what it's like when you get married."

"Yeah, probably. It will be a good practice run for me too."

"You're getting married?" Tina asked.

"Yeah, we just got engaged, so a date hasn't really been set."

"Who's the guy?" Tina asked sleepily.

"He's a writer/director like Patrick, only maybe not as popular."

"He may not be as popular, but he deserves to be. He's damn good at what he does," Patrick interjected.

"How have you managed to do it, become a household name?" Marialena asked, turning to him.

"I've always been really good with the pitch and being able to get people to buy into what I'm selling. And I've gotten incredibly lucky with casting and support from the studios. But in the pitching phase, you have to sell it. Really sell it, to anyone who's listening. Esteban, he's a little on the quiet side, isn't he?"

"He is, a little. Honestly, I don't know how it all works. Do you think it's something I could help him with?"

"I'm not sure. You should be seen more, I'll tell you that much. Get your picture taken from time to time. It will create some buzz."

"That's not really us."

Tina stood up. "I'm going to get ready. I'll be back down in a bit."

Marialena and Patrick nodded. "He's doing fine on his own, honestly. Maybe he doesn't need the help at all," Patrick finished.

"Maybe not. Hey, if you go to the Oscars next year, have you thought about taking your son?" The movie they were working on was inspired by his son's life, and when it was released, it would qualify for next year's Oscars.

"Oh, I don't know. I'd feel as if I'd be using him somehow. I wouldn't want to introduce him to all this. I like that he has his privacy. It's the protective parent in me, I suppose."

Tina came back into the room, announced her shower, and walked out without another word.

When Tina finally emerged, she was dressed in leggings and an oversized sweater.

"You wearing anything under that sweatshirt?"

"A tank, why?"

"Well, it might be hard to take off when your makeup is done. You might smudge something.

Marialena ran up to Patrick's room and grabbed one of his zip-up hoodies and they left. Tina got into the passenger seat and changed sweaters as Marialena drove.

"So, what's your sister's name?" Marialena asked, to be polite.

"Rebecca."

"And you guys were born and raised here in Los Angeles?"

"Malibu, actually. We both moved here for work. My parents are still in Malibu," Tina replied, her voice throaty and deep. She sounded bored, but Marialena thought it was how she always sounded.

Marialena nodded. They arrived at the nail shop a few minutes later, and Rebecca was already inside, flipping through a magazine. You could tell the two were sisters, though they had a different style. Rebecca had more of a punk style, with dyed jet-black hair and visible tattoos.

371

Tina introduced Rebecca to Marialena, and the two shook hands.

"Hey Tina, are you going to wear your hair up or down?" Rebecca asked from where she was sitting, ignoring Marialena.

"I don't know yet. The hairdresser gets to decide."

"I think you should go with it down."

"Yeah, maybe," Tina said, unsure.

"So, you work for Patrick?" Rebecca acknowledged Marialena once Tina was whisked away from them to the other side of the room by the nail technician.

"I do."

"Tell me, is he the real deal?" Rebecca asked.

"What do you mean?" Marialena asked politely.

"I mean him and my sister."

"Well, I don't know, honestly."

"You must know something about his dating habits."

"I really only handle his business affairs, and we don't really talk about his personal life," she said, lying.

Rebecca nodded. "It would just suck if this were all one giant waste of time, you know?" she said, speaking loud enough for her sister to hear.

A giant waste of time? If getting ready to go to the Oscars on someone else's dime was a waste of time, Marialena wondered what these girls did for fun.

"Well, you can go if you need to. I can stay with Tina," Marialena replied.

"No, it's just that I have two little ones at home, and honestly, it feels good to get out of the house for a little while. So, you haven't been working for him long; how do you like it so far?"

372

Marialena shrugged. "It's great and it seemed like a step in the right direction for me. My personal life was headed in a new direction, and working for Patrick just made sense."

Rebecca nodded, satisfied with her answer, because she didn't ask her anything else. She picked up the magazine she had been reading and casually flipped through the pages.

Marialena sent a text to Patrick. "In my next life, let me be a man who gets to put on a black tux and black shoes and be done with it."

"Sure, then you can go bald or gray, you'll wish you had some color in your wardrobe, and you'll want to look sexier in underwear."

"You don't look sexy in underwear? Esteban does," she said, blushing at the thought of sending this to her boss.

"Oh sure, you would say that about him. I doubt you'd say the same about me. Isn't that why you refused me that first night?"

Did he really just go there? Where was this coming from? How did that happen so quickly? She decided to play along with it.

"Hold on, I'll ask Tina what she thinks."

"Haha, that would be a very short conversation. We haven't been intimate with each other."

"Really? I don't want to say I'm surprised, but honestly, I *am* surprised. It's been what, three weeks?"

"Almost four."

"Jesus, it took me a lot less time with Esteban."

"Did I mention he was a lucky man?"

Marialena blushed. What was going on with these texts?

"So, what's been the hold up?"

"It's all her. She wants to wait."

"Really?" Marialena glanced at Tina, having pegged her all wrong.

"Anyway, when you get back, I want to run something by you. Hopefully, we'll have time before Tina and I have to leave. Come and find me."

"That looks really nice, Tina," Marialena said. When Tina was done, Rebecca got up to take a look as well.

"You're going to look amazing tonight. I can't wait to see the hair and makeup."

Tina nodded and smiled at her sister in the reflection of the mirror. "Do you think we'll get stopped on the red carpet?" Tina asked, her eyes on Marialena now.

Marialena thought for a second. "Well, it depends. Most of the bigger stars come later, so it depends on who's around. He's a big deal and he won last year, and people care about that. They might ask him who he'd like to see win tonight."

"He's not allowed to say, though, is he?"

"Sure, he can."

"I guess I never really paid attention."

"If you two get stopped, just smile and look pretty," Rebecca chimed in.

"What if they ask me something?"

"They'll just tell you that you look amazing; they might even ask you who you're wearing, if it's still a thing. But I doubt they'll ask you anything serious."

"Okay, you're all finished here," the nail technician said and stood up. She turned on the fan and aimed it at Tina's nails. "Wait here, ten minutes."

"Are you nervous about going?" Marialena asked Tina.

"No, not really."

A few minutes later, Rebecca came back. Tina looked down at her nails and stood up.

"Don't try to fish out your wallet. I've got this," Marialena replied, pulling out Patrick's credit card.

"So, is it okay if I hitch a ride with my sister?" Tina asked.

"Of course, just keep in mind that our appointment is in twenty minutes, so don't stop anywhere. Not even for coffee. If you want something later, I can pick it up."

Marialena got into her car a few minutes later. She turned up some music and was grateful that Tina was riding with her sister. Since she had texted with Patrick earlier, she was wondering what Tina was doing with him, even though it was none of her business. If Tina had joined her, she might have been tempted to ask her about it.

When she arrived at the hairdresser, she was pleased to see that Tina and Rebecca had just parked. The three of them walked in together.

A few minutes later, a skinny man dressed in a black v-neck sweater that was too small for him approached from a back room. His straight dark hair was in a ponytail and his face was gaunt. Marialena wondered, upon looking at him, how people could live in Los Angeles and be as pale as he was.

375

"Hey, look at you. Getting ready for the Oscars. I'm so proud," he said, as Tina stood up to give him a hug and a kiss on the cheek.

"Hi Robert. You remember my sister, Rebecca. And this is Marialena. She works for Patrick Denny."

"Rebecca, yes, hello. Why don't you come back to me," he said, touching her hair briefly. "I have some ideas for this." Turning to Tina, "So, what are we thinking for tonight?" he asked, taking her by the hand and leading her to a chair.

Rebecca handed her the phone, and Tina pulled up the picture of her in the dress.

"Great bold color. I like it." He paused for a second and played around with different styles. "We could go classy up-do or down and wild. That dress lends itself to both."

When Marialena came back with coffee twenty minutes later, Robert was still working on Tina, which was to be expected. She handed a coffee to Rebecca and set one down on the counter for Tina.

"Her hair is already looking amazing."

"I know, it's too bad Robert can't be a live-in hairdresser. He's a magician."

"So, let me ask you something, how does Tina feel about the age difference?" Marialena asked Rebecca, wondering if that's what kept her from sleeping with Patrick.

"Honestly, she seems fine with it. I don't know, I don't think I could do it. He's twenty-five years older than she is."

Marialena nodded. "My fiancé is twenty-three years older, and honestly, it's fine."

"Are you serious?"

"Yeah, I mean, he looks a little younger than his age, but it hasn't really been a problem, and he's in great shape. It doesn't seem like his age matters, honestly."

"You said he was a director?"

"Yeah, Esteban Gutierrez."

Rebecca took out her phone and googled him. "Oh, you're right. He looks younger than he is. He's very handsome," Rebecca said.

She nodded proudly. "Yeah."

The two girls chatted for a while longer. Twenty-five minutes later, Tina's hair and makeup were done.

"You look stunning," Rebecca said.

Tina smiled and looked down. Marialena was surprised to find that Tina was shy. She had always thought she was moody and that's why she was quiet, but it turned out that she was just shy. She looked at the time; it was almost two. Marialena gave the sisters some space to say goodbye to each other.

When Tina got into the car, she flipped open the mirror. "I feel like a different person," Tina admitted.

"You look incredible," Marialena said.

"You don't think it's too much?"

"Oh, absolutely not. It feels that way now, because you're not wearing your dress. But once you're out there and you're standing next to Patrick in his tuxedo, trust me, you'll feel the part."

The two girls sat in silence the rest of the way. When Marialena got back to Patrick's, she texted him to let him know they were back.

"Okay, come find me in the master bedroom. Tina's dress is in the guest room next to mine. Let her know, will you?"

"Tina, Patrick wants to see me about something. Your dress is in the guest room next to his. Are you going to need help with it?"

"I think so, yeah."

"Okay, I won't be long. I'll knock, okay?"

Marialena sprinted up the steps and knocked on Patrick's door. "Patrick, it's Mar," she said. He opened the door for her and was half dressed. He was wearing his tuxedo pants, but only a white t-shirt, which he wore tucked.

"Hey, so how'd it go?"

"Perfectly. Patrick, she looks incredible."

Patrick smiled as he closed the door behind her and threw on his dress shirt.

"So, I've been thinking about it, and I wanted to ask you first. What would you think if I took Tina to New York tomorrow? Is that too extreme?" he asked, as she sat down on the edge of his bed, feeling a tad out of place in his bedroom.

"Well, that depends how she feels about you."

"How would you take it?"

"If I were Tina?"

He nodded.

"If I hadn't slept with you and I was going with you to the Oscars?" She thought about it for a second. "Let me ask you something, why hasn't she slept with you?"

"She wants to wait, I guess."

"But for what?"

378

"I don't know. She's attracted to me, that much I know."

"Okay, so if you take her to New York, this could become serious, at least for a while. Is that what you want?"

"Sure, why not? She's a nice girl, not to mention beautiful. I like that's she's not terribly fussy or demanding. She's easy to be around."

"She is, yeah. She's very quiet though. And I thought *I* was quiet. Also, I didn't notice this before, she's a little on the shy side."

"Yeah, you're right about that."

"I don't see why you shouldn't ask her. Anyway, good luck tonight," she said as he put on his bowtie, then his jacket. "You look incredible yourself. I better check in on Tina. She might need some help getting the dress on."

"You get to see her undress before I do, no fair."

"She calls the shots," Marialena said with a smile.

She left Patrick and knocked on Tina's door, announced herself, and came in. Tina took off her clothes as Marialena unwrapped the heavy emerald green dress. She held it high, careful not to drag it on the ground.

"Okay, you don't have to turn around. But we're going to step into it, instead of going over the head," Marialena said, carefully bunching up the fabric at the bottom so that it would be easier for Tina to step into without stepping on the gown.

"Before we zip it up, are you going to wear anything over your breasts?"

"No, I think it'll be fine."

"Okay. I'm going to zip this up." The zipper started at the small of Tina's back, and Marialena zipped it up carefully, trying to avoid catching the fabric. It fit Tina like a glove.

"Okay, turn around. Let's take a look."

Tina turned around. Marialena made a small noise. "Oh Tina, it's absolutely incredible," she said as Tina walked over to the mirror.

"The whole ensemble works," she said, admiring herself and fixing her hair.

Marialena handed her the jewelry and asked her if she wanted Patrick to do the honors of helping her with her necklace. Tina nodded. Marialena knocked on Patrick's door.

"Come in," he said, expecting Tina. "Oh, it's you."

"Don't look so pleased. She's ready, but you should help her with the jewelry."

"Oh, of course. Is she ready for me now?"

Marialena nodded. "I'll be downstairs if you need me."

Patrick and Tina emerged a few minutes later.

"Guys, you look incredible," Marialena said, standing up.

"She does look amazing, doesn't she?"

"You don't feel like you're going to trip on your dress?"

"Well, I do. But I'll be careful."

"Walk slowly, Patrick," Marialena reminded him. "Okay, my job here is done. Patrick, let me know what's in store for the rest of the week," she said and smiled. She collected her things and gave Patrick and Tina a hug. "Good luck, guys. Have fun."

When she got back to Esteban's, Henry was on the couch reading the paper. Marialena set down a few groceries she had picked up on the way back.

"So, how was it?"

"Good. Being a woman is a pain in the ass," she said, half joking.

Henry smiled. "Yeah, I don't know how you chicks do it," he said and walked into the kitchen to see what she had picked up from the store.

He held up the kale. "What is this?"

"Kale. For the salad."

"Leave it out or put it in the fridge?"

"In the fridge, please."

"This must be what it's like to have a live-in girlfriend. Eating things like salads at home, watching the Oscars," he said.

"Oh, come on. You make it sound like torture."

"No, it's kind of nice actually. You're relatively easy to live with, and this is the longest I've ever spent with a woman under the same roof. I can see how it was easy for you and Esteban to decide to live together."

Marialena nodded. "He's pretty easy."

"It's weird watching this relationship unfold. Esteban's different with you than he was with Laura."

"He's different?"

"He's smiling a lot more."

"That could be a number of things," she said.

"Sure, he's working again, and for him that's important. But it's also you. What about you, were you different before Esteban?" he asked, curious.

381

"I was lonelier. I'd watch more movies, read more books, that kind of thing. My life sure wasn't like this, helping someone get ready for the Oscars."

"What would you do for fun?"

"I didn't really."

"No friends?"

"You know, I wasn't really close to any of them. I think I shut out all of my high school friends when my parents died, and afterward, I just never really made new ones. I tried for a while, but it all got to the point where trying just got hard. And I had Roxanne."

"Your cousin?"

Marialena nodded, looking a little sad.

"She's on the other side of the country though. How have you managed to be by yourself for so long?" Henry asked.

"I had Esteban's films," she replied.

He smiled. "So, they saved you?"

"No, they gave me hope. I held out for that. And it paid off."

"Well, it's a good thing he can pass for attractive, you know, depending on who you ask," he said, laughing. "He could have been two hundred pounds with a beard down to here."

"Yeah, I got lucky. He's not too neurotic or weird. He's pretty normal, actually."

"Well, I don't know about that. He's quiet. Like way too quiet."

"No one's perfect. Lord knows I'm not."

"Nah, you're pretty normal."

"You know, I feel normal now actually. I didn't for a long time. And I guess, at night, it comes back to me, the old hauntings. They don't let me forget," she said with that sad look in her eyes again.

Henry picked up the can of tomato sauce she'd use for the enchiladas and threw it in the air. "Well, Esteban is coming back tomorrow. Don't worry about it so much. I'm sure it will go away, whatever it is."

"Yeah," she said, taking the can of food from him. "Didn't anyone tell you not to play with food?"

Marialena went to change into something more comfortable, a warm pair of fleece leggings and one of her own flannels. She started cooking, while Henry flipped channels. When everything was in the oven simmering, she sat down with Henry on the couch. The Oscars pre-show had started.

Marialena got up during the commercial break to check on the rice. She gave it a stir and came back.

"Smells good in here."

"You know, you should start learning how to cook. It's not hard."

"Maybe one day," he said.

"You taught yourself how to play guitar, so you could teach yourself how to make dinner every once in a while."

Henry thought about it for a second. "I was going to say that I picked up the guitar to pick up chicks, but that's a lie. I picked it up to play the music I idolized. But I guess girls also dig guys who can cook. Maybe you're right. I should."

Marialena laughed and shook her head. The timer went off. She stood up.

She served dinner and they ate at the table, watching the Oscars.

383

"Oh my god, there they are," Marialena exclaimed.

The woman interviewing Patrick asked him a question and Patrick let out a laugh. He held Tina's hand, who was smiling. She looked absolutely stunning.

"Well, I'm presenting this year, so the pressure is off for the time being. I have to admit, this is nice. I get to come and just enjoy it all, without all the stress."

"I am admiring this emerald," the woman said, referring to Tina's dress. "Who are you wearing tonight? I must say, you look fabulous."

"Thank you, it's a Valentino."

"It's divine. And look, here comes Julianne Moore," the woman said, which was Patrick's cue to exit. He smiled politely and that was it.

Marialena put a hand on her heart. "Wow, she looked beautiful."

"So, you helped them get ready today?"

"I did."

"What did that entail exactly?"

"Getting her nails done, figuring out how to wear her hair and makeup. That kind of thing."

"Did you help her with her dress?"

Marialena nodded, taking a bite of the enchilada.

"And are they a couple?"

"Well, they haven't slept together yet, but I think they might be starting something."

"He hasn't been able to sleep with her yet?" Henry said and whistled. "What's that about?"

"I don't know, to be honest."

"Well, if she doesn't sleep with him tonight, he doesn't have a chance," Henry said.

384

"I don't really want to talk about my boss getting laid," she said.

"Oh come on, he's hardly a boss. He's more like a rich man who's paying you to help his incredible-looking women in incredible-looking clothes," he said, teasing her.

"Hey, I do more than that, thank you very much."

"I know, I'm only kidding. Hey, this is really good by the way, thank you."

"No problem."

They watched the rest of the show and talked throughout. She called Roxanne a little later, and the rest of the night was relaxing and nice. When Patrick presented, he was smooth and confident. Marialena smiled, watching him.

When the Oscars were finally over, Marialena took a shower. When she came out of the bathroom, Henry was in gym shorts and a t-shirt, clothes he slept in around her.

"Ready for bed?" he asked.

She nodded.

Henry went into the bathroom to get ready for bed. When he emerged, Marialena was already in bed. He turned out the light and got in next to her."

"Thanks so much for this past week," she said into the silence. "Thanks for putting up with me."

"No problem. You'll finally be rid of me tomorrow. Are you going to miss me?"

"Yes, of course," she said and curled up to him. She put an arm around him. "You'll never know what this has meant to me."

"Hey, it's okay," he said, placing a hand on hers. He took a deep breath. "Let's not talk about it. Just get some rest. I'll stay until you fall asleep. I have some errands to run in the morning, but I'll be back in the afternoon to see my brother before I leave."

"Okay," she said. "Have a good night, Henry."

"You too, Lena." He already missed how her body felt against his. This was their last night together. He wanted to try to get closer, but he knew it was a bad idea. He was honest when he told Laura that Marialena only had eyes for Esteban. There was nothing he could do. She was asleep minutes later, with thoughts of Esteban on her mind.

Chapter Twenty-five

It was Monday morning, the day Marialena had been waiting for. Henry had left to go to the bank, giving Marialena some privacy. He'd be leaving for Temecula later that afternoon.

When Esteban arrived, Marialena sprinted to the door and greeted him before he set his bags down. He looked amazing, even as tired as he was.

"God, I missed you," she said. He put an arm around her and set down his bags. She kissed him on the mouth, but he cut it short, smiling a small smile. He looked a little distracted. Marialena wondered if he had gotten sick. She had never seen him look so tired before, or scruffy.

"How was your week?" he asked her, walking to the kitchen to get a glass of water. Marialena gave him a perplexed look.

"It was good," she said, leaning against the sofa. "Henry is out running errands. How was your trip?"

Esteban sighed and brought his water out to the sofa. Both of them sat down. Marialena braced herself. Something was off. "It was…eye-opening. I didn't get to work at all. Robert stayed longer, a day longer actually, and the last day I was there I did a lot of thinking. I think we need to talk, Marialena."

Marialena watched him, waiting for him to continue.

Esteban sat down and ran a hand through his hair; he decided to cut right to the chase. "Rob, he uh, he's about eight years older than me. And Marialena, I'd be lying if I told you I didn't see myself in eight years looking just like him. He seemed so much older to me. And I know we've gone over this a few times, but you're going to be thirty-five years old in eight years and I'm going to be fifty-eight. That just doesn't seem *fair* to you," he said. "I've been thinking about it this whole week. Marialena, I can't let you go through with this."

"Go through with what? What are you saying?" she asked, feeling everything at once. Scared, panicked, sad, angry.

"I don't think we should get married," he said.

Marialena sat on the couch, her mouth open. She looked around the room, searching for the right words. "Esteban, look, I love you. I don't care what you'll look like in eight years."

"I think you will. You didn't see this guy. That's going to be me one day, one day really soon."

Mairalena was furious. "I don't care."

"I do!" he said, his voice rising. "I can't do this to you."

"Don't you love me?" she asked.

"Of course. It's not that. I think my love for you is blinding me to the fact that this probably isn't going to work in the long run."

"Why can't you trust me? Why can't you have faith in this?"

"I'm sorry, Marialena. I don't know what to say. I feel terrible about all of this."

Marialena grabbed her keys and purse and left. She was fuming.

When Henry got back to Esteban's an hour later, he found him on the couch with a glass of whiskey in his hand, his eyes bloodshot.

"Hey, welcome back. Everything okay?" Henry sat down on the chair adjacent to the sofa. "Where's Lena?"

"I called it off."

"WHAT?!"

"Look, it never would have worked. You're right. She's too young for me."

"And you suddenly realized this?"

"The guy I went with, Robert. You should have seen him. He's not that much older than me, but I swear I saw myself in him. And I can't do that to her, man."

"Are you fucking kidding me? That guy, whoever the fuck he is, he isn't you."

"Dude, my age is going to catch up with me sooner or later, and Marialena will still be young and beautiful."

Henry stood up and paced the floor. "You're making a huge mistake. Where is she?"

"She left. I don't know."

"You're a fucking asshole, you know that?"

"I'm sparing her the pain. I'm freeing her from this."

"She doesn't need to be freed from anything. She's made her decision."

"A decision she's going to eventually regret."

"You don't know that."

"Hey, this is my life."

"It's hers too."

Henry picked up his keys.

"Where are you going?"

389

"I'm going to go find her."

Esteban called out after his brother. "Have a nice life together. Give her my best, will you?"

Henry was heading out the door, but stopped short. "What did you say?"

"Oh, come on, I know how you look at her."

Henry walked over to Esteban and punched him in the face. He fell back into the sofa.

"What the fuck, man!" Esteban yelled.

"She fucking loves you, man. She's fucking crazy about you. And yeah, I've looked at her. She's beautiful. Sure. But you know what? Even if I was the type of guy who'd try and take her away from you, I couldn't fucking come close to getting her to love me the way she loves you. You know what she told me? She told me that she wants to have your kids. You know how many women have ever said that to me? And what? All this because you hung out with some older guy? Get it together, man. Don't throw this away because you're scared she might stop loving you"

Esteban looked into his lap. "Fuck." Henry sat down next to his brother, not sorry he had hit him. "I don't know what to do," Esteban said.

"She loves you."

"I've blown it, haven't I? I don't deserve her."

Henry pulled an envelope from his jacket and handed it to Esteban.

"That's your share from the restaurant. It's all there. Everything you put in." He held another envelope in his hand. "Do you want to know what this is? A lease agreement between Marialena and me. I'm moving into her apartment next month, and she's moving in here."

"Shit," Esteban said.

"Yeah. We've been pretty fucking busy. It was supposed to be a surprise." Henry looked at his brother, who was downright distraught. "What do you want out of all of this? Do you want to marry her?"

"Yeah, I mean, I love her."

"Let her love you back."

"I can't. I don't know why, but I can't."

"You know how many men your age would share your opinion? Zero. Look, I'm going to go and see if I can find her, but I have to be in Temecula tonight. Do you have a spare key to her place?"

Esteban nodded. "What are you going to do when you find her?"

"I don't know, make sure she's okay. Hold down the fort until you get your shit together."

"I need some time to think. Fuck."

"Figure it out. She shouldn't be alone though. You were right about her, you know that, right? She's all types of messed up at night. She told me what happened. It's not pretty."

Esteban looked at his brother, feeling even worse about himself. "I don't know if I can come tonight. I need to figure out what to do."

"Find a way to fix it." Henry walked out.

He drove over to Marialena's, grateful his brother had given him the key. He didn't call, he just drove. He knew that she would probably turn him away if he called. He didn't even know if she was home, but he had to try.

Twenty-five minutes later he was there and knocked on her door.

"Marialena, it's Henry."

He knocked once more. "I have a key, I'm coming in."

"Marialena?" He called out again. No answer. He checked the bathroom, nothing. He called her and was surprised to hear her phone ringing from somewhere in the bedroom. That's when he saw her purse on the bed. Where was she?

He went outside through the sliding glass door and saw her sitting on the floor, watching the traffic on the busy street below. She was dressed in leggings, boots, and a blouse, but she wasn't wearing a jacket and it was cold.

He took off his jacket and draped it around her shoulders.

"How you doing?" he asked.

"I'm feeling pretty shitty, Henry," she said, staring straight ahead. She held out her hand and handed him the engagement ring in a box. He held it in his hands, turning it over and over nervously. "You wanted me to give that back to Esteban, in case it didn't work out? Well, you can give it back to him yourself," she said.

"He told you about that?"

"Yeah. A few days after we got engaged," she said.

"Listen, Marialena. Forget that. I didn't know you then."

"It's okay. It doesn't matter now. It's over."

"You have to know, this isn't about you. He loves you. He's just freaking out."

"Why are you even here? Don't you have to be back in Temecula?"

She looked at him now, and he could see her tear-stained face, but she didn't look sad. She looked angry.

392

"I want to make sure you're not alone, Lena. Why don't we get back inside, it's cold out here." He led her to the couch where they both sat in silence.

Henry took the ring out of the box. She noticed that his knuckle was bloody and a little swollen.

"Jesus, what happened to your hand?"

"Nothing," he said calmly. He held out his good hand and took her hand in his. "Marialena, listen to me. This week has been incredible." He took a deep breath. He remembered what she had said the other night about making the leap when the time called for it. And hadn't his brother already assumed that he was here for Marialena? Henry took a deep breath. He looked at her lips, drew himself closer to her.

"Marialena, do you remember when you were asking me not to be afraid to jump when the time came?"

Marialena looked into his eyes and nodded.

He pulled her ever so closer toward him and he kissed her softly on the lips, then more passionately. He loved how she felt against him, his lips pressed against hers. He placed a hand softly on her face, and Marialena placed a hand over his hand, breaking up the kiss. She kissed his fingers, tears falling from her eyes.

"Henry, I can't. I'm sorry, I can't."

Henry nodded. He was trembling. He took the engagement ring out of his pocket and looked away for a second, fighting his emotions. He cleared his throat.

"This ring belongs to you," he said.

"What are you doing?"

"Marialena,'' he said, looking into her eyes, close to tears. He looked away, placing his left hand on his forehead. After a few seconds, he looked into her eyes

393

again and cleared his throat, trying to get a grip. He took a deep breath before speaking, trying to decide what to do. "My brother gave you this ring. He just needs to figure out how to jump. Don't take it off. He's going to come back." He placed the ring back on her finger.

Marialena took a deep breath, tears falling from her eyes. "He's not here giving it to me, you are. And you just kissed me."

"I'm sorry, I shouldn't have. Forget that I kissed you. It was a stupid thing to do. But, promise me, don't take this off again. It's yours. You're meant to have it. My mom would be doing the same thing if she were here instead of me. Please believe me, he'll come around." He cleared his throat again and let go of her hand. He sat back against the couch. "Esteban just turned fifty. He's been on this earth for that long. And he's never once been in this position. Getting married, falling in love, it's just cold feet. Look, I know him. He's an over-thinker. He's in his own head too much and always has been. He's just scared, but he'll come around. I know he wants you to have the ring, trust me."

Marialena was crying. "I just wish I could prove it to him. He asked me to move in with him, so that I could be sure. And oh my god, I fell in love with him, so much more than I ever thought I could. Why isn't that enough?"

"We all have our fears."

"I opened up to him more than I would have with anyone else. I think I trusted him more because of his work, and I know that sounds ridiculous, but it's true. I'm not proud of it. But it took off on its own from there. He's been good for me and I can't explain how or why."

Henry shrugged. "I don't know. I don't know what to say. It's a complicated relationship."

Marialena laughed. "I don't think so. I love him, he loves me. What's complicated about that? I'm so sick of people, Esteban in particular, thinking that they know what's right for me. *I* know what's right for me. And trust me, this is right for me."

"He's just looking out for you, Marialena."

"Bullshit. He's not looking out for me. He's scared. He's scared I'm going to turn on him. He has to have some faith in me."

"No, he is looking out for you. He wants to give you more, he wants more for you, more time on this planet maybe. Time he doesn't think he has years from now."

"He's not that old!"

"Don't sit there and try and tell me that twenty-two years isn't a big difference."

"And I'll take ten years with him rather than one or two or forty years with someone who isn't him."

"I know that. I do. And he does, too."

Marialena patted him on the knee. "Well, I guess we'll have to wait and see. But don't think that I won't give him hell for this. I'm sick of this, Henry."

"I know."

"Look, why don't you get going? Don't worry about me, I'll be okay."

"I do have to leave eventually. And I'll get there. I'm hungry, though. Do you have anything to eat here?"

Marialena shook her head. "Not a single thing." She watched him as he opened up the cupboards. She took off his jacket and followed him into the kitchen.

395

"Wanna order some pizza?" he asked.

"It does sound good right now. Yeah, let's get some."

"Salad?"

She shook her head. "No salad."

"Oh shit, look out. No salad!" Henry exclaimed, trying to cheer her up.

Marialena laughed, feeling a little better. "Calm down."

"Oh, I'm never calm about pizza."

"I like it, too. It's my favorite. But it is just pizza."

Henry looked at her seriously. "Are you trying to get on my bad side? I don't understand this; I come over, try to do a nice thing, and she says 'it's just pizza?' I don't think you actually like pizza."

"Oh come on, you came over to cop a feel," she said, laughing.

"I didn't, honestly. It was a bad move on my part," he said, his smile fading.

"That excuse is starting to get old."

Henry put a hand on his heart. "So that's what a broken heart feels like."

"You know what love is?" Marialena asked, ignoring him. "Have you ever had pizza from scratch?"

"Do you think I was born yesterday?"

"Well, I'm just asking."

"Of course I have. It's heaven on earth."

"You should learn how to make it."

"Yeah, let's try and figure that out one day. Right here, in this kitchen."

"I guess the real question is, will it be yours or mine?"

"Oh, mine. Speaking of which," he said, pulling an envelope out of his pocket. "I have the lease."

"Shut up, you got it?"

"Yeah, you want me to hang on to it, or should we sign it?"

"Let's take that leap. Think the pizza place can deliver a bottle of wine?"

"I don't think so, why?"

"Let's see if they can."

"I seriously doubt they can. But I shouldn't drink too much, I still need to drive."

"One glass?"

"A small glass, sure. You're right, we need to celebrate this."

"Alright, we'll order the food, but then we'll walk down to this liquor store before it gets here. We can sign it, then!"

"This means you have to move in with my brother. How do you feel about that?"

Marialena danced where she was standing in the kitchen with Henry. "I don't know. We'll have to see what he does."

"So, you're putting your money on him?"

"I think, yes. I think I'm all in. All or nothing."

"Come on, I'm starving. Let's order some food!"

They ordered pizza and walked to the liquor store for a decent bottle of wine. When the pizza arrived, they dove in hungrily.

"You were so right. This is exactly what I needed," she said.

"Don't you just love it when I'm right?"

Marialena nudged him playfully with her knee. "Don't let it get to your head. Look, why don't you get going. Don't worry about me, I'll be okay."

"Soon." Henry took out the lease and laid it on the coffee table. She picked it up and read over it.

"This doesn't say anything about selling my soul over to you, does it?"

"Not to my knowledge, but we can add that in later if you want," he said jokingly.

"Okay, let's do this." Marialena grabbed a pen and signed it. Then she handed the pen to Henry and he signed it too.

"It's official," she said.

"Congratulations on your new tenant. I think I need to make a phone call. I'll be right back, okay? I'm just going to step outside for a second."

Outside, Henry tried to call his brother but noticed him sitting across the street in his car.

"What are you doing? You just get here?" Henry asked.

"I got here about half an hour ago."

"What the hell are you waiting for?" Henry noticed how bad Esteban's eye had gotten. "Jesus, I'm sorry about your eye."

"It's fine. I deserved it. How is she?"

Henry smiled. "She's okay. Go talk to her. I've gotta get back to Temecula." He hugged his brother. "Good luck up there." Henry walked back to his own car and drove off.

Esteban walked up to Marialena's door and knocked.

398

"What happened to your eye?" she asked, wanting to caress his face.

"Henry," he said.

"Jesus, I didn't know. What happened?"

"I said something I shouldn't have," he said, following her into the living room.

"Can I get you something? Wine?" she asked, feeling like a stranger.

"No, I'm okay. Thanks."

She sat on the opposite end of the couch with her wine in her hand, waiting for him to speak.

"Marialena, I'm sorry. I'm an idiot."

All she wanted to do was crawl into his arms and take him back, but she was mad. The anger took over.

"I did what you asked. I moved in with you. I fell in love with you, and you proposed. Then you go off to god knows where and come back and it's all over. That's no small thing. And what I don't get is that you decided it wasn't a good idea without even talking to me about it."

"I know. I should have. I'm sorry."

"Esteban, I love you," she said, her eyes watering. "I love you so much. Why can't you just accept that?"

"I don't know. I want to. Believe me, I want to."

He inched closer to her, reached out for her hand. She gave it to him, unsure of herself. "I don't want to break off the engagement." He took a deep breath. "But I think I need a few days to screw my head back on right."

She was still mad. She pulled her hands away from him.

"It's just not fair," she said, hating that she sounded like a child. "You get to call all the shots, and no one believes me when I say I'm in love. It's like my voice

399

doesn't matter, and why? Because I'm young? Well, I know what I'm talking about, and I want this."

"I want this too. But I also want more for you."

"More? How is that even possible? You're everything to me. And what, you're allowed to break my heart now, because you're afraid I'm going to break yours years from now?"

Esteban sighed. "Look, I'm sorry. I don't know why we're even talking about this. Marialena, I love you. I don't want to end this. I want to be with you." He caressed her hand. "Look, I need a few days. I just really need to get back into the swing of things, I need to erase this week from my memory." He kissed her hand. "Hey, I missed you too. Like crazy. God, especially at night."

Marialena held his hand tighter. "We should talk about that."

"Yeah, I know. Henry told me a little bit. Is everything okay?"

She told him about the night her parents died, that she felt guilty for not answering her phone, that she was a mess for a really long time, that she dropped out of school, and that nothing made sense.

Marialena shook her head. "I tried meds for a while, but honestly, I hated them. Taking them every night reminded me of what I was missing, what I was doing with my life, and it made me feel worse. I know it sounds crazy, but somehow, just staying awake, I got used to it.

Esteban nodded. "I'm sorry that I've brought this all on you."

Marialena didn't agree. "I'm not sorry. I love you, and if this is what happens when I fall in love, so be it. It's just something I need to figure out. I'm sure it will eventually go away."

"Are you going to be okay tonight?"

"I'll be fine. This isn't anything I can't handle."

"I'm glad Henry was there for you. I'm only sorry I wasn't."

She walked over to him and they hugged, holding on to each other for a long time. She put her arms around his waist, underneath of his jacket, each of them taking deep breaths.

"I'll call you. This will all be over in a few days. I won't let you down again."

Her eyes watered as he kissed her on the cheek and she watched him leave. She closed the door behind him, and missed him more than she had all week. He looked tired and disheveled. He looked as miserable as she felt.

When Marialena got out of the shower, she watched a movie—not one of Esteban's. She couldn't deal with that now. When she needed a comfort movie in the past, she always went for his. But now things were different.

She took off some layers of clothes and went to bed, but grabbed her book, just in case.

Then she heard someone come in the front door and say her name. She turned the light on next to her bed and waited, thinking it was Esteban.

Henry poked his head in the bedroom.

"Hey, thought I'd find you in here," he said as he plopped on the bed.

"What are you doing here?" she asked with a smile. She was pleasantly surprised.

401

"Don't worry about it. So, I heard you two patched it up."

"I guess so, but he needs time, like you said."

"I know it's only for one night, but I wanted to make sure you wouldn't be alone. I have to drive back again tomorrow."

"You came back all this way?"

"We're family. And this is a rough time for you. And me, really. Tonight was awful."

"So, you told them?" she asked, referring to his staff.

"It fucking sucked. I feel absolutely terrible right now, so you're in good company."

Marialena nodded. "I'm sorry."

"I'm glad I came back, I didn't want to be alone, either. Is it cool?"

"Yeah, it is. Hey, do you really think Esteban will come around?"

"I am positive he will. Hey, come here. Let me get under these blankets." A few tears started to fall from her face.

She let herself be held. "Thanks for coming. I should probably throw on some clothes. I'm not wearing any pants," she said, her voice muffled, crying softly into his clothes.

"It's okay. Just stay here for a second. It's going to be okay. I promise."

Marialena let herself be held by Henry. She held him back, happy that he was there, knowing that he was also going through his own problems. She put her hand on his chest, trying to comfort him.

402

"It's not really about the money at this point. And I know it's the right thing to do for me, it just doesn't *feel right.* And I guess I didn't want to be alone tonight, so I came here." He took a deep breath. "I'm beat, though. I don't think I'll have any trouble falling asleep."

She lay in his arms for a few minutes, just listening to him breathe.

"Henry?" she finally asked.

"Yeah?" he asked, his voice deeper than usual. She could tell he was tired.

"When you put the engagement ring on my finger, I totally thought that you were—" She let the sentence hang in mid-air.

Henry exhaled loudly. "I know. I did too. I wasn't sure, to be honest, but it was crazy thinking. You and Esteban should be together." Henry couldn't believe he had almost proposed either. He barely knew Marialena. Still, he knew there was something about her, something special. It was an emotional time for him, and for Marialena too. He wasn't thinking straight. At least, that's what he was telling himself.

"Are you serious?" She propped herself up to see him better. "I thought I was maybe imagining it."

He stared at the ceiling. "You weren't. Don't worry about though."

"Henry," she said again, unsure of what to say.

"Hey, I didn't ask," he said, his voice rough.

"Do we need to talk about this?" she asked.

"What's there to talk about? It won't make a difference either way," he said. For a few minutes, neither of them said anything. Then he asked into the silence, "It wouldn't have made a difference, right?"

"No," she said. "It wouldn't have." She didn't hesitate in the slightest.

Marialena found her way back into his arms. "Henry, I'm so sorry." He put his arm around her as she pulled herself up toward his mouth. "Don't take this the wrong way," she said and kissed him softly on the lips. He held her tightly, their faces touching. "Thank you so much for everything. I'm so sorry."

She slid back down and rested her head on his chest.

"I don't want you to leave, but I also feel like maybe you shouldn't be here," she said.

"I just didn't want you to be alone."

"Henry, we can't do this."

He took a deep breath. "I know. Don't worry, I won't try anything like that again, but I really don't want to drive back tonight. We'll figure the rest out. Please don't tell Esteban, though. He doesn't need to know how I feel about you. I'm sure it will pass."

"I appreciate everything you've done. You can't imagine how much I've appreciated it, but I can't lead you on."

"You're not leading me on. Do you want me to leave? I can get a hotel? I will."

"No, it's okay. You're tired. I'm tired too. I'm glad you came back, really I am."

Marialena stayed in his arms for a few minutes longer, but finally wiggled herself free. Henry got out of bed, changed into pajamas, and brushed his teeth.

When he was gone, Marialena jumped out of bed in her underwear to look for some pants. She looked through her drawers in a panic, realizing that all of her winter clothes were at Esteban's. She found a small pair of shorts and quickly put them on, just in time for Henry to see.

"You're paranoid," he said, laughing. "And I do have some willpower, you know."

She got back into bed and smiled.

"I trust you. Have a good night, Henry."

"Goodnight. Sleep well," he said, wishing he wasn't as tired as he was. He wanted to remember this moment, with her in her own bed.

"You too."

Chapter Twenty-six

The next morning, Henry woke up to find Marialena still asleep. He was mad at himself for slipping last night. He felt guilty. He knew that he wasn't going to come between them, but he shouldn't have told her. He cursed under his breath and lay back down, wondering how this would change things between them.

Marialena woke up to a text from Roxanne. She was alone in bed and gave Roxanne a quick synopsis of the previous twenty-four hours. Roxanne was the constant supportive rock in her life.

"It's nothing I can't handle. But you were totally right about Henry. Just don't talk to anyone about it, okay? Not one word to anyone. Esteban is a famous director, don't forget that. Word gets around."

"I won't say a word. Call me when you can."

Marialena put her phone down and tried to close her eyes for a while. She thought about what Henry said last night. Maybe he was just feeling vulnerable because of his restaurant staff.

Henry knocked on the bedroom door. He was clean-shaven and wide awake.

"Wow, love that water pressure. I'm excited. I can't believe that's going to be my shower every day," he said from the doorway. "I made coffee."

"I don't have any creamer."

"I take it black."

"I know, but I don't. Think we can pick some up somewhere?"

"Yeah, we can grab breakfast before I have to leave."

A half hour later, Marialena was dressed and ready to go, wearing old clothes from when she was younger. All of her newer stuff was at Esteban's. She had started looking more sophisticated when she began dating Esteban, and she welcomed it. It was time. But now she looked at herself in the mirror and felt ten years younger. She came out of the bedroom and realized that all of her makeup was also at Esteban's.

Marialena tied up her hair and put on a Dodgers cap. She looked at Henry. "Don't you dare say anything about the way I look."

She grabbed her purse and a hoodie and they were out the door. Henry was dressed down too, in jeans and a sweater.

When they got in the car, Marialena was interrupted by a call from Esteban.

"Hello?" she asked, her heart racing.

"Hey, I was just calling to say good morning," he said.

"Morning," she said quietly.

"I have to say, it feels weird to be here without you."

"I know the feeling," she said, looking out of the window, feeling awkward in front of Henry.

"So, I talked to Henry last night. He told me he was driving back up to Los Angeles. He make it there okay?" She didn't know that Esteban knew Henry was there.

"Yeah, he did," she said. "Hopefully in a few days this will all be over," she said.

407

"Yeah, I think so. Anyway, I just wanted to say hi. I'll call later, okay?"

"Sure."

She hung up as Henry pulled up to the diner and they both got out. He didn't ask her about the phone call. He didn't need to.

"I have never wanted coffee so badly. Why'd you wake up so early this morning?" Marialena asked Henry.

"Beats me," he said. But he knew the answer. He hadn't intended on telling Marialena how he felt, and now that he had, he was worried that it might alter their friendship or create an uncomfortable situation between them, especially since he was moving into her place. He was restless the whole night.

Henry felt his phone vibrate. It was Esteban.

"Hey, are you with her right now?"

"Yeah, we're out for breakfast. Hey, let me call you back, actually. Give me a second."

When they got to the restaurant, Henry let Marialena go ahead of him while he stayed behind to call his brother back. "So, I was thinking about taking her back to Temecula with me. She could spend the night, and I could drop her off tomorrow at your place. What do you think?"

"Yeah, sure. But what's there for her to do in Temecula?"

"She could hang out at the restaurant, do some light shopping. I don't know. It's a hell of a lot better than sitting around her apartment all alone."

"That's true. Where is she going to sleep? That sofa of yours is rough."

"I'll sleep there."

"If she wants to go, I can spring for a hotel for the both of you. It might be more comfortable."

"Sure, yeah. Hey, if we go, we might need to swing by your place. All of her clothes and shit are at your place."

"Yeah, sure. I have to run some errands later. Come on by in about an hour; I'll leave some money on the table for the hotel."

"All right, cool. How much time do you think you'll need to collect yourself, man?"

"I don't know, two or three days."

"But you're definitely getting back with her, right?"

"Yeah, I am. I just need to be in a better place than I am right now. That fucking trip screwed me up."

"All right, man. We'll be by later."

"Okay. Hey, and thanks. For looking out for her. I owe you one."

"Don't worry about it. Let me ask you something though. She's going to forgive you. Honestly, it's not going to take a whole lot. She's yours, and she wants you back. Don't you think taking this time away might look like the opposite? If you love her, why take the time at all?"

"Because I went over to her place last night, and I had nothing. I need to have something. I need to tell her how I feel, and I need to figure out what I want to say. I sort of rushed through the marriage proposal and it was a big fiasco; I want to do this right. I want to get it right this time, Henry. I want to marry this woman, I really do."

"Okay, your call. Call me if you need anything. I should get back in there," he said.

"See you in a couple of days."

409

Henry came back inside to find Marialena with coffee. She had both hands around the mug and she was smiling.

"Coffee is in my life again and it is so good," she said happily.

He looked at her and smiled. "Hey, so I was thinking. Come to Temecula for a few days with me."

Marialena looked up at him with big brown eyes, unsure of what to say. "What? Why?"

"You could hang out, see the restaurant. Go shopping. We could get a hotel."

"Yeah, but what if Esteban wants to see me? What if he wants to talk?"

"We'll be back in a couple of days."

"I don't know, Henry."

"Okay, confession. That was Esteban on the phone. I might have mentioned it to him. He didn't think it was a bad idea, and the hotel was actually his idea."

Marialena nodded. "So, he's okay with me just running off with his brother?" she asked angrily.

"Marialena, it's not like that. Listen, he loves you. I know that for a fact. I also know he's going to marry you, because he told me. But he wants to start on the right foot again. *It's important to him*. He feels like shit right now, and he knows he fucked up. And it's not such a hot idea to leave you alone while you're kind of waiting around for him to figure it out."

Marialena nodded, taking it all in. The food arrived and she welcomed the silence as she thought.

"Okay, maybe you're right. The idea of me at home alone right now isn't very tempting."

410

"The two of you obviously want to be together, and more than that, you belong together. He's my brother and you're going to be family, so this is what family does."

Marialena nodded, accepting his answer. "I don't have any clothes for the trip."

"Esteban isn't going to be home later. I told him we'd swing by to pick up some things."

They finished their breakfast together and went back to her place so she could pack a few things.

When they got to Esteban's, he wasn't home. Marialena walked into the bedroom and inhaled Esteban's scent from that morning. She lay there for ten minutes without moving, but was interrupted when Henry knocked on the door.

"Hey, sorry. I didn't hear anything. I just wanted to make sure everything was okay."

"Everything's fine. I just miss him, Henry. I want this to be over. I want to hold him in my arms and never let go," she said sleepily, without moving.

"All right, I'll give you some privacy," he said, turning to walk away.

"No, it's okay. This is just torture, anyway," she said, finally getting up. Henry gave her some space as she pulled herself together and packed her bag. When she walked out a few minutes later, she was wearing one of Esteban's knit sweaters and she felt better.

They left a few minutes later. There was a little bit of traffic. Henry hooked his phone to his car stereo and played music, neither of them speaking a whole lot.

A few hours later, Henry got off the freeway and pulled into a quiet suburban area.

411

"I need to change before work," he said.

"We're going to see your place?" she asked excitedly.

"Yeah. Then we can check into the hotel. After that, we'll stop by the restaurant, grab a bite to eat."

Henry pulled into a condo community, much bigger than hers and completely different from Esteban's.

"So, Esteban used to live here?"

"Yeah, a long time ago. Leave your overnight bag here. It'll be okay."

Marialena looked around his place, trying to imagine Esteban living there, with his own stuff. She saw a couple of pictures. "Oh my god, that's you and Esteban and your mom?"

"Yeah, Esteban was about twenty and I was ten."

"This is the first time I've seen a picture of your mom," Marielana said, feeling the weight of her engagement ring on her finger. "My god, Henry, she was so beautiful. How old was she in this picture?"

Henry did some quick math. "Forty-two."

"Wow. She was a knockout. I see some of her in you."

"She's not smiling in that picture, but yeah, we have the same smile too. Esteban looks more like my dad."

"Esteban is so young in this picture, I can't believe it. Look at the both of you." Esteban's hair was short, and he was smiling at something off camera. Henry was sitting next to his mom.

"He had such a baby face," Marialena said. "I can't believe I'm seeing this for the first time. Your mom too. Why doesn't Esteban have any pictures?"

"I'm sure he does somewhere."

412

"Henry, what happened to your dad? No one ever talks about him."

Henry exhaled and sat down on the couch.

"My dad died when I was about five...cancer. It broke my mom's heart. She didn't like us to talk about him. She was so heartbroken. She never really dated or anything after that."

"I'm so sorry," she said.

"Yeah," he said, sighing. "Maybe that's what scares me about being in a relationship. Feeling that way about someone."

"You think so?"

"I don't know."

"Esteban had a lot more time with your dad than you did. I didn't know any of this. Esteban never talks about him."

"They weren't close. I think they had a lot of disagreements growing up. He was hard on Esteban, called him a dreamer. And I was always kind of bitter that Esteban left when he did. I felt like he had abandoned my mom and me. I don't think that now, but I did growing up. We weren't close for a long time."

"Is that why you stuck around in New York?"

"Well, yeah. I couldn't leave her. She never found love again. She never even tried. She was a beautiful woman, but she was devoted to my dad. When she died, Esteban and I got a little closer. And I moved to Temecula when he settled in Los Angeles. I didn't have anywhere else to be. But we still kind of led our own lives." Henry stood up. "All right, well, let me get dressed. I'll be right out. Make yourself at home. I don't have much to offer you; I haven't been to the market in at least two weeks."

413

"I'm okay, thanks." She continued to look around, gravitating toward his guitars. She picked one up, strummed the strings. She looked out on the balcony. He lived on the second floor, like her. There wasn't much of a view.

When Henry came back out, he was wearing a button-down dress shirt. They walked back out and Henry drove to the hotel, where he needed to check them in.

"Okay, we're all set. Here's your key," he said, and he handed her a card. "Take this in case you need it, if you want to come here after you go shopping."

"Thanks," she said. She put it in her purse as Henry drove to the restaurant.

He started to talk about the history of the town, how long the restaurant he took over had been in place, the kind of food they served, and the staff he had. She could tell he was getting excited about showing it to her.

They arrived at the restaurant. The place not only looked old, it felt old. Ten years ago it might have survived looking the way it did, nostalgic and classic, but not here in Temecula, where the population was still growing and new restaurants were popping up all over the place.

Henry grabbed her hand and she let him as he led her into the kitchen. "Hey guys," he said boisterously. "I want you guys to meet Marialena. She's here from Los Angeles and is going to be staying for a few days. So I wanted to bring her here," he said awkwardly as she greeted the cooks.

"Smells amazing," she said, smiling big.

He walked her back out to the seating area and she picked a booth as Henry handed her a menu.

"On the house. As long as you don't order a salad. Please, don't insult me," he said, laughing.

"Okay, no salad, got it," she replied, smiling.

"Good. So, I actually need to work now; I'll be in the office for a little bit. But, if you need me, Jennifer can direct you."

"Okay," she said and ordered a cheeseburger. She took out a book she had brought with her. When the food arrived, she took a big bite. It was delicious.

Henry dropped by her table right before she was done eating.

"How is it?" he asked.

She had food in her mouth as she answered. "So good."

Henry slid into the booth across from her and stole a french fry. "So, what are you going to do after this?"

"I'm thinking about going to the mall soon."

"Okay, I'll be here in case you need anything," he said. "Let me know if you want me to pick you up."

Later, Marialena walked outside and scheduled an Uber pickup to go to the mall.

She looked around a few stores and found a perfect black dress. It was a high neckline turtleneck dress. The skirt went down to the knees and it was long sleeved and fit her perfectly. She was at the mall for two hours, but didn't really see anything else, so she decided to take an Uber back to the restaurant. When she got there, she set her new purchase aside and asked for a red wine. The bartender brought it over and made small talk about why she was sitting alone.

Marialena shrugged. "I'm meeting someone here," she said, not wanting to give away the fact that she knew the owner. She wanted to pay for her drink, fair and square.

"I've never seen you here before. I would have remembered you."

Marialena smiled. "I'm from Los Angeles. I'm just here for a few days."

"Please don't tell me you're here to meet some guy."

"I am," Marialena said, smiling. "And I am also engaged. Sorry."

The bartender put a hand to his heart. "Ah, well. Enjoy the wine," he said and smiled.

"Thanks, I will." She sent a text to Henry, "Did you train your bartenders to hit on all women? Nice business move."

"I did no such thing. Are you back?"

"I'm at the bar."

Henry came around a few minutes later and sat down next to her at the bar. He ordered a beer, and they clinked glasses. At first, the bartender thought Henry was making a pass at Marialena, but then he realized the two of them were there together.

"Hey Mario, her drinks are on the house."

"No, I don't think so; I can pay. Let me pay," she said.

"Mario, don't listen to her," he said. "Hey, so how was your day?"

"Good. I found a dress."

"Nice. Do you need to order some more food?"

"No, I'm good. You?"

416

"No, we can finish these and get out of here. I think I'm mostly done for the day. But you remember Jim from Esteban's dinner?"

"Yeah, why."

"He ran out of milk and asked me to bring some."

"Okay."

"Anyway, you could stay in the car. Don't worry about coming in and putting on a show or anything like that. I don't plan on staying."

When Henry pulled up to Jim's restaurant, Marialena held the door open for Henry.

"I'll be right out," he said as she sat in the lobby and waited.

"Hey, thanks for the delivery. I can drop some off on Monday," Jim said when he saw Henry.

"Sure, man, no problem."

"You know, I never got to congratulate you on your engagement," Jim said, referring to the fact that last time he saw Henry, he mistook Marialena to be Henry's fiancée, and not Esteban's.

"Don't worry about it," Henry said, not wanting to get into a whole discussion.

"I just have one question. How did you find an escort with a driving service?"

"You're talking about Marialena?" Henry asked with a raised eyebrow.

"Oh yeah, that's right. An exotic name for an exotic escort."

Henry laughed. "Now, why would I let an escort drive my car?" Jim stopped smiling. "Yeah, that was my car. Also, you're an asshole. Do you want to tell her you thought she was an escort, or do you want me to?"

417

"What do you mean?"

"She's in your lobby, man. She's spending a few days here in Temecula. We were just on our way back to my place, but made a detour here."

"You're joking."

Henry shook his head. "Walk me out, see for yourself."

When Marialena looked at Henry from across the room, Henry nodded at her ever so subtly and she nodded back, understanding. She stood up and smiled at Henry.

"Hey, that was quick," she said and grabbed his hand as he approached.

"Jim wanted to thank you in person for the delivery. Jim, you remember Marialena."

"Hi. Yeah, thanks." He cleared his throat and took a quick look at Marialena. She looked so different from the night he had seen her out with Henry. She was dressed casually. He felt foolish for thinking she had been an escort. Maybe Henry really was that lucky.

"How are you liking Temecula so far?" Jim asked.

"I like it," she replied.

"Well, I hate to cut this short, but we should get going," Henry said. Marialena waved at Jim and they turned to leave. When they were outside, Henry kissed her on the cheek, knowing that Jim would still be watching.

When they got inside the car, Henry dropped the act. "Fucking asshole. I am so sorry about that, Marialena."

"What? It's okay, but what happened? I could feel the tension."

"The night he met you, he thought you were an escort," Henry said angrily.

"No!" Marialena said, surprised. "Oh my god, did I look like an escort?"

Henry turned to look at her. "What? No, he's just a fucking asshole. But what pisses me off is that he's right about you and I. I mean, we're not together and so that makes him right. Not about you being an escort, just about me and you."

"Fuck him," Marialena said, trying to calm him down. "Henry," she said, putting a hand on his knee. "Don't let him get to you. It was an accident, but it doesn't matter. And if it's any consolation, I'd totally date you if Esteban wasn't in the picture," Marialena said, feeling brave.

"Okay, I won't let him get to me if you won't let him get to you. You were classy and beautiful that night. He was just jealous and trying to hurt me, got it?"

He pulled up to the hotel and they got out without a word. The room was nice and spacious. Marialena plopped on the bed and stretched out as Henry poured them a glass of wine from a bottle he brought from home.

Marialena decided to change into some pjs. She took off Esteban's sweater, her tank top coming up with the sweater. Henry got a good look at her torso before Marialena pulled her tank top back down. There was some tension between them now. She felt bad for him. He seemed quiet and moody. She couldn't tell why he was mad, but could it be the fact that she didn't really belong to him at all? How could she make him feel better? She was out of her league in this area and didn't know what to do or say, but it made her feel terrible that she couldn't think of anything to cheer him up.

Hours later, Henry stirred from a deep sleep when he felt Marialena climb into his bed. She put an arm around his chest.

"What are you doing?" he asked in whisper, doing nothing to stop her.

"Don't tell," she said and she kissed him softly on the jaw, moving her way to his lips. When their mouths met, he moaned loudly and flipped her over on her back passionately. He put a hand up her shirt, but wasn't satisfied. He lifted her shirt right off and looked at her naked breasts underneath him. He fondled one while he put the other one in his mouth.

She spread her legs and he knew that they had passed the point of no return. You can't go back from there. It's all the way now. He took his shirt off and kissed her on the mouth, loving the way her hands and arms felt on his back. She took her shorts and underwear off and he hurriedly did the same.

"Let me look at you first," he said, and she lay back down. Her hair was untamed, and she looked absolutely beautiful. He kissed her collarbone and touched her all over, wanting to make this moment last.

"Come here," she finally said, pulling him toward her. When he entered her, he could tell she had been wanting this as badly as he had. His whole body quivered with the touch of her body around him. His movements were slow and focused, Marialena rhythmically gyrating along with his body. She ran a hand through his hair and that's when he lost it. He told her that he loved her. He said it over and over again. When he was came, he shouted loudly. That's when he woke himself up and noticed that the sun was rising and the light was cracking through the curtains. He lifted his head to look around the hotel room and he saw Marialena across from him, sleeping soundly. Henry rested his head back on the pillow and realized he had had an incredible wet dream. He felt himself and realized he was absolutely soaked in semen and sweat.

"Dammit," he said as he got out of bed and grabbed a pair of boxers from his overnight bag. He cleaned himself off in the bathroom and threw his pants and boxers back in the bag.

Marialena stirred when she heard him in the bathroom. It was just after five in the morning. She looked at Henry now sprawled out in bed, his covers coming up to his waist. She saw, even in the dim light, that he had been sweating profusely. His skin was glistening.

"Hey, are you okay?" she asked, sitting next to him on the bed.

"Yeah, bad dream, I guess."

Marialena ran a hand through his hair, "You're drenched," she said. He turned to his side, his back to her.

"Marialena, I'm fine. Go back to bed," he said curtly.

"Okay," she said a little defensively, and went back to her bed. Henry turned his head.

"Hey, I'm sorry, I didn't mean to—"

"No, it's fine. You're right," Marialena said. He had been sweating profusely, almost as much as Esteban did whenever they had sex. That's when she put two and two

421

together. No, she had to be wrong about that. Maybe he really did just have a bad dream.

Marialena eventually fell asleep, and when she woke up, Henry was gone. She found a note taped to the TV that said, 'Went out. Be back soon. There's breakfast and coffee downstairs. Don't wait for me.'

Henry hadn't been able to get back to sleep, so he decided to drive back home, shower at his place, make coffee, and change his clothes. He didn't feel bad for leaving her, he just felt angry. He was angry he had dreamt about her. He was angry that it made him want her more. He was angry he couldn't have her. It was ten a.m. when he drove back to the hotel.

"Good morning," she said quietly as she watched the morning news.

"Hey," he said.

"You okay?"

"Yeah, I just haven't really been home for a while. Needed to take care of some things. I think I'm going to head to work a little earlier today. I'll probably end up leaving soon. Do you want me to drop you off anywhere?"

"I don't really feel like going anywhere. But I'd rather stay at your place than here. Is that okay?"

Henry looked at his phone, distracted. "Uh, yeah. I guess so. I don't have too much food there," he said as they walked out.

"I can order food. Just leave me your address."

When they got to his place, he gave her his key in case she needed to go anywhere and he left quickly. Marialena sat on his couch, wondering what the hell was up. He was acting strange. Sure, they had spent a lot of time together. She didn't even spend this much free time with Esteban. But this time with Henry was totally different. Maybe this had to do with the run-in with Jim.

She decided to ignore it for now and looked at one of his guitars out of the corner of her eye. Marialena Googled a song, looked up the chords, and replayed them over and over on Henry's guitar, but felt like she wasn't getting it. She put the guitar down for a little bit and went back to her book, but she couldn't concentrate because she kept thinking about the song she wanted to learn. After about two hours, she finally heard the song coming through, but her fingers hurt like hell. She didn't know how long Henry was planning on working, but she was cold and starting to get hungry. She looked in his cupboards for hot chocolate but couldn't find any, so she texted him.

"Why is it that no grown man keeps hot chocolate in his house?"

He replied after a few minutes. "Hot chocolate? Now, why would I want hot chocolate? Am I twelve?"

"It's good for the soul."

"My soul hasn't been good for a long time."

With that, she scheduled an Uber and told the driver to take her to Henry's restaurant.

The hostess walked Marialena to his office and knocked on his door, which was ajar.

"There's someone asking for you," the hostess said nervously, then led Marialena in.

Henry took off his glasses and exhaled loudly as the hostess closed the door behind her.

"Hey," she said casually.

"What's up?" he asked, setting aside some paperwork.

Marialena nodded. Something was definitely up. Instead of asking him outright, she tried changing the subject. "Hey, so I learned how to play the guitar today. It was kind of cool. I might want to get one in the near future. I almost heard a song in there."

Henry nodded, avoiding eye contact. Marialena laughed to herself. "Why can't you look me in the eye?"

He looked right at her when she asked, but he didn't say anything, and it infuriated Marialena. "What's wrong? What did I do?"

Henry shook his head. "You didn't do anything. I just have a lot of work to do, work I've been putting off."

Marialena nodded, but she didn't drop it. She had a feeling it was more than that. "So, this morning, that dream you had—" She searched his eyes before she said anything else, but they didn't tell her anything, so she continued. "That dream was about me, wasn't it?"

"I told you, I have a lot of work to do."

She remembered seeing him go into the bathroom with his gym shorts, heard the faucet for a while, then the toilet, then the faucet again. And he had emerged with a new pair of boxers.

"If you're asking me if I dreamt about you, the answer is yes. Okay, fine. Are you happy?"

"Happy? Are you kidding me? No, I'm not happy. But Henry, I don't want anything to come between what we have. And if you dreamt about me? It's okay. It's part of your subconscious. It's not real. That wasn't me," she said.

"That's the thing though," he said bitterly. "It's *not* part of my subconscious. I do think about those things. I want those things."

Marialena looked away. "I see," she said quietly.

"Look, we've been spending all this time together, and I haven't gone on a date in a while. I think I just need to get this out of my system," he said. "So, I'm thinking about going out tonight. I'm sorry, I know that wasn't the plan. I'll come home early though. I won't stay out late."

"No, it's okay. I get it. You should go on a date. And you're right. We have been spending a lot of time together. And it's all my fault. If I didn't need a babysitter, none of this would have happened."

"It's not your fault, Marialena. I'm here this week because I want to be with you. Are you kidding me? I love being around you. It's been nice. I feel useful again, you know?" he said, his voice softening. "Almost like my life has some purpose. And it's not because of how I feel for you, it's because you're going to be permanent in my life. You're going to be family, and I didn't know how much I was missing that. But this week will be over soon, it's just taking its toll."

Marialena nodded. "I feel guilty."

"Don't. Look, I'm sorry for being an asshole this morning. The dream complicated things. You know—" Henry stopped himself. "No, I shouldn't."

"What? What were you going to say?"

"Nothing, hey listen, you eat yet? I'm starving."

They ate and talked and everything appeared somewhat normal again. He gave Marialena tips on learning the guitar and she listened eagerly, then he gave her a ride to the hotel this time.

Hours later, after she watched a movie and read some more, she got a call from Esteban.

"Hi!" she said excitedly.

"Hey, how are you?"

"I'm good."

"So, for tomorrow, I was just thinking, I want you to meet me somewhere. I'm going to fill Henry in on the details. It's something that means a lot to me and I want you to be there too."

"Okay," she said uncertainly. "You're going to call him now?"

"Yeah, why?"

"Well, he's on a date. Maybe you shouldn't interrupt him."

"This can't wait, and it's important. It won't take long."

"His date is important too."

"His dates are never really that important."

"That's not a nice thing to say."

"No, but it's true. It won't take long; he can go back to getting laid afterwards."

Marialena called Roxanne after she hung up with Esteban.

"Hey, how are you?"

"I'm fine. Alone at the hotel. Henry's on a date and I just got off the phone with Esteban."

"Who's the date?"

"I don't know, I don't think it's serious. Hey, so it sounds like Esteban wants me to meet him somewhere."

"Oh yeah? Sounds like you two are on the mend. Listen, hate to cut this short, but I need to get ready for a big day tomorrow. Hang in there, okay?"

426

"Yeah, okay."

When Henry got home an hour later, Marialena was already in bed with the lights out, but she wasn't asleep. Henry took his dress shirt off and climbed into Marialena's bed with her, but he stayed on top of the covers with his back against the wall.

"Feel better?" she asked him.

"Yeah, hey, come here. I'm really sorry. Marialena, I didn't mean for any of this to happen."

Marialena pushed the covers back, so she could get next to him properly. She noticed a David Bowie tattoo he had on his right arm that she had never looked at properly before, as she sat up with him and he put his arms around her. She rested her head on his chest, thinking this was weird since he had just gotten back from having sex.

"I know. I didn't mean for this to happen either. I'm sorry I can't give you what you want," she said.

"I'm not good at this relationship stuff. I never have been."

"I don't believe that for one minute. You've been amazing with me." Marialena wrapped her arms around him tighter.

"Maybe being close to you will help me be close to someone else. You know, I didn't want to tell you this earlier, but in that dream I had, I told you that I loved you. I've never said that to anyone out loud, ever," he said quietly.

"What does it mean? That you said it to me in a dream?"

427

"It means I think I've kind of been opening my heart to you, or maybe that I am ready to open up my heart to someone."

"You think it's because we've been spending all this time together?"

"Yeah, and you're easy to talk to. You're unavailable to me, so I can trust myself with you a little more. I'm opening up a little more. You're a wonderful woman, and my brother is one lucky man," he said, holding on to her.

"Hey Henry, I know you didn't say it to me, but I love you too." She kissed him on the chest where her face was resting and she felt tears fall from her eyes. "You mean the world to me, and I want you in my life. I'll take the good and the bad. I'm only sorry that I can't reciprocate the same feelings, but I love you and I'm sorry that we have to go through this."

"I'm not sorry," he said, lifting up her face to see her better. "You're helping me grow. Something I should have done a long time ago. Maybe I just needed someone to show me the way."

"Did you talk to Esteban?" she asked.

"Yeah, get this, we're going to meet him in New York. He wants me to be there too. But we have to be there early tomorrow, which means we have to leave tonight."

"New York, tonight?"

"We can sleep on the plane. We're not meeting Esteban until four in the afternoon."

"What? New York? Why like this?"

"He wants to do this for himself, and for you. What do you think?"

"Why, though? God, I'm not getting married tomorrow, am I?"

Henry laughed. "No, nothing like that." Though, he knew what Esteban had in mind.

"Jesus. When do we need to leave?"

"Soon. I want to take a quick shower, and I'll need to check us out of the hotel, then run back to my place and pick up a few essentials."

"Wow. Okay, so we're doing this? I mean, I'm not exactly packed for New York."

"Relax, Esteban knows that and is going to bring some warm items for you."

Marialena was too excited to argue, and besides, Henry had mentioned to Marialena that Esteban had already left for the airport and was due to arrive before Henry and Marialena got to New York.

They arrived at the airport with what little luggage they had. Despite her excitement, Marialena was getting sleepy once they were on the plane. She put her arm through Henry's and put her head on his shoulder. He turned to her as she closed her eyes.

"I love you too, kiddo," he whispered as she drifted to sleep.

Chapter Twenty-seven

When Henry and Marialena arrived in New York, the cold morning air was crisp against Marialena's skin.

"Holy crap," she said to Henry. "This weather is not kidding around." Henry took a coat he had been carrying and handed it to her.

"Here, put this on. Hey, do you feel okay? Do you need to sleep when we get to the hotel?" he asked.

"I think I'd like to know why we're here," she said playfully.

"All in due time, my dear," he said.

He hailed a cab, and forty minutes later they were at the hotel. The place was a little smaller than the last hotel room, but it was a lot more elegant. She saw her clothes and a few pairs of her shoes and boots laid out in the closet and went toward them.

"Esteban was already here," she said, touching her stuff. "Is he here now?"

"I don't know actually. We spoke briefly."

"Maybe he's right next door," she said.

"Sure, but in which direction? Just try and get some sleep. I'm exhausted," he admitted.

After forty minutes of trying, he had a little trouble falling back asleep himself, but could hear Marialena sleeping soundly. Henry felt a text vibrate from the pillow at his side. It was Esteban.

"You guys make it in okay? I thought I heard you come in."

"Yeah, we're here. She's asleep already."

"Hey, let me in, will you? I don't want to knock and wake her up."

"Are you at this connecting door, or will you be at the front?"

"The connecting door."

Henry got up and Esteban was there waiting. The first thing he noticed was Esteban's black eye.

"Jesus, your eye," he whispered. "I'm sorry about that." He cringed.

"I'm not. I deserved it," Esteban said, whispering back. "Man, I really fucked this up, didn't I?" Esteban looked down at Marialena sleeping peacefully.

"Yeah, you did."

"Hey, thanks for everything you've done. Thanks for being there for her. Man, you've been helping out for like a week now."

Henry smiled. "Yeah, it's starting to mess with my sex life a little bit. She's killing my vibe."

"What vibe?"

"Hey, I have a vibe. So, what, you're staying here with us to this morning?" Henry climbed back into bed. "I'm not getting back out of bed again. I feel like shit and I'm tired."

"Yeah," Esteban said, already in pjs. He lifted up the covers and pulled Marialena's long hair off of the pillow. He lifted up her head gently and placed it on his chest. Marialena put her arm around him, but was fast asleep. Esteban took a deep breath, inhaling every scent of hers.

Later, Marialena woke to the sounds of Henry using the restroom.

"Hey, good morning," Henry said.

431

"Yeah, good morning," she said.

"Did you notice anything different while you slept?" he asked.

Marialena gave him a confused look. "Different? How so?"

"You weren't warmer in bed, or I don't know, you didn't sleep any better than usual?"

Marialena shrugged. "I slept really well, but I think I was just tired."

"Esteban left about thirty minutes ago," Henry said.

"He was here?"

"Yeah. He got in bed with you for a few hours, but had to leave to run a few errands for later."

"How did I sleep through that?"

Henry shrugged. "You said you were tired."

Marialena smiled as she thought of him there beside her. She lay back down and closed her eyes happily.

"We should probably leave in an hour."

"Oh, wow. Okay." Marialena looked through the clothes that Esteban had brought for her and tried to piece items together with the new dress she had brought. She was glad he was thoughtful enough to not only bring her boots, but a long pair of socks for her. He was used to this weather, so he knew how to dress for it. She took a shower, then tried on her new dress. It was perfect. The skirt went down to the knees and the lacy sleeves were long, the neck high. She came out when she heard a knock on the door. She looked up as Henry walked to the door and grabbed a bag from someone on the other side. She heard him talking, but she couldn't make out the other voice. They were whispering.

"Delivery for one Marialena Villaneuva," he said and handed her the white bag.

"What's this? Was that Esteban?"

Henry smiled. "Maybe."

Marialena opened the door and ran down the hallway. She saw Esteban walking away from her. She called out his name. He was dressed in a suit and looked amazing in a black trench coat. He had a pair of gloves in his hand.

"Esteban, what are we doing here?" she asked breathlessly, elated to see him.

"This is something I need to do and I wanted you here. But listen, I have to get going. Someone's waiting for me. I'll explain later." He looked into her eyes and cleared his throat. "I brought you some extra winter clothes. I had some help picking them. See you in a little bit, okay?"

Marialena sprinted back to her room and smiled when she saw Henry. He shook his head. "You couldn't wait?"

Marialena shook her head. "Hey, he was the one who snuck into my bed." Marialena peeked in the bag and pulled out a black knit scarf, a black pair of gloves, and a pair of black leggings with a note that said, "Wear these underneath your clothes." She didn't recognize the handwriting, but decided it was a good idea.

When they got into the cab, Henry gave them the address and made sure it was okay for the cab driver to take them that far. "And if we could stop for flowers, that would be great. I think there's a place down the street."

When Henry alerted the driver to the flower shop, he asked Marialena to stay inside. He came back out with two dozen red roses.

"Okay, so it should be right on the left here in a second." Henry set the flowers down and put a hand on Marialena's hand, looking into her eyes. "Esteban felt it was important to see my mom and dad. He wanted you to be here. Marialena, is that okay with you?"

"We're at the cemetery?"

Henry nodded. "He didn't want me to tell you. I'm sorry it's not more exciting, but he really wanted to do this."

"No, this is fine. I wasn't sure what to think, actually. What about you, how are you with all this?" They were his parents, too.

"I haven't been here in a few years. It was time," he replied soberly.

Marialena nodded. She took his arm as they walked. There was a little bit of snow on the ground, but it had been a mild winter, and there hadn't been much snowfall, just some icy patches. She could see two people in the distance, a man and a woman, with their backs to her. The man knelt down and placed some flowers on the grave. It had looked like Esteban, but she didn't know who the woman was.

The woman turned around as they got closer. It was her cousin Roxanne.

"Oh my god, what are you doing here?" Marialena whispered to her, as they hugged each other.

"Esteban asked me to come." Marialena looked at Esteban as she hugged Roxanne. Esteban cleared his

434

throat. Henry pulled Marialena away from the grave as Esteban knelt down.

"Hey Mom and Dad," he said loud enough for everyone to hear. "I brought someone here to meet you. Her name is Marialena, and I love her." Esteban said, then kind of chuckled to himself, "I uh, I messed up, though. Mom, you wouldn't believe this, but I fell in love then got scared and called it off. I'm sorry, Mom. I'm sorry for letting you and the woman I love down. But I love her, and I want to marry her. You would have loved her too. She's great. Amazing, beautiful, funny. She gave me a hard time when I tried to end it; I think you would have liked that about her. She didn't let me off the hook. And all I can hope for now is that she accepts my apology and chooses to accept your ring, because I love her and want her in my life, to be my wife."

Esteban took a step back and stood next to Marialena, who was holding hands with Roxanne. Marialena's eyes had started to water and tears fell from them. Marialena tried to let go of Roxanne, but Roxanne held her tightly and linked her arm in Marialena's, in her own way saying it wasn't over yet. And it wasn't. It was Henry's turn to walk up to the grave. He set the bouquet of roses down on his mom's grave.

"Hey, Mom. It's me, Henry. I'm sorry for not coming sooner." Henry cleared his throat. "Mom, you should see those two together. They give me hope, you know? You can see their love, see it unfold in front of your very eyes. Esteban's right. You would have loved Marialena. No one has ever loved him more, except for you, of course. But she's wonderful and she's giving me something powerful to believe in." He looked around for a second, then continued. "Seeing them together makes me want to settle down and find someone myself. I know that ring on her finger was for whichever one of us got married first, but Mom, I can honestly say I am glad it's on her. She's one of us now. And I wouldn't have it any other way."

He took a step back and turned to look at Marialena, who was still crying softly. She nodded at Henry and took a step forward. It was quiet in the cemetery. She set down the bouquet of roses she was holding.

"Hi, Mr. and Mrs. Guiterrez. I'm Marialena. First of all, let me just say that you have two *amazing* sons. Both of them have been godsends to me and you'd be so proud of them. Henry has been so kind and wonderful." Marialena looked at the ring on her finger. "I am wearing your ring. It's so beautiful, but in a moment of weakness when Esteban broke off our engagement, I am ashamed to admit that I took it off. But the fact that both of your sons have placed *this one* ring on my finger—Esteban to ask for my hand in marriage and Henry to fight for Esteban and me to be together—is not lost on me. I'm so incredibly lucky to have them both in my life."

Marialena paused before continuing. "Can I ask you both for one small favor? Can you look for my parents up there? Can you find them and tell them that I am okay and that I'm happy? Tell them about your sons." Marialena's voice was quivering. "They'll be easy to find," Marialena said, tears falling down her face. "My dad is handsome, loud with a personality you'd just love." Marialena laughed. "He thinks he's funny even with he's not. My mom—" Marialena's voice cracked and she couldn't speak. She broke down into a sob, and

Roxanne held Marialena as she sobbed into her arms. When Marialena was able to speak again, she took Roxanne's hands and tried again, both girls crying. Esteban stood on the other side of Marialena and took her other hand. "My mom, she's an angel. I thought she was one when I was little. She's amazing and kind. You'd love her. Tell them that I'm not alone anymore," she said, struggling to speak. "Tell them that I love them and that I miss them so much." It was just too hard, so she finally said, "Can you do that for me?" Her voice was hoarse.

Marialena turned to hug Roxanne and they held each other for a long time, both of them crying. Henry and Esteban gave them some space.

When Esteban approached Marialena, she cried into his arms. He held her tightly. "I am so sorry," he said.

"I love you, Esteban," she said into his shoulder.

"I love you too." He pulled away from her, wiping the tears from her face. "So, you'll marry me?"

Marialena laughed through her tears. "Let me think about it." She kissed him softly on the lips and put her arms around his neck. "Yes," she said, smiling into his eyes.

Henry and Roxanne walked back to the limo that Esteban had waiting for them, and Esteban walked with Marialena a few paces behind.

"Thank you for doing this, Esteban. I had no idea what you were planning, but this was really beautiful. I'm sorry I got emotional."

Esteban took her hand and kissed it as they walked. "It's okay. I'm sorry too. But I'm glad we did this."

"I'm a mess right now," she said, wiping her tears away.

"It's okay, the driver is going to take us back to the hotel. We'll have some time to clean ourselves up a little bit before heading out again," Esteban said.

"Have you made flight arrangements yet?" Esteban asked his brother when they got back inside of one car.

"Not yet. I was going to do that later. I wanted to leave tonight, but I'm not sure yet," Henry said, running a hand through his hair. "I'm really tired. I'll see how I feel later. Roxanne, what do you think? Should we let these two lovebirds have dinner together? Care to join me somewhere when we get back into the city?"

Roxanne nodded. "Yeah, of course." She kept Marialena's hand in hers. "I'm spending the weekend with these two, so we'll have time to catch up. Let me see this ring properly now that I have a chance." Roxanne held up Marialena's hand. "Oh wow. Esteban, it's absolutely beautiful." Esteban smiled. "It looks perfect on your hand, Marialena. Like it was meant to be."

Marialena smiled and put her hand back in her lap. "I can't believe we're all here. This is so amazing."

Chapter Twenty-eight

Back at the hotel, Marialena splashed cold water on her face and started over with her makeup, which had mostly come off while she had been crying.

Roxanne was sitting out on the double bed, talking to her through the open door.

"You know, Henry isn't bad looking."

"Yeah, he really isn't."

"In fact, I think he's kind of cute."

"Really?" Marialena said, sticking her head out of the bathroom.

Roxanne smiled. "You know, I've never dated an older guy before. I mean, not ten years older."

"Hey, so how long have you known about this trip?" Marialena asked, changing the subject.

"I just found out yesterday. Esteban called me."

"So, last night when I talked to you, you already knew?"

"Yep. I had to get off the phone quickly, otherwise I was afraid something would slip."

"Thanks for being here," Marialena said genuinely.

"I wouldn't miss this."

Marialena continued her makeup as Henry knocked on the connecting door.

"Come in," Roxanne said.

"I was thinking dinner in about an hour. Then we should come back here, because I still need to figure out what I'm going to do about leaving tonight.

439

"Dinner in one hour. Got it," Roxanne said.

"I'm going downstairs to the bar and get another drink. Roxanne, you're welcome to join me if you want."

"Well, I have this wine."

"Leave it. I can finish it for you," Marialena said.

Esteban came in as the two walked out. He was still in his suit. Marialena could taste the whiskey he'd been drinking with his brother as they kissed for a few minutes.

"God, I've missed you," he said breathlessly. "Marialena, I love you so much."

"I have missed this so much," she said, kissing him on the lips. "God, your eye looks bad. We can't go out like this."

"It's okay."

Marialena looked at her makeup still on the bed. Then she texted Roxanne. "Hey, can I borrow your foundation. I want to cover up Esteban's black eye and can probably do a better job if I mix yours and mine."

"Go for it."

Marialena stood up. "Sit down in that chair over there."

"Yes ma'am."

She straddled him and mixed the two colors on her fingers, their faces close.

"I think this is going to work," she said in a whisper.

"You know, I don't think this is the method professional artists use."

"Sssshhh, be quiet," she said, looking into his hazel eyes. "Close your eyes, I don't think it's going to be perfect, but I think it might actually work."

440

Both of them were quiet as she applied the foundation, rubbing it in, careful to avoid his eye. He winced in pain a few times.

"How does it look?" he asked when she was done.

"It looks good," she said, looking into both of his eyes. "It's not perfect, but it's not something you might notice right away."

"Thanks for that," he said and kissed her. One thing led to another. "Let me cancel the car," he said breathlessly. He made a phone call and when he returned to Marialena, she stood up and turned around so he could help unzip her dress.

Marialena took the dress off. They made love for over an hour, each wanting to make it last. By the end, Esteban needed a shower, and so did Marialena. They showered together quickly.

"My god, that was amazing," he said.

"I know," she said, kissing him again on the lips, loving how his wet face felt in her hands.

"You make me feel like a teenager," he said.

"And you make me feel like a woman," she said, kissing him one more time. "Man, I have worked up one hell of an appetite though"

"Tell me about it. How long do you think it will take you to get ready?"

"I need to blow dry my hair...maybe about twenty minutes. Do you still plan on wearing your suit?"

He picked his shirt up off the chair where he had set it down. "Yeah, I think it's still okay."

It was eight p.m. when they finally left for dinner. It was a classy place, but all Marialena had eyes for was Esteban.

441

"I could look at you all night," she said.

"You look pretty great yourself," he said. "But thanks, I've never really liked myself in a suit. I'm too short and stocky. I feel like I'm a kid in his dad's clothing. They just don't look right on me. Not like Henry. Henry looks great in suits," he said, rambling.

"No, you look amazing," she said.

The waiter came by and they each placed their order. When he left, Esteban didn't hesistate.

"So, when do you think you want to get married?"

Marialena smiled. "Well, seeing you like this, here in your home state during winter, I don't know, I think you're a vision right now. I can see us getting married here, in this climate."

"Yeah, I'd like that. So, what? Next year?"

"I could marry you tomorrow."

He smiled. "Me too. Well, think about it."

"I will. I'm just glad that we're here now and together. That's what's important."

"Listen Marialena, if there's anything else you want to pursue, we can talk about it. I will support you in anything you want to do. If you don't want to work for Patrick, you don't have to."

"Thanks, but I think I want to pursue this job with Patrick. You're still okay with me working for him?"

"Oh yeah, I'm not worried about that."

Marialena nodded. "As for the wedding, I want it to be small, and I don't mind if it's sooner rather than later, but let's sleep on it for a few weeks."

When dinner arrived, Marialena asked him about his screenplay.

"How's the writing going?"

442

"Nowhere fast," he answered, taking a bite of food. "I haven't written since before I left for the fishing trip. I haven't even thought about it."

"Well, it's only been a little over a week. You've had some major disruptions in your life. I'm sure that when we go back home, you'll pick it up again. Can you at least tell me what it's about now?"

"Nope, not yet."

"Why not?" she asked, laughing.

"It's just a thing. I don't like talking about it until I'm right near the end, and I'm this close," he said, indicating with his fingers. "I don't want to jinx myself. Give me a little more time, okay? I just hope I'm able to pick it up again and soon. I can't afford not to write at this point in my life."

"Esteban, I don't want to say this to bring you down or anything, but you will get writer's block again one day. It happens. It's natural. I think you've just had a rough couple of weeks. But honestly, it will happen again and you just have to wait until it passes."

"I know it happens, but it was awful. And I just don't want to disappoint you the way I do myself when I can't write."

"Seriously, Esteban. You don't have to worry about disappointing me."

"Well, I know one thing for sure. I don't think I am going to be unhappy ever again. Not with that face looking at me every day."

Marialena smiled. "There'll be days, I'm sure."

"Sure, we'll have our moments. But you know what I'm looking forward to? Lazy Sunday mornings, Friday night movies, coffee in the kitchen. I can't wait for my life to begin. At fifty, I can't believe I'm actually saying that."

Marialena smiled and raised a glass to him. "To the rest of our lives," she said.

When they got back to their hotel room, they could hear Henry and Roxanne in the next room. Every so often you could hear one of them laughing, but you couldn't tell what they were saying or doing.

Marialena put her coat on a hanger.

"Hey, come here," Esteban said. "Are you okay with that?" He wanted to know if she was okay with Roxanne seeing someone like Henry. He knew they were protective of each other.

Marialena sat down on the bed and thought for a second, thinking about everything she and Henry had just been through. She wasn't worried about her cousin, though she knew that's what Esteban meant.

"I don't know," Marialena said, being honest. "I know his track record, but so does Roxanne."

"You've talked to her about him?"

"Yeah, and she's an adult. But at the same time, she means the world to me. I don't know, it's a strange situation. What do you think?"

"I think they're both old enough to know what they're doing. And it's just one night. She must know that. She's going back to Nashville in a few days, so it's not like she can expect anything from him."

"I know, but at the same time, it's him," she said. "Remember what you said about his dates not being important? Well, that's my cousin in there."

"I'm sorry I said that. I shouldn't have. But she's a grown woman."

Marialena smiled. "Yeah, I know." She started to undress and get ready for bed, and so did Esteban.

When Marielana climbed into bed, her phone buzzed with a text message from Roxanne.

"I know we aren't being quiet, and I know this may be weird, but he's a really nice guy and he's been so great tonight. I'm having so much fun. We can talk about this tomorrow. Love you."

Marialena read the text. She wanted to say so much, but all she dared to reply back with was, "Love you too."

Chapter Twenty-nine

Earlier that evening, Henry and Roxanne got in a cab, and Henry gave the driver the name of a restaurant. He looked at Roxanne next to him. She was different from Marialena, beautiful in her own right, but lacked the other-worldly beauty that Marialena possessed. Roxanne was cheery. When she smiled, her eyes smiled too. Her hair was dark like Marialena's, but a lot more curly and wild. When they had been at the bar, she held herself very well. They talked about her work at a busy hotel in Nashville, and he talked about his restaurant. They laughed easily. Roxanne was into him, he could tell. But given their circumstance, he wasn't sure how he felt about her. Things were complicated.

"This restaurant is one of my favorites in the city. I always try to come when I am here, which sadly, isn't as often as I'd like."

"I've only been here twice myself."

"To the restaurant?" he asked, kidding.

"No, the city," she said laughing, the alcohol showing in her cheeks.

He smiled in reply. "Well, it's a good distance from you. How old were you when you left Los Angeles?"

"My parents moved when I was seventeen. I was a senior in high school."

"So, that was, what, five years ago?" he asked. He couldn't help it, he was a natural flirt, which is why it was always so hard for him to be around Marialena. He had to hold back when he was around her.

Roxanne laughed. "Twelve, it was twelve years ago."

"Twelve? Wow. How is it that you stayed so close to Marialena after all that time?"

Roxanne shrugged. "We were inseparable when we were little. Our parents would take these long vacations all the time. Camping in the summer, log cabins in the winter, that kind of thing. We'd sleep together in the same bed. Every weekend, her family came over to our house, or ours went to theirs."

"How did Marialena take to your family moving away?"

"Well, the older we got, the less close we were, but we still adored each other. I think she was more angry that her mom agreed with my mom and thought I could be a bad influence on her, which is totally bogus. Have you ever tried to get her to do anything? It's like pulling teeth, she's so stubborn! But I guess her parents didn't realize that Mar was already set in her ways." She took a breath and looked out of the window, then continued after a brief pause. "She's lightening up a little bit, I've noticed. Maybe that's your influence."

"Our combined efforts, maybe?"

"I'll take that," she said and smiled. "Anyway, when her parents died, she was twenty-one. She took it hard, you know? Anyone would. She was alone. I stayed with her for an entire summer. My mom and dad came out and helped her sell her parents' house, and with that, she took the money to buy her condo. We got close again that summer, but I started to worry about her. Her bright

447

smile was gone, her passion was gone. She dropped out of school and got a job. She said helping people find jobs made her feel better. But I've never stopped worrying about her. Don't get me wrong, Los Angeles is a blast, but I really just love that girl. It's so nice that she's found someone."

"So, you're okay with her marrying my brother?" he asked, searching her eyes.

"Are you kidding me? Look at her, she's thrilled. Who cares about the age difference? She's happy. And she hasn't been in so long. It's long overdue."

"Yeah, I guess she's lucky when you put it that way. Although I'm going to be forty, and I've never found that kind of happiness."

"Well, I haven't either," Roxanne said. "But it's out there, somewhere. I'm just glad she found it. She deserves it. She's a pain in the ass sometimes, but she's my pain in the ass and I love her."

"I know what you mean. I feel this protectiveness toward her. I don't know if it's because of her past, or because she's my brother's fiancée, or because she's wearing my mom's ring. But I feel this weight on my shoulders to kind of make sure that she's going to be all right. And I don't mean that it's a bad weight to carry around. It actually feels good to care about someone again."

When they got out of the cab, Henry paid the driver, and when they entered, Roxanne was touched that Henry had made a reservation for the two of them. He immediately ordered a bottle of red wine for the both of them out of habit. They were in New York City, so why the hell not?

448

"So, this past week with Marialena has been complicated, to say the least," he said, speaking slowly, careful with his words. "I think she's an amazing woman and my brother is lucky to have her." He looked at Roxanne across from him, trying to gauge how far he should go. "Look, I'm not going to lie. There are some feelings there. You know, some of it is the ring she's wearing. When I saw that ring on her finger the first time I met her, I felt this immediate connection. And then it came out that Marialena had trouble sleeping, and I thought about my mom too. How my mom had suffered all those lonely nights without my dad. I couldn't let Marialena go through that. So, when Esteban asked me to help, of course I couldn't say no. And she was so vulnerable when she and Esteban had that falling out. She was tough, sure, but you could see her falling into this dark place. And again, I thought of my mom. It was like I was doing my mom a favor too, by being there for Lena. Of course, it got complicated because Marialena looks the way she does," Henry said, turning the slightest shade of red.

"Yeah, I know exactly what you mean. You can't help but get pulled in to her sadness."

"I just wanted to protect her, you know? And not only that, I could sense the way she looked at me. She saw me as a good guy. Now, I don't know what you know about me, but I don't think I could call myself a good guy. And after I met her, after this past week really, suddenly I felt this change in myself. I wanted to be a good guy, for her, you know? I wanted to kind of own up to her faith in me as a good person."

449

"She thinks the world of you, I know that much. You've really been there for her. I think she needed that. I would have been in your place had I been here, and I am thankful that *someone* was able to be." They were quiet for a moment before she asked the inevitable. "Do you think that you have feelings for her?"

Henry took a rather large sip of wine before answering. Roxanne noticed and gave him a small smile. He looked away before answering. "I don't know. It's complicated. She's in love with my brother. The story just kind of ends there. I could never come between the two of them. Nor would I want to," Henry said, surprised at his own honesty. "I want to have that though. I want to settle down," he continued. "They've kind of inspired me. It's time to grow up," he said with a smile. "I don't know who that person will be, but it's not Marialena. Her path is set with my brother and I am honestly good with that. I'm happy for the both of them. I'm just glad that I'm moving to Los Angeles. I'm glad that I can be close to family again, to be close to her and to Esteban. All this talk about parents and family, it's made me take a look at my life since my mom died, and I don't know, I kind of miss having family around. Esteban lives a few hours from me, but we get lost in our own lives. I think with Marialena in the picture, it will make things easier. I'm glad I'm moving closer."

"You don't think that will make things harder for you, if you do have feelings for her?"

Henry shook his head. "No, I think being around them more often might help inspire me to be the kind of person I want to be. If I stay in Temecula or go somewhere else, I could stay like this forever. That's a scary thought."

"Well, you're honest about everything at least."

Henry shrugged. "I assumed you knew half of it anyway. Why lie?"

Roxanne laughed warmly. "Actually, Mar has said very little about you."

Henry laughed and sat up straighter. "Really, is that so? Did I just gave it all away then?" Henry asked with a self-deprecating laugh.

"No, I mean, I know some stuff. And I get it. Trust me, if anyone gets what you're going through, it's me."

"Yeah, but you're her cousin, and a woman at that. You don't know what it's like to want someone you really shouldn't have," he said, feeling bolder.

"I do though. Whenever I come back to visit her in Los Angeles, we always have nights when we go out. And you know, I think I'm doing a good thing, getting her to wear a pretty dress, to show off her body, and just kind of let go of herself, but then I'm the one who ends up getting the short stick. The way guys look at her when we go out, and I'm not complaining. I'm not. I can get plenty of attention when I want to, but she barely even tries and yeah, guys just like her. I'm over here like, 'Hey dammit, I'm a person, too.'" Roxanne laughed at herself. "It's a ridiculous thing to admit. I get her to go out so that she can meet some interesting people, and end up resenting her for it."

"No, it's not ridiculous. I mean, my brother's famous. Think about what that must feel like," Henry said, smiling.

"Are you jealous?"

451

"Me? No. I wouldn't want his lifestyle. Writing all the time, it's unhealthy," he said, sitting back in his chair and feeling comfortable around her.

"What about the fame?"

"He doesn't buy into the fame part of it. What's there to be jealous of?"

"He has Marialena. You don't," Roxanne said honestly.

"Well...there is that," Henry said, picking up his glass. "No, I wouldn't say I was jealous though. Are you jealous of Marialena?" he asked, the conversation suddenly getting real.

Roxanne thought about it for a second. "No, actually I'm not. I'm happy for her. She's finally getting out there. Working for Patrick Denny took some guts. She left her comfort zone and she's finally living. She might be a little naive sometimes, but no, I'm not jealous. I'm happy for her."

"Okay, enough about our families. Tell me Roxanne, what is life like for you in Nashville?"

Roxanne blushed, the wine getting to her. She shrugged. "Oh, you know. A little bit of this, a little bit of that."

"That sounds vague," Henry said, laughing.

"It's starting to feel like every day is the same, every date, the same thing. The men are even starting to look the same. I miss Los Angeles and its variety."

"In men?" he asked inquisitively.

"In everything! I've been to every restaurant, to every bar. And it feels as if I've run out of men to become interested in." Roxanne gave him a look and laughed. "Okay, that sounds bad. I don't sleep around as much as it sounds like I do, but honestly, I'm sick of it. I'm sick of Nashville."

"So, move," he said smoothly.

"Yeah, you know, moving doesn't sound like a bad idea right now."

"And you'd come to L.A.?"

"Oh, definitely."

"What's keeping you in Nashville?"

"My parents, I guess."

"They have each other though."

"Yeah, they do."

"Roxanne, I don't know you very well and it's not really my place to say this, but if you're not happy in Nashville, then why stay? I know a person who'd be very excited to have you in Los Angeles."

"Not two?" Roxanne asked mischievously.

Henry raised an eyebrow. "Okay, three," he said, smiling. "No, really, do what makes you happy. I'm thirty-nine years old, and you know what I've learned in that time? I have learned that you should do what makes you happy. I sold my restaurant and am moving on," he said with a casual shrug.

"What about you? What are you going to do in Los Angeles?"

"I am going to invest."

"In what?"

"In restaurants."

"Isn't that kind of risky in Los Angeles?"

"Yes and no. There is so much opportunity there."

"But you just closed your restaurant for financial reasons. No offense, but isn't that a risky business to go into for you?" she asked, trying to put it delicately.

"No, I knew when to walk away. And I didn't lose any money. Had I stayed, I would have lost money. Now I get to take that money and invest it in something that has more of a shot at becoming successful. My restaurant was cute, homey, but over the years I've realized that those aren't the moneymakers."

"Sometimes they are."

"Sure, if you're very lucky. I wasn't that lucky." He took a bite of his dinner. "Marialena offered me her place, you know that?"

"Yes, I do."

"If you come back, wouldn't she prefer you living there?"

"Oh, I could never live there."

"Why not?" he asked, curious.

"I knew and loved her parents too. I know Marialena has had some dark days there. I'm afraid that if I took over, those same feelings would come back to haunt me. She is close to me and so were they. You're far enough removed from it, but I miss them too and I'd think about it too much if I were there."

"So, if you come to Los Angeles, you'd be okay with me being in her old place?"

"Of course, but it's not really up to me, either way. Anyway, I'd probably live in the house I grew up in, get some roommates."

"See, you have it all figured out. Sounds like you just need to make the jump."

"Easy for you to say, you're only two hours away."

"A jump is a jump, as far as I'm concerned."

"Maybe you're right," she said, taking a bite of her steak. "It's definitely something to think about."

454

They continued to eat and to talk, laughing easily with each other. Roxanne loved how easy he was to talk to, how honest he was with her. He was incredibly good-looking too, which Marialena failed to mention. She said he was handsome, but not this handsome. She left out his dimpled smile, the way he leaned his head in when he was listening, his scruffy but kempt hair. He had this focus about him, making her feel like the only woman in a room.

When they got to their hotel, things got a little more complicated.

"Hey, so it doesn't look like I'm going to make it out of here tonight. Are you okay with sharing a room, or we could book another room for you?"

"No, this is fine. I don't need another room," she said. "Is it just me, or is it cold in here?" she asked, knowing what it must sound like.

"It is a little drafty. Let me turn the heater on for a bit," he said. He took off his tie and unbuttoned the top buttons of his dress shirt. Roxanne watched him, unashamed.

Henry saw the half open bottle of wine the girls had been drinking earlier and was thrilled for something to do. He poured a small glass for himself and for Roxanne.

"Cheers," he said, sitting across the room on the chair.

"Cheers," she said, not planning on drinking anymore and setting it down after one small sip.

He took a rather large sip, not sure what they were going to do for the rest of the night. "Hey, so how do you think tonight will play out?" he asked her bluntly.

"Between Marialena and your brother, or between you and me?"

"You and me. I don't want to make any assumptions," he said. "You're her cousin and I'd hate to, you know, get in between the two of you."

"Interesting phrasing," Roxanne said, turning red.

Henry laughed. "Okay, you have a dirty mind. I wouldn't want to disrupt anything between the two of you. I've, uh, disappointed her too frequently in the short amount of time I've known her. I'd hate for this to be another strike against me."

"You really care about her?" Roxanne asked.

Henry shrugged. "Yeah."

"And you think she'd fault you if we slept together?"

"I have no idea. She doesn't have the most respect for me in this department, with good reason."

"Look, I know what I'm getting myself into with you. Hell, I warned her against you." Henry laughed when she admitted that. "But I am not my cousin."

Henry took that as a sign and sat next to her, looking her in the eyes. Roxanne put a hand on his dress shirt and unbuttoned one button. He took a deep breath, weighing his options. He put a hand on hers, stopping her.

"I want to, I really do," he said. "God, you have no idea how much I want to."

"So, what's stopping you?" she asked.

Henry smiled and looked down. He laughed to himself and shook his head. Then he got on top of her and kissed her passionately on the mouth, Roxanne's body responding immediately. She took his dress shirt off quickly. He lifted up her skirt and touched her between her legs.

"Wait, hold on," she said and took off her boots and tights. "Much better." He continued where he left off and Roxanne moaned softly. She took off her underwear and he took off his t-shirt. She helped him with his belt and he kicked off his shoes. Little by little, each layer came off as they continued touching and exploring each other's bodies. He paused to put on a condom and they were quiet as he entered her, knowing that Esteban and Marialena would soon be coming home. He felt Roxanne's body quiver under him and pushed himself in further, enjoying how her body responded with the slightest of sounds.

When it was over, he was sweating profusely, and with good reason. He was great in bed. Roxanne bit her lip to keep from yelling as he satisfied her. She went limp in his arms, and he put his arms underneath her back and held her tightly as he finished. A few minutes later they heard Esteban and Marialena's footsteps next door.

Henry rolled off of Roxanne. "That was close," he said, and Roxanne giggled. Henry laughed, embarrassed.

"Henry, wow. That was amazing," she said. "You know, I always wondered if older guys were better at this kind of thing."

"Hey, who you calling old?" he asked with a smile, walking to the bathroom.

"Well, you know what I mean."

"Just so you know, age has nothing to do with it. I've always been that good," he said, laughing.

"Oh sure. Seventeen-year-old Henry was just as amazing."

"Well, I was twenty, but thanks for the compliment."

"Hey, Marialena's first time wasn't with my brother, was it?" he asked.

Roxanne laughed loudly. "What in the world makes you think that?"

"I don't know, the way she carries herself. She's a little reserved, I guess."

"She has her problems sure, but she wasn't celibate. Let's see, her first time was when she was nineteen or so. Maybe eighteen. He was a lot older and extremely good looking. When they had sex, he basically took it to mean they were headed for marriage. She was only eighteen, and she broke up with him right after."

"Was she ever in a serious relationship, I mean, after her parents died?"

Roxanne shook her head. "A few long ones, under a year or so, but not a serious one. She had a few opportunities, but no. I don't think she liked anyone enough."

"Why not?"

"I don't know. I guess she was waiting for someone to open his heart to her. And Esteban sort of did that through his films. I think that's why it was so easy for him. She trusted him before she even knew him. You know, she used to say that the men she met felt like they were entitled to her. Because they asked her out, she was expected to fool around with them. And that kind of rubbed her the wrong way. She was never into that."

"I can see that."

"Hey, I should text her. They can probably hear us making a racket over there. They might be thinking we're up to no good."

"Well, we kind of were."

"God, that timing though," she said, laughing. Roxanne pulled out her phone and texted her cousin. When she got a reply, she put her head on Henry's chest. "Is it okay if I stay here in this bed with you? Tomorrow morning, I'll switch, in case Mar or Esteban comes over. I don't want to make things awkward."

"Yeah, sure," Henry said, still sweating a little bit. And the two of them fell asleep.

Chapter Thirty

The next morning, Marialena woke up before Esteban. She put her arm around him and kissed his shoulder, loving how warm he always was. He was snoring softly.

Marialena threw on Esteban's sweater and her new pair of black leggings and ordered coffee from room service. There was a knock on her door ten minutes later. She heard her phone buzz and Esteban stirred in his sleep. She had received a text message from Roxanne.

"Hey, Henry's in the shower. Are you awake?"

"Yeah, want me to come by?"

"Yeah."

Marialena knocked on the door and found Roxanne in the bed she was in yesterday. She was in a dark blue two-piece pajama set.

Marialena set the coffee down and crawled into bed with her cousin, something they did often when they were teenagers. Roxanne handed her a pillow.

"Don't be mad," Roxanne said.

"I'm not mad. I just, I don't know, I just wish…look I don't want you get hurt."

"I know what I got myself into. But I want to make sure you're okay with it."

"Yeah, I mean, why wouldn't I be?"

Roxanne bit her lip. "He really cares about you."

Marialena looked at her cousin, feeling a little embarrassed. "I know. What did he tell you, exactly?"

"He said that he could see himself through your eyes, and how he didn't want to disappoint you. How, for some reason, he wants to try and change to match what you see in him. He thinks it's partly because of the engagement ring, but again, you're also you. Mar, you're beautiful, kind, and sexy. That got all mixed up in those feelings. When we came up here, he didn't want to sleep with me. He stopped, and I kind of convinced him that it was okay."

Marialena thought for a second, thinking about what she had just said. "You deserve someone who *isn't* mixed up with all those feelings."

Roxanne laughed. "Honestly, I've known you for my entire life and I've always played second fiddle to you. I'll always be into someone who wonders what it would be like to be with you."

"That's not true."

"Yes, it is actually."

"Rox, listen to me. You are worth someone who makes you feel the way I feel about Esteban. I just don't know if that person is Henry."

"I know that person isn't Henry too. I just wanted to get laid, and I feel sort of guilty now that I picked him."

"Guilty? Why guilty?"

"I don't know yet, I haven't figured it out. But he's great, from what I've seen so far. And I wouldn't mind a fling, but it's not worth talking about at this stage." Roxanne exhaled. "Listen, I do want to talk to you about something else. I've been thinking a lot about it. You know, everyone is taking these giant risks. Henry sold his business, Esteban is in love with a twenty-seven-year-old, and you're in love with a fifty-year-old man. Mar, I'm

461

not happy in Nashville. I've been thinking about it for a long time, and maybe it's time I take the jump. Maybe it's time I move back to Los Angeles."

"Roxanne, oh my god."

"I know, I know. Nothing is set in stone, and Henry and I talked about it a little, but honestly, I've been thinking about this for a really long time. My parents are leasing out their house and that lease ends in April. I know they'd let me live there. I'd have to get a roommate or two, but I think I want to do this. And get this, Henry said he knew a few people who work in the hotel business. Nice places, classy places. Can you believe it?"

"Holy shit, you in Los Angeles?"

"I know."

Henry walked out of the bathroom with a towel wrapped around his waist and nothing else. He saw the girls in bed together. "Woah, hey now. That's not an image I'll be able to get out of my head any time soon," he said and grabbed a pair of pants and boxers and walked back into the bathroom. The girls giggled.

"That's my cue," Marialena said and got out of bed. She went back into her room and kissed Esteban on the mouth while he was sleeping. He smiled without opening his eyes.

"Everyone's up. We should have breakfast together. I'm not sure when Henry is leaving, but it would be nice to do something while all four of us are still here," she said.

"Yeah, let's find out when he's leaving." He opened his eyes and stretched.

Marialena nodded and texted him.

"I booked a flight eariler, it's not until five," Henry replied back.

"Okay, good. We're all doing breakfast."

"I know just the place," he texted back.

Henry picked the place and the men talked excitedly about their memories from that restaurant. "I once took this date there when I was, oh, I don't know, eighteen. We went for dinner and she smoked an entire pack of cigarettes that night. We must have had ten cups of coffee," Esteban said, reminiscing.

"Yeah, that place is like that. You sort of forget what time it is. Part of it is that the service takes so damn long, but that's also the beauty, because you *can* get lost in conversation."

The restaurant was more laid back and casual. And very loud, there was definitely a buzz. There were posters of movies covering every inch of the walls. It was a place that always sparked a conversation, and there was always something new to see. Marialena immediately eyed one of Patrick Denny's films. She thought about texting him. Unfortunately, there wasn't a poster for any of Esteban's movies, but he didn't seem to mind.

"Wow, look at this place," Roxanne said. "This is probably what Marialena's dreams look like."

Marialena laughed. "Yeah, pretty close."

It was a Saturday so there was a little bit of a wait. But when they were finally seated, everyone ordered coffee and talked about movies—favorites and least favorites, holiday movies, movies they liked when they were younger. Someone walked past Esteban and stopped.

463

"Excuse me, are you Esteban Gutierrez?" Esteban smiled. "Oh wow, I love all of your movies."

"Thank you. That's very kind."

"Coming out with anything new soon?" the passerby asked.

"I'm working on a screenplay now, actually."

"Oh great, I look forward to it."

"It's almost like you belong to the public. That must be so weird," Roxanne said. "I could never do it. Do people ever stop Patrick Denny?" Roxanne asked Marialena.

"Daily," Marialena said.

"And do they pretend like you're invisible?"

"They think I'm his girlfriend some of the time. Once someone thought I was his daughter, but mostly no one cares who he's with."

When the waiter brought the check, Esteban gave him his card. Marialena put her head on Esteban's shoulder and he put an arm around her. When the waiter came back, he was accompanied by a short, balding man with a huge smile on his face.

"I understand you're Esteban Gutierrez. My name is Sergio Martinelli, the owner of this establishment. We have a poster here for you, if you'd care to sign it. We haven't had the honor of putting it up yet. It's new, actually. But since you're here, I thought maybe we could put it up today."

Esteban smiled. "Yeah, sure. Why not?"

Sergio rolled out the poster for "Paris in the Dark." It was glistening. Esteban signed the poster, adding 'Writer, Director' underneath his signature.

All eyes were on them as the owner made an announcement. "Ladies and gentleman, today we have the writer and director of a fine film called 'Paris in the Dark.'" The crowd clapped as Sergio held up the signed poster. "Please join us as we make room to add this poster to our collection. Sadly, one must come down for another to go up, but such is the way of life."

They sat in their seats as a poster was taken down, a romantic comedy from the late 90's. His poster was adhered to the wall and there was a round of applause from the crowd. Esteban stood up and bowed slightly. Henry, Roxanne, and Marialena clapped along with everyone else.

"Thank you for joining us today, Mr. Gutierrez and company," he said, as people continued to take pictures of them. Esteban waved and thanked the owner for his kindness.

Esteban laughed at they left. "I felt like I just won an Oscar. That was great."

"You belong up there, Steven," Henry said.

Esteban took Marialena's hand. "Thanks for putting up with all of that."

"Are you kidding me? That was awesome. Not to mention, it *is* my favorite movie."

"It really is," Roxanne said, smiling. "She's not kidding."

"Oh, I know she's not kidding. She made me watch it on Christmas Eve," Esteban said.

"She made me watch it too." Roxanne said, feigning annoyance.

"Excuse me for trying to spread the word about a talented man who made an incredible film!" Marialena said, defending herself.

Roxanne and Henry walked ahead of them, lost in conversation while Esteban and Marialena walked hand in hand, feeling lucky in love.

They continued to walk for another hour, Roxanne with Marialena and the two brothers up ahead. They were already making plans for when Roxanne moved to Los Angeles.

"We could have beach days in the summer. God, I would kill for a beach day right now," Roxanne said. "Plus, if I move, I could help out when Esteban is out of town, you know?"

Marialena shrugged. "I'm hoping it will go away. I feel bad. I think Henry might have gotten those mixed feelings about me because he had to stay and watch over me."

"Nah, I don't think so. I think it just made you two closer, that's all. It's good to have that bond."

"Yeah, but at what expense?"

"He'll get over it. When you and Esteban are married, he'll have to."

When Esteban announced it was time to go to the bookstore, Henry decided he'd stay behind. He needed to check in on work and get ready for his flight.

Esteban, Marialena, and Roxanne made it to the bookstore and it took a little longer than they thought. Each of them wanted to look around and really take their time there, checking out different sections and levels of the store. Marialena bought a few books, some t-shirts with the images of her favorite books, and Esteban spent over two-hundred dollars on some books that he arranged to have delivered. While the others were still shopping, Marialena snuck out and called Henry.

"I'm not interrupting anything, am I?"

"No, what's up?"

"So, you and Roxanne?"

"Yeah?"

"I don't know…" she trailed off, losing her confidence.

"Okay," he said, unsure of what to say next.

"It's just strange. I mean, with everything you and I talked about. Your dream the other night. I guess I don't know how to feel about everything."

Henry took a deep breath. "Marialena, what do you want me to say? That I have feelings for you? Yes. But what am I supposed to do? I can't do anything about it," he said, glad that this conversation was taking place over the phone and not in person. He couldn't bear to look at her right now. Her big brown eyes, the tears that always looked like they'd be falling. She was so vulnerable around him; all he wanted to do was pick her up and take her with him somewhere for the rest of his life. But he couldn't do that.

"And that's what makes this awkward. It's just that she's my cousin. Aside from you and Esteban, she's all I have," she said, bringing him out of his reverie. "I don't want anything to get weird among the three of us, especially if she's planning on moving back."

"Weird. You wanna talk weird? I have a crush on my brother's fiancée. That's weird."

467

"So, we're weird," she said quietly, taking a deep breath, unsure why she had even called him. "Just don't treat her like shit, okay? That's all I ask."

"Wait, who says I did? Or will?"

"No one. I just want to make sure you don't."

"Are you kidding me? You don't need to say that to me. Look, Marialena, I don't know what you want me to say."

"I don't know either. I'm not really asking for an explanation or an apology."

He took a deep breath. "Then why are you calling?"

"I don't know, honestly. I'm just... It's not that I want her to get hurt. I know she's tough, unlike me. But it's not a great feeling knowing that the man who slept with my cousin has feelings for me." There, she said it.

"I'm sorry. I know. You're going to be family, and I want to protect that more than anything," he admitted.

"Henry, I care about you too. I guess that's why this is so hard. I want to be in your life, and I want you in mine."

"And we'll have that."

Marialena took a deep breath. "I don't know why this is so hard."

"What's hard?"

"Us. I feel guilty. I think that's what I'm struggling with."

"Guilty? None of this is your fault."

"Bullshit."

"We talked about this before, Lena. I *wanted* to be there this week, and it was a *great* week. I don't regret it in the slightest. And I actually can't wait to move to Los Angeles. Not because of my feelings for you, but because

468

having you in my life has been wonderful, and you're going to be family. Let's just focus on that, okay? Don't feel guilty. If anyone should feel guilty, it's me."

"Let's agree to disagree," she said, seeing Esteban coming out of the store with Roxanne. "Hey, we're leaving now. You're going to stick around for us before you leave, right?" she asked, suddenly realizing that she wouldn't be seeing him for a while. He'd be flying into San Diego while she and Esteban would be flying into Los Angeles. She suddenly felt sad at the thought.

"Yeah, if you can make it back in time. Otherwise, I have to jet," he said matter-of-factly.

There was traffic on the way back to the hotel, and Marialena was anxious to see Henry off before he left. They had been gone three hours when Henry finally called Esteban.

"Hey, so I'm not going to be able to wait for you guys to get back. I'm headed to the airport. Give my love to everyone."

"We're about a block away from the hotel," Esteban said.

"I'm already on the sidewalk trying to get a cab." Henry could hear Esteban repeat the message to Marialena.

"Wait, I want to say goodbye. Tell him to wait for me."

She got out the cab and ran to find Henry in front of the hotel. When she got to him, she was out of breath and gave him a big hug. He lifted her off the ground.

"Did you finally figure out you were marrying the wrong brother?"

She smiled, but looked into the traffic with a frown on her face, unable to face him.

"You don't really believe that, do you?" she asked, suddenly serious.

Henry laughed. "What? I was kidding."

"No, you've said that a couple of times now. You don't really want to marry me, do you?"

"Hey, Marialena, relax. It's a joke."

"I have to know, is there some truth to it?"

It was Henry's turn to look away. He shrugged. "I don't know. Why are you asking me? What does it matter?"

That's when Henry saw Esteban and Roxanne in the distance. They were a block away but in no hurry to catch up to them. It looked like Esteban was window shopping. Something had caught his eye, and suddenly he and Roxanne were out of sight.

"Just answer the question, Henry. It *does* matter."

"It *doesn't* matter. But okay, maybe. I don't know actually. Maybe not, Marialena," he said, unsure of what the right answer was.

"Look, what if the universe is trying to tell me something and I'm just not listening? What if it's supposed to be you instead of Esteban?"

Henry put his hands on Marialena's shoulders. "The universe?" he asked, looking into her eyes. "Marialena, what is your heart telling you?"

"My heart is telling me to be with Esteban, without a doubt, but I can't shake this feeling all of a sudden that I'm not listening to the universe, and it's supposed to be you instead."

"Marialena, I'm pretty sure the universe is telling you that you're at the right place at the right time, with Esteban. Not with me. Listen to your heart. It's not me."

"How are you so sure?" Marialena asked, tears welling up in her eyes.

Henry sighed. "The night I put that ring on your finger, I had a plan. I was going to slam Esteban for breaking it off, and I was going to ask you to take a leap of faith, with me. And when I kissed you? Remember? I knew then what I was going to say. But when I took the ring out, I was going to ask you to hold on to it, that I'd ask you to marry me one day. But I couldn't. I froze. I chickened out, Marialena, and then I just thought about what my mom would have said in my place. She would have wanted you and Esteban to be together."

"But maybe you didn't ask me out of respect for Esteban."

Henry shook his head and turned away. "No, that's not why I didn't ask you." He turned to look at Marialena again. "Marialena, I didn't ask you because I didn't think I would be able to do what my brother does for you. I didn't ask you, because I'm not so sure I can make you happy the way he does." He put a hand on her chin. "Marialena, this is *my loss*, not yours. I *couldn't* do it. And anyway, say I had done it, say I had asked you to take a chance on me? Lena, you know as much as I do that you still would have picked Esteban. And so, Esteban wins. Not just because he was able to take the leap, but because *he* has your love. I'm so sorry for making you question that. If you and I were meant to be together, it would have happened."

471

Henry saw his brother and Roxanne again, each with a cup of coffee. Esteban held a red package against his chest. As Esteban got closer, Henry smiled to himself.

"You know how I know the universe is telling you to do the right thing?" He motioned toward his brother. She turned around and they both saw Esteban holding a red heart-shaped box. "Follow your heart, Marialena."

Marialena turned around as tears fell from her eyes.

When Esteban and Roxanne got closer, Esteban offered his cup to Marialena. "We just walked by a Chocolatier. This place has the best chocolate ever. I know it's not Valentine's Day, but I figured, why not? I got you a hot chocolate too." He saw that Marialena had been crying. "Hey, what's wrong?" he asked, as she took the hot chocolate in her hands.

Henry laughed. "Esteban, you just made all of Marialena's dreams come true."

"How so?" Esteban asked, confused.

"Did you know that she bugged me about not having hot chocolate at my place a few days ago?"

"Yeah, that sounds like her," he said, looking into her face as she looked away, avoiding his eyes.

"Marialena, I bet that's going to be the best cup of hot chocolate you've ever had. The universe knows what it's talking about," Henry said and winked at her.

Marialena took a sip of the hot chocolate. It was good. It was *really* good. With that, she gave Henry another hug with one arm. Henry and Esteban hugged warmly.

"Thanks for everything, brother," Esteban said.

"No problem."

Henry hugged Roxanne. "Let me know what you want to do about Los Angeles. I'll make some phone calls."

"Thanks," she said.

"Hopefully we'll see each other again."

"I'd like that," she said.

They stood a few feet away as Henry hailed a cab. He waved to the three of them before he got inside. They saw him off and walked back to the hotel.

"Sorry. We needed a heart-to-heart. I realized I wouldn't be seeing him for a while. It's been an emotional rollercoaster," she said, talking to both Esteban and Roxanne. "Thanks for the hot chocolate. How'd you know that I've been craving this for days?"

Esteban shrugged. "I know what's in your heart."

"Yeah, you do," she said, promising herself never to question her love for Esteban again.

Henry drove off, headed to the airport. He looked out of the window and thought about Marialena, wondering if he had just missed his chance.

Firstly, I'd like to thank my parents. My mom for taking me to the library when I was a young girl because I always needed *more* books. She always found the time! Thanks to my dad who celebrated my birthdays by taking me to bookstores and letting me buy however much I could carry out. Dad, now I have my own book! You'd be so proud!

I would also like to thank my friend Gaby Goose, who was my very first reader and saw this vision with me from start to finish.

Thanks also to Kristina King, who read the early stages of this and helped flesh out some details with notes of her own.

Thanks to my editors, Blair Schuyler and Samantha Talarico.

And a big shout out to John Franklin Pickett III, Jeff Kazmierczak, John Daski, Emilie Hancock, Alessandro Saini, and all my friends and family for your love and support through this one.

I would also like to thank Crazy Ink their endless hard-work, love and support. Erin, thanks so much for EVERYTHING you've done. And thanks to Taylor Henderson who directed me your way. Forever grateful!

About the Author

I grew in Los Angeles as an avid reader of books, and a life-long dream is to have my own library filled with thousands of much-loved books – all dog-eared from being read over and over. I am also a huge film enthusiast and music lover, and my passions converge in my writing. I love that books, films and music can transport us to magical places, can let us live incredible adventures, and even make us fall in love.